LOVE'S IMPOSSIBLE CHOICE

MEKONG BELLE

BILL LYNCH

HELLGATE PRESS   ASHLAND, OREGON

MEKONG BELLE
©2023 Bill Lynch

Published by Hellgate Press
(An imprint of L&R Publishing, LLC)

Hellgate Press
72 Dewey St.
Ashland, OR 97520
email: sales@hellgatepress.com

Interior Design: L. Redding
Cover Design: Getcovers.com

ISBN: 978-1-954163-79-9

Printed and bound in the United States of America
First edition 10 9 8 7 6 5 4 3 2 1

AUTHOR'S NOTE

Mekong Belle: Love's Impossible Choice is a love story...

T HERE ARE PLENTY OF EXCELLENT war stories written by Vietnam veterans. This is not a war story. Nor is it a memoir about my experience as a naval officer with the Riverine Forces in the Mekong Delta, or an account of my return to Vietnam fifty years later as a visitor.

All those things influenced the story, but are not what inspired it. Love did. The sweet and irrepressible people of Vietnam did. And perhaps, most of all, music, and the people who play it, did.

Those of us who served in Vietnam brought our favorite music with us and played it on portable record players, recorders, and the radio. If we brought guitars, we played for whoever would listen. Music was present in every barracks, mess hall, tent, bunker, hooch, and foxhole.

When I returned to Vietnam decades later, everything had changed, except the music, and the sweet and welcoming nature of the Vietnamese people, who for the most part, seem to have forgiven us in our misguided attempt to inject ourselves into their civil war.

Their welcome and the fact that the music we brought with us back then was still there with them, both in its original form and infinite updated variations, gave me a warm feeling. Perhaps something good was accomplished after all.

1

After I returned home, the feeling remained. The writer in me struggled with how to express it. When the inspiration finally came, I was watching a musical review in the middle of a vineyard in my home town.

Sonoma Valley, Jack London's famous "Valley of the Moon," where I'm fortunate to live and work, is not only the birthplace of California's wine industry, it is where Broadway intersects with the wine country. In 2011, a group of seasoned Broadway actors, singers, and dancers established Transcendence Theatre Company in the remains of the old stone winery at Sonoma's Jack London State Park. And it was at one of their shows, in the middle of a song from the musical "South Pacific," that an idea popped into my head. "My Vietnam tale should be a love story set to music."

I've always been a sucker for good love stories, sappy romantic comedies and musicals, including those, like *South Pacific*, set in World War II. Why not one set in Vietnam? With the exception of *Good Morning Vietnam*, all the rest are war stories. Even the Korean War had *Sayonara*, definitely a love story.

Driving home later, I realized I had one really big problem – I was remembering those examples as they appeared on film or stage. I was neither a composer nor a screenwriter. I'm a journalist, with thousands of news stories, and columns plus two history books on my resume. None of it prepared me to write a love story, let alone a musical.

Still, I couldn't get the idea out of my head. So, as scenes played out in my mind, I wrote them down. The more I wrote, the more the story unfolded before me. I couldn't compose music, but had plenty in my memory. The soundtrack from *American Graffiti*, or any one of a half-dozen "Golden Oldie" albums from the 1950s and '60s, provided all that was needed.

The plot is all fiction, bordering on fantasy. There were no Navy ships serving as showboats in Vietnam, nor were there sailors assigned to perform musicals. The characters, except for some historical political figures, are all fictional.

What I believe is true, is the love that actors, dancers and musicians express when they perform. It is that love I tried to bring out in the characters who were the performers in this story.

I also relied on old memories, saved letters I wrote to home, and a journal I kept while in Vietnam to illustrate some of the combat and naval action. None of it should be regarded as precise or accurate enough to be a true account of my specific Vietnam War experience.

Nor did I fall in love with a beautiful Vietnamese woman, although many American GI's and sailors did. That part of my story can be attributed to the fact that I am a hopeless romantic with an active imagination and a fondness for love stories, including those where characters, like Romeo and Juliet, face nearly impossible choices.

A choice, volunteer or be drafted, was how most of us ended up in Vietnam. We were the children of the greatest generation. They saved the world from fascist tyrants. We were imprinted with their sense of duty. Without the draft, most of us wouldn't have chosen to join the military, but neither could we choose the other alternative and run away. We chose to serve. And thus, we found ourselves in a country we knew little about, engaged in a fight we did not understand, with a people with whom we had no quarrel.

The characters in my story are, for the most part, a reflection of the Americans with whom I served, and the Vietnamese I got to know – good people making the best of a situation in which they were forced to make impossible choices, or had no choice at all. I chose to remember what they did for love.

MEKONG BELLE

1

Vung Tau, Vietnam, November 1967
••••••••••••••••••••••

THE ANCIENT WOODEN PIER, REEKING of fish guts and smoke, vibrated from the beat of a thousand feet. Men and women stood or rested on their haunches haggling over all manner of meats, fish, rice, fruits, and vegetables. Their words were foreign, but there was no mistaking their intent. I'd landed in the middle of a Vietnamese market.

I scanned the crowded waterfront and listened to the murmur of voices, tingle of bells on carts, cries of gulls, and coughs from one-lunger motors on weathered sampans and wondered if this was the normal way people did business here. Like most young Americans sent to Vietnam, I knew little about the country, its history, culture, and people.

The scene before me reinforced the odd feeling I'd had ever since reporting to my Navy ship that I'd passed through a time portal into a weird Asian "Brigadoon" on a wartime mission to the twilight zone.

The ship, built for amphibious landings during WWII, was undergoing an unusual transformation. It would become the Navy's only "showboat," its mission to bring live musical shows to troops stationed upriver in the jungles of the Mekong Delta.

It sounded crazy to me at first, but the plan was well underway when I reported to our ship and met her captain, Lieutenant (Lt.) Baillier, during a rehearsal with the crew. They were incredibly talented. The message was clear. The USS *Bell County*, LST 888, was going to be a showboat and, as one of its officers, I was expected to get with the program.

Everyone on board was involved in some way. Band and chorale practices were held daily. Music played over the ship's P.A. from reveille to midnight. We became accustomed to performing our routine duties while singing.

By the time I took my first steps ashore in Southeast Asia, I almost expected the people there to provide background music. Instead, a man in tattered pajamas, his lean, weathered face shadowed by a conical hat, shouted at me from the seat of his bicycle rickshaw. "Mister! You like ride. Real cheap."

I hesitated a second to see if he and the people on the dock would break out in song. They didn't. So I asked for directions.

"Can you tell me where I can find a bookstore?"

He scrunched his face in thought for a few seconds, then grinned. "Maybe Saigon," he said.

Wouldn't you know that the first Vietnamese person I met was a wise guy? I smiled, but didn't say anything. Then, he nodded his head in the direction of the waterfront and added, "Try Rue de Paris. Some French stores there."

"Can you take me?"

"Not now. Market in way. Too many peoples. You walk that way." He pointed toward a gap between buildings along the wharf.

"Thank you."

"Okay, Joe. Maybe later you need ride to good place to eat."

I'd taken the ship's shuttle boat to the pier in hopes of finding a place to buy an English/Vietnamese dictionary and a map of the village.

I waved thanks and headed in the direction he pointed. My time was limited. I had to be back at the ship in less than three hours. I assumed somewhere in the bustling little port town there'd be a store or newsstand selling books and maps.

Vung Tau was going to be our homeport for the better part of a year. Learning as much as I could about it seemed like a good idea. I'd also promised my Aunt Celie that I would send regular reports to her. It was an obligation I could not ignore. Celie adopted me after my parents died in a car crash when I was twelve. She never married but applied herself to parenting me with the same determination and energy she put into running her newspaper. The one unique thing she required of me that no other kid had to do was to write a daily "news story" about something that happened around me each day It didn't have to be long, but the lead had to include the five w's and h (who, what, when, where, why and how). It was her way of training me to become a journalist.

Celie also played the piano, loved musical theater, and bought tickets for us to Broadway shows that passed through San Francisco. Music was the medium through which she expressed her love. But when she tried to teach me piano, I rebelled and chose the guitar. As a peace offering, I learned the chords to most of her favorite show tunes so I could accompany her when she played them on her piano. What a strange coincidence it was that I ended up on the only ship in the Navy assigned to produce a musical show.

The Navy and Vietnam had not been in the plan for my future. She wanted me to study journalism and take over the family newspaper. I wasn't sure what I wanted to do and chose the beachside campus of UCSB, where I majored in English (and minored in surfing,) while remaining undecided about a career.

The draft hung over the head of every American male approaching eighteen. College could delay it, but short of running away to Canada, there was no way to avoid it. When the time came, I chose the Navy. The Navy made me an officer, postponing my need to decide on a civilian career for at least three and a half years.

My aunt continued to demand reports from wherever I was stationed. She said she wanted to run them in the newspaper.

"Auntie, I'm a naval officer, not a war correspondent."

"We get enough news about the war. Tell us about the things we don't usually see on TV– the people, the country, what it feels like being in the middle of it all. Make it personal," she said.

Personal it was. The transition from college to military was sudden and life-changing in every way imaginable

One day I was on "Campus Beach" at UCSB free as a bird and the next I was on a ship where my entire life was controlled by the Navy. Our leaders in Washington said it was to help the people of South Vietnam fend off Communists. But not a single minute of OCS was dedicated to Vietnamese history, culture or language. I wondered, "How can we be partners with people we did not know, whose language we can't speak and whose culture and history we do not understand?" In my case at least, it appeared that I would be making music, not war.

Nevertheless, I wanted to learn as much as I could about Vietnam and its people during my tour. The shore excursion was the first step toward that goal.

Dodging dockworkers wheeling carts filled with live chickens, dead fish, green vegetables, bags of rice and other consumables, I moved along the waterfront toward the gap pointed out by the rickshaw driver. The way was crowded with vendors squatting in tin-sided shacks under makeshift awnings, haggling mostly with old women, many already burdened with heavy sacks of rice and other commodities.

The gap was at the intersection where a narrow street led away from the wharf.

I let myself be carried along with the natural flow of shoppers away from the water. Adapting to the pace of the crowd, I was able to pull off to the side, check out the wares and then rejoin the movement. Nothing resembling books or maps were offered.

As some people peeled off onto other alleys, I continued walking until my street intersected with a much wider one so different from that which I'd exited that I was momentarily disoriented.

It was a wide, Parisian-style boulevard, nearly deserted, and shaded by large trees planted along a well-kept sidewalk. I saw no street sign, but assumed it must be Rue de Paris. Many storefront names were in French, reminding me that this country had once been part of French Indochina.

Relieved to be out of the claustrophobic confines of the alley, I strolled along the sidewalk looking into windows. Most of the buildings were locked, their spaces and shelves empty. If the French ever did business on the street, they were long gone.

I saw a woman with long, straight dark hair wearing an ao dai, a traditional Vietnamese dress, enter a store a half block ahead of me. I quickened my pace to follow her through the door.

"Bonjour monsieur," a Vietnamese woman behind the counter said as I entered.

"*Bonjour, Madame*," I replied.

It appeared to be a gift and stationary shop, but the shelves were nearly bare and the merchandise looked dated and worn.

"*Puis-je vous aider?*" She was asking me something in French, but I didn't understand.

"I'm sorry. I don't speak French or Vietnamese," I said, then added, "I am looking for a book. A dictionary."

"Ah, *un dictionnaire, oui.*"

She walked over to the shelf on the far wall, grabbed a small red book and brought it to me. It was a French-Vietnamese dictionary.

"Yes. *Oui*. But, I need this in English. *Anglais.*"

"Perhaps, I can help." A British-accented voice appeared to

come from an apparition in white standing near the store's large front window. It was the woman who had preceded me into the store, but backlit as she was, I could only see her eyes. They were large, beautiful, and locked on mine.

She stepped out of the light and touched the book in my hands. "You want to buy a Vietnamese/English dictionary. Is that right?"

Still beguiled, I managed to stammer a reply. "Ah, oui, yes, that is exactly what I'm looking for. Thank you. Oh, and if she has a map of the city for sale, I would like to buy that too."

She turned toward the store clerk and spoke in Vietnamese. The clerk replied and shook her head.

"She has a city map, but it is in French. She doesn't have the English dictionary in stock, but knows where she might get one. Can you come back tomorrow?"

"Yes, and the map, even in French, would be helpful. Thank you. And, yes I think I can come back tomorrow. My ship is here for a while. I'm American."

She smiled that I had stated the obvious.

"I know you are not French."

"I guess my accent gave me away. My French is limited to a few words. I studied Spanish in school, but can't speak that very well either. But, if you don't mind me saying so, you speak English better than me." I knew I was babbling like an idiot, but wanted to prolong our conversation for as long as possible.

"Thank you, but your good manners, not your accent, gave you away. You speak respectfully. It is a quality that we do not always see in French men here."

I knew there was a story behind the edge to her voice, but decided it wasn't the time or place to request more information.

"My name is Rob. Rob Allen. It is very kind of you to help me, Miss…"

"Marquis. I am Melanie Marquis," she said.

"Mademoiselle Marquis, *merci.* Without your help, I was destined to wander the city searching for something I might never have found."

"Do you need the dictionary for your job?" She asked.

"Yes, sort of. I'm a Navy officer. The dictionary is to help me understand Vietnam and its people. I want to learn some Vietnamese words and phrases and try to talk to people. I write news releases for my ship and my aunt has requested that I write home about Vietnam, its culture and people."

"Your aunt wants to know about our culture and people. Is she a teacher?"

"No. She's a journalist. She wants to run my reports in the local newspaper to give readers more than the usual war coverage they see on television."

Melanie's beautiful eyes widened with interest when I mentioned the newspaper.

"So you are a journalist?"

"Not a professional like my aunt. I've studied journalism and worked at the newspaper while I was in college. But the war and the Navy interrupted my career plans."

Just then the store clerk said something to Melanie, who then turned back to me.

"I'm sorry. She says she wants to close for lunch now. And I am late to work. I have to go too. It was nice meeting you Rob."

"It was my pleasure, Melanie. Thank you for helping me."

She nodded and said, "*A bientot.*"

"Wait," I whispered, but she'd already turned and started out the door. I wanted to chase after her to ask where she worked, but feared it would make me as rude as the French men she so clearly despised.

The clerk's voice startled me, breaking the spell. "*A demain?*" (tomorrow), she asked.

"*Oui.* But the map, can I buy the map?"

She looked confused. Then I remembered the words. "*Le plan de la ville?*"

"*Oui. Voilà,*" she said, handing me a piece of paper folded several times.

"*Merci. Combo? Combien?*"

"*Non, non. Monsieur. C'est gratuit.*" (Free)

"*Merci. Merci beaucoup, Madame.*"

"*De rien Monsieur, a demain.*"

I nodded."*Oui, Madame. A demain,* merci."

It was the most French I spoken since I bid adieu to Louiselle, the French Canadian nurse I'd met in Newport months before. She did her best to teach me French during our brief time together. I left the store thinking she would be proud of how well I managed.

I looked at my watch. There was just enough time to find my way back to the waterfront and catch the next shuttle back to the ship. The throng of shoppers had thinned so that I could examine my surroundings.

It helped me understand why my first impression was so disorienting.

The nearly abandoned boulevard on which I discovered the little French boutique and the narrow street leading back to the wharf were worlds (and decades) apart. It was as though Vung Tau existed on two planes, one ancient, another a fading shadow of French occupation, neither acknowledging the civil war fought with modern weapons just beyond the horizon. The best the residents could hope for was to be unimportant enough to be ignored and bypassed by all sides. Americans like me, sent there to help, really didn't have a clue how.

I wondered how our crew of misfits, as musically inclined as we might be, could do any good. An optimist by nature, I hoped my chance encounter with Melanie might shed light on that question. In a way, she rescued me that first day. Hers was the welcoming smile in a city of strangers. I knew nothing about her, except that she had the most captivating eyes and spoke three languages.

Would I ever see her again?

When we parted, she said *"A bientot,"* not *"au revoir."*

The first meant, "see you soon," the latter, "goodbye." On that difference I pinned my hopes.

Waiting for my ship's shuttle boat to arrive, I was determined to find the time the next day to pick up the dictionary and also persuade the store clerk to tell me where she worked.

Unfortunately, my time was not my own. It belonged to the Navy. It was the first lesson I learned when I reported my ship, the *Bell County* at the naval base, Subic Bay, Philippines, one month before.

She was tied to a broken-down wharf at the far end of the base. Unlike a sleek destroyer, she looked like a dumpy cargo vessel. An industrial-grade crane was chained to her long, flat, main deck. A four-story superstructure rose from the stern.

I'd seen ships like her on old WWII newsreels of the D-Day landings. One paragraph in my naval history manual revealed that LSTs were built by the hundreds during World War II. Nearly as long as a football field and sixty feet wide, they had large, hollow interiors designed to carry tanks, trucks, and other equipment, and could sail all the way to shore during amphibious landings. There, the bow doors could open and the vehicles could drive off.

Those features made them perfect for transiting the rivers of Vietnam, where they supported the mission of the U.S. riverine forces. It meant I would be sailing muddy rivers rather than the deep blue sea.

A hard rain was falling the day I arrived in Subic Bay. I teetered on the rotted pier boards, wiping the water out of my eyes and squinting through the mist trying to figure out where I was supposed to board. My once clean, starched, tropical white uniform clung to my skin. There was a stain near the crotch where I'd spilled coffee.

I was dead tired, swaying on my feet after more than thirty-six hours on airplanes and buses. I needed sleep.

I was startled by a voice from behind. "Excuse me, sir."

A short, thin young man with dark hair and light brown complexion smiled as I turned toward him. He was in civilian clothes and holding an umbrella.

"Are you looking for the *Bell County*?" he asked.

"I think I found it," I said nodding toward bow where the numbers 888 were painted.

"Yes, sir. You must be Mr. Allen. I'm Reyes, steward third class. Let me help you get aboard."

He picked up my duffel and guitar case and walked toward a gangway that rose at a 45-degree angle toward *Bell County*'s main deck fifteen feet above us. A sailor wearing a rain slicker and standing under a makeshift shelter snapped to attention and gave me a sharp salute.

"Ensign Allen reporting for duty. Request permission to come aboard," I said returning his salute.

"Permission granted, sir. Welcome to the *Bell County*. I'm Adkins, ship's quartermaster."

"Thank you, Adkins. I'm glad to finally get here."

"Yes, sir. The Captain (Capt.) and XO are off the ship. But the duty officer, Mr. Walton, is in the wardroom. Reyes can take you to him."

We entered a hatch in the ship's superstructure and walked down a steel passageway to a curtain-covered doorway. Reyes knocked on the outside wall, pushed back the curtain, and entered.

"Mr. Walton, our new officer, Ensign Allen, has arrived," he said.

Ensign John Walton looked up from a paperback copy of James Michener's *Tales of the South Pacific*. When he put his book down and stood up, he had to duck to avoid hitting the ceiling. Low overheads didn't trouble me, but John was well over six feet tall.

"Welcome. I'm John, John Walton." His eyes focused on me for a few seconds. "What happened? You look like you've been dragged through the swamps or something."

I extended my hand.

"Hi John. I'm Rob. And yes, I not only look like shit, I feel like it, too."

I gave him a summary of my thirty-six hour journey – the plane delays, spilled coffee in my lap, rain, unintentional mud puddle baths, and so forth.

"I stink. I need a shower. Then, I want a bunk where I can catch some z's."

"Sorry. The Captain told me to have you report to him at the Pink Palace as soon as you get in."

"The Pink Palace? Whatever or wherever it is, I can't show up looking and smelling like this, and I need some time to catch up on my sleep."

"No sweat. We can fake it for a few hours. He just went over there about an hour ago, and it is probably going to be a long night. So, we're just going to say that you arrived three hours from now. That'll give you time for a shower and a few hours of shuteye. Reyes can drive you over after that."

"Jesus. that's not enough time. I need more than a couple of hours. I haven't slept for two days."

"Get used to it. The Navy owns your time, including how much you sleep."

He headed out the wardroom door. "C'mon, I'll show you your quarters, the head, and the shower."

Officer's country barely covered 800 square feet, including the corridor and wardroom, which also served as the officer's mess. There was a compact communal head with one shower, two sinks, two urinals and two toilets. The stateroom had just enough room for a bunk, a built-in desk, and a locker in which we could hang our uniforms. A small porthole was the only source of outside air or light. They'd managed to squeeze in a second bunk. I realized I would be sharing that tiny space with another officer.

Tight quarters or not, all I wanted was to take a shower, crawl into that bunk, and stay there for a day or two.

My head hit the pillow thirty seconds after my shower. I was dreaming that I was cuddled up with Louiselle, my French Canadian girlfriend, when she began poking me with her finger.

"Not now, *ma cherie*. *"Je suis trop fatigué,"* I muttered. The poking continued.

"Mr. Allen. Mr. Allen. We got to go see the Captain." The voice didn't belong to Louiselle.

"Go away. I just got to sleep a few minutes ago."

"I can't, sir. It's been almost three hours and we've got to get going now."

Reyes finally came into focus, and I remembered something about meeting the Captain at a pink place.

"O.K. I'll get up, but my duffel is still packed and my uniforms probably need ironing. It's going to take a while for me to get ready."

"No sweat, sir. Your bags are unpacked and your uniforms are ironed. But, you don't need them now. We wear civvies in Olongapo."

"Huh?"

"Olongapo City. It's the town next to the base. That's where the Pink Palace is. When we go off base, we're allowed to wear civilian clothes."

I understood that Reyes was just doing his job. He was a steward, and his duties, like mine, were rigidly bound by traditions that dated back to the Revolutionary War. We all had to know our place and behave accordingly. He was informing me of where I was supposed to be and what I was supposed to wear. He also ironed my uniforms and put out my civilian clothes.

He was one of two stewards assigned to serve the ship's seven officers, doing everything from serving our meals and washing our clothes, to making up our bunks and cleaning our staterooms. He was also a fighting sailor. At general quarters (battle stations) he was part of the gun crew. And, as I would soon learn, he was assigned to our ship because of his amazing contra-tenor voice.

Reyes had laid out my only aloha shirt and a pair of khaki cotton slacks.

"This is what I'm wearing to report to the Captain?"

"Yes, sir. It's what we wear off base."

I had no reason to doubt him and was dressed and ready to go in ten minutes.

"Oh, and the Captain wants you to bring your guitar." He picked up the case and headed toward the main deck.

"My guitar? What is it with this Captain and my guitar?"

I followed Reyes off the and the pier toward a Navy gray 1959 Ford Crown Victoria parked just beyond the broken chain link gate.

2

Subic Bay, Philippines
••••••••••••••••••••••

R EYES WAS CARRYING MY GUITAR for the same reason
I'd carried it halfway across the globe – because the Captain
had ordered it so.

His order was in a message I received following my graduation
from Officer Candidate School. It read:

> *Congratulations on your commission. Welcome to the Bell County. Upon*
> *completion of your training, proceed to our ship. Bring your guitar.*
>
> —Lt. E.W. Baillier, Commanding Officer

Getting to the ship had been a long, sleepless, trans-continen-
tal/trans-Pacific, ordeal for me and my guitar. What use the Navy
had for either of us, I still didn't know.

Now I was in a car riding through Olongapo City, a corrugated
tin and plywood ramshackle town of titty bars catering to sailors.

Four blocks outside the base entrance, Reyes stopped in front of
a knockoff of a New Orleans brothel. I followed him through the
front door. The dimly lit, hazy interior could have been any number
of music clubs I'd seen on Frenchmen Street in New Orleans. But
this was Olongapo City, far, far away from the Big Easy.

On a small, elevated stage in the far corner, a pianist was pounding out Fats Domino's "I'm Walking," accompanied by a drummer and a big, heavy-set, bearded guy on stand-up bass.

A tall man with salt and pepper hair appeared to be polishing glasses while dancing behind a bar that ran the length of the wall on my left. The center of the room was filled with small cafe tables and chairs arrayed on a dark bare wood floor. Except for two young women seated closed to the stage, the tables were empty.

Reyes waved to the bartender and walked toward the stage.

The pianist ended the song with a flourish and stood up.

"Reyes!" he shouted. "Are you and the girls ready for your number?"

"Yes, sir. We are. But I brought your new officer with me."

In that instant, I realized the guy with a voice like Fats Domino was Captain Baillier.

"Rob Allen, the guitar playing surfer from sunny Santa Barbara? Well, it's about time," he declared, stepping off the stage and walking toward me.

I panicked, not remembering the rules regarding saluting while in civilian clothes, so I just stood there at attention. He solved my dilemma by smiling and offering his hand. "Welcome to our crew and lovely Olongapo."

"Yes, sir. Thank you, sir." It was all I could manage to say, nearly struck dumb by how far this was from my imagined first meeting with my commanding officer.

"Relax, Rob. We're all Navy aboard ship. Here, not so much." He paused, then added, "But just to keep things comfortable, you can still call me Captain."

I understood that although he used the word "can," he meant "will."

I always called him Captain.

No more than 5'8", Capt. Baillier was about my height and

slightly built. He had closely cropped dark hair, green eyes, a dark, almost golden brown, complexion and a warm smile. His accent, straight out of the bayous of southern Louisiana, suggested he was French Cajun, but I would learn later that he proudly cited Native and African Americans as part of his family tree.

It was hard to tell his age, but when he smiled the lines around his mouth and eyes told me he was well into his thirties. He was dressed even more casually than I in blue jeans and white tee shirt, over which he wore an unbuttoned, short-sleeved floral patterned shirt.

While he was speaking, the drummer came down from the stage and walked up next to him. The Captained turned toward him and said, "This is Lt. Lewis Luccero, our XO, sometimes known as 'Triple Lew.'"

The XO was gaunt, a half-foot taller than the Captain and at least five years older. His thinning blondish hair was streaked with gray. Although not as effusive in his welcome, his soft smile and friendly light blue eyes suggested they belonged to a kind person.

"Welcome, Rob," he said extending his hand. "How about a drink?"

Before I could respond, the Captain clapped his hands

"OK. Let's take a break. Reyes, you're up in fifteen." He joined the XO in walking me toward the bar.

The huge bear of man who'd been strumming the bass fiddle was already standing there with a beer in each hand. He offered one to me as I walked up.

With a thick black beard, a full head of curly black hair and dark eyes, magnified by thick, rimless glasses, he looked like a mad scientist turned backwoods moonshiner. He was as tall as the XO but outweighed him by 100 pounds.

"Welcome to our Pink Palace, surfer boy. I'm Harry Haggert and this is San Miguel, our fine local brew."

"Harry is the ship's engineering officer," the XO said.

I guessed he was also the ship's jester.

The Captain and XO ordered bourbon straight.

With drink in hand, the Captain nodded toward the bartender. "The distinguished gentleman behind the bar is Master Chief Clem Graham, now retired, who, along with his beautiful wife, Cecile, are the proud owners of the Palace."

Gesturing toward me, he added, "Chief, this is Ensign Robert Allen, the newest member of our crew."

Retired Chief Clem Graham was a strikingly handsome black man with a smile that could melt an iceberg. He may have been retired, but didn't look like he was much past forty.

"Hello, Rob, welcome to the Palace." He extended a hand so huge that it literally engulfed mine. His soft voice belied his size.

I could not have imagined a more exotic setting for my induction into the crew of my ship. Dozens of questions rattled around in my sleep-deprived brain as I shared the first of many drinks with the men who would be my closest companions for at least the next twelve months.

"Did I walk in on some kind of rehearsal?" I asked the XO.

"You didn't get my letter?"

"No, sir."

"That's military mail for you. After the Captain sent you a message telling you where to meet us, and asking you to bring your guitar, I decided you needed more information. I sent a longer letter telling you more about our mission."

"I'm still curious why he mentioned my guitar," I said.

"As you can probably tell, music is a big deal with the Captain. He's from New Orleans. To him, music goes with life on the water like chili peppers go with food. So, since he took command of the ship six months ago, he's been rebuilding her crew with the idea of taking it on a special mission – bringing live music and good food to our troops in the war zone."

"Wow! And the Navy is letting him do that?"

"Not exactly. At least not yet." He glanced at the Captain.

"Go ahead, Lew, I think you understand the whole picture better than I do. I'm just the talent." He walked over to Reyes and the two girls and left the XO to finish the story.

"Let's go to one of those tables. I'll explain what we're trying to do."

Nodding toward his boss, the XO, continued, "The Captain is being modest. He's the most talented musician I've ever known and this is his plan all the way. His biggest fan is Admiral Kirkpatrick, commander of all the amphibious ships in the Pacific. The Admiral was his CO back when they were both Navy divers. They're still good friends. The Admiral has a thing about making his brown-water Navy as well-respected as the blue-water."

I didn't understand the reference – "brown-water Navy."

"In this war there is a 'blue-water Navy,' the carriers, destroyers, cruisers, and others who do their work from miles offshore. Ships like ours spend most of their time much closer to the fighting, in the rivers where the water is brown. We're part of a big fleet of small boats all manned by U.S. sailors."

I nodded that I understood.

"Brown-water sailors and their craft get the low end of the stick and all the worst berths in port. We're ignored for most of everything else that you might consider a perk over here. The blue-water boys get whatever goodies there are. When Bob Hope and his entourage come around, he plays for the blue-water crews. We're lucky to hear the show on Armed Forces Radio. Admiral Kirkpatrick wants to do something special for the sailors under his command to let them know they're appreciated." He paused and took a sip of his bourbon.

"One more thing, the Admiral plays the saxophone and he's a huge New Orleans jazz fan."

I smiled at the image of a Navy admiral playing the sax in some smoke-filled nightclub.

"One night several months ago, when he and the Captain were jamming right here at the Palace, Clem shouts over to them, 'You guys are great, you should take your show on the road.'"

"It was said in jest, but the Admiral looked over and shouted back, 'Chief. You're absolutely right.' That night, Admiral Kirkpatrick and Captain Baillier hatched a plan to bring their show to the long-neglected sailors of the brown water navy in Vietnam."

"So the Admiral and the Captain formed a band to take to Vietnam?"

"More than that. The Admiral asked Captain Baillier to put together an entire show, a musical review to be performed by the ship's officers and crew. He also wants the ship to serve good, hot food during their show to troops that have been eating nothing but cold C-rations for weeks."

"It's amazing that the Pentagon agreed to that," I said.

"It hasn't, he replied. "At least, not yet."

Leaning forward in his chair and lowering his voice to a con-spiratorial whisper, he added, "The trick was to figure out a way to fit the show and chow into our military mission. And that's where Captain Baillier's idea of finding officers and enlisted men who were musicians came in."

He paused, went over to the bar, and returned with another bourbon, plus a bottle of San Miguel for me.

"The plan was to find crew members who could play music, then produce a show that we could bring to remote bases. Of course, there are still some details being worked out," he said.

I was growing increasingly alarmed as I realized what the XO's explanation implied.

"So you're telling me that the Admiral approved this idea?"

"Not only that, he also wants to sneak in and play with the band whenever he's in country," the XO answered.

The reason for the guitar request was suddenly clear. I realized I was way out of my league. "Oh shit! Captain Baillier thinks I'm a musician," I blurted out.

"Is that a problem?"

"Yes! Huge! Awful! You're going to be pissed." I grabbed the beer bottle and took a long swig, then gasped out a hasty confession. "I'm not a musician; at least not a good one; nowhere close to the Captain, or you, or Harry. I played rhythm guitar in a pick-up fraternity band. I can't even read music. I know some chords, but I couldn't play a real song to save my soul."

"Relax. We know."

His response was not what I expected.

"How? How could you know something like that?"

"Simple. Every officer needs a security clearance. You must pass a thorough background check. The Navy actually sends agents to your hometown and your former schools to talk to teachers, friends – anyone who knows you. We just added some questions."

"So you know I'm not a real musician. Yet the Captain asked me to bring my guitar. I'm confused."

"All will be revealed in time. Our ship has at least four guitarists in its crew, including two that are very good. We don't need you to play in the shows. The fact that you play the guitar is a plus. You understand and enjoy music. You will appreciate what we are trying to do."

"Yes, sir, I do. I'm just trying to figure out how I'm going to fit in."

"You're a writer, a journalist. You've written song lyrics. You managed your college band and organized events and shows. Your creative writing professor at UCSB said you have a vivid imagination. We need that kind of talent too, because no Navy ship has

24

ever done what we're trying to do and we're not quite sure yet how we're going to do it. We need you to help us tell our story."

Just then, the Captain clapped his hands. "Okay. Break's over. Let's get back to work."

Reyes, along with the two young women I'd seen at the tables, were the next act and did a perfect rendition of "Boogie Woogie Bugle Boy," written by Don Raye and Hughie Prince and made famous by the Andrews Sisters. I wondered how the women figured into the ship's mission. As far as I knew, Navy ships had all-male crews. That was just another in a long list of questions rattling around in my head after the conversation with the XO.

For the next two hours a variety of singers and musicians from the crew arrived, performed, and then joined a growing audience drinking San Miguel. The level of talent surprised me. These were not sailors who happened to play music, but musicians who happened to be sailors.

"How in the hell did the Captain find these guys?" I was still pondering that question when the lack of sleep got to me and I nodded off.

"Wake up, surfer boy. It's show time." Harry was shaking my chair. Most of the crew was gone and Clem was wiping down the bar.

"Looks like the show is over," I said.

The Captain was playing something on my guitar. He stopped, stood, and handed it to me.

"Your turn, Rob."

This was my audition. Sober, I'd have been terrified of exposing my mediocre talent to an audience of accomplished musicians. But the San Miguel did its job. I made my way through "The House of the Rising Sun." Nobody gagged.

My performance didn't secure a spot on the stage, but apparently earned me a yet-to-be-determined supporting role.

That first night with my shipmates in a smoky saloon in

Olongapo City, I learned that making music would be our mission above all else. We were in uncharted waters. There was no manual on how to turn a Navy ship into a showboat. But, as tired and confused as I was, I contributed to our mission by suggesting our ship's show business handle, which all present unanimously approved. She would be known as the *Mekong Belle*.

By the time we dropped anchor in Vung Tau Bay, the *Mekong Belle's* transformation into something resembling an old-time Mississippi River showboat was well underway.

3

Vung Tau

•••••••••••••••••••••

T HE RICKSHAW DRIVER WHO'D DIRECTED me to
Rue de Paris earlier that morning was gone when I got back
to the dock. I wanted to thank him and ask his name. I was certain
he would be a rich resource of information about Vung Tau.
Perhaps he knew where Melanie worked.

The ride back to our ship, which was anchored in the bay, took
fifteen minutes. The only other returning passenger was Signalman
Third Class Edward Archer, with whom I often stood watch on
the ship's bridge.

"Why are you heading back so early, Archer?"

"I've got the 1600 to 2000 watch. I just went into town to look
around."

Archer, a lanky black man born and raised in New York City, was
good at his Navy job, which was using semaphore flags and signal
lights to send messages across the water as fast as a man could talk. But
it was his excellent tenor voice and ability to mimic the lead singer of
every R & B song ever recorded that got him assigned to our ship.

"Are you going back on liberty after watch?" I asked.

"Me and LaMo are going to a club that he knows. Barker's got
evening watch, so he can't come."

Clayborne La Motte and Charles Barker, both black, were also signalmen. I had plenty of time on the ship's journey from Subic Bay, Philippines to South Vietnam to get to know Archer and LaMotte, with whom I stood watch in four-hour shifts. Singing would not be allowed on most ships while standing watch. On the *Bell County*, it was encouraged.

We sang whatever came into our heads. I preferred pop numbers by the Beatles or songs like Bobby Darin's "Beyond the Sea." Archer and La Motte favored popular soul and old doo-wop rock. Our interests converged with groups like the Drifters and The Five Satins.

Their voices were better, so I followed their lead. On a good night, with the right selection of songs, time passed quickly.

"Do they have live music at that club in Vung Tau, Archer?"

"Yes, sir. LaMo says they got a couple of black Frenchies and some locals who can really rock it."

"Black Frenchies?"

"You know, from Algeria or someplace like that. They don't speak English, but they sure can sing it."

Archer and I had just gotten back on board the ship when the day's plans were changed.

The XO came on the ship's PA announcing, "We're lifting anchor and heading to the ramp. All hands man your stations."

Bringing a ship into a dock, where too much speed meant crashing into something and too little meant drifting off course, was like steering a tiger by his tail, only instead of a tiger, it was an enormous, fat, sluggish, steel whale, the length of a football field.

At these times, our Captain was the opposite of his usual relaxed and affable self. He did not drive the ship as smoothly and naturally as he played jazz.

Jaw clenched, body stiff, he paced from one side of the bridge to the other, checking both sides for danger while gauging the

28

ship's progress on its intended course, then barking out orders for speed and rudder position changes.

Another officer relayed those orders through a voice tube down to the wheelhouse one deck below. That officer was Lieutenant Junior Grade O.J. Jackson, from Atlanta, GA, the operations officer and my direct supervisor.

He was cool, quiet, and reserved, the picture of what you'd think a naval officer should look like; except when he put on his thick, horned-rimmed glasses to read the charts. Then, he looked like the guy who does your taxes.

As our ship moved toward the ramp at Vung Tau, O.J. was at his usual spot on the bridge relaying the Captain's orders to the wheelhouse. My only job was to watch and learn.

When the ship got closer to shore, the Captain's commands came louder and faster.

"All engines ahead one third. Right ten-degree rudder. All engines stop. Port engine ahead one third."

Ships do not stop or turn on a dime. Each command had only a slight effect.

It was nerve-wracking to watch. I could not imagine how I would ever be able to judge distances, speed, wind, and tide to make that kind of approach safely.

The closer we got, the slower the ship moved, until it seemed a tiny breeze could blow it off its mark. Then, the bow gently kissed the center of the ramp and the deck crew tied off the stern. It was over.

Everybody exhaled. Tension left the Captain's face.

"Mr. Jackson, you have the deck. Finish securing the ship and prepare to open the bow doors," he ordered as he took the ladder that led down to his cabin.

"Aye, aye, Captain," O.J. replied.

Most ships tie to a pier. Our ship could do that, but had been designed to also "beach out" with its bow touching shore or a man-made ramp. Then it could open its bow doors, exposing a large, hollow interior hold, in which large amounts of cargo, and/or vehicles could be stowed. Ramps were designed to make it easy for forklifts to drive in and out of the ship's hold carrying pallets loaded with food, beer, gasoline, and ammunition.

If the *Bell County* had been just another LST the shore-based forklift operators would have her fully loaded in less than a day. But our ship's conversion into a showboat required further development. For that, the Captain had been authorized to stay on the ramp two extra days.

Turning an old Navy ship into a showboat required experience normally found on Broadway stages and Hollywood movie sets. The unlikely genius directing our effort was Chief Boatswains Mate Michael John McNally, aka, "Chief Mick," a Navy veteran of more than twenty-five years. He was a short, pot-bellied, weather-beaten, forty something, with no discernible neck, and both of his thick, muscled arms sported tattoos. His overly large head appeared to be balanced on broad shoulders slightly hunched from a lifetime of hard work. Freckles and deep lines marked the leathery skin of a face that had seen many long days in the sun, and his nose was smashed from numerous bar fights. One of his front teeth was missing, indicating that he'd not taken advantage of the excellent dental care available to all sailors.

Quick to laugh and quicker to shout menacingly at a sailor who moved too slowly, his speech was oddly lyrical in its use of colorful profanity and creative malapropisms.

After the Captain, there was no other man on board who had more say over what happened on the *Bell County* than Chief Mick. The Captain, XO, and other officers issued orders. Chief Mick saw that they were carried out.

When the Captain said he wanted to turn the ship into a showboat, the chief just nodded and said, "Aye, Aye, Captain. We'll get it done." All he needed was a description of what was wanted.

While the ship was still docked in Subic Bay, the XO handed him a rough diagram of a portable stage. By the time we reached Vung Tau, Chief Mick and his men had designed and built it from spare plywood and pallets. Broken down, it was easily secured to the bulkhead of the main hold.

The final test was to come when the chief and his men brought the parts onto shore and turned them into a stage on which our ship's show would be presented.

As good as he was at his main job, I got to know the chief in a different setting.

He and I stood next to each other at the ship's choir practices, held in the mess compartment. The choir was the XO's way to get more sailors involved with the show.

We started with the "Navy Hymn." The choir director asked who knew the words. Chief Mick was one of a few.

"How about giving us the first stanza, Chief?" the director said.

Without hesitation, the no-neck, old salt began: *"Eternal father strong to save, whose arm hath bound the restless wave. . ."*

All of us stared in disbelief. He had an angelic Irish tenor voice.

He just grinned, showing that big gap at the front of his mouth, and kept singing.

Even on a ship loaded with extraordinary musical talent, the chief more than held his own.

Now that we were on the ramp, he put his talents to finishing the stage on which the *Mekong Belle* would present its first show.

The Difference between a Fiddle and a Violin

●●●●●●●●●●●●●●●●●●●●●●

E NSIGN ANDREW COHEN REPORTED TO the ship the day before the *Bell County* departed Subic for Vietnam. He and I were classmates and liberty buddies at OCS, but I lost track of him after we graduated. While I remained in Newport for communications school, he was sent to engineering school in Norfolk, Virginia.

Andrew had a music degree from UCLA, played the violin, and spoke fluent French, from a year studying in Paris. He was smart and sophisticated but didn't like getting his hands dirty. I doubted he'd ever looked under the hood of a car, let alone seen the giant diesel or steam engine of a ship.

Naturally, the Navy made him an engineer.

Handsome, impeccably groomed, slender, slightly above average height, and dark-haired with an olive complexion, he was the guy who women eyed with more than usual interest.

Thanks to Andrew, I met Louiselle, the French-Canadian nurse. He dated her roommate, Claire.

We met the two women halfway through OCS while we were

on weekend liberty in Newport at a local nightclub. Andrew overheard them speaking French.

"*Bonsoir mademoiselles, pouvons-nous vous acheter un verre?*" He asked if we could buy them a drink. They were from Quebec City. They also spoke English, but considered themselves French to the core. Andrew won them over immediately.

I didn't speak a word of French, but stood there nodding and smiling. Louiselle smiled back and touched my hand, "I will teach you to speak French *mon cher*."

She was a slender brunette with dark brown eyes that sought and held mine. She had high cheekbones, a generous mouth and a Lauren Bacall voice with which she made even common words sounds sexy. "*Si'l vous plait*" (please) and "*merci*" (thank you) sounded even better when they came from her.

I had no idea what this lovely, charming, young woman saw in me, but I was totally smitten. She was a sweet, engaging and affectionate companion who taught me just enough French so that certain phrases always remind me of her.

Both women were more sophisticated about relationships than either Andrew or me. They knew that ours would end when the Navy sent us on our way. I expressed hope that Louiselle would wait for me. She made it clear that wasn't going to happen.

After we graduated from OCS, Andrew had to say goodbye to Claire.

I stayed on at the communications school in Newport for another three months, finally bidding *au revoir* to Louiselle and boarding a plane for Little Creek, Virgina, for amphibious training. From there, I would eventually fly to Southeast Asia to report to my ship.

Louiselle and I exchanged letters for several months, but time and distance conspired against a continuing relationship. The same issues ended Andrew's connection with Claire.

He was surprised to see me when he reported to the *Bell County* in Subic Bay.

"I can't believe we got assigned to the same ship. When they changed my orders, I thought that yours were probably changed too," he said.

"I don't think it's a coincidence."

"What do you mean?"

"I'll explain later, but first I need to introduce you to Lt. Luccero, the XO."

Triple Lew was shuffling some papers when I brought Andrew down the narrow corridor to his stateroom.

"XO, our assistant engineering officer, Andrew Cohen, has arrived."

"Ensign Cohen, welcome aboard the *Bell County*," he said standing and extending his hand. "The Captain's ashore, but he'll be back in a few hours."

"I see you brought your violin," he added, nodding toward the small case Andrew carried in his left hand.

"Yes, sir, as you requested. And I got your letter explaining why. I hope you got my reply that I was classically trained. I don't play fiddle."

"You know the difference between a violin and a fiddle?" the XO asked. Before Andrew could respond he added, "A violin doesn't get beer spilled on it."

A look of discomfort crossed Andrew's face. "Ah. Yes, sir. If you say so, sir," he said stiffly.

The XO replied gently. "Don't worry, Andrew. Nobody's going to force you to play music you don't like. That part of your job is entirely voluntary. Just give us a chance to show you what's possible."

With that, we were dismissed and I took Andrew to our tiny closet of a stateroom.

"Like I said. No coincidence. You're here because of music. So am I, sort of, although I'm not a real musician like you."

"But they want me to play the fiddle." He said it as though they were asking him to pick up dog shit with his bare hands.

I pulled back the curtain to our stateroom.

"Jesus! How are we both supposed to fit our stuff in here?" Then he glanced at the bunks, adding, "I assume I'm on top."

"Good guess. This is just where we sleep. The wardroom has two comfortable easy chairs."

Andrew, never "Andy," had a fastidious side, which was why he chose the Navy. He imagined himself in his dress white uniform, white gloves, and polished brass, drinking champagne and greeting guests in French at some naval ambassador post.

Instead, he was jammed into a stuffy, steel, broom closet, with a less-than-neat roommate, destined to be grubbing around in the bowels of the ship's engine room getting grease on his clean, freshly starched uniform.

Like all of the ship's officers, he was also required to stand watch as the Officer of the Deck, a responsibility he found frightening to the point of nausea.

After his first time, he declared, "I hate being the OOD. It makes me nervous. I just know I'm going to run the ship aground."

He did not enjoy our voyage from the Philippines to Vietnam, but having arrived, we were about to go on our first evening liberty in Vietnam, and I was anxious to tell him about the interesting woman I'd met that morning while shopping for a dictionary.

"Andrew, you won't believe what happened to me when I went into Vung Tau this morning. I met the most incredible woman. She speaks three languages, including English, and in addition, she is drop-dead gorgeous."

"Right. After weeks at sea, any female is going to look beautiful compared to the ugly mugs of our shipmates. I have a more important concern. What are we supposed to wear for dinner at the governor's mansion tonight?"

It annoyed me that he showed no interest in my story about Melanie.

"Dress whites, with swords," I said.

"You know. My dad is a butcher. He taught me how to sharpen all manner of blades. I'm going to stick my very sharp sword where it hurts most if you don't tell me what we're supposed to wear for dinner with the Captain," he said.

"Your dad was a butcher? I thought for sure he was a broom handle maker and stuck one up your ass the day you were born."

He threw his pillow at me.

"Here's the deal. The Captain invited, aka ordered, us to accompany him and the XO to dinner tonight. Civilian clothes are required. I only have one pair of non-Navy khakis and two shirts: a short-sleeved aloha and a light-blue long-sleeve. Everything else in that tiny locker is Navy. So, I'm wearing the khakis and the blue shirt."

"Okay. Fine. Tell me about the woman," he said.

"No time now. I've got to go see the XO. You have about an hour to add more starch to your already starched collection of button-down shirts for tonight's soiree. Then we have choir practice." I said.

The XO was coming out of his office as I approached.

"Good, you're here."

The ship's office was little more than another small closet squeezed in between the officers' head and a compartment where we stored the extra stuff that wouldn't fit in our staterooms.

There was room for two people, one at the desk, one standing in the door.

He went to the file drawer, grabbed a folder from which he pulled a sheet of paper, and handed it to me.

It was an excellent rendering of the *Bell County*.

"That was done by Ortega," he said.

Ortega was our other steward. Younger than Reyes, he'd reported aboard just before we left Subic.

"It looks like he's got some skill," I said.

"Notice his calligraphy too. I think Ortega has a talent we can use," he added.

"Okay," I said

"I want you to rough out a handbill announcing our shows. We'll assign a couple of the crew to hand them out. I'd like it to be general enough that we can add dates, times, and places in a space at the bottom."

"Okay, how do we get them printed?"

"O.J. will take care of that. There's a print shop on the base tender. They have one of those new A.B. Dick quick-print presses. He knows somebody there."

"Aye, aye, sir. When do you need it?"

"Yesterday."

"Yes, sir."

His request was not unexpected. I'd already been noodling around with some ideas. Ortega's artistic skills were just what I needed.

I found him in the small galley next to the officer's mess, showed him my rough draft for the handbill, and explained what I'd like for artwork.

"I want a drawing of our ship, but I want it to look like an old-fashioned Mississippi River paddle wheeler."

Ortega looked puzzled. "Patti wheel?"

I realized that this guy, barely eighteen, had never been out of the Philippines and had no idea what I was talking about.

"A showboat, with a big wheel on the back," I replied, my poor artistic skills failing me as I tried to enhance the rough outline I was showing him.

"Showboat? Oh, like "Old Man River." I saw the movie. My parents love it."

"Yes. That's it. Can you make a drawing of the ship that makes it look like a riverboat?"

"Yes sir."

I gave him my rough drawing that included the wording: "Showboat coming. *Mekong Belle*. Live music from Dixieland to Rock 'n Roll. USS *Bell County* (LST 888)."

There was room to hand-print, or stencil, a day and time.

While I was talking to Ortega, Harry found Andrew ironing his dress shirt in the storage compartment. I was passing the compartment and heard Harry's wisecrack.

"Don't forget to iron your boxers too," he said.

Andrew and Harry, were opposites in every way. They'd gotten off to a rough start. Andrew did not know how to take Harry's humor. He was repelled by the grime that the engineering officer wore on his uniform, almost like a badge of honor.

"The man cannot speak without yelling," Andrew said. "I don't get his jokes. And, I've never seen him in a clean uniform."

"And yet the engineering compartments, the engines and generators are spotless," I said.

"Yes. I think he uses his shirt to do most of the cleaning," Andrew said.

"I agree about the uniform, but you're reading him wrong. Harry is rough around the edges, but a real creampuff inside. His men respect him. Heck, I think they actually like him. That's why the engineering spaces always look squared away."

Just before choir practice, Andrew came back to our stateroom, a puzzled expression on his face.

"What's up, roomie?"

"Harry said the strangest thing to me, and I haven't a clue what he meant."

"What was it?"

"Welcome to the black gang."

I knew what the black gang was, but I wanted to hear more of Andrew's story.

"Tell me more."

"When we got out to the ramp, we spotted Chief Mick getting chewed out by a base supply officer.

"We heard him say that our stuff wasn't authorized cargo. Then he stuck his finger in the Chief's face and demanded that it be removed immediately. I don't know how the chief kept so calm. He looked like he was enjoying himself.

"Anyway, Harry walked over and introduced himself to the lieutenant. Then the guy started ranting at Harry about our crates and pallets junking up his pier."

I'd already learned that Navy supply corps personnel and regular Navy sailors had a relationship borne out of necessity, not love. To sailors, the shore-based supply guys were tight-assed bean counters. To them, sailors were pirates who could not be trusted.

"So what happened next?" I asked.

"The officer's last name was Burlocker. Harry kept calling him Buttlicker. The guy's face got redder and his voice got higher. He kept repeating that our stuff was unauthorized and had to be removed.

"Harry took a step toward him, folded his arms across his chest and asked 'Why?' I thought the guy was going to blow a gasket. He shouted 'What do you mean why?'"

"I'm surprised that Harry didn't throw him into the bay," I said.

"That's when I said something," Andrew said.

"What?"

"The word 'why' is used as an inquiry, a request for a reason. For example: Why are you being such an ass?"

"Before the guy could turn on me, Harry stepped between us and spoke up. 'Okay, Lieutenant. We'll move 'em,' he said. And just when I thought he'd given in, he added a final word, 'tomorrow.'"

"That set the guy on another tirade, until Harry took a step toward him. Then another. The supply guy shut his mouth and backed up. Harry kept moving forward, not saying anything.

"The lieutenant continued backward until his retreat was stopped by a pallet resting on the blades of a forklift. He kind of fell/sat down on it while Harry towered over him.

"Then Harry said, ' Okay. Tomorrow, it is.' He nodded at me. We turned around and headed back toward the chief, who'd been standing with several of the ship's crew watching us. 'Carry on chief,' Harry said as we passed him."

I pictured Harry, as big and burly as a bear, standing over the stunned supply lieutenant.

"The guy was still sitting on the pallet when we walked back up the ramp into the ship. I asked Harry if we were going to get into trouble. He said, that the supply guys were a bunch of pussies and wouldn't have the guts to do anything."

"He's probably right," I said.

"Anyway, Harry actually thanked me for speaking up. When I replied that Buttlicker was a fucking asshole, he let out a loud guffaw, put his arm around me, and said 'You got that right Andrew. Welcome to the Black Gang.'" Andrew paused and spread his hands wide. "What the hell did that mean?"

"Black gang is old Navy slang for the sailors who work in the engine room. It refers to the dark, oily places below decks where they work. It's an honorific they bestow on themselves." I said.

In his wildest imagination, Andrew could never have seen himself in any gang. Yet, from that day on, he carried that distinction with pride. I even saw diesel and grease stains on his uniform on rare occasions.

Andrew and I couldn't change the Navy, but it was surely changing us.

Having answered his question, I saw the tension leave his face.

"Now, tell me about that beautiful woman," he said.

I gave him a summary of my morning searching for the book, and how I ended up at the store where I meant Melanie.

"Her name is French, but she is Vietnamese," Andrew said.

"Yes. At least I think so. She spoke Vietnamese and French to the store clerk, and perfect British English to me."

"Sounds like a cultured, sophisticated woman. I wonder what she sees in you."

"Fuck you, Andrew."

He laughed. "Okay. How about I go back to that store with you tomorrow? I can use my French to ask the clerk if she knows where Melanie works."

"Thanks. I'd appreciate it. Now, I want to bag a few z's before choir practice."

"Oh Happy Day"

Eternal Father, strong to save,
Whose arm hath bound the restless wave,
Who bidd'st the mighty ocean deep
Its own appointed limits keep;
Oh, hear us when we cry to Thee,
For those in peril on the sea!

—First stanza, US "Navy Hymn"

"STOP!" REYES HELD UP HIS HAND. "The 'Navy Hymn' needs a full, deep sound, like the rumble of a ship's engine, building to the next to last line; then, all engines ahead full. Let's start again."

Choir practice was after lunch every day.

The choir was the XO's idea, for two reasons: If our shows were performed on Sundays, opening with the choir would mollify the chaplains. It also got a lot more of the men involved.

The crew's mess, one of the largest interior compartments of the ship, had interesting acoustics. It was like singing in the shower.

The crew's taste in music ran from rock and roll to country. But the choir only practiced the "Navy Hymn," "Star Spangled Banner," and "Amazing Grace." We were getting restless.

"No matter how we sing it, it still sounds like we're at a funeral," groused one of deck crew.

"Yeah. Can we at least do a rockin' gospel with some kick in it?" Archer said.

Reyes started to respond, but his co-conductor, Melvin "Doc" Hodges, spoke up first.

"You're right, Archer. The band shouldn't be the only one having fun. Let me think on it. But we still need to work on the songs we've been given, because that's what the Captain and the XO want," Hodges said.

I learned about second-class medical corpsman Hodge's pre-Navy history from the XO. He's finished at the top of his class with a B.S. in biology at Morehouse College, GA. His intent was to go to medical school, but his med school application didn't get far enough, fast enough, probably due to racism at the nearly all-white medical schools to which he applied.

He got his draft notice instead, forcing him to join the Navy.

Few Navy recruiters, especially in the South, saw black men as potential officers. They didn't even suggest he apply for OCS. Hodges thought about applying anyway, but a friend, already in the Navy, suggested that with his degree in biology he could advance quickly as a medical corpsman, which could be his eventual ticket to medical school.

As the only medical technician on board, he was virtually our ship's doctor, an experience that would eventually get him into medical school. He had the physique of a long-distance runner, which he had been at Morehouse. On the *Belle County* he led calisthenics every morning. He was part of our crew because he was a talented pianist with a fondness for jazz.

Perhaps the most popular man on the ship, and in spite of the Navy tradition discouraging fraternization between officers and enlisted, Doc was also as close to the Captain and XO as any of us. He was the CO's understudy on piano and collaborated with him on musical arrangements and show programing.

Doc's musical talents were not limited to the piano. He played electric guitar better than anyone on the ship. Even the Captain was amazed when he pounded out a perfect imitation of Jimi Hendrix's "Purple Haze."

Doc's musical diversity made him the perfect choir director. Reyes, who had a lot of church choir experience as a boy, was his assistant.

Together, they made a good team and the choir was rounding into shape.

"How many of you know, 'Oh Happy Day?'" Doc asked.

Most of the black choir members raised their hands. A few white guys, myself included, also raised theirs.

"It's an old gospel song rearranged and released by the Edwin Hawkins Singers. It's upbeat and the lyrics are easy. All you got to do is follow."

Then he started clapping his hands and tapping one foot.

"Those of you who know it, join in." He started singing.

"Oh, happy day. Oh, happy day. Oh, happy day. Oh, happy day. When Jesus washed, when Jesus washed. . ."

It was one of those songs where the lead sings a line, then a second group echoes it. With each new chorus, the choir got more confident and the harmony came together.

Soon, everybody was clapping, singing, and dancing around the mess hall. Even the cooks in the galley joined in by banging on pots with metal spoons, adding to the rhythm.

Halfway through the third stanza, the Captain and XO walked in.

Before anyone could shout "Attention on deck!" and stop the music, the CO motioned Doc to keep it going.

Then he smiled and started clapping. The XO joined in.

The mess hall rocked for several more minutes until Doc brought everybody to a big finish. There were shouts of joy and high-fives all around.

"Doc," the Captain said, "I think you should add that to your song list." Then he turned to the XO, "You agree, Lew?"

"Absolutely, Captain," the XO replied enthusiastically.

"Aye, aye, Captain," Doc responded smiling then pointing to Archer, the signalman, who had spoken up. "We can thank Archer for the suggestion."

Back in our stateroom after practice, I asked Andrew if he was going to come to the band rehearsal later.

"Probably. But, I've got the mid-watch tonight, so I want to get some sleep before we go to dinner."

"I know the feeling, but I really want to see if everything works. This is our first big test. Besides, I saw you singing, clapping, and jiving with the rest of us at choir practice. Fiddle, or no fiddle, you're into the music."

He grunted, then climbed up into his bunk and closed his eyes.

I stared at him, waiting for an answer.

"Okay. Wake me up when you head down," he said.

Making good music was the key to turning our ship into a showboat, even if not all of us performed on stage. Many played supporting roles. Chief Mick trained some sailors in packing, unpacking, and assembling the stage parts and crates, including the one that contained the Captain's small upright piano.

Others worked on technical stuff, like getting power to the microphones and amplifiers. An enthusiastic team helped prepare and serve food during our shows. A significant number practiced musical numbers they hoped could be added to our show. This was, after all, a group of men who thought of themselves as musicians first, sailors second.

They all wanted to be part of the show.

"I'm walkin', yes indeed, I'm talkin'…" The first Vung Tau band rehearsal started at 1600 as planned. The Captain was well into his Fats Domino routine and the ramp area was filling up with sailors from nearby ships and warehouses. Except for a couple of microphones by the piano, the music was not amplified, yet it was heard all over the base.

The band opened with a Dixieland version of "Bill Bailey Won't You Please Come Home?" At the Captain's insistence, I had written lyrics for a second verse, which was supposed to serve as a musical invitation to our show.

"Rob, we want to send a message to our troops that we're playing for them – the guys, our brothers, especially the ones stuck way out in the boondocks where they get pounded by mortars and sneak attacks every night."

I knocked the verse out in a hurry the night before the practice and handed it to the Captain in the morning.

He gave it a quick glance then replied. "This'll work for now."

It was shit and we both knew it. But there was no time for improvement.

I cringed when they used it, but nobody seemed to notice how truly bad the lyrics were:

Won't you come on my brothers?
Won't you come yell"
We'll play the whole day long.
We make the music sunny. We make it free.
We hope that you'll sing along.
Remember those rainy evenings,
They stuck you out,
In a shit hole that was close to hell?
Tonight with a beer,
Sweet sounds you will hear.
My brothers come and cheer with Belle!

Andrew and I were standing with the crew to the right of the stage. Chief Mick was putting cans of beer into a tub of ice, from which the sailors were invited to help themselves.

Ships like ours hauled a large variety of cargo up river, including ammunition, gasoline, food, candy, soda pop and beer. The candy and beverages were destined for small PXs at the remote bases where they were sold to the soldiers there by the supply corps.

Sometimes, pallets broke in transit. When they did, their contents were reported "lost." It wasn't a coincidence that the most frequent accident happened with beer pallets.

The bogus damage claims were one of many reasons why the supply corps guys thought we were pirates. We gave the beer away free to the guys stuck upriver under fire. We made lots of friends with our brothers in arms.

As the sailors enjoyed the beer, the practice continued.

After the CO ran the band through several Dixieland jazz numbers, the doo-wop quartet came up.

They started with "Sh-Boom" and followed it with "Why Do Fools Fall in Love?" Signalman Archer nailed the falsetto lead originally performed by Frankie Lyman.

The band finished with "When the Saints Go Marching In." The entire crew and most of the sailors who had wandered over to watch were clapping and singing along.

Everyone applauded, whistled, and cheered, many coming over to the bandstand to shake hands with the musicians and thank them.

I noticed Reyes handing something out to anyone who passed by the stage. It was the handbill. At the bottom, someone had hand printed: "Dress Rehearsal Tomorrow (Sunday) 1100. Free Music. Free Food. Free Beer"

"Holy Shit! Did you see this?" I showed the handbill to Andrew.

"Wow! We're going to have a beer bash tomorrow. And we've invited the whole Navy; at least the ones here in Vung Tau."

"I bet you anything that the base brass didn't approve this. The Captain and XO must have been secretly planning this all along."

Harry walked over as we were looking at the handbill. "They clearly have the biggest and brassiest balls in the fleet," he said.

"Do you think Lt. Asslicker will try to shut us down?" Andrew asked.

"That's Lt. Buttlicker. Please. Show the guy some respect," Harry said. "Hmm. I think we need a plan in case he shows up unannounced," he added.

A few minutes later we saw him huddled in close conversation with O.J. and Chief Mick.

"Andrew. Those three are cooking up something," I said.

"Harry is always cooking up something," he said.

"It's time for us to get ready for our dinner in Vung Tau."

6

A Reunion with Melanie
● ●

I T WAS A SHORT DRIVE from the base to the restaurant
through the heart of the village. Local residents shopped and
milled about chatting while their children played.

"Don't they know there's a war going on?" Andrew asked.

"They know. But Vung Tau is generally considered a no-fire
zone by all sides. Vietnam has been at war for centuries. First with
the Chinese, then the Japanese and the French. Now it's South
versus North, the Catholics against the Buddhists, Americans
against the Communists. Vung Tau is where they all take a break
from fighting," the XO said.

His explanation confirmed my earlier feelings that the village
had an "other-worldly" vibe.

We turned into a quiet, tree-lined neighborhood that looked
similar to the one on which I'd strolled in the morning.

The former governor-general's mansion was a two-story,
French-colonial structure painted white, and surrounded by a fence
and garden. A hand-painted wooden sign at the gate read: "*La
Fille du General*" (the General's Daughter).

Andrew and I followed Captain Baillier and Lt. Luccero up
the walkway to an expansive front porch where several small groups

of men in civilian clothes were conversing over cocktails. A woman in a silk ao dai, her back to us, was taking orders for more drinks.

Captain Baillier stepped onto the porch and called to her.

"*Bonsoir,* Melanie, *ca va?*"

She turned and smiled, then looked toward me, nodding in recognition. My heart skipped a beat.

She kissed the Captain lightly on both cheeks. "*Bonsoir mon capitaine,*" she said, then switched to English. "My mother said you were coming tonight."

Turing to the XO she said, "Lieutenant Luccero, it is nice to see you again."

She paused, looked at me, then Andrew, and turned back to the XO, "And who are these handsome young gentlemen?"

"Mademoiselle Marquis, may I present our two newest officers, Ensign Robert Allen and Ensign Andrew Cohen. Gentlemen this is Miss Melanie Marquis, daughter of Madame Simone Marquis, the owner of this lovely establishment."

Andrew stepped forward and took her hand.

"*Enchanté, Mademoiselle, C'est un grand plaisir de vous rencontrer*"

She answered him in French, then looked back at me.

"So that's what you meant when you said *a bientot,*" I said.

"Yes. When you mentioned the *Bell County,* I hoped that you might be here with Captain Baillier tonight."

Speaking to Melanie, I said, "Andrew and I are roommates. I told him about meeting you today. It was very kind of you to come to my rescue."

She nodded and offered us each an arm. "You are most welcome. Allow me to escort you to our dining room."

Andrew whispered in my ear. "I will never doubt your taste in women again. She is *trés magnifique.*"

The mansion dining room was in the large central courtyard open on one side toward the beach in the distance. Strings of small white lights were strung across it. There was a fountain in the center. A small bandstand with a piano sat in a corner next to the building. A warm, light breeze floated in from the bay.

Vietnamese men, smartly dressed in white trousers and long-sleeved white shirts, and women, most barely five feet tall, wearing ao dai's, were busily attending to diners.

Melanie led us to a table next to the bandstand. As soon as we were seated, a waiter appeared with four glasses of champagne and announced that they were "courtesy of Madame Marquis."

The Captain raised his glass. "*Salute*, gentleman. Here's to the success of the *Mekong Belle*."

"*Salute!*" we all said in unison.

"Madame Marquis has requested that we enjoy the set menu. It shows off her kitchen's talent for blending the best of French and Vietnamese cuisine. I told her we were in her hands," said the Captain.

Our meal began with crispy crab rolls and a papaya salad, followed by lemongrass chicken, roasted duck breast and a fish called "Ca Hop," accompanied by fried rice, green beans and noodles.

"This duck breast is as good as any I had in Paris," Andrew said.

"The chefs here were trained in Paris," said the Captain.

"Wait until you taste the French pastries they serve for dessert," the XO said.

The conversation around the table ranged from the quality of the food, and beauty of the setting to the big show rehearsal set for the next day. As we were talking, I noticed that musicians were taking their places on the bandstand. They were children. The oldest was perhaps fifteen, the youngest ten or eleven.

"The band members are all kids," I blurted in surprise.

Andrew had noticed too. We both looked at the Captain for an explanation. But before he could respond, a slender, elegantly dressed woman took the stage and spoke into the microphone.

"Dear guests, welcome to the General's Daughter. I am Simone Marquis and it is my great pleasure to present a very special concert by the students of Saint Genevieve's Church school.

"I want to thank my friend Captain Baillier of the USS *Bell County* and members of his crew, who have offered extra instruction and arranged for donations of instruments and music to the school's program."

That explained the Captain's absence from the ship earlier in the day. He had been over at the orphanage school helping prep the young musicians for this performance.

The group consisted of a pianist, a cellist, and three students on violin. They began with Vivaldi's "Spring" from his *Four Seasons* concerti.

The dining crowd was enraptured. As the last note died, everyone stood and applauded and each child took a bow. Andrew was smiling and clapping enthusiastically

Madame Marquis came back onto the stage.

"Thank you for your kind applause. Now we are in for a special treat courtesy of Capt. Baillier," she said gesturing toward our table.

The Captain went to the stage and took the microphone.

"*Merci beaucoup,* Madame Marquis, it is nice to be back here in Vung Tau again, and it has been a great pleasure working with these wonderful students." He paused for minute and nodded to one of the students, who reached down by the side of the piano, picked up a violin case and handed to the Captain

I heard Andrew gasp, and looked at him quizzically.

"That's my violin," he whispered. "What's going on?"

I shrugged and waited to hear what the Captain was going to say.

"Now, I'd like to call up Ensign Andrew Cohen, one of the newest members of my crew, and ask him to join me as first violin to perform our excerpt from Mozart's *Concerto for Violin, Piano and Orchestra.*

"Although I did not tell him about this command appearance here in Vung Tau, it is a piece that he is most familiar with. He earned special recognition at UCLA for his mastery of this and other pieces by Mozart. Come on up Andrew."

The expressions on Andrew's face moved from surprise and terror to grim resignation. He stood and stiffly made his way to the stage. While he was opening his case and preparing to play, the Captain continued.

"Most of you are aware of the good work that Madame Marquis, her staff, and the sisters at Saint Genevieve's are doing. Many of us, including our brothers in the Australian Navy, try to support them whenever we're in port. We believe in the power of music to bring us together."

He sat down on the bench next to the young Vietnamese pianist and nodded to Andrew, who had managed to get over the surprise.

The Captain demonstrated that he was not just a jazz guy. But, more surprising was my virtuoso roomie; I had no idea he was that good. The Vietnamese youngsters demonstrated competence beyond their tender age. When they finished, the audience gave a standing ovation for the second time that evening.

The Captain stood and offered Andrew his hand. He said something that I couldn't hear, but Andrew's thank you was easy to read on his lips. When he came back to the table, the XO stood, shook his hand and patted his shoulder. "Great job, Andrew," he said.

"Andrew," I said offering him my hand. "I've never heard a violin played better."

All of the tension left him as he collapsed into his chair. He grinned. "You don't get out much, do you."

He was right about my limited knowledge of classical music. But there was no doubt that the Captain, XO, and the audience agreed with me.

Madame Marquis came to the table and added her praise. "You were fantastic Andrew."

"Merci Madame, le plaisir etait pour moi," he replied.

"Now, you're just showing off," I whispered to him.

"All that talent, and you also speak French with an excellent accent," she said.

Andrew blushed. *"Merci, Madame,* but whoever taught those kids deserves the credit. They're very good,"

Seeking to turn the attention away from himself, he added, "I can't believe the Captain. I knew he was great with jazz, but I had no idea he was classically trained."

"My grandmother was a demanding teacher," the Captain said as he rejoined the table. "She made me learn the classics first," then added, "we must introduce you to Sister Wolfgang."

"Did you say Sister Wolfgang, Captain?" I asked.

"Your Captain makes a little joke. Her name is Sister Josephine. She is Mother Superior at the orphanage, and the school's music teacher – a most remarkable woman," Madame Marquis said.

"And she is as married to Mozart as she is to God, " the Captain added.

"How does a school in a small city like Vung Tau manage to operate a music program that's so sophisticated?" Andrew asked.

"It began in the 1930s when Paul Dourmet, the Governor General of French Indochina, built this mansion. He persuaded the French government to pay for the construction of a church, convent, and a school.

"The first Ursuline Sisters to arrive included several idealistic young women who were also musicians. Through their music, they were able to attract local residents and convert their children." She paused and looked at the Captain as if to see if he wanted to add anything.

"Don't forget the most important people in this story: the governor's wife, his daughter, and you," he said.

"Of course. It was the general's wife, Madame Dourmet, who had the most influence. In fact, her youngest sister was one of the original nuns here. Also, the first priest was secretly in love with Madame Dourmet and would have done anything to make her happy.

"The sisters recognized the need to add an orphanage to their school, and that these orphans would depend on them for everything, including teaching them skills with which they could survive when they became adults. So, in addition to the basics, the church school became a vocational training center specializing in music, cooking, and hospitality."

She stopped and waved to a nearby waiter.

"Would anybody else like coffee? This story is going to take a little longer."

Andrew and I both said yes; because we had watches to stand later. The Captain and XO ordered cognacs. Melanie, helped the waiter bring our beverages, then moved toward the empty chair next to me. I stood to pull out the chair for her. She smiled. "Merci, Robert," she said quietly, her eyes holding mine for a few seconds.

Her mother continued with her story.

"Madame Dourmet's daughter, Antoinette, who was only twelve when they first came to Vung Tau, also attended the school, as did several other children of French citizens working and living in the area at the time. The Ursulines were inspiring teachers and created a wonderful, integrated program that formed strong bonds between the Vietnamese and French children; so much so, that when the time came for the older French students to travel to France to continue their education, they didn't want to leave their classmates behind.

"Thanks to the governor's wealth and connections, many of the convent school's best Vietnamese students were also sent to France, some to music academies, some to cooking schools and several to university.

"Antoinette was finishing her university in Paris with the intent of becoming a music teacher. But her mother became seriously ill. She and the governor returned to France so she could see a specialist. She died six months later.

"Eventually the governor had to return to his post here. Antoinette asked to return with him. I was her best friend at the University and she invited me to go with her. The governor was a kind and decent man and accepted me into his home here as though I was part of the family.

"Antoinette took up where her mother left off with the school. I joined her in that task and eventually taught there too.

"When the governor was called back to France several years later, Antoinette went with him, promising to return once her father was settled into his new position in Paris. He left me in charge of their home and to manage his interests at the school.

"Back in France, Antoinette met and fell in love with a young Parisian man whose family was quite wealthy. I flew back to Paris for their wedding.

"While I was there, she and her father met with me and asked if I was interested in a permanent position as manager of their business interests and property in Vietnam. Having fallen in love with the country and its people, I said yes.

"Tragically, a year after she was married, her father was assassinated by a crazed anarchist. Antoinette was his only heir. In settling his estate, she determined that I should inherit what I had been managing. Included in that gift was a large endowment to support the school and orphanage, as well as enough to manage this property."

Madame Marquis went on to tell us why and how she turned the former governor's residence into a restaurant.

"Several of the students sent to Paris, returned to Vung Tau. Two of them had been trained at Le Cordon Bleu, and then worked in several restaurants in the city. They came home because they needed to care for their families. But there was no work for French-trained chefs in this small city. It was they and my daughter, Melanie, who gave me the idea of creating The General's Daughter as a fine dining restaurant. I named it in honor of my friend, Antoinette."

I saw no wedding ring on her hand, and the delicate question on the tip of my tongue related to how she came to have a daughter. She looked at Melanie, who nodded and said, "Go ahead, Maman, it's okay."

"Melanie, whose parents perished in a boating accident on the Mekong, was a ten-year-old orphan when I came here with Antoinette. She was a sad little girl, but incredibly bright and full of curiosity. Something clicked between us, and she became my shadow. She had an incredible gift for learning languages and quickly mastered French and English. By the time she was 16, she was among the school's best students and we were as close as any mother and daughter. Not long after, the adoption was approved.

She went to Paris, where she studied at the Sorbonne before returning here two years ago."

By the time Simone finished her story, it was nearly 2300 hours. I knew Andrew had the mid-watch.

The Captain stood up. "Madame Marquis, this has been a delightful evening and we appreciate your wonderful hospitality, but I know Andrew has the midnight to 4:00 a.m. watch and needs to get back to our ship."

"Of course. It has been my pleasure," she said. She turned to Andrew who was also standing.

"Andrew it was a delight to hear you play tonight. I have a small favor to ask," she said.

"*Oui, Madame, je suis a votre service*," Andrew replied.

"Merci Andrew. Would you consider coming to the school in your free time, if your Captain and XO permit, and give some instruction to our young violin students?"

"It would be my pleasure, Madame. If you hadn't asked, I was going to offer."

The XO nodded at the Captain, then declared that he would see to it that there was time for Andrew to join the growing list of crewmembers from the Belle, including its CO, who were volunteer music teachers at the orphanage.

While Andrew and the XO walked toward the door, leaving the Captain and Madame Marquis in close conversation that hinted that their relationship was more than just about teaching music at the orphanage, I lingered trying to figure out an excuse to see Melanie again.

She beat me to it.

"Rob, I have a favor to ask you."

I nodded affirmative. I would have done anything she asked.

"Could you meet with me sometime? I could use your help with my writing," she asked.

"Of course, I would love to meet with you. But, I'm not an experienced journalist."

"No, but you are exactly what I need. I studied literature and short story writing in Paris, but they didn't offer journalism. I bought a journalism textbook and I have drafted some practice articles, but I need someone to read them and give me tips."

The XO and Andrew had stopped at the front door and were looking back at me impatiently.

"You have yourself a coach. Whenever you're ready, I can read what you've written and offer suggestions. Is that okay?"

"Oh yes. *Merci beaucoup.* Oh. And don't worry about your dictionary. I will pick it up for you." She kissed me on both cheeks. Then added "*a bientot.*"

The XO gave me a curious look, while Andrew just smiled, and muttered "Ooo, la, la."

"Shut up, Andrew," I shot back as we walked down the sidewalk.

7

The Show Must Go On
••••••••••••••••••••••

I HIT MY RACK WHILE Andrew took the officer of the deck watch on the ramp. I still felt Melanie's warm lips on my cheek and the touch of her hand on my arm.

I had a hard time shutting down my brain. Was there more to her request than an interest in journalism? How could I get time off the ship to see her? What about her mother, Madame Marquis, and the Captain? Where they involved? Do Melanie and her mother realize that there is no place for them to run if the war moves south?

It seemed that I'd just fallen to sleep, when I was awakened for my turn on watch.

Afterward, there was just enough time to eat breakfast and help set up for the ship's dress rehearsal at 1100.

O.J. was just finishing his breakfast as I entered the wardroom.

"Good morning, Rob. How was your dinner at the General's Daughter last night?"

"It was the best meal I've had in a long time; maybe ever. The mansion is beautiful. And we heard some amazing local kids playing Vivaldi and Mozart."

"I heard that you were a hit with Madame Marquis' daughter," he added dryly.

"Hit? Probably not. But she did ask for my help. Did you know that she wants to be a journalist?"

He took a last sip of his coffee, stood up, and put his cup down. "No. And I bet her mother doesn't know either."

"Is that a problem?" I asked.

"Could be. This war has a lot to do with old grievances between the French, their Vietnamese Catholic converts, and the non-Catholic and communist Vietnamese who want them out of the country.

"Thieu, the current South Vietnamese president is a Catholic, but his government is as corrupt as his predecessors. They don't like journalists. They tolerate ours, but treat their own like shit unless they kowtow to the government's storyline.

"If Melanie becomes a journalist, and if she ruffles any feathers, she could create problems for herself and her mother, Catholic or not."

He started to leave the wardroom, but stopped, and turned around.

"And one more thing, the Communists also hate journalists. You need to tell Melanie she is headed down a dangerous path."

Then, he was out the door.

O.J.'s comments tempered my enthusiasm for coaching Melanie in her choice of journalism as a career, but not my happiness about the prospects of seeing her again.

After breakfast, I headed down to the ramp to make surethat our Electrician's Mate, Murdock, was following through on all the last-minute checks of the electrical gear for the show.

On my way I passed by the crew's mess and the galley. The Captain was standing next to our ship's cook, Freddie Wing. They were sampling something from a large steaming pot.

"Perfect as always Freddie. Do we have enough rice cooked to go with it?"

"Yes, Captain. But it must be kept hot here until the last minute. Then, we rush it to the ramp to serve," Wing replied.

I'd been surprised at the quality of the food on our ship. Navy cooks are generally good, but Freddie Wing was a master. He was the second generation in his family to be a cook in the U.S. military. Fred, Sr., his father, emigrated to the U.S. from China in 1939. He was working in a San Francisco restaurant when the Japanese attacked Pearl Harbor and immediately joined the Army, which designated him as a cook.

A top general discovered and commandeered him to be his personal chef. Freddie After the war, he opened his own restaurant in Napa.

Freddie Jr. grew up in that restaurant kitchen, then spent high school summers with his uncle, who was a chef in New Orleans. By the time he was an adult and joined the Navy, he was already an accomplished chef in his own right.

By good fortune, Freddie was sent to the *Bell County* where his New Orleans training quickly endeared him to the Captain, with whom he regularly collaborated on the ship's menu.

As I passed them, the Captain saw me and waved me over.

"Rob, come here and taste this."

Freddie handed me a clean spoon and I dipped it into the dark, rich, peppery- smelling stew. It was every bit as delicious as it was fragrant. There was quite a bit of cayenne that added extra kick as well.

"Jesus! That's really good. What is it?"

"Shrimp étouffée, just like my grand-mere used to make," the Captain said. "Freddie has a knack for Cajun cooking,"

"Is this what we're serving at the rehearsal?"

"Yes, this over rice." Freddie said.

"How? I mean. In what?"

"Your boss, O.J., has taken care of that," the Captain said.

"He snagged a shipment of disposable bowls and plastic forks and spoons that the Army sometimes uses."

With that, he turned back to take one more taste of the bubbling étouffée, and I continued on my way to the ramp. It occurred to me that the *Bell County* was the most unusual ship with the most uniquely talented crew in the Navy. But I wasn't certain if the Navy would accept what was coming next.

* * *

By 1030 hours, all the electrical gear had been checked out, pallets were stacked to serve as food service tables, and members of the ship's choir, scheduled to perform first, were starting to mingle around the bandstand.

I noticed that Harry, the engineering officer, was talking intensely to a small group of crewmembers and gesturing toward the ship.

At 1100 exactly, Reyes took the stage and tapped on the mike. A small crowd of fifty to sixty sailors from the base and nearby ships had gathered.

"Welcome everyone to the first performance of our show before a live audience. I want to remind you that it is just a rehearsal. We're still getting our act together. As a reward for showing up and supporting us, there will be hot chow and free cold beer served immediately following the last number. Enjoy the show and stay for the food."

The sailors whistled and applauded.

"How 'bout some beer now?" one sailor yelled.

Reyes glanced over at the XO, who nodded approval.

"Okay, the beer is in a big tub of ice on the starboard side of the ramp. Go help yourself. Just one per sailor for now, guys."

The rush for the beer took several minutes. During that time, Doc and Reyes hustled the choir onto the stage.

As the mob around the beer tub dispersed, we began the "Navy Hymn."

The sailors jumped at attention. Some saluted.

As we neared the second stanza, a jeep drove up and stopped just behind the last row of sailors. It was Lt. Buttlicker. With him were two burly shore patrolmen who looked like they meant business. The lieutenant pointed toward the stage and said something to the SPs.

Just when I thought our show was going to be shut down before the conclusion of the first number, Harry and John approached Lt. Buttlicker.

They seemed to be explaining something and pointing to the ship's open bow doors. The lieutenant followed one of our sailors up the ramp and into the ship as the hymn ended.

John offered the SPs each a cold beer and brought them to a row of folded chairs set up close to the stage. Seated on either side of them where the Captain and XO. I had no idea what Harry had cooked up.

Everyone stood at attention as we sang the Star Spangled Banner. Then Doc stepped to the microphone.

"I know you all have been to church today," he said, then paused while a small ripple of laughter ran through the gathering. "But, just in case you were on watch or something, we're gonna bring a little church to you. Feel free to clap and sing along with us."

Then he started clapping his hands, and began the lead;

"*Oh Happy Day. Oh Happy Day. When Jesus Washed. When Jesus Washed….*"

We left everyone clapping as we left the stage and the Captain and his band came on and went right into "Won't You Come Home Bill Bailey?"

The Captain had been working with Reyes and Doc to keep

the show moving. It was pretty damn professional. There was virtually no delay from number to number. I thought they'd canceled the Andrews Sisters' "Boogie Woogie Bugle Boy" number, until Reyes and two other crew members came on stage to roars of laughter from the crowd.

Reyes, the diminutive Filipino, Archer the lanky African American and no-neck Chief Mick came to the microphone in bizarre "drag."

Their fake long hair had been fashioned from several mop heads. The chief's was dyed red. Reyes and Archer easily fit into women's skirts and blouses with balloons for breasts peaking over the top buttons. The chief was decked out in a muumuu. Bright red lipstick and overdone eye shadow completed the look. Laughter continued until the band started playing and the trio started singing.

They looked like a joke, but their voices weren't. They were amazing. And so was John on the trumpet. The number turned out to be the hit of the day. The rest of the show ran smoothly and everybody joined in the final parade around the yard as the band played "When the Bell Comes Sailing In."

By that time, Freddie and his assistants had set up the food service line and were spooning étouffée onto warm rice for the sailors, who eagerly lined up for it plus another free beer. The XO made sure that the two shore patrol guys were at the head of the chow line.

Harry was standing with Chief Mick and John near the ramp as the last of the sailors were passing through the food line.

"Chief. You are by far the sexiest Andrews Sister," I said.

"Don't get too cocky, Mr. Allen. You're going to be called on stage soon enough."

"Chief, I have neither your talent, nor your good looks."

He laughed.

"John. Is it possible that you could play "Reveille" like that every morning?" I asked our deck officer.

"Only if the Chief and Reyes sing along. Of course, I'll need the Captain on piano and the XO on drums too."

Just then the Captain and XO walked out of the bow doors and down the ramp toward us. Between them was the slightly disheveled supply lieutenant blinking as his eyes adjusted to the bright sun.

"Don't you worry, Lieutenant. We'll make sure our stuff is back inside the ship by 1600 today. We've got to move off the ramp by 1800," the Captain said as they walked by.

I looked at Harry, who was grinning as he watched the lieutenant catch up to the two SPs, who quickly hid their beers when they saw their boss approaching.

"Harry, what did you do?" I asked.

"I think he misunderstood me. I told him the Captain would like to meet with him on board the ship. He must have missed the part when I added '...after the show.' One of the crew gave him directions to the Captain's cabin. He got lost and was accidentally locked in the ship's rope locker."

"So that's our story?" Andrew asked.

"The show must go on," said Harry

Just then the Captain approached our group.

"Great job everybody. The *Mekong Belle* is ready for action," he declared. There was joy in his voice.

After dinner, I wrote my first report to Aunt Celie, describing my first day in Vung Tau, meeting Melanie, and about our ship's successful rehearsal.

A Change Is Gonna Come

●●●●●●●●●●●●●●●●●●●●●●●●

CHIEF MICK AND THE CREW had the bandstand and instruments stored and secured within thirty minutes of the last dish of étouffée being served. The Bell County's ramp was raised and bow doors closed.

At 1730 hours, the ship backed away from the ramp and began its journey south and west toward the mouth of the Mekong River system and the Song Tien Giang, its tributary. It would take us to My Tho, one of the larger cities in the Mekong Delta.

Timing is important when approaching the river because a bar of silt builds up where it meets the sea. Ships can get stuck if they try to cross at low tide. We didn't want to cross the bar in the dark because there were no buoys or lighthouses marking the way.

The plan was to arrive near the mouth just before dark, drop anchor, and wait until 0600 when the tide was right to begin our transit.

With a wind at our backs, we arrived at the anchorage well before dark.

The Captain called a meeting top critique the show with all officers not on watch, plus Doc, Reyes, Chief Mick and Wing, our cook.

"You and your crews proved that we can do this. We can bring a live musical show and hot chow to almost any spot we can set our ramp on. I'm proud of you all."

Starting with Fred Wing, he went around the room asking for suggestions for improvement. Everyone was positive and enthusiastic. Most of the suggestions had to do with adding something to improve either the flow of the show, or the setup and takedown.

The Captain, whose musical taste was formed in the rich cultural soup of southern Louisiana, asked the group if they liked the song choices.

The Captain's ancestors, Cajuns, who had fled British-controlled Canada in the 18th Century, shared the swamps and bayous with Native Americans and freed or escaped black slaves. While Cajun music is rooted in the songs of French-speaking Acadians of Canada, it evolved in Louisiana into something unique, borrowing heavily from the African jazz styles of the co-inhabitants of the region.

The Captain said he was concerned that his music didn't reflect the taste of the majority of the Belle's typical audience. The average age of most of the soldiers and sailors in Vietnam was around twenty-two. Their taste ranged from pop, soul, rock and roll to country and western.

"Our music is good, and most guys will be happy to hear it played live," Doc said. "But we might consider including a couple of current pop hits," he added. "It's the music that connects all of us to home." He paused, looked at the Captain, who nodded back. "And one more thing, even if the brass doesn't like it, we have to add the most popular song here, our Vietnam anthem."

Everyone knew the song he referred to – "We Gotta Get Out of this Place," written by Barry Mann and Cynthia Weil, and recorded by Eric Burdon and the Animals. It was by the far the most played and requested by American servicemen in every boat, barracks, hooch, and foxhole in Southeast Asia.

Nobody had to say anything. We all knew Doc was right. The Captain stood and closed out the meeting.

"Thanks, Doc. We have some work to do. There are great artists out there putting out hit songs, including Stevie Wonder, Aretha Franklin and even the Beatles, and the Beach Boys. Let's fill in our show with a few more songs that our audience listens to on Armed Forces Radio."

One thing was certain, the *Mekong Belle* had more than enough outstanding musicians and singers to do it. I wasn't good enough to perform one of those numbers on stage, so I had to be content with singing in the choir and playing my guitar in private. There was an isolated open-air spot on the main deck just aft of the officer's quarters that I used as my personal space for reading, napping or playing guitar. It was a place where I could play without exposing my paucity of talent.

When the meeting broke up, I grabbed my guitar and went there to watch sunset just west of the river mouth. As I sat there watching the water move along, the song "Old Man River" popped into my head. It was an easy number with just a few chords, so I started playing and singing.

When I got to the part *"You and me, we sweat and strain, bodies all achin' and racked with pain,"* a voice behind me said, "You realize you're white, don't you?"

It was Archer, the signalman with whom I often stood watch.

"Archer, you discovered my secret."

"So what are you doing singing a black man's song?"

Archer and I had previous discussions about race during our early-morning watches together. I admitted to him that I was raised in a lily-white community and had no idea what it was like to be a black man, particularly in culturally rigid institutions like the military.

His tongue-in-cheek question fit right into the tone of our earlier conversations.

"'Old Man River' was actually written by two white Jews, Jerome Kern and Oscar Hammerstein," I replied.

"Yeah. I know. But it was sung by a black man."

"So. You've seen *Showboat?*"

"Yeah. I didn't like it much, but some of the music was okay."

"What didn't you like about it?"

"It wasn't real. It's what you all think black folks are about. It looks down on us. It's insulting."

"Were any parts of it real?"

"The pain, the misery, and the shame were all real enough, but the reasons weren't. It was a white people's story with black people as props."

Archer's critiques, so different than mine, made it clear how much I didn't understand about what it was like to be black in America.

Showboat, as dated as it was, was a musical I enjoyed not only for its music, but also for what I thought was its sympathetic portrayal of its black characters. Clearly, he saw it differently.

"Does my singing 'Old Man River' offend you?"

"No. It's not like that. It's just…I don't know…like me trying to sing like Elvis Presley."

I laughed and almost fell off my chair. I stood and held out my guitar.

"I'd love to hear you sing like Elvis."

Archer laughed too. "Thank you very much," he said in a fairly accurate Elvis voice, waving off my effort to give him the guitar.

"Actually I was just sitting here looking at the river and that's what triggered my memory of that song," I said.

"When you look out at the water, what pops into that musical head of yours?" I asked him.

"Do you know 'A Change Is Gonna Come' by Sam Cooke?"

"I know the tune and I love the song. I really like Sam Cooke, but I can't hit those high notes."

"If you can play me the chords, I'll show you what a real black man's river song sounds like."

He sat down next to me.

I asked him to hum a few bars to get me started in the right key, and then nodded I was ready. I played it slower than Cooke's original because I was still figuring out the chord changes, but Archer followed right along.

To this day, the memory of his beautiful rendition of that song gives me chills of pleasure and brings tears to my eyes.

"A change is gonna come, oh yes it will."

When the last verse and chorus was finished. We both just sat there in silence, each of us in our own thoughts about what that song meant to us. Then a voice from behind made us both jump. It was Doc.

"You boys should take that show on the road."

"Hi Doc. It looks like my secret spot is no secret anymore," I said to him as he walked over to where we were sitting.

"Oh. I've seen you out here before. But, with all due respect, the sound was never quite as sweet as it was just now."

"No offense taken. Archer makes even a hack like me sound good."

"You know. I was thinking, as you two were playing, that we could work this into the show. It might be a good way to add just a little more soul to our showboat."

"Doc. I'm ready, anytime you can convince the Captain to give me a solo," Archer said.

"I agree that Archer should do it, but with a better musician behind him. I'm just not good enough for the road yet," I said.

"Still. You two actually work well together. Let me think on it and get back to you," he said turning to walk away. Then he stopped. "Oh yeah, I forgot. The XO is looking for you."

With that, our musical interlude was ended, and Archer and I went about our duties. I had the 2000 to midnight watch and was looking forward to getting at least five hours in my rack afterward before we weighed anchor and headed upriver.

I found the XO in the wardroom having a cup of coffee with the Captain.

"Doc says you wanted to see me, XO."

"Yes. We're trying to figure out how we get the word out about our shows once we get upriver," he said.

"How much time do we have?" I asked. "I mean in between the time we open the bow doors, offload our cargo and have to clear the ramp."

"We don't know," the Captain said.

"What's the normal procedure?"

"Offload as fast as we can and get back out into the safety of the middle of the river," the XO answered. "But if nobody is behind us waiting to offload their stuff, we could probably stay there for a few hours, assuming the base wasn't under attack."

"It takes us about an hour to set up the band and a half hour to take down. The full-length show is about an hour long, and then there's the food service. We're well into three or more hours if we do it like we did in Vung Tao," the Captain said.

We spent the next half hour reviewing the average time it takes to offload cargo, how we could expedite the food service, and whether or not the officers in charge of the bases would allow us to interrupt their work and let their men attend our show in the middle of the day.

"What about doing it at night?" I asked.

They both shook their heads.

"The nights belong to Charlie," the XO said.

I knew he meant the Viet Cong.

"Even in daylight we might have to back off the ramp in a hurry if bullets and mortar rounds start flying. We must be anchored as safely away from potential attack as we can before the sun goes down," the Captain said.

"They attack the bases every night?" I asked.

"No. Not every night, but often enough to keep everybody on edge. A big target like the *Belle*, all lit up and playing Dixieland, would make an inviting target. We'd have no way to back off the ramp in a hurry if shooting started. We can't maneuver in the dark," he replied.

"So our music could be our own death knell," I said. And then an idea popped into my head.

"Death knell. That's it. We'll get the word out like we used to in our town when someone died."

They both gave me a quizzical look.

"I live in a small town. Our newspaper is published every Thursday. If someone dies and their funeral is set for a day before the next paper is published, we have to get the word out by other means. So we print abbreviated obituary handbills with funeral place, dates, time, and post them on telephone poles all over town. It gets the word out in a hurry."

They seemed interested so I continued.

"I suggest that we get a stack of handbills ready. When we know the time for the show, Ortega fills then in by hand. Then I send out a couple of sailors with the handbills, tacks, and tape, and tell them to post them around the base as quickly as they can. They should also leave a stack at the base mess hall."

The Captain stood.

"Excellent idea, Rob. Make it so. You and the XO can work out the finer points. I'm going to find O.J. and see if we can send a message to the base commander so he doesn't blow a gasket when he reads one of your handbills."

9

Bright Music for the Brown-water Navy
••••••••••••••••••••••

I T WAS OVERCAST AND RAINING heavily as we pulled anchor and moved across the sand bar to enter the river. Visibility was poor, but there wasn't much to see anyway. The lower Mekong Delta is at sea level, with the horizon flat in every direction.

The river mouth was a mile wide, but gradually narrowed, then wove like a drunken snake through a vast and featureless flooded plain studded with tulles and scattered patches of stunted trees. There were no buoys or lighthouses, no navigational markers of any kind. Some of the turns were close to 300 degrees. The water was too muddy for us to see the bottom, but we knew that silt built up on the edge of every sharp turn and added to the risk of our ship running aground.

We had charts marking the deepest part of the channel. They could not be entirely trusted because heavy annual floods moved the silt around. The Navy issued us a chart book, with each page covering about an eighth of a mile of river. It used whatever meager landmarks there might be, tree trunks, large snags, and wrecks of old boats, as navigation points, advising that at any given time those points might have washed away.

The good news was, weather permitting, we had unimpeded views to the horizon in every direction.

Our bridge, from which we navigated the ship, stood nearly four stories above the water, and our shallow draft allowed us to go safely where many ships half our size would have gone aground.

Nevertheless, we proceeded very slowly not wanting to risk getting stuck hard in the thick mud no more than a foot or two below the ship's bottom.

Judging from the amount of debris floating on the chocolate brown current, we determined that there must be flooding upstream. Most of the flotsam appeared to be water hyacinths and pieces of bushes and trees. The Captain stationed a sailor with a 30-cal. carbine on the bow, directing him to shoot into every large clump of anything that looked like it might brush against the ship. The Viet Cong hid mines in the stuff hoping to damage Navy ships coming upriver.

Although it would have been impossible for the VC to sneak up on us during daylight hours, we had all six of our machine guns manned.

When we got further upstream, the banks were lined with heavy brush and larger trees, behind which a hostile force could hide in ambush. From there all the way to the base at My Tho, all guns, including the 40mm, were manned. In spite of the heat, we all wore flak vests and helmets.

It would have been suicidal for someone to shoot at us from the riverbank, because the 40mm and .50-caliber machine guns could literally mow their cover down to the ground. That was the point of being at battle stations. In theory, our readiness discouraged sneak attacks, at least during the day.

Going cautiously against the heavy river current took longer than expected. We didn't arrive at My Tho until mid-afternoon.

At a wide bend in the river, into which several other tributaries came, there was a mile-wide bay of relatively calm water.

In that bay was the largest mobile riverine fleet in naval history.

At the center of the bay was the *Hampton County* (LST 1122) at anchor. Next to it was a large, dark green, two-story barge. Attached to the barge was a series of connected floating docks where heavily armed small boats, mostly painted dark green, were berthed. The *Hampton County* served as a "mother ship" for the fleet, while the barge was a barracks that housed many of the brown water Navy sailors.

A motley mix of riverine forces craft moved back and forth on the bay, while Vietnamese sampans wove slowly in and out of the traffic. The Navy boats included modified WW II landing craft mounted with large guns. There were also newer, heavily armed, fifty-foot-long swift boats, plus the much smaller, fiberglass PBRs (Patrol Boat, River). I even saw a couple of PACVs (air cushioned vehicles). They were fast, barely touching the water as they moved, but they made an ungodly racket the enemy could hear for miles.

It was too late for us to get to the base ramp to offload our cargo before dark. For security reasons, no ships were allowed on the ramp after sunset. We were ordered to moor alongside the Hampton County, where we would spend the night, then proceed to the ramp the next morning.

After we were securely alongside the mother ship, Andrew and I stood on the main deck watching the various boats motoring about the bay.

"There must be more than two hundred boats here," Andrew said.

"Yeah, and some of them look like they were in the first wave at Okinawa twenty-two years ago," I said.

"Yeah, but so was our ship," he added.

At the start of the Vietnam war, the Navy used WW II craft like ours, because it didn't have anything else specifically designed to fight a war in rivers.

The first smaller river boats were simply old landing craft with guns awkwardly mounted where space allowed. The newer "swift boats" were an improvement, but almost too big for the smaller channels in the Mekong Delta.

PBRs were the workhorses. They were extremely fast, agile and could go just about anywhere. But they were made out of fiberglass and didn't hold up well when hit by the Soviet-made RPGs (rocket propelled grenades) used by the Viet Cong and NVA forces.

Their main job was to stop and search the thousands of sampans that transited the Mekong and its tributaries every day. The Vietnamese locals were known to use their boats to transport weapons and ammunition, willingly or under threat of execution, to Viet Cong cadres in the area.

The mission of the fleet comprising the Mobile Riverine Forces (aka Brown Water Navy) was to interrupt the Viet Cong's lines of communication and resupply. The larger, more armored craft in the river fleet were used to cover the PBRs, while overhead the "Seawolves," a squadron of helicopter gunships, piloted by Navy volunteers, added air cover, weather permitting.

As we were watching the beehive of activity on the bay, one of the air-cushioned PACV's pulled into a berth next to the barracks barge. Two sailors got off first, followed by a tall, lanky officer who looked very familiar. It wasn't until he took off his hotshot aviator dark glasses that I realized it was Alex Anderson, another classmate from OCS. He was decked out as some kind of jet-jockey wanna-be with his fatigue pants tucked into a pair of calf-high lace-up jungle boots and a .45-caliber pistol strapped to his waist.

Andrew saw him too.

"Alex. What the hell kind of ugly beast are you flying?" he shouted.

Alex looked up, squinted, then a big grinned spread across his face.

"Hey guys. What are you doing here?"

"Bringing fuel for that gas-guzzler you're driving," I replied. "Come over for dinner, we'll tell all."

"Okay. Let your watch know I'm coming. They get tight-assed about security around here at night," he said, then turned and headed for the barracks barge entrance.

When I checked with the XO to confirm that it was okay if Alex joined the wardroom for dinner, he told me that the Captain of Hampton County, the LST serving as the brown water navy mother ship, would also be joining us.

"Anything new on what's happening tomorrow?" I asked him

"Nope. O.J. sent a message to the base commander. We haven't gotten a reply. We're hoping the CO of the *Hampton County* can fill us in on what to expect. Maybe your PACV pilot buddy will know something."

"Okay. In any case, I'll have handbills ready as soon as we know if the show is on," I said.

After I left the XO's stateroom I returned to mine. Andrew was already snoring in the upper bunk. He had the mid-watch. I was scheduled to follow him on the 0400 to 0800. It was a good time to bag some Zs.

Andrew and I greeted Alex as he crossed the gangway between the *Hampton County* and our ship. He'd changed from his PACV pilot's getup to regular Navy tropical khakis, the standard uniform of the day.

"I was really surprised to see you guys today," he said. "I've lost touch with just about everybody from our class. How did you two end up on the same ship?"

"It is a long and bizarre story. But first, I'd like to hear how you became a PACV pilot," I replied.

As we walked toward the wardroom, he told us more.

"It's not that complicated. I volunteered for helicopter pilot training before we graduated from OCS, but there weren't any openings. BuPers asked if I was interested in a new experimental craft program the Navy was going to try. I said yes. After OCS, I spent four months learning how to pilot the PACVs, and then got assigned to this squadron."

The wardroom was empty, and the stewards were just finishing setting the table for dinner.

We offered Alex one of the two easy chairs and I grabbed a third chair from the table.

"Before we fill you in on our stories. Tell us what piloting one of those things is like."

"They're fast, wild, and noisy. When they're flying right, they skim over the water without any drag at all. They're incredible. We can attack and then maneuver out of danger faster than the enemy can react," he seemed to hesitate.

"But?" Andrew said

"They are a pain in the ass to maintain and prone to breaking down at the worst possible time in the middle of nowhere."

"Do you get shot at a lot?" I asked.

"Sometimes, usually as we're moving away. We operate with the PBRs or swift boats nearby, and there's air cover from the Seawolves. The VC haven't been interested in taking us on directly."

"Okay. Enough about me. How did you two guys get here?"

Andrew and I each told our tales.

"The *Mekong Belle*? A Navy showboat? You've got to be kidding me. That's what you guys are doing here?"

Alex seemed to think we were pulling his leg.

Just then, the Captain walked in with an officer who I assumed was the Captain of the *Hampton County*.

We stood to attention.

"As you were," the Captain said.

Gentlemen, this is Captain Overway, CO of the *Hampton County*.

"Captain this is Ensign Rob Allen my communications officer,

Ensign Andrew Cohen, assistant engineering officer, and this must be PACV pilot Ensign Alex Anderson."

Captain Overway smiled. "Yes. I know Alex quite well. He is the pilot of one of those noisy contraptions the Navy hopes will stay working long enough to do some good."

He appeared to be at least five years younger than our Captain. In fact, I would have guessed he was only a year or two older than me. In any case, he was affable and seemed happy to be joining us.

"The word has gotten around fast that the *Bell County* serves the best chow in the Navy. Alex and I appreciate being invited," he added graciously.

He was in for a treat. Freddie, the ship's cook, had found a resource in Vung Tao for fresh Mekong River catfish. He served us a Louisiana "blackened" version of that dish over rice with some vegetables that appeared to be greens mixed with diced bell peppers.

It was hot, spicy and delicious.

"Do you eat like this every night?" Captain Overway asked, smacking his lips and reaching for his glass of water to cool his palate.

"Our cook is a master at turning regular Navy chow into something a lot more interesting. But he's not always so heavy-handed with the cayenne. For me, the hotter, the better, but not all of our crew likes food that hot."

"Your crew gets the same food?" the CO asked.

"Of course. Maybe Freddie puts a little more pepper on my plate, but other than that, it all comes from the crews mess. What they eat, we eat."

"Hmm. I could get used to this," Captain Overway said patting his stomach.

"How do you think the guys stationed here, including the Marines and others on shore, would like it?" The XO asked the *Hampton County* CO.

"Are you kidding? If they knew you served chow this good and could find a way on board, your ship would be swamped."

"That's what we want to ask you about tonight," the Captain said taking charge of the conversation.

He explained how the *Bell County's* supply mission had been expanded to bring music and good hot chow to the guys stuck out in the boonies.

"And you're telling me the admiral is behind this? As commander of the entire Pacific amphibious fleet. I'm surprised he hasn't sent us all orders to help you make it happen."

"Well. That's the thing. He wants it, but he hasn't brought the idea to his boss yet He's waiting for us to show that it can be done without interfering with our main supply mission, or anybody else's mission." Captain Baillier explained.

"Hmm. So what are you planning?"

"The idea is to put on a show and serve some chow at the ramp immediately after offloading our regular cargo. Our goal is to provide a short, but memorable, break from the grind, fear and danger of war."

"Sounds like the devil is in the details and the timing."

"We've got a routine that allows us to set up a show, deliver it plus hot chow, break everything back down, and store it back aboard in less than three hours."

"So, you'd stay on the ramp an extra three hours to put on the show?"

"Yes. And serve hot food to the sailors, Marines, and soldiers who can make it to the show," the XO added.

"I see two additional problems. How do you get the word out fast enough to attract a crowd? And, if you can do that, who keeps the officers in charge of the base or ship from going ballistic when everybody stops working to go to the show?"

"You got it right. Those are our challenges," the Captain

answered. "Rob here has an idea for getting the word out quickly. I think it might work. But the second matter, mollifying the various COs, is a more complicated issue."

The Captain paused, as the stewards cleared the plates, and began serving dessert and coffee.

"What's this?" Captain Overway asked, a look of pleasure on his face as he took his first taste.

"Key lime pie."

"Well, you might start addressing challenge number two by sending every unit commander a slice of this pie."

By the time everyone had finished the pie and coffee, the Captain returned to the subject of the show.

"What do you know about the base CO here?" he asked Captain Overway.

"The Turtle probably won't be a problem. The Marine Captain in charge of perimeter security might be though."

"The Turtle?" the XO asked.

"Yeah. His name is Jones. He's a supply corps lieutenant commander that's getting close to retirement. He's a short-timer, with less than sixty days before he ships home. The sailors tagged him "the turtle," because his office and bunker are part of a Quonset hut that he's heavily sandbagged. He holds up in there and only rarely sticks his head out to see what's going on. Sort of like a turtle."

"Why would the Marine officer be a problem? We wouldn't be trying to get his men to break ranks and leave the perimeter."

"That may not be the objection. He gets a bug up his ass anytime one of our ships stays too long on the ramp and it gets close to nighttime. He thinks LSTs are way too big and way too attractive as targets for mortar and rocket attacks after dark."

Talk around the table shifted to the status of the brown water fleet and whether or not it was working.

The general consensus of Captain Overway and Alex was that

it was hit and miss so far. Night attacks, especially when weather kept our Huey helicopters on the ground, were their biggest worry.

Alex stood and said he had an early mission the next morning. Andrew and I agreed that we'd try to catch up with him later, and then excused ourselves from the wardroom, so we could get some sleep before our watches.

We both hit our bunks and were out in less than five minutes. I didn't even hear Andrew get up to stand his watch.

My wake up at 0330 came way too soon.

Because we were tied up next to the *Hampton County*, my watch as OOD allowed me to move around, rather than just confine myself to the bridge. A quartermaster stood watch at the gangway between the two ships, and another crewman had the engineering watch below decks. Because we were in a war zone, we also had two men on the bridge, a signalman, and a gunner's mate manning the .30-caliber machine gun.

My main job was to walk around and make sure all the guys on watch were awake.

It was a warm, but cloudy night. From time-to-time parachute flares shot into the sky above the base. The light from the flares reflected off the low cloud layer casting an eerie glow on everything below. A few cooking fires were visible along the shore where most of the village of My Tho was still in slumber. The water was flat calm and the scene so serene that I had to remind myself that I was in the middle of a combat zone and that any moment explosions and gunfire could shatter the peaceful quiet of the early morning.

Had the VC attacked the base or any of the vessels anchored in the middle of the river, we would have gone to General Quarters with all guns manned, the engines fired up and the crew ready to throw off the gangway and lines so we could maneuver.

Fortunately, it remained quiet. At 0500, I saw Alex climb into his PACV, fire up its noisy engines and follow a small flotilla of PBRs up the river. As exciting as being a pilot of one of the PACVs might be, I was glad to be where I was, on a all-steel, well-armed ship, rather than a scantily armored rubber raft with unreliable engines.

At 0630 the tweet of a bosun's pipe sounded through the ship's PA system with the usual morning wake up call.

"Reveille, Reveille. All hands heave to and trice up. The smoking lamp is lighted in all berthing spaces."

That announcement was made every morning on every ship in the Navy. It took me a while to find out that the phrase "heave to and trice up" was a carryover from the days when sailors slept in hammocks and had to heave themselves out of them and secure the ends to a trice (hook) on the bulkhead.

Whatever its origins, everyone on board not already up and on watch was called to get up, eat breakfast and go to work.

We were scheduled to head for the ramp at 0800.

10

Trial Run in the Combat Zone
● ●

A HEAVY, DAMP OVERCAST HUNG over the water. There was not a ripple of wind. Across the bay, the inhabitants of My Tho were up and smoke from their cooking stoves rose from a long line of small wood and bamboo houses along the shore.

A few fishermen in sampans were casting their nets at the mouth of small channels that ran out from the bay like spokes of a wheel.

The flotilla of PBRs, PACVs and other craft had not returned. I heard the sound of a helicopter in the distance. There was a distinct absence of explosions or sounds that indicate a firefight was close.

Because the ship was scheduled to head to the ramp at 0800 just as my watch ended, I was relieved in time to use the head and eat a quick breakfast.

As I was finishing my coffee the XO came into the wardroom and sat down.

"We still have no response from the base commander. But, if everything goes as expected, our cargo should be offloaded by 1100. That means we're scheduling the show to start at noon."

"Aye, aye, sir. I'll get the handbills done and have a couple of my men ready to head out to post them as soon as the bow doors open. Do I say anything about chow or beer?"

"Chow, yes. Beer, no. We gave most of it away in Vung Tao. There are no pallets of beer to break in this shipment."

"What's on the menu?"

"Muffuletta sandwiches and shrimp po-boys."

When I first joined the crew, I had no idea what either of those popular New Orleans sandwiches were. But, because they were among the Captain's favorite lunches, I had several opportunities to enjoy both. The most amazing thing about them was the fresh-baked bread that Freddie and his mess assistants managed to produce with the ship's ovens. By far, the po-boys were my favorite.

At 0800 all hands were called to their stations and the *Bell County* disconnected from the *Hampton County* and slowly maneuvered across the bay toward the narrow channel that led to the loading ramp. The Captain carefully and gently touched the *Bell County*'s bow to the shore. Our ship's engines continued to idle, in case we needed to back off in a hurry.

By 0845, we were on the ramp, the bow doors were open and the forklift from the shore base was already moving into our cargo bay to offload the pallets stacked there.

I sent two of my radiomen out with three-dozen handbills on which Ortega had quickly and neatly printed the time of our show. They carried thumbtacks and tape so they could attach them to walls, gates and any other spot where people would see them. In addition, I asked them to put a dozen on a table at the base mess hall.

I stood to the side of the ramp with Chief Mick, who was examining a bare patch of mud where he might set up the stage. While he was walking off the area, I waited for my two men to return from their handbill-posting mission.

A loud clank came from behind me inside the ship's hold. It was followed by a burst of profanity. I walked up the ramp to see what was going on. The forklift driver was beating on the forklift engine compartment with his hat and swearing a blue streak.

Chief Mick, who was right behind me, stepped up.

"What the hell are you yelling about sailor?" he shouted.

"This mother-fucking forklift crapped out again Chief. This is the fourth time this week. It just stops running right in the middle of an offload."

"Fix it. We've got to get the rest of this shit offloaded ASAP," the chief ordered.

"I would if I knew how Chief. I just drive it. Our only mechanic had to make a run upriver an hour ago to fix that god-damned PACV again."

At that moment, Harry and Andrew walked up. The chief filled them in.

"Machinist Mate Smith can probably fix it. I'll send someone to get him down here," Harry said.

"Just in case he can't, or if it takes too long, we've got to move it out of the way so we can get our stage and chow service set up," Chief Mick noted. "I'll get a bunch of hands and we'll push it down the ramp and off to the side."

"Okay," Harry said, then turned to Andrew. "Go tell the XO and Captain that we may have a problem, but we're working on a solution."

It took a half-dozen men to push the heavy forklift down the ramp and out of the way.

While Smith, the machinist, started tinkering with the forklift, Chief Mick got his crew to use a hand truck to move cargo pallets out of the way so he could get to the bandboxes.

At 1130 the forklift was still broken down. Smith had no clue what was wrong with it. The bandboxes were all out on the dirt and Chief Mick and his men were quickly transforming them into the stage. I told Murdock to break out the electrical cable for the mikes and amps.

The Captain, XO and Freddie, the cook, came down to a scene

of semi-organized chaos. Pallets of cargo still took up most of the ship's hold, and there was little room to maneuver. Sailors were setting up the stage and Murdock was pulling electrical cable down the ramp. Smith had the engine cover off the forklift and various engine parts stacked on the driver's seat.

"I was going to serve the food just inside the bow doors. There, where all of those pallets are stacked. I need to find another spot," Freddie declared.

At just that moment, one of the two sailors I'd sent out with the handbills jogged up out of breath.

"We've got a problem, Mr. Allen. The base commander saw me posting one of the handbills on his office door and demanded to know who had authorized it. I didn't understand if he was talking about the handbill or the show."

"So what did you tell him?" I asked

"I'd told him I would find out, gave him a smart salute, turned and ran back here."

The Captain and XO overhead the conversation.

"Lew, go and find Lieutenant Commander Turtle, or whatever his name is, and invite him to join me in our nice, safe, steel-covered wardroom for a confidential briefing."

"Confidential briefing?" the XO responded, paused in thought, then laughed. "You're going to use the key lime pie trick aren't you?"

"You know the old saying about getting more flies with honey? I'm hoping a delicious piece of Freddie's key lime pie will bag us a turtle," the Captain replied.

"Aye, aye, Captain," the XO said and then headed in the direction from which the crewman had run.

What the Captain intended to do if the base commander accepted his invitation he did not say. I assumed he was not planning to lock him in the rope locker as we'd done with the supply lieutenant in Vung Tao.

Ten minutes later the XO, returned with the base commander. The man sailors called "the turtle" looked to be an identical twin to Ernest Borgnine. He was the only one wearing a flak vest and helmet. The XO escorted him past us, up the ramp and into the bowels of the ship on the way to the wardroom. Our preparation for the concert continued. We knew the Captain would persuade the turtle to let the show go on.

Freddie found a spot near the broken-down forklift to set up his serving tables. The sandwiches were all made in long loaves and then cut into individual servings.

No utensils were needed and two large containers of hot coffee and a stack of paper cups completed the service.

"What, no dessert?" exclaimed Harry in mock surprise when he saw how Freddie had set up the food service.

Freddie, didn't miss a beat. "Of course there's dessert, lieutenant. What is your favorite New Orleans snack?" he asked the burly engineering officer.

"You made pralines!" Harry shouted with joy. "Freddie, you're the greatest cook in the Navy," he declared. Then asked, "Okay, where are they?"

"Staying fresh in the galley. They will come down after the sandwiches are served."

Harry looked satisfied, but I suspected he was plotting a way to sneak into the galley and grab a couple of those nut and sugar confections before the show started.

Meanwhile the Captain's meeting with Commander Jones, aka the turtle, was going better than expected.

I followed, as the XO brought the commander into the wardroom, the Captain was being served a cup of coffee and a piece of pie. He stood, shook Jones's hand, and offered him a seat across from him.

"Commander. You're just in time for a little snack. Please join me for one of our chef's finest creations, an honest-to-god, key lime pie, made with fresh limes."

The commander smiled and accepted the Captain's offer without hesitation. He turned out to be an easy-going, middle-aged Navy supply corps vet of nearly 25 years, who was counting the days until his retirement.

"I know the men call me the turtle because I spend most days and nights in my fortified hooch. That's because I have a family at home depending on me to get out of here alive and in one piece. Once you're a short-timer, inside sixty days, you get superstitious," he told the Captain.

With the commander thoroughly enjoying his pie, the Captain found it easy to explain the extra mission on which the entire crew was working. Although he was not yet authorized to say that he had Admiral Kirkpatrick's authority to proceed, he did indicate that the admiral was considering approving it.

Jones didn't need much convincing. "Whatever you need Captain, just let me know," then he paused and held up his hand. "But, I expect you to express your gratitude by offering me pie every time you visit."

By the time they'd finished their meeting, sailors from around the base and started to mill around the ramp. Several boats that had been berthed next to *Hampton County* brought the ship's sailors, including its Captain, over to the ramp.

Our Captain spotted him getting out of one of the landing craft and waved him over.

"Captain Overway. I'm glad you can make it. You're just in time to join Commander Jones for a front-row seat for the show." He pointed to a row of folding chairs that had been set up close to the bandstand.

Reyes took the microphone and the Captain and other band members started taking their places on the stage.

"Thank you all for coming to see *Mekong Belle*'s first road show. We have two missions. The first is bringing the usual stuff, food, ammo, gasoline, etc. upriver to you guys in the boonies. The second is to bring some joy with us in the form of hot chow and great music. Bob Hope and those other USO tour types may be too chicken to come here, but the crew of the *Mekong Belle* isn't. So enjoy the show. After which, we will be serving you lunch made by the finest cook this side of New Orleans."

Without waiting for applause, the Captain hit the first note of "Won't You Come Home Bill Bailey?" and the show was on.

The crowd standing near the ramp doubled as the first song came to a big finish. The boats that went upriver before dawn were now squeezed into spots along the shore, their crews joining the audience.

I looked for Alex, but saw neither him nor his PACV.

Each performance went smoothly and the crowd applauded enthusiastically.

The Andrews sister trio in drag was the hit of the show. They'd managed to master a second song, "*Bei Mir Bist du Schon*" and presented it as their encore.

Next, Harry, Doc, and a couple of sailor guitarists from the deck crew, came on and did a loud, feedback-heavy intro to "We Gotta Get Out of This Place," with Archer and LaMotte getting the entire audience to sing along.

After the finale, Reyes came back on stage, introduced the band, then pointed to where Freddie and his men had set up lunch and invited everyone to enjoy the food.

Commander Jones and Captain Overway shook hands with the band and told Captain Baillier how amazed they were at the talent of the crew.

"You guys are professionals. I can't believe you were able to find this much musical talent on one ship," Commander Jones exclaimed. "You've got to get the Admiral to make your musical mission official."

"He wants to. I think he needs us to prove that our show won't interfere with our regular mission."

The base commander looked at the CO of the *Hampton County* and they both nodded.

"You can count on us to communicate that fact to the admiral right away. You have no idea how much you have lifted morale here. We want you to come back and do a show as often as you can.

"Now, I want to go try one of those shrimp po-boys before they're all gone."

Just then, I felt a tap on my shoulder, and turned to see Alex smiling at me.

"Alex! I was worried about you. I heard your jet flamed out."

"Yeah. So what else is new? But I got a tow back from one of the LCUs. I actually caught most of the second half of the show. You guys are great."

"I'm glad you made it. Come on, let's get in line for some chow. I think you're going to love it."

The end of the line was close to the forklift. Our ship's machinist was working with a sailor who looked like he'd been dipped in mud. They each had a sandwich in one hand as they used the other to work on the engine.

"Is that the guy who fixes your PACV?" I asked Alex, pointing to he muddy one.

"Yes. That's machinist mate second-class O'Halloran. Without him, most of us would be dead in the water."

"He looks like he's been swimming in the mud," I said.

"Yeah. He actually crawled on his belly and got under the PACV to see if something was clogging the vents or tubes or something. He said it was such a mess under there he needed to pull it entirely out of the water. That's why we needed a tow and it took so long to get back."

By the time we'd made it through the chow line and eaten our sandwiches, the two machinist mates had the forklift ready to run. The chief and his hands were already disassembling the stage and stacking the crates off to the side, so the unloading could proceed. The light was fading and we'd stayed on the ramp far longer than anticipated.

As the small boat crews returned to their craft and Freddie closed down the food service, a Marine gunnery sergeant came up to where Alex and I were standing.

He saluted, and we returned his salute.

"Excuse me, sir, but are you in charge of that ship?"

"No, Gunny. But I'm one of the officers on board. What can I do for you?"

"I'm supposed to relay a message that you need to be off the ramp in forty-five minutes." Then he hesitated. "That message was from my CO. I just want to add my thanks. Your show and lunch were the best things that have happened here in months."

"Gunny. I'm glad you enjoyed it. That's why we are here. I'll inform our ship's Captain about the deadline and see if we can get the rest of the cargo off the ship by your CO's deadline."

"Thank you, sir."

"My pleasure, Gunny."

He saluted again, I returned his salute and he walked away toward the perimeter of the base.

"I don't envy those guys. Standing night watch on the edge of the jungle has got to be the scariest duty of all," I said to Alex.

"You got that right. At least we have a way to maneuver away if we have to. They have to dig in and hold the line. As far as I'm concerned they're the bravest men over here," he said.

I had no desire to trade places with them, but I felt ashamed that I served in relative safety while they were exposed to constant danger. With everybody hustling, we unloaded all the cargo and cleared the ramp with five minutes to spare. It was too close to dark to head down river to Vung Tao, so we moored alongside the *Hampton County* for the night.

I was assigned the 2000 to midnight watch, which turned out to be even quieter than the watch I stood earlier. Fifteen minutes after my watch ended, I was sawing logs in my bunk. If nothing unusual happened, I would get at least six hours shuteye, the longest I'd had since we arrived in Vietnam. I went to sleep thinking of how I could manage to squeeze in another coaching session with Melanie when we returned. Just the thought of being with her made me happy.

11

You Don't Have To Stay Forever
●●●●●●●●●●●●●●●●●●●●●●●

A S THE SUN ROSE OVER the Mekong, *Bell County* was disconnected from *Hampton County* and headed downstream toward Vung Tau. It was a bright, clear, hot day with just enough cooling air from the ship's movement to keep us from roasting on the sunbaked steel deck.

We made good time, crossed the bar at high tide, and turned toward Vung Tao, arriving at midday. Because another LST was on the ramp, we were ordered to anchor in the bay. I was free until my watch started at 2000 hours. Anxious to see Melanie, I jumped on the ship's first shuttle boat into town.

The bicycle rickshaw driver I'd seen on my first day in Vung Tau, was in the same place. This time I accepted his offer of a ride, and told him I wanted to go the General's Daughter."

"It not open yet. Many other bars open. I take you," he said.

"No. I know somebody who works there. It's okay."

He seemed to understand. After we agreed on a fare, he started pedaling. In less than ten minutes we pulled up at the restaurant's front gate.

"Xin cam on," I said, adding a healthy tip to his fare.

"Thank you. Your Vietnamese is good, like my English. I am Ernest, as in Hemingway. I happy be your driver."

"Your English is much better than my Vietnamese, Ernest, as in Hemingway. I am going to be here a while. Maybe later, I'll need a ride. My name is Rob. Thank you."

"Okay Mr. Rob. *A bientot.* See you later, alligator."

I laughed and waved as he peddled away.

I walked onto the restaurant's porch, through the lobby to the patio. The staff was setting up for dinner. Melanie and her mother were standing near the fountain in the center of the patio talking.

As I approached, Madame Marquis noticed me first and waved.

"*Bonjour,* Robert, *bienvenue.* You are back from your voyage. All goes well?"

"*Oui, madame. Ça va bien, merci,*" I answered, surprising myself that I remembered a proper reply in French

Not sure if Melanie had informed her mother about asking for my help with her writing, I said I was just in the area to hoping to familiarize myself with the town. "I wanted to visit the school and then walk around the village and see the sites. I'm hoping you will give me some suggestions."

Melanie replied quickly. "I would love to be your guide for the afternoon. The church and school are just a few blocks from here. We can go there first."

"Excellent idea. I don't need Melanie here until later," Madame Marquis said.

"She will introduce you to Father Daniel and Sister Josephine. Some of the children may still be in practicing their music," she added.

Melanie excused herself, saying she needed to change before we took our walk, returning ten minutes later in a floral sundress. Her sandals were color-coordinated with the dress and her long black hair was tied back with a matching ribbon. She took my arm as we walked out the door and down the walk. I was so happy I felt like skipping.

"Thank you for volunteering to be my guide," I said.

"We heard your ship arrived and I was hoping you'd stop by," she said.

"You were looking forward to seeing me again?" I replied hopefully.

She squeezed my arm and spoke quietly in my ear. "Yes, of course. I must help you in your quest, and you have agreed to help me with my writing. We have much to do."

"You know, I haven't been able to stop thinking about you," I said, wanting to take her into my arms right there on the sidewalk. Just then, I heard someone clear his throat behind us. It came from a middle-aged man wearing black trousers, a white, short-sleeved shirt, and a cross on a cord around his neck.

"*Bonjour,*Melanie," he said. Then turned to me, "*Monsieur,*" he added curtly.

Melanie looked slightly embarrassed but quickly recovered.

"*Bonjour,* Father Daniel. We were just on our way to the church and school. May I introduce you to Ensign Robert Allen, he is one of the officers from Lt. Baillier's ship, *Bell County.*"

"How do you do, Robert," the priest said in a thick French accent, nodding toward me but not offering his hand.

"It is a pleasure to meet you, father. I've heard a lot of good things about your parish."

"Well then, we should stroll along quickly so you may enjoy the last part of the string ensemble practice. The children are truly exceptional musicians." He stepped up, took Melanie's arm, and moved forward leaving me behind.

She glanced back to make sure I was following and mouthed an "I'm sorry."

When we reached the end of the first block, Melanie managed to free herself from the priest's grip and turned around to me.

"This neighborhood was once occupied by the French," she said. "Many of these homes are still owned by French people, but they never come here anymore," she added, then turned to the priest.

"Father, I promised Robert that I would show him around Vung Tao and tell him some things about local history."

There was some kind of tug-of-war going on between her and the priest, who seemed annoyed that she stopped to point things out to me.

"The people who made this village a wonderful place are back in France. It is very sad," he said.

"Perhaps the people of Vietnam think it is still a wonderful place, and intend to make it even better," she replied defiantly.

The priest harrumphed, then added, "Perhaps. We shall see. Come along, we must hurry if you wish to hear some of the music."

This time Melanie hung back, took possession of my arm, and indicated we would walk together. He turned and walked ahead. While his back was to us, she kissed my cheek and whispered, "He is a nasty old man who should also go back to France."

We continued to walk, but at our own pace, letting the cranky priest move away. Melanie's closeness dominated my senses. I could have been walking on hot coals and not noticed.

True to her promise, she pointed out the more interesting old homes, some now the residences of local Vietnamese government officials.

The old French Catholic Church stood prominently at the end of the block. Unlike European Catholic churches and cathedrals, the architecture looked much like that of the former Governor's mansion, except it had a three-story façade topped by a bell tower.

On each side were two long dormitory buildings. One was the convent, the other the orphanage, behind which was the school.

Father Daniel led us toward the two-story wing on the right, through an arched entryway, and into an auditorium that included a small stage.

A student orchestra, including some members of the string ensemble that I'd seen at the General's Daughter, was playing a piece that sounded familiar. I thought it might be Mozart.

They played for another fifteen minutes. At the conclusion, the conductor, whose back was to us, and whom I assumed was also a student, rattled off some instructions in rapid French.

When she turned toward us, I realized that she was not a student but a tiny older woman, several inches short of five feet tall. She wore a simple, black, full-length dress and a black and white wimple. I guessed that she was well into her seventies, if not older.

"*Bonjour* Sister Josephine, your students sound as wonderful as ever," Melanie said to the nun who squinted in our direction, before finally putting on the glasses that hung around her neck on top of the cross that also hung there.

"Ah. *Bonjour ma chere,* Melanie. *Ça va?*" she said quickly walking over to us and giving Melanie a kiss on each cheek.

Pointedly ignoring the priest, she turned to me and said in English, "And you must be Melanie's friend, Robert. She has spoken highly of you."

I wasn't sure whether one shakes hands with a nun, or bows. She solved my dilemma by offering me her hand.

"It is a pleasure to meet you, Sister. Melanie says that you are the genius behind these wonderful young musicians."

"I am just a teacher and servant of God. He gave the music to Mozart and Beethoven. I simply help translate."

"Sister Josephine is a true servant of God," Father Daniel said intruding into the conversation.

Both women ignored the priest. I sensed a tension between them.

"I am Robert's tour guide for the afternoon. I would like to show him around the school and then we will walk through the village," Melanie declared.

"*C'est bon.* Oh, one more thing Robert, Captain Baillier, and your ship's doctor, Corpsman Hodges, are here today also. Enjoy your visit," she concluded, turning back toward her students.

Leaving the priest to his duties, Melanie and I went down the stairs to the ground floor where there were several classrooms on either side of a long hallway.

No students were present, but we heard voices from a room at the far end of the hall. They came from a small office set up as an infirmary. Doc Hodges was in the process of putting a bandage on the elbow of a Vietnamese boy who was around seven years old.

"Melanie, Mr. Allen, nice to see you," Doc said as we peeked in the door.

"This is Chi. He fell and dinged up his elbow. But he's all fixed now." He turned back to the boy. "Okay Chi. Here are two more bandages for you in case this one falls off. Try to keep your elbow out of the dirt for a few days. You can go back to your room now."

After the boy left, Doc invited us in, indicating that we could sit on the bench against the wall if we wanted.

"So Doc. This is what you do in your free time."

"Yes. I volunteer here and at a free clinic operated by a Christian NGO from the states at the local hospital. Almost all of the corpsmen from our units and the Aussie units do."

"Sister Josephine said the Captain was here too," I said.

"He was. But, I think he went over the General's Daughter to see Madame Marquis."

"What does our Captain do here?"

"Mostly, he gives Sister Wolfgang fits. All of the kids want to play the piano like he does, banging on the keys like Jerry Lee Lewis and Fats Domino."

"So, he teaches piano?"

"You could say that, although the sister wouldn't. The sounds that come out of the classroom when he's teaching are not Mozart."

We left Doc to attend to another child who had walked up and knocked on the door jam.

We strolled through the dormitory next, and then into a large space that appeared to be a combination library and playroom. There were some children seated at tables reading and doing homework while others were engaged in chess and other board games.

When Melanie entered they all started shouting her name.

"Are you some kind of rock star here?" I asked.

"It wasn't that long ago that I was one of them. Almost all of us who went to school in France returned and became tutors and helpers. Some of us still teach here."

"Do you?"

"Yes. I teach English and creative writing."

"You must be really good. All the kids love you."

"Most of these children not only lost their parents, but also their homes and other relatives. That's why they're here. The school, the nuns, the teachers, and tutors are all part of the only family they have."

"So, you're like a parent to them," I said.

"More like a big sister, but I think the nuns, particularly the older ones like Sister Josephine, are closer to being their mother."

"I understand. I lost my father and mother when I was 12. My only other relative, my grand aunt Celeste, adopted me. She became my mother," I said.

"I'm sorry Rob. I know you never get over losing your real parents." She took my hand. "It seems that fate has brought two orphans together."

We exited the school buildings and stepped onto the street that would take us into the center of Vung Tau.

"Sister Josephine and you seem to have a bond," I said.

"She saved my life," Melanie replied firmly. "If it wasn't for her, I would probably be dead, or somebody's sex slave."

"What do you mean?"

"After my parents died, I was living on the streets, begging for food, and sleeping under overturned fishing boats on the beach. I caught pneumonia. A fisherman found me unconscious and brought me to the orphanage. Sister Josephine, took me in and nursed me back to health."

"And when did your mother, Simone, come into the picture?"

"She was already here, working alongside her friend, the governor general's daughter. Both of them took turns helping Sister Josephine nurse me back to health. It was my mother who first started to read to me as she sat by my bed. Soon, her visits and reading became the highlight of every day."

I saw a look of sadness cross Melanie's face as she told her story.

"Do you remember your birth parents?"

"Yes," she said, almost in a whisper.

"I'm sorry. Of course, you do. That was a stupid question."

"It's okay Rob. Of all people, you would understand. I'd like to tell you what I remember, just not right now. Not today. I want to enjoy our time together and show you my village."

"Okay. Just one more question so I don't tread where I shouldn't. What is the deal between you, Sister Josephine, and Father Daniel?"

She sighed, then shrugged. "Let's just say that he is what you would call a "dirty old man." Sister Josephine has made it her mission to protect all of the girls in the orphanage from his advances."

"He molests the girls?"

"I don't think he's ever gone that far, yet. Sister Josephine has caught him sneaking peaks at the adolescent girls as they shower. He targets the more physically mature girls for hugs, and his hands sometimes wander where they shouldn't."

"Dirty old man sounds like the right description. Has he ever tried anything with you?"

"Just once, when I was thirteen and still attending the school, although I was living with my mother. I was walking alone down the hall. He came up behind me and put his arm around my shoulder. His fingers touched my breast. I ducked out from under his arm and ran all the way home."

"Did you tell your mother?"

"Of course.

"So what did your mother do?"

"She walked directly to the school, found Sister Josephine, and told her what happened. Then, the two of them confronted him. They warned him that they would do everything in their power to have him defrocked and sent home in disgrace if he ever stepped out of line again."

"Wouldn't it have been better to report him and get a new priest?"

"Maybe, but Sister Josephine was worried that it would be her word against his and might backfire. All of the sisters could be recalled and the orphanage closed. Fortunately, Father Daniel is afraid of Sister Josephine. As long as she is here, he will behave."

I was trying to calculate in my head how long this uneasy truce had existed. I wasn't sure how old Melanie was.

She must have read my thoughts.

"It's been almost eleven years. I'm twenty-three. He's still a dirty old man, but fortunately, still very much intimidated by Sister Josephine."

"I'd say he seems a little intimidated by you as well."

"He knows that my mother and I, and all of the sisters here, are watching him. If he crosses one of us, he knows he'll answer to all. We also make sure that all of the girls are instructed on how to protect themselves from unwanted advances from men, including those who wear a priest's collar."

Our conversation, although bordering on uncomfortable, showed me an entirely new side of Melanie. Contrary to my first impression that she was shy and naïve, I now saw a confident, sophisticated, and strong woman, well capable of standing up for herself.

As we walked toward the center of Vung Tau, she began pointing out local sites, including a remarkably ornate and well-kept Buddhist temple.

"Most Vietnamese people are Buddhists. Even some of us who are Catholic observe Buddhist traditions," she volunteered.

"Do you?" I asked.

"Yes. The church rescued me and took me in. My mother adopted me and I actually have French citizenship. But I am also Vietnamese, and Vietnam is my home."

"You spent five years in school in France. That must have been a huge change from your life here."

"I was sixteen when mother took me there. Paris was like some kind of magical place that I'd only read about. The sounds, the lights, the crowds of people, the traffic, and the huge buildings overwhelmed me at first. It was never home to me, but I got used to it."

"Did you have a lot of friends?"

"I went with four other students from my school here. Two girls and two boys, but except for one of the other girls, we were all sent to different schools in the city. Only Cam and I went to the English/French school. An English woman was one of my teachers. She insisted we learn to speak her language properly, without a Vietnamese or French accent.

I was about to ask more about her Paris experience when a middle-aged woman shouted something in Vietnamese at Melanie. She stopped, looked, smiled, and then responded to the greeting.

The woman who'd called out to her was standing in what

appeared to be a small grocery store with its front open to the street.

Melanie took my hand, and led me to where the woman stood. She put her hands together as though praying and bowed to the woman, then spoke something rapidly. The only part I understood clearly was my name.

I'd memorized a few Vietnamese words, like *"sin chow"* (hello) and *"kahm uhn"* (thank you), but was certain I mispronounced them.

The woman turned to me and smiled, put her hands together, and bowed, saying something that sounded like *sin chow*.

Doing my best to imitate her gesture, I replied *"Sin chow,"* then added in French, *"Enchanté, Madame."*

Whatever I did must have been correct, because she smiled with delight and said something in Vietnamese to Melanie that made her giggle.

They chatted for a few minutes and I smiled and nodded whenever the woman looked toward me.

As we moved on down the street, Melanie said. "Mrs. Tien likes you. She says you have a kind face and good manners."

"She also said something that made you giggle. What was that?"

"She said you were also handsome in the right ways."

"I understand handsome, but in the right ways. What does that mean?"

"It is hard to explain. Perhaps we can say it is a matter of taste. You have a look she likes."

"And do you?" I asked. "Do you agree with her?" I then put my hands together as though praying, bowed to her, smiled and whispered. "I hope this is true with all my heart."

She laughed, punched me lightly in the arm, then grabbed it and pulled me along with her.

"Of course. You don't think I would introduce an ugly American to my friends do you?"

We spent the next hour walking around the side streets of the village, notably avoiding the streets closest to the beach where most of the bars and clubs catering to U.S. sailors were located.

Melanie introduced me to several more store owners who were selling their wares on the sidewalks in front of their shops.

I couldn't help but notice how relaxed and natural she seemed to be and how friendly all of the people were to her.

"You seem to know everybody in this neighborhood. They know you, but they're calling you by a different name. It definitely isn't Melanie or Mademoiselle Marquis. It sounded like Jean," I said.

"Gian," she said. "That's what you would call my first name. My Vietnamese name is Tran Vi Gian. Tran is my family name."

"Is it hard to have two names? You're Melanie Marquis at the mansion and at the school, and then Tran Vi Gian here in town? Does that ever get confusing?"

She stopped and looked at me. She was frowning.

"What? Was that a rude question? If so I apologize. I'm just trying to understand." I said, anxious not to upset her.

"No. It's okay. You ask me something I am asking myself. Can I ever be the French woman my mother wishes me to be, or will I always be the Vietnamese woman I really am? I do not believe I can be both."

"That sounds like a difficult dilemma. I can't imagine what it's like for you, especially when there are Vietnamese fighting on both sides and the French are considered the villains who created the problem."

"Robert. It is even more difficult and complicated than that. But let's not talk of such serious things right now. Come on. I want to take you to my friend Cam's music club. It is called "Café New Orleans," and has the best music in town."

Melanie's determination to change the subject kept me from

asking the question that weighed on me most, "Are Americans helping or hurting the Vietnamese people, like the ones I just met in Vung Tau?" Getting an answer would have to wait.

We had to cross the main drag where all the bars were, but then took a turn on a side street and down a half block, where a brightly painted sign signified we'd arrived.

There was a closed sign on the door, but Melanie ignored it and walked in with me right behind.

A female voice shouted from deeper inside the club, "Gian, is that you?"

"*Salut*, Cam. Yes, it is me and I brought a friend."

A young Vietnamese woman I judged to be close to Melanie's age came toward the door.

She was Melanie's height, but slightly stockier in build, and her hair was cut shorter. She had a pretty face and a delightful lilt to her voice.

I was surprised that they both seemed to prefer speaking English to each other rather than Vietnamese.

"Cam. This is my friend, Robert, he is an officer on Captain Baillier's ship. I'm showing him around the village. Rob, this is my very best friend in Vung Tau, Cam. She and I went to France as students together."

I was about to extend my hand when Cam moved forward, hugged me, and kissed each cheek in the French style.

"*Bonjour*, Robert, and welcome to Café New Orleans. Your Captain is one of our best customers and sometimes a guest performer."

"It's a pleasure to meet you, Cam. You have a very nice place," I replied.

The two girls exchanged small talk, mostly in English with a few French and Vietnamese words thrown in. Then Cam turned to me.

"The club doesn't open for a few hours but you're just in time to hear our band rehearse. You and Gian can sit down here and I will bring you a beer."

While we were talking, the musicians, two guitarists, a trumpet player, a pianist, and a drummer were setting up on the stage along the back wall of the club. They took only a few minutes to tune up and then went right into some New Orleans soul music, followed by a Bob Marley song, and finally, a joyful, rhythmic rendition of "Iko, Iko."

I noticed that the piano player and the lead guitarist were black and spoke French to each other between songs. I guessed, "These must be the 'black Frenchies' Archer was talking about. New Orleans is the club that he were going to.

After their set, they all came over, greeted Melanie warmly, and sat down with us. Cam handed them beers. When she told them that I was from the *Bell County*, they all raved about "*Le grand capitaine* Bill. He's the best!" They declared.

The conversations around the table were a rich and rapid blend of French, Vietnamese, and English that I only partially followed.

Speaking directly to me in English with a heavy French accent, the pianist said "You know your friend, Melanie is a *bonne chanteuse*, a very good singer."

"No. I didn't know that. I've never heard her sing."

"No? *Alors!* Then you must." He stood and urged his band back to the stage and pointing to Melanie, said, "Your friend Robert must hear your beautiful voice."

"I am not a singer," she protested, but Cam took her hand and led her to the stage.

She seemed to compose herself. Smiled at me then leaned over and said something to the pianist who nodded.

With the band playing softly enough to allow her voice to ride on the notes, she delivered a hauntingly beautiful version of Dusty Springfield's "You Don't Have to Say You Love Me."

She seemed to be singing directly to me, and at that moment I was willing to consider every option I could to stay with her forever.

Then, a more immediate reality intruded when I glanced at my watch. I would have to sprint to the dock to catch my boat back to the ship. I didn't even have time to walk her home. I thanked Cam and the band, and without thinking if it was appropriate, I embraced Melanie and kissed her on the lips. I felt her body melt into mine.

"I've got to run. I cannot miss the boat or my watch. I'm sorry," I said

She held my hand for a few seconds, then let it go.

"It is okay, Robert. You will come back soon?"

"Of course. You know I will," I said, looking back one last time, then went out the door and began to run toward the breakwater where the boat back to the ship waited until I jumped on, panting to catch my breath.

The 2000 to midnight anchor watch left me four hours to stare at the horizon and the stars. Melanie's sweet voice played over and over in my mind: *"You don't have to stay forever…"*

I wondered if she chose that song as a message. The part about not staying forever was particularly troublesome; because both of us knew I would eventually be sent home, while Melanie was already home.

When I finally got to my bunk, I had a hard time falling asleep.

12

The War from a Different Angle
••••••••••••••••••••••

THE *BELL COUNTY* PULLED ANCHOR as the sun rose and was docked at the Vung Tau loading ramp by 0700. Dozens of pallets were lined up and a forklift operator was waiting to load us.

"We have orders to get loaded quickly and head upriver. We're going to a small fire base near Can Tho on the Song Hau Gian," the XO informed us.

"They're almost out of food and ammunition and it's farther away than My Tho. Our plan is to load before noon and beat the tide change to the river mouth."

I was disappointed. Spending the evening in Vung Tao with Melanie was off the table.

"Are we going to do a show there, XO?" Harry asked.

"Maybe. It depends on the base commander and the threat level. The base was attacked several nights last week. For security reasons, they may be a little reluctant. I don't blame them. But, we'll be ready just in case they say yes."

There was no word on whether Admiral Kirkpatrick had gotten approval for the *Bell County*'s musical mission. That meant that we had to ask permission to perform at every base.

At 1100 our main cargo hold was full and our ship's crane was lowering the last of the remaining pallets onto our open main deck. They were securely tied down, the ramp was pulled in, and the bow doors closed.

We were just about to pull in the gangway, cast off the lines and back out, when someone from shore hailed us. There was a passenger coming aboard.

A thin, dark-haired man in an ARVN (Army of the Republic of Vietnam) uniform saluted the quartermaster and requested permission to come aboard. The silver bar on his collar indicated his rank as a first lieutenant.

As I watched from the bridge, the XO walked out to greet him. He was smiling. They knew each other.

His name was Hoang Binh, a courier operating out of ARVN headquarters in Saigon. He said he was carrying documents for the ARVN commander operating with the American forces near Can Tho. Once we cleared the ramp and were underway toward the mouth of the Song Hau Gian, the officers not on watch joined the Captain and XO in the wardroom to meet Lt. Hoang.

He was five and a half feet tall and wiry, probably in his thirties, but had an old face, marked by an abundance of worry lines. His posture suggested he was weary, physically and mentally.

He and the Captain were speaking French when Andrew and I entered the wardroom.

"Ah. Here are my two newest officers, Ensign Rob Allen and Ensign Andrew Cohen. Gentlemen, this is Lt. Binh Hoang. Binh and I met when I first arrived in Vietnam. He has been on several rides up and down the rivers with us."

We shook hands. Andrew said something to him in French, which the lieutenant acknowledged, but then switched to English, which he spoke with a crisp British accent.

"My parents sent me to study law in France, but I ended up studying for two additional years in London," he explained.

I was curious how a Vietnamese lawyer trained in France and England, ended up as an Army courier, hitching rides with the U.S. Navy. Instead, the conversation around the table centered on the war and how things were in Saigon and further north. The only war news we got was from a heavily censored Armed Forces Radio.

"President Thieu is confident that we are winning the war, and that the communists are losing heart. With your help, we are cutting off their supply lines and weakening the rebels like those in this area."

His statement sounded like something read off a cue card. There was little conviction in his voice, and he seemed reluctant to look any of us in the eye. Conversation finally came around to less heavy topics and I asked him how a lawyer ended up as a courier in the Vietnamese Army.

"You could say I was drafted," he answered, relaxing for the first time.

"Well. That makes two of us," I said with a laugh.

"Military service is compulsory here like it is in the U.S. University graduates can join as officers. And if you are Catholic and have friends in the regime, you can advance quite rapidly."

He paused and looked around to see if there was any reaction to what he said. Seeing only interest, he continued.

"My father was a Catholic and a successful businessman in Saigon. He could afford to send me away to school. But when the coup ousted Diem, anyone who'd ever done business with his regime, as my father had, was suspect. I returned home with the idea of being an Army lawyer. Unfortunately, I found that I too was suspect.

"I was allowed into the officers' corps, but my options were limited and have remained so. Still, I am serving my country as best I can."

I waited to see if anyone else was going to ask him a question. When no one did, I spoke up.

"Lieutenant Hoang," I began, but he interrupted.

"Please, you can call me Binh," he said.

"Okay. Binh. I'm probably like a lot of guys sent here who have no idea why or whom we're fighting for. They say it is to prevent the Communists from taking over all of Asia, but I'm wondering if that is what the Vietnamese people, at least the those in the south, think?"

He looked at me for several seconds then down at his hands folded together on the top of the table.

Before he could answer, the Captain cut in.

"Gentlemen, Binh is a friend. He is a good guy and a straight shooter. Speaking frankly to us on the subject of this civil war could get him into serious trouble. So whatever is said here, stays here."

"Thank you, Captain. You're right. Officially, there is only one answer that I can give, and that is the one President Thieu and Vice President Ky want us all to give.

"The truth is far more complicated. It isn't just about Communists versus Catholics, or Buddhists against the government, or French sympathizers versus those who hate the French. It's all of those things and more. It is also rich versus poor, and city dweller versus peasant farmer, educated versus uneducated." He paused, and took a sip of coffee.

"And there is one very important thing. It is about an independent Vietnam, free of the French, free of the Chinese and, yes, free of Americans."

"Is there a book that explains all this so we could understand?" Andrew asked.

"Yes. There are actually two I would recommend, both by Bernard Fall.

The first is *Street Without Joy*, about the Indochina War from 1946 to 1954. And the second is *The Two Vietnams*, his political and military analysis of our current situation.

"Dr. Fall was born in Vienna, but migrated to France as a child. His family was Jewish. The Gestapo killed his father and his mother was sent to Auschwitz where she died. At 16, he joined the French resistance, then the French Army. After the war, he studied political science in France and America, earning several degrees as a specialist on Indo-China. He spent time with the French troops here and was at Dien Bien Phu. More recently, he was here observing ARVN and American troops as a war correspondent. He was killed by a mine last February while he was with an American Marine platoon near Hue.

"He was pro-French and pro-American, but understood that for the Vietnamese on both sides, this is a battle for independence. I wish your president would read his work."

"Can I assume you studied Fall's writings when you were in France and England? You seem to have an extraordinary mastery of it." I said.

"Yes. Dr. Fall was a guest lecturer in London while I was there. I attended every one of his presentations."

The conversation in the wardroom continued on through lunch with those of us who had a watch to stand coming and going.

By the time our ship reached the mouth of the Song Hau Gian River, it was getting dark and the Captain chose to drop the anchor and wait until morning to proceed. There was just no way he wanted to try to navigate upstream in the dark.

The conversation around the dinner table continued to be a Vietnam history lesson for most of us. It was fascinating and informative.

Binh managed to squeeze in some questions of us and about how we came to be officers on the *Bell County*.

Then he smiled and said, "How about your secret mission? How's that going?"

We all looked to the Captain.

"It's the worst kept secret this side of Vung Tau," he said laughing. "I told Binh about it the last time he was on board. In fact, I tried to recruit him to perform with us. He plays the violin."

Andrew, looked up surprised. "You play the violin too. I guess there are no music assignments for violinists in your Army either."

"Andrew. You know that there is an open invitation for you to join our band anytime you are ready," the Captain interjected.

"Yes sir. I know. I'm thinking about it seriously."

Then Andrew turned to Binh, "Where did you study?"

"I started here in Vietnam when I was a little boy, but as I got older, my teachers discouraged it, and I put it away. When I went to Paris and studied history and law at the Sorbonne, my roommates were both musicians, one was a cellist. The other played violin. They encouraged me to start playing again and helped tutor me. I was never very good, but played for my own enjoyment. I still do, when there's time."

The conversation then switched to music, the ship's band, and what we hoped to accomplish with it.

By 2200, I was looking for a way to gracefully excuse myself and get caught up on sleep. The XO caught me yawning and spoke up.

"Binh, our stewards have made up a bunk for you in our storage space next to the ship's office. It isn't much, but it is a place to get some rest for the night."

"Thanks, Lew. I've had to sleep in far worse quarters believe me. I'll be fine. In fact, I'm going to hit that rack right now if you will excuse me."

We all thanked Binh for handling all of our questions so gracefully. I agreed with the Captain that he was definitely one of the good guys.

As I was headed down the passageway toward my stateroom, the XO said, "By the way, if you or Andrew are interested, I have copies of both the books Binh mentioned. You're welcome to borrow them any time."

"Thanks, XO. I would. Could I start with *Two Vietnams?*"

He went into his stateroom and returned a few seconds later and handed it to me.

I took it back to my stateroom, intending to start reading right then, but fatigue hit me as soon as my head hit the pillow. The next thing I remember I was waking up at 0330 to get ready for my watch.

It was dark. There was no moon, but the skies were clear and bright with millions of stars. The air was warm and only a slight breeze rippled the water. There were no signs of any ships or movement on the flooded delta lands at the river's mouth.

Archer had the watch with me.

"How are you enjoying Vung Tao so far?" I asked him. "I think I was in that club you told me about. Was it the New Orleans?"

"Yeah. That's the place. Lots of guys from the ship stop in. The Captain even came by one night and played a few numbers with the house band."

"That group is really good. I listened to them rehearse yesterday," I replied.

"It's a great club if you like music. No bar girls are allowed, just good music, good beer, good times," he added.

"So you avoid the local bar girls?"

"The girls a sailor like me meet in those places are just trying to make a living. They're doing whatever they have to. I'm pretty sure they're pimped by the guys running the bars. It's a sleazy, degrading thing and we're the ones taking advantage of it."

"This war creates lots of poor, desperate people. Everyone does what they have to, just to survive," I said.

"And what are we doing about it? The money we pay our troops is supporting pimps and crooks. I don't think that helps this country," he added.

"I agree," I answered.

Changing the subject slightly, I added. "Binh, that ARVN officer who hitched a ride with us today, doesn't have anything good to say about the war either. Have you met any Vietnamese people?"

"No. Not really. Just some of the bartenders and waitresses. A couple of the guys in the band at the New Orleans club are Vietnamese and we've talked about music, but not about the war or anything like that."

"I'd like to know what they really think about us being here in their country," I said.

Just then I heard someone step onto the bridge and clear his throat. It was Binh.

"I hope it's okay for me to be up here. That compartment is stuffy and I was having a hard time sleeping."

"It's okay. The hardest part of what we're doing is staying awake. Company helps. This is petty officer Archer, one of our signalmen, and the best rhythm and blues singer this side of the Pacific."

Archer saluted the ARVN officer and said hello.

Binh returned his salute and said, "Hello Archer. Nice to meet you. Please relax. I'm just a guest here."

"Yes, sir. Welcome to the bridge. And, if you don't mind me asking, where did you learn to speak such good English?"

Binh laughed, then said, "In jolly old England, where else?"

It was Archer's turn to laugh. "Man, I've got to go there when I get out. If I could talk like you, chicks would be all over my ass."

Navy tradition and protocol required an invisible wall between enlisted men and officers. Officers addressed enlisted men by their last names, never first. They addressed officers by last name also, but preceded by either by the officer's rank, or Mister. It was the Navy's way to make it clear that the enlisted ranks were subordinate to officers, and that we could be friendly, but never friends.

The reality was different.

I spent more time talking with Archer and other enlisted men on watch than I'd ever had with fellow officers, including my roommate. These conversations were all over the lot on subjects ranging from religion, and politics, to food, music, and sex. At some point, a friendship forms whether the Navy says it should or not.

The trick was to know when and where it was okay to be friends, and when we had to be strictly Navy.

An easy watch on a quiet night was friend time.

It was obvious that Binh and Archer were comfortable with each other and I didn't have to worry about protocol.

"I hope you don't mind, but I heard your question about what Vietnamese think about your presence here. I'd like to give you my opinion."

"Yes. Please. It is something I've been wondering about since we got here, I said."

Archer nodded in agreement.

"In truth, there's no consensus among Vietnamese on that question. We don't agree with each other on many things, especially government, which is why we're in a civil war.

"The communists don't want you here. But even that is not absolute. There was a time when they wanted you to help them kick out the French.

"Thieu and his supporters are Catholic. They also wanted the

French to leave Vietnam, but they hate the communists. Thieu's way of governing is no more democratic than the communists. Both sides maintain control through the use of brutal force and intimidation."

He paused, took a sip from the mug of coffee he brought with him and then continued.

"The majority of Vietnamese civilians are caught in between, mere pawns in a cruel game over which they have no say. We are being killed and wounded at several times the rate of actual combatants. Most of us are sick of war. In South Vietnam, we hope the Americans can stop it. But even if you are successful, which is doubtful, in the end we want you to leave. Vietnam is our country. We don't want to be an American colony any more than we wanted to be French."

"Are the Viet Cong fighting in the south really communists, or do they see themselves as patriots fighting for the independence of their country?"

"Both. Some are Communists, some just go along because they see it as a better choice. In either case, they see this as a fight for the independence of Vietnam," Binh answered.

"I've heard that the VC are everywhere, including in Vung Tau. They could be waiting on us in a bar one night and shooting at us the next," Archer offered.

"I think that is true," Binh replied.

"Shit. If it's that obvious, why are we here? The VC couldn't do what they do unless the people who we're supposed to be fighting to protect are protecting the people we are fighting."

"Archer. You've said it better than I could. That is America's dilemma, and also that of many Vietnamese. We have friends and family fighting on both sides. We lose no matter which side we choose."

As the glow of pending dawn appeared on the eastern horizon, it seemed that we'd run out of things to say.

Binh yawned and said he was going to try to sleep for a couple of hours and left the bridge.

"You know Mr. Allen, that Vietnamese officer is a good guy, but he sure said some nasty shit. This war is fucked up and we aren't doing much good for anybody, except the folks making ammunition and body bags."

"I know, Archer. I know," I replied, exhausted by the weight of that realization. We were in the middle of a conflict we did not understand with little power to change the outcome.

13

Binh's Mekong Suite
●●●●●●●●●●●●●●●●●●●●●●●

A NDREW CAME INTO THE WARDROOM shortly after reveille to find Binh working on what appeared to be a musical score spread across the table.

"You're a composer," Andrew declared matter-of-factly.

"Not really. I'm an amateur. I started writing short suites while I was in France. My two roommates were kind enough to help me."

"Do you mind if I take a peek?" Andrew asked.

"Not at all. I'd like to know what you think."

Andrew picked up the first few pages and read them, hearing in his mind what the notes would sound like when played.

He looked up, smiled. "Binh. This is good. Are you going to write it for a full orchestra? I imagine it would be really good that way."

"I'm going to try, but it's slow going. I have no experience. No music education other than violin lessons when I was a child. Right now it is more of what you would call a hobby."

"Well, You're off to a good start. There's something familiar with the style though. I can't put my finger on it."

"Are you familiar with the work of Ferde Grofé?" He asked

"Of course. The *Grand Canyon Suite*, the *Mississippi Suite*, among others. Yes. I used to listen to the *Grand Canyon Suite* and imagine it through the music. Then I saw a Disney feature using the music and I was hooked."

"Me too. My father had a collection of LPs of American music, among them was a collection of Grofé's work. When I started practicing the violin, I used to try to play parts of it by ear."

"So what is the inspiration for your suite?"

"The Mekong, the river that is the life's blood and center of the heartbeat of South Vietnam. I confess, that I am borrowing a lot of ideas from Grofé. But, I'm using a tonal scale that is easier on Vietnamese ears."

Just then the Captain walked into the stateroom.

"Is it finished?" he asked Binh.

"You know it isn't, Captain. But I'm closer than I was before."

"I was trying to whistle that part you call the 'Buddha Cave.' I know it was written for a flute and violin, but whistling works pretty good too," he said smiling. "Who knows, one of these days, young Vietnamese musicians will be walking down the street whistling parts of your *Mekong Suite*."

"Captain, I think Binh has written something pretty good. I'd love to hear it played," Andrew said.

"Me too," he said then glanced at his watch. "Okay. We've got an hour before we weigh anchor. Go get your violin and come back here," he said and then left the wardroom.

When Andrew returned with his violin, the Captain was seated on a stool at the end of the table. An accordion was in his lap.

We all knew that in addition to all of the other instruments he played, the Captain was a virtuoso on the accordion. "It was my first instrument," he declared the first time he ever played it for us in the wardroom.

Binh looked at the Captain, then at Andrew, then back at the Captain.

"You really want to try this?" he asked holding up his composition."

"Not all of it. I was thinking of the 'Birth waters' piece," the Captain said. "What do you think, Andrew?"

Andrew checked out the sheets of music the Captain had chosen, did a quick read through. "Sure. I think we can do it."

I was just coming off watch and heard beautiful sounds coming from the wardroom.

The Captain was playing a slow, lilting melody with single keys on his accordion. After several bars Andrew's violin floated along above the notes like a bird over the water. The sound was captivating.

I had no idea what they were playing, but I wedged myself into the wardroom where Harry, O.J. and the XO had already taken their places to listen.

The melody sounded strangely familiar, but I was certain I'd never heard it before. There was an Asian quality to the notes, exotic but pleasing to the ear.

Andrew and the Captain had only played together one time, as far as I knew, and yet they were completely in sync.

Binh was sitting at the table, his eyes closed, and moving his hands as though conducting an invisible orchestra. The worry lines disappeared to be replaced by relaxed serenity.

Everyone in the room was captivated. When they stopped twenty-five minutes later there was silence for several seconds. Then everyone started talking at once.

"What was that?" Harry asked.

"I didn't know an accordion could sound like that," I added.

"Nice job, Andrew," the Captain said.

I looked at Binh. Tears were running down his cheeks. He whispered something that I didn't catch.

"Did you write this, Binh? It's beautiful," I said.

He looked up and smiled. "Yes, but this is the first time I've heard it. I don't know what to say. I wasn't sure it was any good. Yet, the way the Captain and Andrew played it was perfect."

He turned to both of the musicians, "I'm very grateful to you both. You've inspired me to keep working on it."

Harry and John went over to the table and looked at the sheets arrayed in front of Binh.

"Holy shit, it's a whole frigging symphony," Harry exclaimed.

"Not quite. It's more of a suite, a collection of related pieces."

"What's it called?" John asked.

"For now, I'm calling it *The Mekong Suite*," Binh answered.

"And sweet it is," Harry replied. "I think you need to take this on the road."

Binh looked puzzled. "On the road?" he said

"You know. Find a way to have an orchestra play it," Harry added.

"I agree," a chorus of voices replied.

"You are all very kind to say so, but it's not finished and even if I could finish it, there's a war on, and no orchestra to play it, even in Saigon," Binh replied.

O.J. spoke up for the first time. "I have an idea."

"O.J.? You have your scrounger face on. What crazy scheme is running around in there?" the Captain asked.

"It involves you getting on the good side of Sister Josephine."

"Sister Wolfgang? She's already accused me of corrupting her students. I doubt I have any influence on her."

O.J. nodded he understood, but held up his hand. "Hear me out."

The Captain smiled, and nodded for him to continue.

"As long as it doesn't involve any more broken beer pallet claims for a while. The supply guys are already on my ass about that," said the XO.

"No, nothing like that," O.J. said. He stood and spread his arms like he was unveiling a banner.

"We stage a benefit concert – a big fund-raising event for the school's music program. We do it at the General's Daughter, charge admission, with the proceeds going to the orphanage for instruments, more music, and whatever. It would be billed as a joint effort co-sponsored by ARVN and the U.S. Navy. It's great public relations," he said.

"So, you want us to play Binh's suite at the concert?" said Harry.

"No. Not us, or at least not most of us. The students. The student orchestra will play it." He added. "I think the Captain and Andrew should be part of it too, but that's up to them."

Looks went around the room, all ending up on the Captain, who stood and clapped his hands together.

"Yes," he said. "O.J. has once again pulled a wild hare out of his hat. Gentlemen, we have some planning to do."

Binh remained seated, a look of panic on his face. "But wait. I haven't finished. In fact, I'm unsure how to finish. Not only that, I have to go back to Saigon as soon as we return to Vung Tau."

"Binh. What if I got you temporarily assigned to the *Bell County* as a liaison?" the XO asked.

"How could you possibly do that? Binh asked.

"I couldn't. But I know someone who could," the XO answered. Then glanced at the Captain.

"Admiral Kirkpatrick," the Captain said. "I'll get a message to him tonight. He'll love the idea of the benefit concert. In fact, I'd bet my bars that he'll find a way to attend and make some of the fleet's other big shots join him."

Binh looked around the table in disbelief. "Of course, If you would do all that for me and my little piece of music, the least I can do is finish it as best I can. But I could use some help from you, Captain, and Andrew."

"You've got it, Andrew and the Captain said in unison.

Enthusiastic conversation continued for the next ten minutes.

"I hate to break this up, but high tide has arrived. It's time to pull the hook and head upriver. O.J., call the crew to stations," the Captain said.

"Aye, aye, Captain," O.J. replied then went to the ship's P.A. system and picked up the microphone. "All hands man your stations to weigh anchor and get underway."

It was a clear day and the ship made good time up the river to the base at Can Tho.

Smaller than the one at My Tho, it looked less like a military post and more like a makeshift encampment scraped out of the jungle. There was one small Quonset hut and several large tents set up in the muddy clearing. A half-dozen PBRs and a couple of armed landing craft were tied up to a wooden dock at the side of the ramp.

A small contingent of sailors and Marines were waiting for us as we pulled into the ramp. They began unloading us immediately.

It looked like we'd have plenty of time before dark to put on a show. The XO and Binh left the ship; Binh to report to the officer in charge of the ARVN base; the XO to find the Navy base commander and see if he would approve a concert on the ramp for his men.

I had the deck watch. The Captain and O.J. were in the radio room composing a message for Admiral Kirkpatrick requesting his help in getting Binh posted to our crew for an indefinite period.

I noticed that the soldiers on shore were wearing their helmets and flak vests. Most were either carrying their rifles or had them stashed next to them while they moved the pallets around. Exhaustion showed on their faces and in their posture. They were stressed out and sleep-deprived.

It reminded me of how lucky I was to have been assigned to a ship that provided shelter, safety, a dry place to sleep, and, so far, no middle-of-the-night wake up calls courtesy of Charlie.

I saw the XO and Binh walking quickly back toward the ship. They didn't look happy.

I saluted as they walked up the ramp. The XO stopped.

"As soon as the last pallet is off the ship, notify the Captain. We've been advised to get off the beach and down river before dark," he said.

"Aye, aye, XO," I replied, knowing two things: The show wasn't going on, and this base was not a safe place for us.

Less than an hour later, all was offloaded. I notified the Captain and all hands were called to their stations to move off the ramp.

Once we were headed downriver, the Captain ordered us to general quarters, which meant that all guns were manned, water-tight compartment doors were shut, and the ship was prepared to return fire if fired upon.

My station at G.Q. was on the bridge with the Captain and O.J. The XO was stationed one deck below in the wheelhouse with the ship's quartermaster.

Sailors manned each of the machine guns, including the two 30cal guns mounted port and starboard on the bridge.

John, the deck officer, was in charge of the 40mm gun crews and stationed on the bow. We had two twin mounts forward, and one in the stern. A team of sailors manned each. If we had to start shooting, reloading the guns quickly was a labor-intensive, heavy, hand-to-hand process.

It was the first time we'd been at our battle stations for real since we arrived in country.

All the gunners and John were connected to the ship's hard-wired intercom system and wore headsets. They were WW II vintage and you had to shout through them to be heard, but they worked most of the time.

The Captain didn't appear to be particularly tense, but he was checking out every aspect of the ship's readiness.

As we moved downriver, he explained to all of us on the bridge why.

"The base commander and the ARVN commander were in a meeting when Binh and the XO checked in with them. They were preparing the base for a major assault, expected tonight or early tomorrow morning. They've been hit by with probing attacks for the last five nights. They believe the big one's coming next. They thanked us for the supplies and advised us to get out ASAP. And they meant out of the river too. Apparently, there are sapper squads working along the shore. They've already sunk two PBRs and wounded three crewmen."

We all nodded that we understood.

A second later, several shots rang out from the direction of the ship's bow. Everyone tensed until the bow gunner on the ship's communication net reported that he was shooting at some suspicious flotsam.

Nobody relaxed until the ship cleared the bar at the river mouth and we secured from general quarters. The regular underway watch took over and the ship's course was set for Vung Tau.

'14

When the Goingobatch Breaks
•••••••••••••••••••••••

F OR A SHIP BUILT TO make a single landing on one beach more than two decades before the Vietnam War, the Bell County was in damn good shape. She had crossed the Pacific from San Diego, weathered the heavy seas on the fringe of a typhoon, made two round-trip voyages between Vietnam and the Philippines, and survived numerous runs up muddy, debris-clogged rivers in the Mekong Delta.

I was the OOD nearing the end of my 1200 to 1600 watch as the ship steamed at its top cruising speed of nine knots, which meant that we would easily make it to Vung Tau before dark.

Archer was the signalman on the bridge with me. It was quiet. There were no ships on the horizon.

Suddenly, we both were startled by what sounded like a truck hitting a telephone pole. Black smoke started pouring from the ship's exhaust stack. The ship's speed dropped suddenly and the bow swung to the right.

"Helmsman, return to heading 030," I yelled through the voice tube to the wheelhouse one deck below.

"Heading 030. Aye, aye, sir. There's a problem in the engine room, sir," the helmsman added.

Just then, the ship's intercom phone chirped. It was the engine room several decks below. The petty officer on duty said our starboard engine just blew.

I called the Captain's cabin. As I waited for him to answer, he stepped onto the bridge.

"Captain on the bridge," Archer shouted.

I put down the phone and saluted.

He returned my salute. "Starboard engine blown," he said. He knew without being told.

"I heard it go…felt the ship pull to starboard. Harry is already on his way to the engine room," he added.

"What do we do now?" I asked.

"Just stay on course. We can get by with one engine, it just takes longer to get where we're going." It surprised me how calm he was.

"Aye, aye, Captain," I said, as he left the bridge.

At 1600 John Walton relieved me. As I walked past the wardroom, I saw the CO, XO, Harry, Andrew, and the senior engineering petty officer sitting at the table.

The petty officer was describing the damage.

It seemed to make sense to those listening. To me, it sounded like "Beowulf" in old English.

"The starboard fram feasceaft funden and frofre gebad, and then hyran scolde slip-snotted the goingobatch."

Andrew listened intently, pretending he understood every word.

"Right," I thought.

"Captain. We don't have the parts to replace the fram or the goingobatch. We're going to need the tender to make us the parts," Harry said.

Tenders were the most amazing ships in the Navy. They were large, floating machine and repair shops that could fix, replace, or replicate virtually any part of any ship. The machinists and technicians on board were the best in their trades. Considering how far we were from home, without tenders, many of our ships would have been left to rust wherever they broke down.

Fortunately for us, there was a tender, the USS *Markab*, tied up to a dock next to the supply base in Vung Tau.

"Harry, write up a report detailing the damage. Give it to Lew and he'll send it to the CO of the *Markab*. Ask if we can pull in alongside her to make access easier and faster," the Captain said.

When the meeting broke up, Andrew and I headed back toward our stateroom.

"Okay, Mr. Assistant Engineering Officer, tell me about that cracked fram cylinder and the burned bango-what's-it, in terms that an English major can understand."

Andrew screwed up his face. Thought for a few seconds, then replied.

"We'll you see the fram bone is connected to cylinder bone, and its connected to the bango bone, and the bango bone's connected to the engine bone…"

"Now hear the name of the lord," I sang along with his knockoff of the old spiritual, "Dry Bones."

"You don't know shit about what's wrong with that engine do you?" I added.

"I know it's broken and we don't have the parts to fix it. And I know we're going to get it fixed when we get to Vung Tau."

"Good enough for me," I replied, dropping into my bunk to for a nap before dinner.

I was just dozing off when Andrew's voice came from the upper bunk.

"What the deal with you and Melanie?"

"We're friends," I said hoping to keep the conversation short so I could go to sleep.

"Just friends? Not the way you look at her. I've seen that look before."

"Yes. But there's not much I can do about it, is there? We won't be in Vietnam that long, and even when we're here, we're up the river or some other shitty place most of the time."

"Yeah. That doesn't change the way you feel though, does it?"

"Actually, it sort of does. I feel confused, torn, frustrated."

"Because?"

"Okay. Because I really like her. She's smart, sophisticated, speaks three languages and she's beautiful. She's also very sweet and seems to like me."

"And that's a problem?"

"Yes. If I fall in love with her, and her with me, what are we going to do, runaway to Thailand together?" I leaned out to make my voice heard clearly.

"You and I are in the Navy, in the middle of a war. If we don't get killed, we get to go home. She's Vietnamese. This is her country. She's already home."

"It's not such a nice home right now. She's also a French citizen because Simone adopted her. She could go to France any time she wants," he argued.

"I'm not sure she wants to go to France. I got mixed signals when I asked her about her experience there."

"But if she loves you, France is a place where you could both be together."

"That sounds like your dream Andrew. I know you would love to live in France. Maybe you should ask her?"

"Come on. She likes me, but she really, really likes you. Besides, I've met someone else."

"Who? Where? We've hardly been on liberty."

"I met her at the orphanage."

"You've fallen for a nun?" I exclaimed.

"No. A nurse," he stated firmly.

" I went to the school to meet with Sister Josephine about

helping teach violin. While I was there, I met Kaneli, a nurse attached to the Australian Navy base. She volunteers at the school clinic. I've got a tentative date for dinner with her whenever we get back in."

"What is it with you and nurses?" I asked. "And Kaneli sounds Polynesian."

"Fijian, actually. Her father is Australian. Her mother is from Fiji. Kaneli is a lovely blend – tall, exotically beautiful and funny. She speaks with an Aussie accent and knows lots of jokes. I think you'll like her."

"But, your romance here is likely to go no further than mine," I said

"Yes but, to quote Emily Dickinson, 'The heart wants what it wants.'"

"You're quoting Emily Dickinson now? I would have expected Puccini, or even John Luther Long," I replied.

"Puccini? John Luther Long? As in *Madame Butterfly*? I never took you as an opera buff."

"We English majors have our secrets. In any case, I doubt that either of our women friends would choose to be a 'Cio-Cio-San.'"

I drifted off to sleep, but it wasn't *Madame Butterfly* I thought of. Instead it was the movie *Sayonara*. Marlon Brando played a U.S. fighter pilot on leave in Japan during the Korean War. He falls in love with 'Hana-Ogi,' a beautiful Japanese geisha. His buddy (played by Red Buttons) and his Japanese girlfriend commit suicide because the Army wouldn't let them get married. At the end of that bittersweet movie, Brando's character asks Hana-Ogi to marry him.

My dream shifted.

I saw Melanie seated on a small stool dressed in a kimono, playing odd-looking Asian fiddle, and singing along with Binh's Mekong Suite.

A really loud, rude guy was shouting something from the audience.

"All hands to anchor stations."

I'd slept for over two hours.

We made it to Vung Tao. But, we were unable to get approval to pull alongside the tender. Instead, we had to anchor in the bay until a space could be cleared for us. That wouldn't be until the next day.

After we secured from the anchor detail, I found Andrew changing into his civvies.

"You have twenty minutes to get cleaned up, changed, and make the first boat into Vung Tau. I'm going to try to catch Kaneli at her barracks, and then we can go to dinner at the General's Daughter. Maybe Melanie can take time off to join us."

I was already thinking about catching the boat and didn't need any further persuasion. Once on shore, we caught a three-wheeled cyclo-taxi to the hospital. The Australian nurses' barracks were next door.

There was an armed guard in front of the barracks. Andrew looked hesitant about what to do next.

"What is Kaneli's rank and last name?" I asked him

"Lieutenant, Martin. Why?"

"Just let me handle this," I said.

As we approached the door, the guard eyed us suspiciously.

"Good evening, Corporal, would you please tell Lt. Martin that doctors Cohen and Allen are here to escort her to the presentation," I told him.

"Presentation?" the corporal repeated, hesitation in his voice.

"Yes. Dr. Cohen and I are presenting a new technique on transo-hygenic lymphoid replacement tonight at the hospital. Lt. Martin is our chief assistant."

"Ah. Yes, sir, but I can't leave my post. You can go in, though. Lieutenant Martin is in room 115 down the hall to your right."

"Thank you, Corporal," I said.

Once we were inside, Andrew said, "Transo-hygenic lymphoid replacement? What the hell is that?"

"I don't know, and neither does the corporal. But it got us in the door and the rest is up to you Dr. Cohen."

Room 115 was at the far end of the hall. Andrew knocked. No answer. He knocked again. No answer. He knocked harder a third time.

"Alright, alright, ya bloody bastard. I just got off a twelve-hour shift I was in ma swag, and I'm nuddy. Gimme a sec."

The door opened. The light in the room was out. All I saw was a tall, dark person with a massive head of hair standing in the shadow. "Crikey. Andrew!" A woman's voice cried out, then her arms enveloped him and pulled him into the room.

I felt like I should shut the door and let them be, but Andrew managed to blurt out, "Kaneli, this is my shipmate, Rob. We've come to take you to dinner."

I was sure Kaneli had something far more interesting in mind for Andrew, but she uncoiled herself from around his body and smiled at me.

"G'day, Rob. It's nice to meet one of Andrew's mates."

She was wearing a hospital gown and apparently nothing else, and not the least bit concerned about what peaked out.

She was at least two inches taller than Andrew. Her body was thin, her legs and arms long. But it was her eyes that got my attention. They were feline, big, amber, and nearly glowing. Her golden-brown skin was silky smooth and her hair was a lush mane of ebony curls. Her high cheekbones and wide mouth completed an exotic, statuesque picture, suitable for a movie poster about the queen of the Amazons.

I heard a moan from behind her.

"Knock it down. I'm tryin' to sleep here," another female declared.

"It appears that we've come at a bad time," Andrew said.

"Oh, that's alright. We can sleep some other time. Come on, Meg, wake up. We've got a couple of mates who want to take us to dinner," Kaneli said.

She turned to Andrew.

"Meg's my roommate," she said.

Andrew looked at me. I shrugged.

"Okay, Rob and I can wait outside, until you're ready to join us," he said.

"Naw, Naw. Just grab a spot on the swag. We'll be ready in a jif," Kaneli answered, switching on a small lamp on the dresser at the far side of the room.

Meg appeared to have finally gained consciousness and was squinting in our direction trying to figure out who we were. She put on her tortoiseshell glasses and glared at us for a second, then smiled, shrugged and got out of bed. She was barely five feet tall and wearing a tank top tee shirt and panties. Her blond hair was long and straight. She reminded me of the British actress, Julie Christie.

Neither one of them showed a hint of modesty as they rummaged around in the closet, throwing things about, and slipping into their clothes. They each took a turn in the bathroom to finish their makeup and hair, and we're ready to head out the door in less than thirty minutes.

It had been an entertaining half hour watching the transformation of two tired, rumpled, sleep-deprived women into a drop-dead gorgeous pair of femme fatales.

There was a group of bicycle rickshaws at the end of the parking area. Before we got in, Kaneli stopped, turned to us, and announced, "I've got a better idea than the General's Daughter. That's just too stuffy for me tonight. Let's go to Ollie's Beach Bar," she declared.

Andrew looked at me. I knew he was thinking that I wanted to see Melanie tonight. He was right, but I was worried about showing up at the General's Daughter with what appeared to be a date, even if bringing Meg wasn't my idea. I gave in. "Sounds good to me," I said. Andrew relaxed and nodded.

"Let's go," he added, jumping in one rickshaw with Kaneli. Meg and I followed in another.

"What's Ollie's Beach Bar?" I asked Meg as our driver peddled down the street and into town.

"A fella named Oliver runs a restaurant right on the sand. It's just a shack with some barbies. The coldies are Australian and the shrimp and lobbies are ripper."

In spite of the slang, I understood the gist of what she said.

"What's your favorite place round here, Rob?" she asked.

"We've only been here a few weeks. I've been to the General's Daughter once, and a club called the New Orleans once. That's it."

"You need to get out more often," she said laughing. "Are you married and trying to stay true to your wife?"

"No. I'm not married. But our ship has to follow Navy orders. That's why I don't go out more. We haven't had much time here in Vung Tau. How about you?"

"Me? Well, I guess you noticed the ring on my finger, eh? My hubby is a pilot for Trans Am. I haven't seen him in three months."

I hadn't noticed the ring, and wasn't sure how to react to her revelation.

"Don't worry, Rob. He's not going to show up here," she said, squeezing my arm.

We heard Ollie's Beach Club before we saw it. The heavy vibration from drums and a base guitar came at us through the palms lining the beach. As we got out of our rickshaws and crossed over a slight hump of sand where the trees were planted, we spotted a large bonfire around which were tables with chairs. A three-piece Vietnamese combo, a drummer, bass guitar and lead guitar, were cranking out the last bar of an eardrum-busting version of Dick Dale's "Misirlou."

As we got to the tables, Kaneli waved to a barefoot Vietnamese guy with shoulder-length bleached-blond hair wearing baggies, an open aloha shirt and a string of puka shells around his neck.

He came over and she gave him a big hug. "Ollie these are our friends from the U.S.A., Andrew and Rob. We brought them here to taste the best lobbies in Vietnam. Mates. This is our host, the one and only Oliver," she said.

We shook hands and he offered us seats at the nearest table.

"Chips and coldies all around," Kaneli ordered.

"Just for a while, until we get used to it, could you girls please provide translations," Andrew said.

"And I thought U.S. naval officers were a smart lot," Kaneli declared.

"I think I know," I said. " A coldie is a beer, a lobbie is a lobster, a barbie is a barbecue, and chips are French fries. How am I doing so far," I said.

"Good on ya, Rob," Kaneli replied.

Oliver served us our beers and chips, and we ordered four lobsters.

As conversation flowed around the table, I learned that the two women had attended nursing school on a military reserve program that paid their tuition in exchange for two years of service. They were roommates and close friends. After graduation they were sent to different cities to complete their hospital training.

Meg, whose last name was Jones, met and married her husband, Jack, while Kaneli had stayed single. Yet the women remained in close contact via letters and phone calls.

Meg's husband's international flying assignments meant he was gone more than half the time.

She decided if he was going to be gone so much, she could too. She persuaded Kaneli to join her in accepting an assignment to duty in Vietnam. The deal included combat zone pay and four weeks of paid vacation, including flights to virtually any place in Asia.

While Meg was talking, I had a chance to study her. She was quite pretty in a sun-drenched beach bum sort of way. Her bright blue eyes contrasted with a very tan face, shoulders, arms, and legs. The only spots not tan were little white areas around her eyes, to which she had applied some interesting shades of purple eye shadow.

She was short, with surprisingly broad shoulders, small breasts, and a very nice rear.

"What?" She said. "Do I have something stuck in my teeth?"

"No. I was just thinking how pretty you are," I replied honestly.

She looked surprised, started to say something, then stopped.

"Did I say something wrong?" I asked.

"No. I'm just not used to sweet talk. You Yanks are a lot nicer to Sheila's than most of the Aussies I meet down here. They'll tell me I have a nice bum and try to get me in the swag. I know what they're about."

"Let me guess. Swag is a bed," I said

"Right you are, Rob," she said, then leaned over and kissed me.

I was pretty sure what that kiss implied. But she was a married woman and Australian, my translation could be way off.

Just then, Oliver showed up with our lobsters displayed on a large platter accompanied by a bowl of what tasted like real melted butter. We ordered another round of beers.

What followed was something out of the eating scene in the 1963 movie *Tom Jones*, starring Albert Finney – lots of licking, sighing, slurping noises, and groans of pleasure.

It was the best lobster I'd ever eaten, especially the parts slippery with butter that Meg fed me personally with her fingers.

By then every table was filled. The band came back on and played a set of surf songs by Jan and Dean and the Beach Boys. We had another round of beers. The women took off their sandals. Andrew and I took off our shoes and socks. They insisted we try dancing in the sand with everyone else.

Our bodies gyrating around the bonfire cast shadows suggesting an ancient tribal ritual. Our dance moves weren't smooth, but the night was warm, the beer was cold and the music was loud.

At the end of their set, the lead guitarist got on the microphone and thanked everyone, "And now, I want to ask you all to applaud and help me urge one of Australia's best female vocalists, Meg Jones, to join us for a song."

Andrew and I looked at Meg, then at Kaneli, who nodded toward Meg and mouthed "yes."

Meg waved her arms, indicating she did not want to do it. But the crowd, the majority of whom apparently knew her, kept cheering until she stood up and went to the stage. The lead singer handed her his guitar.

"You all know that Chou here is a master on this Stratocaster, but what he just said about me is a croc of shit," she said, nodding toward the guitarist. Everybody laughed and started chanting, "Meg! Meg! Meg"

"Okay. You asked for it, so here it is, my favorite American rock tune. I'm playing it in honor of our two Yank friends, Rob and Andrew."

With that, she went into the full opening rift, of Chuck Berry's "Johnny B. Goode." Not only could she play the guitar like a true rocker, her voice was rock solid and on key.

By the last bars of the song, everyone was standing up and singing with her,

"Go, go, go Johnny go…Go, go, go Johnny go!"

When she finished with a flourish, the crowd remained standing clapping, shouting, and whistling.

The shouting turned to chanting. "One more song! One more song!"

"Okay mates. One more, but you're all singing along with me, cause you all know it by heart."

She hit a couple of chords to set the tune, then started singing:

Once a jolly swagman camped by a billabong
Under the shade of a coolibah tree
And he sang as he watched and waited till his billy boil
You'll come a Waltzing Matilda with me.
Waltzing Matilda, Waltzing Matilda
You'll come a Waltzing Matilda with me
And he sang as he watched and waited till his billy boil
You'll come a Waltzing Matilda with me"

Andrew and I and Kaneli joined the crowd, locking arms and swaying together as we all sang loud and clear, chorus after chorus.

I'm sure half of Vung Tau heard us too.

When she finally hit the last note, everyone cheered, hugged and then went back to drinking beer.

Just another night with the Aussies, I guess.

A light rain was starting to fall as Meg returned to our table.

Andrew and I both hugged her together.

"My god, I had no idea, you were a rock star!" Andrew declared.

"Yeah. In journalism we call that burying the lede," I added. "You were absolutely fabulous."

"Lads, thanks a lot, But I'm not a star of anything. I played in a college band back home. We got lucky, made a single that hit the charts for a while. One time only. We were what you call a 'one hit wonder.'"

"One is better than none," Kaneli shouted.

"Absolutely," I agreed. "And Chuck Berry would be proud that his song was played so well here on the beach in Vietnam, far from those woods back in New Orleans."

"Speaking of New Orleans, why don't we head over to it and get out this rain," Andrew said.

"The New Orleans Club? That's one of our favorite dance spots," Kaneli answered. "It's only a couple a blocks from here."

15

All I Have To Do Is Dream
●●●●●●●●●●●●●●●●●●●●●●●

T HE SKY OPENED UP AS we got to the street in front of the beach. We dashed from doorway to doorway along the way, and made it to the front of the New Orleans club partially soaked. It was enough for me to notice that Meg, dressed in a knee-length floral shift held up with spaghetti straps, wasn't wearing a bra.

She noticed where my eyes had drifted and whispered in my ear, "And, I'm not wearing any knickers neither." She cackled, took my hand, and dragged me through the door.

The club was packed. Cigarette smoke swirled in the dim lights. A familiar voice carried easily across the room from the stage. It was the Captain. He was pounding out "Great Balls of Fire," standing, like Jerry Lee Lewis, as the New Orleans house band jammed along.

"Hey, it's Rob and Andrew!" I heard someone shout. I saw Harry, John and the XO seated at the table nearest the stage. Next to them was another table filled with more sailors from the *Belle County*, including Doc, Archer and Reyes.

We walked over. Shouting over the blast of sound coming from the stage, I attempted to introduce Meg and Kaneli.

Just then the Captain ran his hands down the keyboard ending the song in a flourish. The joint erupted in applause and cheers.

The bandleader announced a break, and the Captain joined us at the table.

"Good evening, Captain," I said, then introduced Meg and Kaneli to him and the group. This time they all could hear me. I was going to ask them if Madame Marquis had agreed to host the benefit, but was interrupted when Harry and Andrew grabbed four extra chairs from a nearby table and brought them so we could join him.

"You missed our big move this afternoon," Harry said.

"What do you mean?" Andrew asked.

"Not long after you both took the first boat in to Vung Tau, we got a message from the C.O. of the tender. They cleared a berth for us on the pier just in front of them."

"But a bunch of us had already left the ship. Wasn't that a problem?" I asked.

"No, not really. Because we only had one engine, a tug came to keep us from accidentally drifting off line. Once we got close to the pier, the Captain drove the ship dead slow and the tug kept our bow from swinging. We kissed the pier as gently as you would a baby's ass. Or should I say a beautiful Aussie's ass?" Harry said with a grin.

"So who's got the watch?" I asked, noting that just about all of the ship's officers were in the club.

"O.J., but it's an easy watch. The ship is out of commission. We couldn't go anywhere if we wanted to. So the Captain gave just about everybody liberty. O.J. and a half-dozen of the crew are left on board for security and in case of an emergency."

"So, I don't have to stand my watch?" Andrew asked, adding, "I was scheduled for the 0400 to 0800."

"No. Nobody does. Tomorrow is Sunday. John relieves O.J.

tomorrow at noon. The rest of us have the whole day off," Harry said with glee.

That news should have made me happy, but something had been nagging at me ever since we entered the New Orleans Club. I'd seen everybody, except the person I most wanted to see.

Cam, the club owner, brought four beers to us. She gave me a sideways glance that was the opposite of warm and friendly.

There was no sense in trying to explain to her that my arriving at her club with Meg on my arm was not how I intended to spend the evening.

I had no excuse. I chose to go along with Andrew and Kaneli. Meg was pretty and sexy, signaling clearly what would be in store for me later in the evening.

I could not deny that I had gone along willingly.

I sipped my beer and tried to block out the guilt I felt about betraying Melanie, rationalizing that we were not a couple, that neither she nor I made any kind of declaration that we were anything more than friends.

But, there was that kiss; the one I gave her the last time we were here, and the way she held me close just before I ran off to catch the boat back to the ship.

"Hey!" a voice and a nudge broke my reverie. "Are you drifting off on me?" Meg asked.

"No. Sorry. I guess I didn't get enough sleep last night," I said.

"Well then, you just have to keep moving. Let's dance," she said pulling me to my feet as the band retook the stage and began their set with the Doors' "Light My Fire."

At the end of the number, I saw Reyes go to the stage and say something to the bandleader, who then grabbed the microphone. Speaking English with an accent suggesting French/Caribbean roots, he declared: "*Bonsoir, mes amis*. We have beaucoup musicians here from the *Bell County*, plus an Australian pop chanteuse in our midst. Perhaps if you applaud she will sing for us. What do you say Madame Meg Jones?"

This time Meg didn't hesitate. She stood up, grabbed Kaneli by the hand, and marched to the stage with her in tow.

The bandleader handed her the mike and joined everyone in clapping.

"Contrary to that announcement. I'm not a *chanteuse*. I'm Australian," she declared to another round of cheers.

"And this exotic creature here is my mate, Kaneli. Together tonight we're going to be the Everly Sisters." Then she leaned over and said something to the bandleader, who nodded and said something to the rest of the band.

A sad, lonely chord reverberated though the club, and all conversation stopped.

Then two women, in perfect close harmony, began:

"Dream, Dream, Dream, dream..."

It could have been anybody's song, but it had special meaning to every sailor in the bar. Far away from home, standing lonely watches, and yearning to be with a loved one, dream was all they could do. When the girls finished, more than a few guys wiped tears from their eyes as they applauded.

I heard Doc shout at Reyes, "You've found your two other Andrews Sisters."

The party was just getting started. Next on stage was the *Bell County*'s doo-wop group with Archer as the lead, singing "In the Still of the Night." As they began, I suddenly knew what I had to do.

I leaned over and whispered in Meg's ear, "I'm sorry. But I have to go."

She looked at me. Then smiled. "Go on, mate, you've been thinking about her all night. I'll be good here with all your mates."

I kissed her on the cheek, then told Andrew I was leaving and asked him to make sure she got back to her barracks okay. I didn't answer his question. "Why are you leaving?"

I didn't know if I could explain.

Rain was still falling, but lighter than before. There wasn't a rickshaw in sight.

I vaguely recalled how to get to the General's Daughter and started walking in that direction. A half-hour later, it started raining hard again. I'd obviously missed a turn. Then, the weather turned really foul. Lightening flashed and water came down in sheets. A heavy wind lashed the palms. I found partial shelter in the doorway of a storefront. Even though the air was warm, I was soaked. The wind gave me chills.

"What the fuck am I doing?" I shouted into the storm.

For a few seconds, the rain slackened and the wind died. Across the street was a small grassy park and beyond it I saw lights on a building that looked familiar.

Lightening flashed and I recognized it as the old governor's mansion. I sprinted across the street and grass toward it. Heavy gusts of wind blew the rain in my face, adding more water to my already saturated clothing.

I reached the gate, ran up the walk and steps onto the porch. The restaurant front door was unlocked. Several members of the staff were cleaning and looked at me curiously as I entered.

Water dripped off my hair into my eyes, a puddle forming at my feet.

A young Vietnamese man I recognized as one of the people who waited on us the first night, crossed the hall carrying a load of dirty tablecloths and napkins.

"Excuse me," I said. "I'm looking for Melanie. Is she still in the restaurant?"

He looked at me without expression for several seconds saying nothing.

Then he smiled. "Oh, you are friend of Captain Baillier. Yes?"

"Yes, my name is Rob. Rob Allen."

"I'm sorry Mr. Allen. Mademoiselle Marquis retire for evening," he replied bowing.

"It is very important that I speak to her," I said.

"I'm sorry, sir," he said, bowing again and then continuing down the hall.

I had a vague idea of where the mansion's living quarters were. To get there, I had to go back outside and around to the other side of the building.

The rain beat down on me and the wind howled, but I found the front door and rang the bell. I added a series of hard knocks for emphasis.

There was a light on in the foyer, but nobody came to the door.

I rang the bell again, then knocked again harder.

"Melanie, it's me, Rob!" I yelled.

Finally, I saw a light go on in the stairwell. Melanie came down the stairs. She was wearing dark silk pajamas. She opened the door.

"Rob. What are you doing here?" She looked like she'd been crying.

"I had to come see you," I gasped, shivering slightly as the wind picked up behind me.

She sighed, opened the door wider and pulled me inside, closing the door behind me.

"You are soaked to the skin and it's late. I was already in bed." She hesitated, looked down at her feet, then back at me. I saw hurt in her expression. "I know your ship arrived this afternoon. Your Captain was here. I waited for you," she said angrily, tears pooling at the edges of her beautiful eyes.

"I'm sorry. That's why I had to come. That's why I had to talk to you."

"So say what you have to say, and then you can go," she said coldly, turning away.

"Please look at me. I want to say this to you, not your back."
She turned around.

"There is no good excuse for not coming earlier. It was my intention. I thought Andrew and I would be here with his friend, Kaneli, and that you might join us for dinner. But then Kaneli had a roommate and the roommate wanted to come, and then we went to a beach place instead, and I was stuck, and..."

"Stop!" she interrupted angrily. "You don't have to explain anything to me. You have no obligation. We are not engaged. Just go."

"But I want to explain. I do feel obliged. I know we're not engaged. Heck, we haven't been on a real date, or had dinner together, or danced. I don't know enough about you. And you don't know me." I paused, wiped the water from my eyes, sighed and continued.

"And that's the thing. I want all those things. I want to go on a real date with you, have dinner with you, dance with you, hold you and kiss you, at least one more time.

"I know it's crazy. I'm an American sailor. You are a Vietnamese woman. There is a war going on. A future together is an impossible dream. And yet, it is all I can dream about. . ."

She interrupted me again, this time with a kiss.

"You can talk later. Now you must get out of your wet clothes and wrap up in a blanket. I will find something dry for you to wear. There is a bathroom down the hall on your right. Take off your wet clothes in there," she ordered, suddenly business-like.

She pushed me in the direction of the bathroom. I went in, stripped off my shirt, pants, underpants, shoes, and socks, hung the wet garments on a towel rack, wrapped the blanket around me, and peeked out the door.

She was still standing in the parlor doorway looking at me as I padded toward her, my bare feet leaving wet marks as I went.

"I'm sorry," I said. "This was a stupid, crazy thing to do. I had no right to come here in the middle of the night and upset you. If you can loan me a dry shirt and pants, I can find my way back to the ship."

She didn't say anything, but pulled my arms apart, opened the blanket, and then snuggled her fully clothed body against my naked one.

I felt her warmth take away the last of the storm's chill.

"What about your mother?" I whispered in her ear.

"She flew to Bangkok on a buying trip this morning," she answered, taking my hand and leading me up the stairs.

16

What Wakes Us?
●●●●●●●●●●●●●●●●●●●●●●●

MELANIE'S SWEET SCENT AND THE warmth of her body aroused me to consciousness. We had fallen asleep as one. I dared not stir lest I break the connection. Instead, I allowed my mind to drift back to the previous night.

No words were spoken. The only light was from a small lamp in the hall.

I sat on the bed, the blanket still over my shoulders and watched her undress. She leaned down and kissed me, then pushed me down on my back. Quickly moving onto the bed, she used her knees and hips to nudge me toward the middle before positioning herself straddling my middle.

She seemed comfortable being in charge and I was more than willing to go along.

We made love in slow motion, softly, gently, and totally on Melanie's terms. There was no need for verbal instructions. When her movements quickened, I followed.

I was surprised by her stamina. While I needed periodic recuperation, she didn't. It didn't seem to matter. Our bodies were inseparable. I don't know who fell asleep first.

Now, I was awake, remembering, and clearly recuperated. I felt Melanie stir. Then her hips pressed against me. We made love again; then drifted off again; then made love again.

I was drifting somewhere in a hazy fog. A voice was calling me.

"I'm hungry." They were the first words she'd spoken since she led me upstairs.

"I'd be willing to starve a little longer just to stay right here," I said.

"I'm *really* hungry," she said, disentangling herself from me and rolling out of bed.

She reached down and pulled my arm, forcing me to follow her. I wanted to pull her back on top of me, but I acquiesced and followed her from the bedroom to the shower.

It wasn't big as showers go, but enough to share and give us room to gently wash each other. That too became an additional opportunity for blissful distraction, until she insisted we must pause for sustenance.

"You realize I have no dry clothes. My wet ones are in the downstairs bathroom," I said as we toweled each other off.

"Hmm?" she muttered. "Wrap that blanket around you, sit on the bed, and wait for me." She put on a silk robe and walked out the bedroom door, returning in less than two minutes with my clothes, dry and neatly folded.

"Our maid must have found them early this morning."

"What time is it?" I asked.

"Past eleven," she said.

"Wow, we slept a long time."

"I don't think we spent much time sleeping."

"You didn't for sure. You're insatiable."

"It's been a while. I needed to catch up."

"I thought your moves were a little too good for a rookie," I said.

"A rookie?"

"It's an American sports term for a beginner, a new player."

"Oh, a *débutante* you mean."

"Yes, something like that."

"Paris changed that. I lived with a Frenchman for my final six months there. His name was Thierry. He was three years older than me, handsome, charming and sophisticated. I fell in love with him."

"Do you ever think about going back to be with him again, to live in France?"

"I might have stayed, but a month before I earned my diploma, he left me for another woman."

"I'm sorry. The guy had no idea what a mistake he made," I said.

"I think it is the way of French men. They get bored and cast their women aside frequently," she said with bitterness in her voice.

"Let's not talk of this anymore. I'm still hungry. Get dressed, and we'll go find something to eat."

The part of the mansion in which Melanie and her mother lived was expansive and included a large first floor kitchen with a twelve-foot high ceiling and an enormous marble-topped island in the middle. A ten-burner gas range and two large ovens sat along one wall facing a walk-in cooler on the opposite wall. A basket of fresh croissants and a bowl of fruit, including fresh strawberries, sat on the counter.

"The restaurant is closed on Sundays, but it is a tradition that our baker makes croissants for us Saturday night before he leaves," Melanie explained, as she poured hot water from a kettle into a medium-sized French press coffee maker.

While we waited for the coffee to steep, she instructed me to take the croissants and fruits to the screened patio just off the kitchen. There was a small round table with four chairs around it.

She followed me with plates, coffee cups and utensils.

The storm had passed. The sun was shining and the air already getting warm. A ceiling fan mounted in the overhang whirred softly keeping us cool. The strawberries were the first I'd tasted since I left California, and croissants were never served on the *Bell County*. For a few minutes our focus was on the food. All of my senses were enhanced.

I watched Melanie as she took little bites of her croissant, then a bite of a strawberry. She too, seemed lost in her senses. She caught me watching her and smiled.

"What?" she asked.

"I was just thinking how wonderful you, and this food, tastes," I said.

She kissed me. I tasted the strawberry on her lips.

"What would you like to do today?"

"Go back upstairs for a rerun of last night."

"Now who's insatiable?"

"Okay. How about a compromise? We go back upstairs, make love, then you show me more of Vung Tau."

"I think that is an excellent compromise. Just let me have one more croissant," she said.

As lovers, we'd crossed some kind of barrier. Inhibitions vanished. The feelings I dared not express out loud could now be spoken. I felt like I'd awakened from a long, dreary winter to the most beautiful warm spring day ever. Melanie was equally expressive with her body, but I sensed that she was not as head-over-heels, beguiled as I.

Back in her bedroom, sunlight filtered through the shutters providing enough light for me to see and caress her lovely body, first with my hands, then my lips and tongue as she stretched and sighed with pleasure.

We both fell asleep again. I was dreaming that we were fishing together on the banks of a river so wide we couldn't see the other side. I felt a tug on the fishing line, then a nudge against my hip. Melanie's voice woke me.

"Okay. We can't stay here all day. What would you like to see of Vung Tau?" she said.

I opened my eyes and tried to focus on her question.

"Actually, I'm interested in two things. The first is, I'd like to meet more local people, like the lady who ran the little grocery store that you introduced me to. She was so nice. So friendly."

"Yes. We can do that. What's the second thing?"

"If there is a place here that plays music using traditional Vietnamese instruments, I'd like to visit it too," I said.

"There is a school here dedicated to preserving Vietnamese culture, including art and music. I'm sure they accept visitors. Why does that interest you?"

I told her the story about Binh and how we discovered that he was also a musician and trying to be a composer. I explained that he was almost finished with a suite using the Mekong River as its central theme, and how Captain Baillier decided to help him not only complete it, but also to see it performed.

"If the music school is close enough to walk to, I can explain the rest on the way there," I said.

We showered, dressed, and were soon strolling along a shaded street toward the central part of Vung Tau as I told her more about Bihn's composition.

"He calls it the *Mekong Suite*, and I only heard small pieces of it. But I liked it. The problem is that on his own, Bihn could never get it played by a real orchestra. It was O.J.'s idea to put on a concert for the benefit of the school and orphanage."

"Benefit concert? I'm not sure I understand," she said.

"The Captain is going to ask your mother if the General's Daughter will host a concert featuring the school children playing

Binh's suite. Everyone who attends would be asked to make a donation to the school as the price of admission to the concert."

"Oh. That's why he came by yesterday afternoon," she
responded. "He asked for my mother, but she'd already left."

"Do you think she'll like the idea?"

"Of course. She likes your Captain very much and trusts him.
And, she would do anything for the orphans and the school. It is
the main reason she came back to stay. And it is why she works
very hard to make the General's Daughter a successful business.
The profits go to support the school," she paused. Then continued.
"But what does that have to do with traditional Vietnamese music?"

"Binh's suite was inspired by a western composer named Ferde
Grofé, who wrote several musical pieces with themes involving
nature, including our own great river, the Mississippi, and the
Grand Canyon."

"Yes. I saw a Disney movie in Paris that used music called the
Grand Canyon Suite.

"Exactly," I said. "But Binh's piece is also influenced by your
culture. He's managed to blend western tonal scales with those
played on traditional Vietnamese instruments. It's a captivating
sound. I think you'll really like it."

"I see. So the children at the orphanage can play it with their
instruments, but you need musicians who can play on Vietnamese
instruments," she said.

"Exactly. Binh's piece requires them, if it is to be performed
the way he intends," I said. "And one more thing, we're going to
need your help to persuade them to participate."

"I think this is a most interesting idea, and so generous of you
and your shipmates."

"I've done very little except agree with everyone else. It's really
Capt. Baillier's leadership that makes it possible."

"You and he are very much alike. You're both sweet, kind,

gentle men, who really care about people, including Vietnamese. We are most fortunate to have you on our side."

"I just hope we are doing more good than harm."

"Here, right now, you are about to do a great deal of good." She took my hand, "Let's go find some musicians."

As we continued our walk, I wondered at this amazing and beautiful woman on my arm who had so clearly mastered two different cultures. I'd observed how she interacted with her Vietnamese friends, how relaxed and at home she was with them, and how much they liked and respected her. At the same time, she seemed entirely at home as a Western-educated woman, fluent in English and French, plus all the social and cultural subtleties that true fluency requires.

Which was her true self? Was she holding back? If she had to choose, which would it be?

17

The First Time Ever I Saw Your Face
••••••••••••••••••••••

"TELL ME MORE ABOUT BINH'S music," Melanie said. "The parts I've heard grabbed me. I can't tell you why. But listening made me want to hear more. The Captain and Andrew, who know music, say it's good."

"Andrew is going to be working with him to finish it," I added.

"Andrew seems like a nice guy," she said.

"He is. It took me a while to get to know him.

"We met at Navy Officer Candidate School. We were in the same class. At first, he didn't mingle much with the other cadets."

"He has good manners, and speaks fluent French," she said.

"Yes. And some guys took that to mean he was stuck up and pretentious."

"He isn't," she answered.

"You're right. It took us a while to learn that. During our first week as raw cadets, the discipline and hazing is pretty intense. Some upperclassmen were experts at spotting guys who didn't fit in and then they'd bully them.

"Were you bullied?" Melanie asked.

"Not exactly, but Andrew saved me from getting kicked out of OCS for fighting with a bully."

"What happened?"

"During the first month of OCS, cadets are confined to base. We must remain in uniform. One day, a small group of us decided to go over to the Navy base coffee shop. As we were walking there, three upperclassmen in civilian clothes passed by. One of them stopped and shouted, 'Don't you cadets salute your superiors?'

"We stopped, looked at the three, but said nothing. Then the guy who had shouted walked over to me and repeated his question. He was a big guy, a half-foot taller than me, with a thick neck and a thicker head.

"I looked up at him, shook my head, and turned to walk away, still not saying anything."

"Why wouldn't you answer him?" Melanie asked.

"He was being a jerk. He wasn't in uniform and I wasn't sure if I was required to salute him. I wasn't going to give him what he wanted, but I didn't want to start a fight either. Doing that could get me thrown out of the program."

"What happened next?"

"He yelled something and put his hand on my shoulder. I turned around, figuring avoiding a fight was no longer an option. That's when Andrew stepped in.

"Excuse me sir," he said, "But naval regulation 2005.7 b, says that saluting an unknown person in civilian clothes is not appropriate. We don't know you. You are not in uniform. As far as we know, you could be an unauthorized civilian on base harassing Navy recruits. Now, there are six of us, and three of you. If you don't take your hand off of my friend and fellow cadet, we will be forced to subdue you and call the Shore Patrol."

"Andrew was as tall as that asshole, but not nearly as muscular. I doubt that he'd ever been in a fight in his life. But he stood with me and stared the guy down."

"Did either of you get in trouble?"

"No. I asked Andrew how he knew so much about Navy regulations.

"He said he didn't. He had no idea if such a rule existed. He was bluffing and hoping that the thick-necked asshole didn't know Navy regulations any better than he did."

"Andrew was willing to take a risk for you," she said.

"Yes. That's when I knew that Andrew was not only a nice guy, but that there was a good man under that priggish front he sometimes shows."

"He's definitely no prig. In fact, he told me quite a lot about you and your French girlfriend."

I stopped and looked at her. She was smiling at my discomfort.

"He told you about Louiselle?

"When? I didn't know you'd even talked to him since the first night dinner."

"I was at the school teaching when he came to talk to Sister Josephine. Afterward, he walked me home. I asked him how you became friends."

"It's true that we seem to like the same things: music, good wine and beer, and of course, the company of interesting women," I answered.

"Was your Louiselle such a woman? Is she the one that taught you all those interesting things?"

"Taught me?" I repeated out loud. "Oh." I added, realizing what she was asking.

"Yes, you could say that. She was a very kind, sweet person, and patient with my inexperience. She was also pretty and I really liked her; so much, that I asked if she would move to California to be closer to me."

"What did she say?"

"No. In fact, I think she understood all along that our love affair would have to end as soon as the Navy shipped me out. I kept suggesting ways for us to stay together. She kept saying no. She was far more realistic than I."

Melanie's expression turned serious and she looked into my eyes. "And which of us now is more realistic?"

It was a rhetorical question, but I understood why she posed it. I wanted to believe in a magical future where we could be together. I was fairly certain, her vision was far clearer.

"It is a lovely day and I am with the most beautiful girl in the world. Right here, right now is the only reality I wish to consider," I said, taking her hand and continuing our walk.

"Buddha says, 'Do not dwell in the past, do not dream of the future, concentrate on the present moment,'" she said.

"Buddha is wise," I answered.

We walked along in silence until we got to a main intersection on the edge of downtown, but instead of turning left toward the business center, we took a right, crossed the street and turned left down a narrow side street that looked like a back alley.

Half way down the little street was a large gold and red Buddhist temple centered in a well-groomed open space surrounded by gardens.

Next door, past the bamboo fence that marked the far side of the temple grounds, stood a simple, single-story wooden building with a thatched roof. Its bucolic serenity was enhanced by a koi-filled pond surrounded by a neatly groomed garden.

A stone path wound through the garden to a wooden porch. A young Vietnamese woman was sweeping it as we approached.

She looked up, first at me, then at Melanie, smiled, and greeted Melanie by her Vietnamese name, Gian.

Melanie responded in Vietnamese, then switched to French to introduce me.

The woman's name was Hahn Nguyen.

"*Bonjour, Monsieur,*" she said bowing slightly.

Trying my best to remember the little bit of French Louiselle had tried to teach me, I bowed and replied *"Enchanté, Mademoiselle Nguyen."* Then I added in English, "I'm afraid I've used all the French I know."

She laughed and replied, "That's okay. I speak a little English too. And, please call me Hanh. *Mademoiselle* is much too formal."

While Hanh prepared the tea, she asked Melanie in English about her mother and how the school and Sister Josephine were doing. They carried on their conversation, primarily in English.

Once tea was served and the three of us sat around a small table just inside the open doorway looking out onto the garden, Melanie explained the reason for our visit.

Hanh turned to me, "Would your friend Binh be able to come here?"

"Yes. He's been temporarily assigned to our ship and I'm sure our Captain would allow it." I answered.

"It is my father, Nguyen Van Lu, who can help him. He is the headmaster of the school here, which teaches classic Vietnamese art and music. He is at the school now, but he will be back later. If you both can stay for dinner, we can discuss it," she said.

I looked at Melanie, who smiled and nodded approval, and then she said something to Hanh in Vietnamese.

Hanh replied in English, "It will not be imposing at all. It will be nice to have company, and the children will enjoy it."

"How many children do you have?" I asked.

"Six, but they're not mine. They're students here and board with us because their homes are far away."

"I understand. It will be a pleasure to meet Master Lu and the children then," I answered.

We sipped our tea, and she asked about where I was from and how I happened to be in Vung Tau; how I met Melanie, and about my interest in music.

When I got to the part about my interest in music, I described the *Bell County*'s musical mission, adding that my roommate Andrew, our Captain, and several others on our ship were the real musicians, while I was more of a member of the supporting cast.

"I play the guitar, but I'm not very good and I don't perform in the shows."

"I believe you are being modest," she answered, getting up and walking over to a small closet on the opposite wall. From it, she removed a guitar and brought in back to the table.

"Why don't you play something and let Melanie and me decide," she said handing the guitar to me.

I feared she would be disappointed. But I had asked this very nice woman for a favor and did not want to appear ungrateful.

"With great humility, which you will learn is justified, I will attempt a little tune, but only if you in turn, will play for us," I said.

She nodded, and said "Of course."

"Okay. This is a song written by an Englishman, Ewan Maccoll, that I heard performed at my college by a little-known gospel folk duo, Joe Gilbert and Eddie Brown."

Then I turned toward Melanie. "All of the words came back to me that night when you sat down next to me at the General's Daughter. I wish I could sing it as beautifully as Joe and Eddie, but I'll do my best."

I hit the first chord and began.

"The first time, ever I saw your face…"

I must have done a pretty good job, because both women were crying by the time I finished. I heard soft clapping from behind me and turned to see a very thin, older man with grey hair and a wispy grey beard, smiling. He was dressed in a white shirt and black pants. It could be no other than Master Lu. I stood up intending to introduce myself and offer him my hand.

"Please, please, sit back down. I enjoyed that very much," he said in perfect British English. "I actually met Ewan MacColl when I studied in London, he wrote that for his future wife. Seeger, I believe was her last name."

"Thank you Master Lu. I am Rob Allen, a friend of Melanie's."

"Yes. The way you looked at her as you were singing, I assumed she is a very good friend," he said, a twinkle in his eye.

Melanie bowed to him and said something in Vietnamese, which he acknowledged, then his daughter spoke.

"Melanie and Rob have come to ask a favor and I have invited them to stay for dinner, father. I knew that you would approve."

"Of course. It seems I arrived at a most auspicious time," he replied.

"Yes sir. In fact, your daughter has agreed that if I played a song, she would follow," I said handing the guitar back to her.

"Okay. But Melanie must join me. She knows the words in English and in French. You may have heard it performed in English by Rod McKuen. The famous Jacques Brel also recorded it in French. We will do a little bit of both for you."

She strummed a few chords and then began in English:

"If you go away on this summer day…"

She nodded to Melanie, who continued on in French. When they finished, it was my turn to wipe tears away and applaud.

"That was beautiful. Thank you, Hanh," I said, and then turned to Melanie.

"You have surprised me for a second time. What a lovely voice you have."

"Merci beaucoup mon cher, toi aussi," she answered.

"Perhaps after dinner, Father and some of his students will play something traditional for us," Hanh said, adding, "Father would you show Rob and Melanie around the temple and school, while I finish preparing dinner?"

"Of course. It's been a while since you've been here Melanie. Rob, have you ever visited a Buddhist temple?"

"No Master Lu, I haven't."

"Well then, we should start our tour," he said standing and pointing in the direction toward which we should go.

18

Joy Follows Like a Shadow
• •

M ASTER LU KEPT UP A running commentary as we walked
through the temple and then the school next to it. I learned
that while approximately ten percent of Vietnamese are Catholic,
close to eighty percent are Buddhists.

He described an on-going conflict, sometimes violent, between
the Buddhists and the South Vietnamese army controlled by Gen.
Ky and Thieu, the two current rulers of South Vietnam, who
allow only Catholics in government positions while persecuting
Buddhist leaders.

That dispute had little to do with the larger civil war involving
the Communist North and the South Vietnamese regime. In fact,
it drastically undermined the South's credibility with the general
population, a situation that the communists took advantage of in
securing support in the south.

The temple was maintained by a small group of priests who
kept a low profile, avoiding government harassment

It appeared that many South Vietnamese citizens, particularly
Buddhists, had as much to fear from their own government as
from the Communists and the leaders of North Vietnam.

I was already reading Bernard Fall's book *The Two Vietnams,* and beginning to understand what a vulnerable and helpless feeling it is for people trapped in the middle of such conflicts.

The people in the middle could care less about the "Domino Theory," America's alleged reason for going to Vietnam. Our justification that we were there to protect the Vietnamese people from the communists didn't square with how we made it easier for corrupt thugs like Ky and Thieu to terrorize them.

Master Lu's comments confirmed that feeling.

The school, while technically part of the temple grounds, was not run by the priests, but by Master Lu and a few assistants, mostly musicians and artists, who worked as volunteers, relying on a small tuition and donations from a few wealthier local residents who believed in preserving the culture.

"How many students do you have Master Lu?" I asked him.

"More than one hundred, from ages six to fifteen. But most do not attend every day. They are from poor families who need their children to work with them."

"Are there any students who show promise as artists or musicians?" Melanie asked.

"Oh yes. We have many who especially enjoy the art. And a few are quite good for their age and willing to put in the work and practice on the music."

"But you do have some who like it?" I asked.

"Yes. We have a core of ten youngsters, mostly girls, who have stuck with it and are quite accomplished. In fact six of them will be joining us for dinner," he answered.

As we walked through the music room of the school, Master Lu pointed to several of the instruments used, including the *"Dan Nguyet,"* and two other string instruments the *"Dan Day"* and the *"Dan Chi."* He also showed us a long horn-like trumpet he called a *"Ken Bau,"* plus a variety of flutes made of bamboo.

In addition, there were several percussion instruments, some bamboo, and some metal gongs.

"Our girls are quite good on the strings, while the boys prefer the *Ken Bau* and the flutes," he noted.

As we exited the music room, his daughter announced that it was time for dinner.

A large round table and benches were in the center of the room and on it were an array of small bowls containing sliced vegetables, rice, chicken and diced peppers and other things I couldn't identify.

Six children, four girls and two boys, stood next to Madame Nguyen. They bowed as we came in. She introduced each to us both. Melanie smiled and greeted them in Vietnamese. I smiled and said hello.

While they responded to Melanie in Vietnamese, they surprised me when they answered me in unison, in English, "Good evening, sir."

I smiled and said good evening back, bowing as I did. This prompted several giggles from the girls.

Each place at the table was set with a small bowl next to which were chopsticks. Hanh started by passing the bowls of food, one at a time. I noted that she used both hands even though they were small enough to be held in one hand. As they went around the table, everyone seemed to observe this two-handed practice. It was like handing someone a gift.

Not knowing the dining etiquette of Vietnam, I did my best to observe and follow.

It was a slow, friendly affair, with lively discussion, especially once Melanie broke the ice by speaking directly to the children and telling them in Vietnamese that I would love it if they practiced their English on me.

Through this exchange, I was asked my name several times;

then I asked theirs. They asked how old I was, where I was from, and if I knew Mickey Mouse.

Master Lu and his daughter seemed to enjoy the questions and my answers as much as the children.

More food was passed around and one of the older girls offered to help me improve my chopstick technique. She came over, kneeled beside me, bringing her food bowl and chopsticks with her. Using her limited English, she attempted to lead me by the numbers, with one being the proper way to hold the chopsticks, all the way to five, putting the food into my mouth.

This effort led to hysterical peals of laughter from the other kids as I repeatedly failed, particularly in steps four and five.

What had started perhaps as a regular dinner had turned into a party filled with joy and the laughter of children, something I had not expected to see when I was sent to war.

As Hanh cleared off the bowls, Master Lu said something to the children, who all stood, bowed then left the room, returning a few minutes later with their instruments.

In the meantime Hanh returned with tea and some kind of little rice cakes. I noticed that the children eyed the cakes with happy anticipation, assuming they would share in them following their performance.

Three of the girls were on the string instruments, the fourth played a flute, while the two boys teamed up on what appeared to be a set of large bongo drums. At Master Lu's count, they began.

I cannot say that I understood what I heard. The scale was so distinctly different and the sounds so alien that I could not have known whether or not the children were accomplished or just beginners. But there were pleasing parts and I recognized that there was a form and composition that kept them together.

They played several songs, some quite loud and animated, others softer.

When they finished. I applauded enthusiastically, as did Melanie.

Master Lu nodded. They stood up, bowed, took their instruments back to the music room, returned, sat down and enthusiastically began devouring the sweet, honey-flavored rice cakes.

The girl who had attempted to teach me the chopsticks looked at me and said, "Now, you play for us. Yes?"

I looked around the table, hoping to be rescued by Melanie or Hanh, but they were clapping too. Master Lu smiled and nodded enthusiastically also.

"Okay. But I am not nearly as good as you are," I said.

Hanh handed me her guitar again.

"I'm going to ask Melanie to join me in this song. And I think, some of you may know it. It is all about music, and can help you learn English.

The name of the song is "Do-Re-Mi," it is from a musical called *The Sound of Music*. Perhaps you know it?"

"Do Re Mi," one of the girls and one of the boys repeated. Two out of six wasn't bad.

"Okay. Those of you who know the song, must sing along. Those who don't must try." Turning to Melanie, I asked her to translate what I said so the kids all understood.

They all clapped their hands, nodded and squirmed in their seats eager to begin.

I started with a C chord and then recited the simple Do-Re-Mi-Fa-Sol-La-Ti-Do on key. Then started the song:

"Do, a deer, a female deer…"

What followed was a rollicking, often garbled songfest, chorus after chorus, sometimes halted so that Melanie could explain what a deer was, or to explain sewing with a needle. By the time we finished, all of the children were standing and dancing around the table as they sang along, enthusiastically shouting each of the notes as they came up.

I signaled the end by running through the scales several times and strumming the final chord.

The kids wanted more, but Master Lu, was saying no, that it was time for them to go to bed.

Each of them came over and bowed to Melanie and me. They were so delightfully happy and sincere, I wanted to hug each one, but wasn't sure if that was proper. I did, however, shake hands with each of them, American style, after returning their bows. They said thank you. I said thank you. Then good night, which they repeated, bowing. I bowed. They said thank you again. And so on.

Their playful delaying tactic worked until Hanh rose and herded them out.

While she was getting them settled, we sipped tea and I finally had time to talk to Master Lu about why I came.

But first, I wanted to know how this man who had spent several years studying in Europe ended up teaching traditional Vietnamese arts in a tiny school on the outskirts of a small city.

"I was born right here in Vung Tau. My father owned a shipping business that controlled a lot of the cargo boats that brought goods from this port up the river to Saigon and returned with other goods to sell. Our family was quite wealthy by local standards. I was sent to the best schools, some of them taught by the French. My grandfather, who lived with us, was a famous musician and composer, a virtuoso on many of the instruments the children played tonight. He wrote two of three pieces they played for you."

"So, you learned music from him, and western languages from the French?" I replied.

"Yes, although as a boy, I resisted his strict teaching methods, and preferred the music being taught at the French school. I started taking violin lessons there as well."

"What happened when your grandfather found out?" Melanie asked.

"He surprised me by encouraging me, saying that knowing the music of other cultures was an excellent way to become better in one's own."

"So how did you end up speaking such perfect English?" I asked.

"My mother died when I was twelve, leaving just my father, grandfather and me in our home. It stood where the temple stands today.

"When I was sixteen, my father sent me to school in France. In addition to my regular studies in French, history, and mathematics, I also studied English and music. My English professor, a woman, who also played violin, encouraged me apply to Oxford. I did and was accepted. I stayed there four years."

"Then you returned home?" I said.

"Yes. Unfortunately, my father's business had fallen on hard times. The French partners he brought into the company in hopes of expanding it misled him and managed to take control. They forced him out, paying him a small pension. Shortly thereafter, he became quite ill.

"When I learned of this, I left England and came back here."

"Was there anything you could do to get his business back?" I asked.

"No. By the time I arrived, he was bedridden. The doctor said it was lung cancer, but I also think his heart was broken. He died three months later."

"I'm sorry," I said.

"That was many years ago, and I've had a good life since then. I met my wife, who had been my father's nurse. She was a musician also, and we had one lovely daughter, Hanh, whom you have met."

"The temple is built where your family home was. I didn't know that," Melanie said.

"Yes. After my father's death, I found out that my grandfather had left me a sizable cash inheritance. As my father's only child, I also inherited this piece of property, debt free. I was raised as a Buddhist and accepted that I was destined to do something with what I had been given. I built the small house we are in now and the buildings that are now the school. I gave the rest of my property as a gift for the temple. In honor of my grandfather, I started a school dedicated to the traditional arts he loved."

"And your wife?" I asked.

"She also taught music, and art. She died two years ago. I miss her, but hear her in the music our students play every day."

"I'm sorry," I said, expressing my condolences a second time.

"Thank you, but I am grateful for the life we had together and the happiness it still brings into our lives. Now. What is it that you wanted to ask me?"

I told him about Binh, how he became a temporary part of our crew, and how, in a way, our ship's mission intersected with Binh's Mekong Suite. And that we were trying to find a way to actually have it played in concert in Vung Tau.

I concluded my summary explaining that Binh's composition called for a blend of western and eastern musical instruments, and that's why we needed his help.

"You have no idea how fantastic that sounds to me," he said beaming with excitement. "As Melanie knows, I often visit the orphanage school and listen to Sister Josephine's music students. I've wondered what it would be like if some of my students and hers got together and played something. Karma has once again smiled on us."

"Then you'll help?" I said hopefully.

"Yes. Of course. Whenever you are ready. I would love to meet Binh, your Captain and your friend Andrew, who you say also plays the violin. What a special evening this has been," he said smiling.

His daughter returned to the room and he told her that we had cause for a special celebration, which prompted her to go to a cupboard, pull out a dusty bottle in which there was amber colored liquid and four glasses.

It turned out to be a very strong liquor made from distilled rice wine. We clicked glasses and Master Lu offered a toast, "Buddha says, 'We become what we think and joy follows like a shadow that never leaves.' This evening has brought great joy. Thank you Rob. Thank you Melanie."

After we said goodnight and began our stroll back to the mansion, the joy of that last toast was still with me. Melanie felt it too.

"Do you think we can make this happen?" I asked.

"Oh, yes. You have won a strong ally in Master Lu," she said

"I hope so. I really like him, and his daughter. And I loved the kids."

"They loved you too. I doubt that they've met many Americans, and certainly no one like you. I want to be there the first day they sit down next to the students at the orphanage to play together," she added.

"I hope the Captain was able to convince Sister Josephine to go along?" I said.

"She makes a big fuss about his corrupting her students. But in truth, she loves it and knows how much more they enjoy music because he opens their eyes and ears to a whole different world."

"I can't wait to tell the Captain and Andrew about Master Lu," I said.

"Do you have to return to the ship tonight?" she asked.

"No. It's late and I don't have to be back until noon tomorrow." I said turning toward her. "I was hoping that you might invite me to sleep at your house tonight."

"Sleep?" she replied leaning her head on my shoulder.

"Well, maybe now and then," I said.

Our pace quickened in anticipation of what we both were thinking.

19

Back to Reality

• •

T HERE WERE A FEW LIGHTS on in the garden and in the foyer as we arrived at the mansion. Someone had left a note on the hall table for Melanie.

"My mother is flying back tomorrow. She should be home by mid-afternoon," she said after reading the note.

"I have to return to the ship before noon tomorrow. You won't have to answer any awkward questions," I said.

"Awkward?" Melanie said. "You think my mother would disapprove?"

I hesitated, not knowing if I had offended her. "Well, probably."

"She knows that I lived with my French boyfriend in Paris. And she can hardly be critical of me for having a lover in my bedroom when she has one."

"Your mother has a lover? Who?"

"You cannot be that unobservant. Are you sure you don't know my mother's lover?"

I thought about it for a few seconds.

"Oh shit! It's the Captain isn't it?"

She smiled. "But of course. She is quite enamored with your Captain."

"Does he know that you know?" I asked.

"Yes. He often joins me in the kitchen for coffee before going back to his ship. We exchange pleasantries and he asks me how my writing is coming along and I ask him about his music."

"But you don't discuss his relationship with your mother," I said.

"He is a good man and makes my mother happy. That's all I need to know," she answered.

"Still, it would have felt really awkward if I came out of your bedroom and ran into him coming out of your mother's," I said.

"There's little chance of that. My mother's quarters are actually downstairs off a hallway at the far side of the building. It is almost like a separate residence and has a small garden attached. It is quite private and allows for some discretion."

I still felt uncomfortable, and it must have shown on my face.

"Rob. You make me happy. My mother already knows I've had my eyes on you. She will be happy for me."

"You had your eyes on me?"

"You don't think all this happened by accident do you?" she answered, wrapping her arms around my neck and bringing her lips close to mine.

"Oh my God. You mean you schemed so that I would become your sex slave?"

"It didn't take a lot of scheming. To use an American expression: 'You are easy.'"

She kissed me, and pushed her body into mine, to which I responded in kind.

She broke the embrace, looked down, took my hand and led me toward the stairs, adding. "See what I mean."

Experience earned the previous night enhanced our lovemaking and made us bolder in our exploration of each other's pleasure centers. I especially liked touching and stroking the soft skin on Melanie's thighs and stomach.

"Do you know that you are covered in fur?" I said.

"What? No, I'm not. Asian women are known for their silky-smooth skin," she replied.

"Perhaps. But with the light behind you, I can see hundreds, maybe thousands, of microscopic hairs on your skin. They're white, almost silver. Like a newborn kitten."

"Hmm. Well, if I'm like a newborn kitten, you are more like a monkey, with your hairy legs, arms, and chest," she said.

Making monkey grunts, I reached out, pulled her closer, and nibbled lightly on her neck. She squealed.

We made love once more; then fell sound asleep.

Streaks of early morning sunlight reflected off the bedroom wall as I came out of a dream. In it, I was trying learn a Vietnamese song on the guitar and Melanie was helping me, but she kept leaving the room and I'd lose the melody. I woke up calling her name.

"What?" I heard a voice from the pillow next to my head.

She was lying on her back, her hips were nestled against mine, but her eyes were still closed.

"What?" she asked again, this time opening her eyes.

"I was dreaming about you. That you left the room, and I was calling you back."

"I'm here, and now that you woke me up, what do you want?"

"You were teaching me a Vietnamese song. But that can wait," I answered pulling our bodies into a perfect spoon position."

"Hmm. What was the song?" she asked, adjusting her position, her hips moving rhythmically with mine.

"I don't remember. I think that's why I was calling you. It may come to me at any moment."

After we made love, neither one of us seemed eager to get out of bed. But, I knew that I would have to get up soon and figure out how to get back to my ship. Melanie's mother would be arriving sometime after noon.

Our refuge, our special place, where there had been only us – no duty, no war, and no leaving – was drifting away with the morning mist. Reality was creeping in on the narrow shafts of morning light that found their way through the shutters.

"Okay," she said getting out of bed and pulling me up toward the shower with her. "You have one more thing to do for me before you go back to the ship."

"Oh good. I love helping you scrub all over," I replied.

"No, although that's nice too. I want you to read some of my stories and tell me what you think."

"So, you really are interested in becoming a journalist?" I asked.

"Yes. I have an interview with the World Press Service in early January. I need to send them some samples of my writing before then. I want to make sure it's good."

Our conversation continued as we dried off after showering and got dressed.

"Would you have to leave Vietnam to work for them?" I asked.

"They need someone who speaks Vietnamese, French and English to work with their team covering the war here in Vietnam. I would start as an apprentice and an interpreter, but they said I would get a chance to contribute to stories and write some on my own."

"Wow. That's fantastic. But it could also be dangerous. War correspondents have been killed over here, including Bernard Fall, one of the best. Does your mother know what you are planning?"

"Not specifically. She knows that I want to be a journalist. She doesn't know about the job interview."

"Hmm. That might be a difficult conversation. She won't like the idea of your being in harm's way."

"I know," Melanie said, her tone suddenly sad as she looked into the mirror and ran a brush through her beautiful long black hair.

What I didn't say was that I didn't like the idea of her being in danger any more than her mother would, and not just that. The correspondent's job would give her one more reason to stay in Vietnam, while I was already working on a plan to convince her to leave so we could have a chance of being together after my ship returned to San Diego.

We went downstairs to the kitchen. There were no fresh croissants, but there were lots of eggs and a baguette that was fresh enough to slice for French toast.

I prepared the egg batter while Melanie made coffee.

I started reading her stories as we ate. She watched me anxiously as I turned each page.

They were surprisingly good, too wordy, but brevity in a journalistic style can be learned from a strict editor. Her focus was on the Vietnamese people and the impact of the war on their lives. There was a lyrical quality to her writing that made me want to read more about her subjects.

"These are good, Melanie. Really good," I said.

"But? There must be something I can improve on."

"That's true of all journalists. Perhaps, you can tell exactly the same stories, but force yourself to eliminate all unnecessary words."

"Unnecessary?"

"Yes. Assume that your editor tells you he likes your story, but instead of the space your story takes now, he or she only has half the space. Whether you are writing for a newspaper, magazine or even some kind of broadcast, space and airtime is always limited. Telling a good story with as few as words as possible will get you published more often."

"Hmm. Okay," she said. "I can work on them over the next few days. Will you read them one more time before I have to send them in?"

"Of course," I answered.

Just then, we heard the front doorbell ring. Melanie went to answer it.

She returned to the kitchen. The Captain was with her.

Instinctively, I jumped to my feet.

"Relax, Rob. This is just a social call," he said.

"Yes, sir. I was just helping Melanie with her writing," I said, hoping that would suffice as an explanation for my presence in her kitchen at that hour of the morning.

He didn't seem surprised or concerned.

"Good. I actually came by to see when Simone would be returning. I haven't asked her yet about the benefit concert we'd like her to host."

"She should be back by mid-afternoon, Captain," Melanie answered. "Oh, and Rob told me about what you would like to do, and that it will benefit the school. I know my mother will love it."

"I believe you're right. But I still must ask," he said.

"Captain, I have some good news about our concert. Thanks to Melanie, I think we've found musicians who play Vietnamese instruments."

"Really. That is good news," he replied

Melanie handed him a cup of coffee, he joined us at the table, and we briefed him on our meeting and dinner with Master Lu.

"He's anxious to meet you, Binh, and Andrew and begin working on the project," I concluded.

He seemed genuinely delighted at the news. We talked about how the next step after Madame Marquis' approval would be to win over Sister Wolfgang.

"I think that will be easier than you think," Melanie suggested.

"I hope you're right, Melanie. This could be a wonderful event if we can pull it off," he said.

I got up and bussed the dishes to the sink.

"I've got to make my way back to the ship this morning. So I'd better get going," I said.

"Your timing is perfect. Reyes is parked out front in the ship's car waiting to take me back. I just needed to check in with Melanie so I could set up a meeting with her mother. You can come back with me."

Then, he turned to Melanie. "Tell Simone that I'll be back around 1600, but don't say what it's about. Let me tell her, if you don't mind."

"Of course, Captain. She will be happy to see you," Melanie answered.

She came over to where I was putting the dishes onto the counter and gave me kiss on each cheek. "*Merci beaucoup*, for all your help Rob," she said, her lips lingering on my skin just a little bit longer than necessary.

20

Folie a Deux
●●●●●●●●●●●●●●●●●●●●●●

I FOLLOWED THE CAPTAIN TO the ship's car.

Reyes jumped out and opened the back seat door for him. I went over to the other side.

"Reyes, drive us over to the school. I want to show Mr. Allen something."

"Aye, aye, Captain," Reyes responded.

"Have you ever heard the French expression, '*Folie a deux*,' Rob?" he asked.

"No, sir," I answered. "My guess is that it has something to do with two fools."

"You're close. It refers to a shared delusional belief, a mutual craziness."

I realized that he must be referring to Melanie and me, and had seen through my explanation that I was giving Melanie a journalism lesson.

"Captain, Melanie and I are both aware of the obstacles in the way of our having a lasting relationship. But we're not crazy."

"I wasn't referring to you and Melanie. I was talking about you and me." He replied.

"I'm not sure I understand, sir."

"Melanie must have told you that Simone and I have a relationship. It's been going on for months. I can't criticize you for becoming involved with a local woman if I'm doing the same thing. Besides, it is not a secret. I'm sure most of the crew knows."

"I still don't understand the *folie a deux* reference," I said.

In the meantime, the car had arrived in front of the church.

"Park here, Reyes. Mr. Allen and I are going for a short walk."

We got out. Captain Baillier pointed toward the walkway that ran between the church and the convent, "We're going this way," he said.

As we walked between the two buildings, he continued his explanation.

"We're not breaking any Navy regulations. Simone and Melanie are both adults and French citizens. France is an ally of the United States. Neither of us is sleeping with the enemy."

"Yes, sir, but. . ." I started to say.

"But, you and I are not free to do as we want, whenever we want. We both must follow orders; orders that could take us away any time at a moment's notice. We might want to be with our women, but that will not be possible. We will have to leave. We have no choice."

"Yes, sir. But that doesn't change how I feel about her, and how she feels about me," I answered, already saying far more about how I felt than I had intended.

"I get that. Simone and I feel the same way about each other. But that doesn't change the fact that you and I, in less than a year or sooner, will be leaving the women we love behind in this dangerous place, and we won't be able to do anything to stop it."

We had reached the end of the convent building and I noticed, for the first time, that there was a separate, smaller, single-story brick structure behind it.

The walkway led to the building's solid wood front door. There was a bolt on the door, but no lock. The Captain opened it, and directed me to walk ahead. He threw a light switch and I saw that it was some kind of storage space, in which there were a number of old desks and chairs, as well as crates of canned goods, stacks of blankets, and various other materials.

Stone steps on the left side led down to some kind of basement.

"When the original French architects designed the church and convent, this was a combination cooler, food storage building, and wine cellar, because no self-respecting Frenchman, especially a French priest, would be anywhere without an excellent cellar of his own," the Captain explained.

I looked at him curiously, not understanding why he was showing me an old wine cellar.

"As much as I hope that our military will be able to protect the South Vietnamese from a communist takeover, I believe it is going to get a whole lot worse before it gets better. Honestly, I'm not sure we'll succeed. Binh believes, and I think he is right, that the North has been successful in building support for the communist cause in the South, even in Vung Tao. Fighting could break out here at any time."

I was beginning to understand what he was implying.

"But we're the targets – us, the Australians and the ARVN units. Not local civilians, right?"

"Yes and no. We will be targets, but so will any locals allied with us and/or formerly allied with the French," he answered.

"Oh, shit," I said, realizing that he was talking about Melanie, her mother, and probably their entire staff at the General's Daughter. The old mansion would be a prime target.

"Won't the church and school be targets too?" I asked.

"Probably not. The work that the nuns have done for local orphans is widely known, and they have many supporters among the local population. I believe they will be left alone."

"So, what does this have to do with you, me, and our shared craziness?"

"I've already had conversations with Simone and Melanie about my concerns for their safety in the event of an attack on Vung Tao. I've told them that at the first sign of any fighting nearby, they should come here and stay until the fighting is over. I've had the same conversation with Sister Josephine. She has already stocked the cellar with extra water, food, candles, blankets, and other provisions.

"There is plenty of room for all of the students, nuns, and several dozen other people, including Melanie and her mother."

"Sir. That's not crazy. That's sounds like a good plan," I said.

"A better plan, as far as I'm concerned, would be to put both women on the next plane out of here and tell them to wait for us in France. But Simone has already said no to that idea several times, and Melanie won't leave either."

"Yeah. And now she wants to be even closer to the action," I said.

"What are you talking about?" he asked.

I told him about Melanie's pending interview with the World Press Service and what it would mean if she got the job.

"Simone is not going to like that at all," he said. "Maybe she can talk Melanie out of it.

In any case, that brings me around to the crazy part. Let's start walking back to the car."

As we came back out into the sunlight, he described what he called a "Hail Mary Rescue Plan."

"According to Binh, Viet Cong strength is growing in the Mekong, and an all-out attack on all the major cities could happen anytime in the next three or four months. We will probably be in the middle when it happens. We haven't received any alerts from our brass yet, but we could any day."

"Yes, sir, but I doubt the Navy is going to order us to rescue the owners of a restaurant in Vung Tau."

"The chances are fifty-fifty that we will be in port should an attack happen. If we are, I will dispatch you and two armed sailors to the school to protect Navy personnel who might be there teaching. You will see that they take shelter and protect them until it is clear. On the way, you will go by the General's Daughter to make sure that no military personnel are trapped there, rescuing any civilian personnel as well."

"That does sound kind of crazy, and stretches the definition of our mission out to the fringes. But it's better than just hoping that they're going to be okay," I said.

"This plan is not written down anywhere. It is between you and me. I hope it is not needed, but if it is, I know you are as committed as I am to protecting the people we both hold most dear," he said putting his hand on my shoulder.

"You can count on me, sir," I said.

"I know I can Rob. Now let's get back to the ship and see how our repairs are going."

As we walked back I asked him one more question.

"What are we going to do long term? We've got to persuade them to leave before it really gets bad here," I asked.

"Yes. But we're dealing with two strong-willed, dedicated and independent women. That too is crazy-making and there's not a darn thing either of us can do except keep trying."

21

Only God Knows What's Next

●●●●●●●●●●●●●●●●●●●●●●●●

ON THE WAY BACK TO the ship, we talked about arranging a meeting between Binh, Master Lu, and Andrew to go over the music and to confirm that his students could participate.

The Captain had already met with Sister Josephine. She readily agreed to the concert. The next step would be for her, Master Lu, Binh, and Andrew to work on the musical arrangements.

Admiral Kirkpatrick acquired approval from Binh's CO at ARVN headquarters in Saigon for him to be temporarily assigned to *Bell County* as its Vietnamese liaison officer.

The Captain had a list of things to do, including returning to the mansion later to confirm with Simone Marquis that she would host the charity concert at the General's Daughter.

A date was still pending, but sometime in mid-January was the target.

The pier next to the ship was cluttered with pallets, cables, and hoses. Harry and Andrew were standing near the gangway as the Captain and I walked up. They snapped to attention and saluted him.

"As you were," the Captain said. "How are the engine repairs going Harry?"

"The new parts should be here by tomorrow morning, and we might have them installed by tomorrow afternoon. By Wednesday, we should be ready to test it," Harry replied.

"Good. Keep me informed of any new developments," he said, heading up the gangway.

I stopped to talk with Harry and Andrew.

"And where did you disappear to Saturday night?" Harry asked.

I looked at Andrew, who shook his head indicating that he had not said anything to Harry about me and Melanie.

"I had an important personal matter to attend to."

"I bet. It must have been really important for you to have left that hot Aussie girl stranded with a bunch of horny sailors at the New Orleans Club."

"It was important, and Meg is more than capable of handling herself. My guess is she was the belle of the ball," I said to Harry. Then turned to Andrew. "I assume Meg make it back to her barracks alright."

"Kaneli and I had to pry her away from all the guys she wanted to dance with, but we succeeded. In fact, there was a telegram waiting for her when she got back. Her husband has a three-day layover in Hong Kong. She flew out Sunday afternoon to meet him there," Andrew replied.

"Is Binh around? I have some good news for him."

"Yes. He's in the wardroom working on his music. He's almost finished. What's the good news?"

I told them about how Melanie set up a meeting with Master Lu, and that the Captain had already gotten the okay from Sister Josephine, and that things were looking good for using the General's Daughter as the venue for the concert.

"You've been a busy boy," Harry said.

"Yeah. Now, I've got to go change into my uniform, check in with O.J., and find out when my next watch is."

"Actually, Andrew and I and most of the crew just got back to the ship a little while ago. Everybody has been on liberty and the watch schedule is kind of in limbo. I'm going to have to babysit the engine repair work, so the watch may be on me. The XO has called a meeting for all officers in the wardroom for 1300 hours. We'll learn more then," Harry said.

"Okay. I think I should still check in with O.J. and then tell Binh about Master Lu."

"Rob, after you see O.J., come get me. I want to be there when you give Binh the word," Andrew said.

I found O.J. in the radio room. He briefed me on what was happening in the operations department, which wasn't much, and I gave him a synopsis on what I had done regarding the charity concert arrangements.

Andrew and I found Binh in the wardroom busily scribbling on various scores spread in a line from one end of the dining table to the other.

"Binh. Have you left this spot since I last saw you forty-eight hours ago?" I asked.

He smiled sheepishly. His eyes told me he hadn't gotten much sleep.

"Now that it is so close, I want to finish it. I will rest after it's performed." he said.

"I've found your Vietnamese instruments and musicians."

"You have? That is wonderful. But how did you do it? There are no orchestras here in Vung Tau."

I told him how Melanie had taken me to the music school, and about our meeting with Master Lu amd his students.

"Master Lu is very enthusiastic about your project, and looking forward to meeting you and working with you on the concert. I think you will like him," I said.

He listened politely to everything I told him about our meeting, the dinner, the kids playing for us, and the sing-along. I added that if it were not for Melanie, we would never have had this good fortune.

"I'm sorry. I understand everything, but who is Melanie?" he asked.

"That's right. You haven't met her. She is the daughter of Madame Marquis, the owner of the General's Daughter, where we hope to hold the concert."

"So, she is French?" he said.

"Actually, she's Vietnamese, but Madame Marquis adopted her when she came to the school as an orphan. She spent several years attending school in Paris, and returned recently to help her mother run the restaurant. She also teaches at the school."

"I see. So she is a musician too."

"No, although she has a beautiful singing voice. She volunteers as an English and French teacher at the school."

"And you say that Master Lu's school is next to the Buddhist temple. This too is most fortunate. I believe there is good karma in what we are doing."

"Melanie can set up a meeting whenever you are ready."

"I am ready now. The music is done. I'm just working on a few corrections. Only the final arrangements are needed, and that depends on what instruments and musicians we have at our disposal."

"Okay then. I'll try to contact Melanie tonight and see what she can set up for tomorrow or the next day." I was happy for the excuse to see her.

After lunch, all of the *Bell County*'s officers remained in the wardroom until the Captain spoke up.

"We've got quite a bit to cover, but before I turn the details over to Lew, I want to thank all of you for getting behind O.J.'s crazy scheme - the benefit concert featuring Binh's Mekong Suite. We have some more good news about that and several other things. I'll let Lew fill you in."

"Thank you, Captain," the XO began. "First, you all know that Admiral Kirkpatrick got approval for Binh to be a liaison with our ship for at least the next ninety days."

The Captain then stood and offered the ARVN lieutenant his hand, "Binh, on behalf of our entire crew, welcome."

"Thank you, Captain. I am honored," Binh replied.

"The second piece of fantastic news is that the Admiral has gotten approval for our musical mission," the XO continued.

Everybody cheered and clapped.

"Somewhere, deep in the bowels of the Pentagon, there is a person with a heart," Harry declared.

The XO added, "We are now officially ordered to put on our shows, so long as it doesn't interfere with our primary mission, or endanger any base where we perform. We are required to get each base commander's approval, and they are instructed not to stop us unless our performance would seriously interfere with base security or its primary mission."

"That allows them quite a bit of wiggle room," Harry observed.

"Yes it does, but without a base commander's full support, our shows will not be attended. So we'll live with it," the XO said.

"The Admiral has also signed off on our benefit concert featuring Binh's music," he continued. "In fact, he is planning to invite South Vietnam's leaders in Saigon to attend. He wants to make this a shining example of how our two countries are working together to preserve Vietnam's culture. He also plans to attend. He'd liked to get CINCPAC (Commander in Chief Pacific Fleet) to come too, but that is just a maybe at this point."

"Wow. This plan is moving fast. Have we set a date yet?" O.J. asked.

"January 15, plus or minus a day or two. We don't want it to interfere with the usual celebrations of Tet, the lunar New Year on January 30," the XO answered.

"It's almost Thanksgiving, so we have about forty-five days to put the whole thing together, and that's in between our regular mission up and down the rivers, plus our musical shows. It's going to be a busy holiday season for the *Bell County*," Harry declared.

"Most of the concert prep work will be done by Binh who will be working with Sister Wolfgang and her students and our new Vietnamese music partners," the Captain added.

"Binh is now under my command, at least temporarily. That means I can assign him to spend virtually all of his time on the concert, which I'm certain he won't mind. Am I right Binh?"

"Yes, Captain."

"Okay. Andrew and Rob, I want you to concentrate your extra time on working with Binh and Madame Marquis on the details of the concert. O.J., you will be the overall supervisor of the event, which means that Binh, Andrew and Rob report to you. The XO and I will work with Doc and Reyes to keep refining our regular shows and the food we serve. A lot depends on where our mission schedule takes us. We won't know that until our broken engine is back on line. Harry has the watch for the next twenty-four hours, during which I hope he delivers some good news about that engine. Any questions?"

"What about Thanksgiving?" Harry said.

"That's going to depend on where we are. Freddie is working on finding the birds, stuffing, and all of the ingredients for a real Thanksgiving dinner. But right now we don't know if we'll be here, up a river, or somewhere else in Vietnam. It could be just us or we could also be serving a bunch of guys on some ramp in the boonies. We'll be prepared for whatever happens."

After the meeting broke up, the Captain asked me to see him in his cabin.

"I'm heading back into town to meet with Simone at 1630 hours. I want you to come so you and Melanie can confirm a date with Master Lu for the meeting with Binh."

"Aye, aye, Captain."

I returned to my stateroom where Andrew was lying in the top bunk reading through some of the loose sheets of Minh's musical score.

"Are you going to see Kaneli tonight?"

"She doesn't get off her shift until after 2000 hours, but yes. I'm meeting her at the New Orleans club at 2030 or so. How about you? Are you seeing Melanie tonight?"

"I hope so. The Captain wants us to set up a meeting with Master Lu and Binh for tomorrow. I need Melanie's help. After that, if she's not needed to work at the General's Daughter, maybe we could join you at the New Orleans."

"That would be great. I'd like Melanie and Kaneli to meet."

"If we don't show up, it means that she couldn't get away, or that the Captain has some other job for me later."

"Things must have gone pretty good with you and Melanie. You literally disappeared for a day and a half. I was sort of worried, but no bodies washed up on the beach, so I assumed you were okay."

"It didn't start well. In fact, I got lost after I left the New Orleans Club. The rain was pouring down. I couldn't see shit, and I wasn't sure where I was. Then, when I finally found the mansion, Melanie was really pissed at me for not coming sooner and I thought she was going to throw me out."

"Obviously, she didn't."

"Nope. In fact, it was the best thirty-six hours of my life. How about you and Kaneli?"

"She's an amazing woman. I've never known anyone like her – so wild, open, free. She knows exactly what she wants and is not shy about going for it."

"Yes. She doesn't seem like the kind of woman you would be attracted to."

"What does that mean? She's smart, clever, gorgeous, and funny as hell."

"I know. But you are a reserved, fastidious, button-down, French-speaking, tight-ass, who irons and starches everything, including your skivvies. She seems your exact opposite in every way."

"Fuck you. Kaneli likes my tight buns, and I don't iron my underwear."

"I have to admit you've changed a lot since you were inducted into the Black Gang. That must be what Kaneli sees in you —the new macho engineer with the scent of fuel oil and engine grease in his hair."

"And what on earth does an intelligent, sophisticated, beautiful woman like Melanie see in a barely adult-height country bumpkin in scruffy old khakis and an ugly, wrinkled Hawaiian shirt?"

"It must be my sharp wit and silver tongue"

"Wit? No. Tongue? Maybe, but only if you know how to use it properly?"

Not wishing to get into any intimate details, I let our banter cease.

"Rob?" Andrew said a little while later. "You know we are two of the luckiest guys in the Navy. Here, in the middle of a war, we've found two amazing women. And what's even more amazing, they seem to like us."

"You're right. I plan on making the most of every minute I have with Melanie, because only God and the goddamn Navy knows what's in store for us next."

22

Sweethearts Stranded in a Storm
•••••••••••••••••••••••

I T WAS AN UNUSUALLY CLEAR and windy day in Vung
Tau as Reyes drove the Captain and me toward the General's
Daughter. The palms swayed heavily along the beach and the bay
was filled with whitecaps. The wind provided natural air-condi-
tioning, with the added benefit of keeping the mosquitos away.

"I'm planning to stay at the mansion tonight," the Captain
volunteered, tactfully not asking my intentions.

"Yes, sir," I said. I wasn't sure how I was supposed to respond.
There was an awkward silence.

"It's okay, Rob," he said. "We're in a very unusual situation. I
know that. I don't expect you to do anything to change your relationship with Melanie, wherever it is at this point. And I'm not
going to change mine with Simone. Life is too short."

"Yes, sir. It's just that it's really awkward to think that we might
both end up in the kitchen with Melanie and her mother tomorrow
morning, as though it is all perfectly normal."

He laughed. "Yes, I see your point. But you're forgetting that
Simone is a sophisticated *femme Parisienne*. The fact that her adult
daughter is sleeping with you doesn't shock her. In fact, I'm sure
that she and Melanie have already discussed it ."

"You're probably right. Melanie didn't seem particularly concerned when I asked about her mother's possible reaction. In any case, I'm not even sure Melanie will want me to stay tonight."

Our car pulled up to the mansion. "You're about to find out," he said.

A gust of wind nearly blew the car door out of my hand. The Captain looked toward the eastern horizon and frowned.

"Do you feel it?" he said.

"The wind?"

"Yes, but also the change in air pressure. Maybe it's just an old sailor's superstition, but I think we may be in for a blow."

He turned back to the car, opened the door, and said something to Reyes. Then rejoined me on the walkway up to the mansion.

"I ordered Reyes to tell the XO and Harry, to secure everything on deck, put out extra lines to the pier, and close all exterior watertight doors tonight, just in case."

Is it typhoon season here?" I asked.

"No. The season normally only lasts until October. But typhoons have occurred in Southeast Asia in virtually every month of the year. Our ship couldn't outrun one even if both engines were running. She is as safe as she can be right where she is. I will suggest that Simone and her staff be prepared in case the weather gets worse."

Simone Marquis must have seen us coming up the walk, because she opened her front door and came out to the porch to greet us.

"*Bonjour, mon capitaine, bonjour* Rob," she said smiling and giving us each a kiss on each cheek.

"*Bonjour Madame Marquis*," I replied.

"Rob. This time you must call me Simone. I think we will be seeing you here, *beaucoup de temps, no?*"

"Ah. *Oui, Madame*. I mean, yes, Simone, you will."

Just then a strong gust of wind blew her long and reddish-blonde hair across her face and she grabbed the porch railing for balance.

"Ooh! This is not good," she declared.

"You're right. Outdoor dining will not be an option tonight. In fact, I think it's going to rain."

Just then, Melanie opened the door and beckoned us all to come inside.

"We have fresh coffee in the kitchen," she said.

The small kitchen table was set with coffee service for four. A large plate of what looked like extra-large biscuits was sitting in the center.

"We have fresh ginger scones also," she said.

"Ginger scones? I don't think I've ever had any kind of scone before," I said.

"Wait until you taste them. They're delicious," she said. For emphasis she put her arms around my neck and kissed me.

"That's sweet ginger on my lips, *mon cher*," she added.

Any reservations I had about disclosing our intimacy were canceled by that kiss. Simone, didn't seem fazed by it. She accepted the chair the Captain pulled out for her. I did the same for Melanie. We passed around the platter of scones, while Simone began pouring coffee.

I took a bite of the scone. The dough tasted like a normal buttery biscuit, but the tangy ginger added a whole new dimension.

"Hmm!" seemed to be the most frequently uttered sound for the next several minutes.

"I've got to get this recipe to Freddie. These are unbelievable," the Captain said.

For a few minutes, we talked about the difference between a biscuit and a scone, and agreed it didn't matter.

"Simone," the Captain said changing the subject. "I'm sorry I missed you the day our ship arrived. How was your trip to Bangkok?"

"I ordered everything I needed and got the first available flight home. I don't like that filthy place, but it has the best markets for what we can't get here. In that respect, my trip was successful," she replied.

"I'm glad you're back. Has Melanie told you anything about why I stopped by?"

"Yes, and even without hearing any of the finer details, I love the idea. It is such a kind and generous thing you are doing for the school. Of course I want to help in any way I can. And yes, I would be honored to host the concert here at the General's Daughter."

"Merci beaucoup, c'est magnifique. But, I actually can't take much credit. It was O.J.'s idea. It's Binh's incredible music, and Rob, Andrew and Melanie have done more work on it than I have so far," he said.

Simone stood up and went over behind his chair leaned over, wrapped her arms around him, nuzzled his neck, then kissed his cheek.

"You are such a dear, sweet man. It's you who lead us," she whispered, loud enough for us all to hear.

He pulled her around and down so she sat on his lap. He kissed her then said. "Well, I guess there's no sense in hiding our feelings from the kids."

I nearly spit out a mouthful of coffee suppressing a laugh. It came out as a snort. Melanie blushed slightly, then recovered, smiled, and reached for my hand. The signals were all sent and received. The four of us could be as we wished to be with each other. Nothing more needed to be said.

A loud slapping sound of a wooden shutter hitting the wall broke the mood.

"I think we should get busy battening down the hatches," the Captain declared.

"Batten the hatches?" Simone looked puzzled, then smiled. "*Oui. Fermez les ecoutilles.*"

Her chief assistant came into the kitchen and said something in French. Simone nodded and said, "*Oui.*" He hurried out.

"Danh, our manager, has ordered the staff to bring the tables and chairs in and lash down the awning and covers. All of the storm shutters can be pulled in and closed from the inside.

"Melanie, take Rob upstairs and start closing those shutters. The Captain and I will close most of the downstairs. We'll leave some open here in the kitchen for light as long as we can. I will also pull out the oil lamps, candles and matches. We're going to need them if the power goes out," she said.

We all jumped to our tasks. When we got to the top of the stairs, Melanie stopped turned around, and gave me a long, deep kiss.

"That's just to let you know how happy I am that you're here," she said.

"I couldn't have said it better myself," I answered.

There were a surprising number of windows. Pulling in and locking the storm shutters required us to open each screen, then reach out, grab the handle on each shutter, pull it in, and then fasten its latch to the inside frame. Then, we closed the screen, but left the actual windows open so that air could flow in.

It took us nearly forty-five minutes to get them all done.

Daylight still leaked into each room through the louvers of the shutters, but it seemed later than it actually was.

"I was hoping you could take me to Master Lu's home today so I could arrange a meeting for him and Binh. It would be a nasty walk in this wind. I guess it will have to wait until tomorrow," I said.

"It's not that bad yet. We can drive," she said.

"Drive what? We sent the ship's car back."

"We have a little jitney that we use to take our linens to the laundry in town. It's small, but there's room for the driver and a passenger. If we take that, we can be at Master Lu's in five minutes."

Downstairs, the Captain and Simone had finished their work and were headed toward the restaurant to see if the staff needed help.

We told them our plan.

"Rob. Keep an eye on the east. The storm is probably not going to arrive until later, but if the sky starts to look really flat and dark gray, get back here quickly," the Captain warned.

"And don't stay there long. That open truck won't protect you from the storm." Simone added.

The laundry jitney was little more than a flimsy light metal cab built over a three-wheeled motor scooter. A small bed extended over the back wheels. There was a windshield and roof, but no side doors.

The wind seemed to have died down as we headed out from the mansion toward town. We didn't see anybody until we turned down the little street to Master Lu's house. All along there we saw people pulling in their awnings and nailing boards onto their windows.

We pulled up in front of Master Lu's home and saw him and his daughter, Hanh, working to fasten their own window shutters. Hanh saw us first.

"Melanie, Rob. What are you doing here? There's a storm coming," she shouted in the wind.

"I needed to speak with Master Lu. We won't be staying, although if you need help securing your home, we can stay."

"No, these are the last shutters to be done. We've been through this before. My father built our home on high ground with a strong foundation and framing. We will be fine. Come in. Let's get out of the wind so we can talk."

Master Lu finished latching the last shutter and followed us inside.

"Well. Your business must be very important for you both to go out in weather like this," Master Lu declared.

"Yes. Master Lu. It's good news. Our concert is moving forward. We have a tentative date for January 15, with a day or two on either side open as alternatives.

Binh's score is done. He asked if he can meet with you as soon as possible, at your convenience of course."

"I can meet with him tomorrow, depending on the weather. It would be best if he got here between three and three-thirty in the afternoon. That way, he could hear the children during their music practice. Then we could talk after that and he could join us for dinner."

"That sounds perfect. I know he would love that. Would it be okay if my fellow officer, Andrew, joined him? Andrew is an excellent musician, a violinist, and is helping Binh with the music."

"Certainly. If the weather doesn't allow a meeting tomorrow, we can do it the next day," he answered.

A noticeable howl from outside was getting louder and there were intermittent banging sounds coming from the streets as loose boards and shutters rattled in the wind.

Melanie glanced at me, concern on her face.

"I think we should go before things get worse. Thank you for agreeing to meet with Binh and Andrew, and thank you again for your hospitality and courtesy last night. It was a wonderful evening," I said.

"You are most welcome. Now get going before the rain arrives," he said.

We bowed to Master Lu and Hanh and quickly made our way to the jitney. I glanced in what I thought was an easterly direction. The sky had an ominous, bluish gray tint. The air was warm in spite of the wind and smelled of ozone and salt water.

Papers and other loose trash blew into the open sides of the little truck as we backed it out.

We turned onto the street leading to the General's Daughter. Without warning, the sky opened up and the rain came down in torrents. Visibility went to zero. Lighting flashed east of us. I slowed to a creep, not wanting to run off the road.

Another gust of wind pushed the truck to the right, which was fortunate because a large tree branch landed in the street where we would have been.

Water streamed down Melanie's face. "Go faster!" she yelled.

"Okay, but tell me when to turn into the driveway. I can't see shit."

Again, lightning flashed, this time closer, followed by a loud clap of thunder.

A pile of large palm leaves suddenly appeared in front of me. I swerved just in time to avoid them. The passenger side tire sunk into the roadside mud.

Down shifting to the jitney's lowest gear, I gunned the engine, and the wheel jumped back onto the pavement and we shot ahead.

"Turn here!" Melanie shouted pointing to my left.

"Here? I can't see anything."

"There," she said her hand extended in front me.

I saw a small post that must have marked the back driveway to the mansion. Trusting her directions, I turned. I spotted the lights at the back of the General Daughter's big kitchen and knew that we'd made it. I pulled in as close to the back door as I could and we both jumped out and scrambled up the steps through the door into the restaurant's warm, dry interior.

We were soaked to the skin and had a generous collection of wind-blown debris sticking to us. Melanie stared at me and a look of alarm crossed her face.

"You're bleeding," she said putting her hand to my left cheek.

"That tree branch must have grazed me when it fell. I was so busy dodging and weaving, I didn't feel it."

She got a clean dishtowel from a drawer, put some water on it and padded my cheek.

"Does it hurt?" she asked.

"Yes. I'm going to need a lot of special care tonight," I said leaning into the cloth she held to my cheek.

"You're such a baby." Her tone indicated she was relieved I wasn't seriously hurt.

I kissed her, and she dropped the cloth and put her arms around my neck, pressing her body into mine. Just then Simone and the Captain came into the kitchen.

"You two are all wet," Simone declared with some concern.

"But, otherwise they both appear to be perfectly fine," the Captain added.

23

Singing in the Rain
●●●●●●●●●●●●●●●●●●●●●●●

I GOT OUT OF MY wet clothes and dried off. Simone found a pair of busboy uniform pants, and the Captain loaned me an extra shirt he had stashed in Simone's room.

It was dark outside. The storm continued to rage.

The four of us gathered in the kitchen and were discussing what we should have for dinner when the lights went out. Simone lit candles that she had staged around the kitchen.

"Whatever we prepare, we'll be dining by candlelight," she said. "There are plenty of fresh vegetables and two baguettes left-over from lunch."

"Let's keep it simple. If we have eggs, cheese, and a little bit of cream, I can make a delicious vegetable frittata," the Captain volunteered.

"Oui," declared Simone, "And with the baguette and some wine, we will have a feast."

The gas range was working perfectly.

While the Captain and Simone prepared the frittata, Melanie and I started setting the little table in the kitchen.

"*Non, non*. For this special night with the four of us, we will eat in the dining room," Simone ordered.

"*Oui, Maman*," Melanie responded. "Shall we use the silver, China and crystal too?"

"Of course," her mother replied.

Melanie led me to the dining room, which was between the kitchen and the living room. It had a large set of French doors that opened to another private patio. They were shuttered against the storm. In better weather they could be opened to let in fresh air.

"This was where the governor general hosted large dinner parties for wealthy French planters and local dignitaries. We very rarely use it anymore," Melanie said.

She retrieved the China, silverware and crystal from a large antique carved oak armoire.

"Rob, bring a dish towel from the kitchen. These things are dull and dusty from lack of use. I want to clean and shine them a little. Oh. And in the hall linen closet, there is a cream-colored tablecloth on a hanger. Bring me that, too."

"Aye, aye, *ma cherie*," I said, saluting as I returned to the kitchen.

She also found a Sterling silver candelabra and a drawer full of new candles, which she added to the center of the table.

"Where do you keep the wine?" I asked

"Follow me," Melanie said, leading me down the hall past the linen closet to another door. Behind it, a narrow set of stairs led down into the dark.

"Wait. I'll get us some candles." She returned a half-minute later with a lit candle for each of us.

At the bottom of the stairs was another door, which opened into a four-foot by eight-foot space lined with rocks set in mortar. The floor was a mix of gravel and sand. The ceiling was the first floor of the mansion. Ancient wooden wine racks lined three sides of the small room. Dusty bottles filled most of the spaces.

While Melanie held both candles, I checked out the collection.

"Most of the labels are unreadable. And they're all French. I don't much about French wines."

"The governor general was very rich. You can be sure that they are all very good wines," Melanie said.

"I was born and raised in Calfiornia's wine country. But most of our wine makers came from Italy. Thanks to a Brit who ran a local French restaurant, I know a few names. But if they're not here, I'm just going to have to guess."

My Brit friend was very proud of his Bordeaux wines, particularly those from Chateau Lynch-Bages. It was the only French wine label I could remember. With Melanie holding the candles close, we went along each rack, twisting the bottles to see if we could read the labels. We were getting near the last rows when the light fell on a design that looked familiar.

"Move the candle just a little closer," I said.

"Holly shit! I found it. There's an entire row of Chateau Lynch-Bages here."

"Do you have any idea how valuable this rack of wine is? I bet each one of these bottles is worth at least $150," I said.

"These have been here since before I arrived. My mother never comes down here, nor do I. We get our wine from a Thai liquor distributor."

"Well, tonight we are all in for a treat." I grabbed three dusty bottles of Chateau Lynch-Bages Paullic 1947 and indicated that she could lead us back upstairs.

I took the bottles into the kitchen to dust them off.

"Captain, you won't believe what I found," I exclaimed as I put the bottles down on the counter next to the range in front of him.

He leaned over, squinting at the label in the dim candlelight.

"Where in the hell did you get this?" he said incredulously.

"There's a cellar down some stairs off the hallway. There must be seventy or eighty cases of wine in it, all French, mostly Bordeaux, and I didn't see anything newer than 1950," I answered.

I knew that growing up in New Orleans, his knowledge of French wines would be far more extensive than mine.

"You picked a couple of good ones," he said.

"Honestly, it was the only label I recognized."

"We'll probably need to decant it."

"I know. I can do that while you finish the frittata. I'm going to see if Melanie can find me a corkscrew and a nice carafe."

By the time the frittata was ready to serve, the table was set and the first bottle of wine had been decanted into the beautiful crystal carafe that Melanie found in the armoire.

While the table was set formally, we served family style, passing around the frittata, bread, additional sliced vegetables, and sliced cheeses.

When each of us had a full glass of wine, the Captain spoke.

"Here's to the two most beautiful women that two lonely sailors could have ever hope to find. We are most blessed by fair winds to have landed at their door, and twice blessed that they took us in."

The wine was well balanced, with just enough tannin, acid and very slight fruity sweetness to rest gently on my tongue and stay smooth all the way down my throat. It was surprisingly light, not more than twelve or thirteen percent alcohol.

It went perfectly with the Captain's frittata that was generously spiked with multiple cloves of garlic, sliced squash and some kind of leafy greens.

Our conversation ranged from compliments of the food to the wine. We wondered at the age of the oldest bottles. I'd taken a quick look aided only by candlelight. What might come from a more diligent search with a good flashlight was something worth considering.

As we finished the first bottle of wine, I opened the second to let it breath before decanting.

"What about dessert?" The Captain asked. "There must be some pastries somewhere in the kitchen."

"*Je regret*, there are no pastries. But we do have *mousse au chocolat*."

Melanie stood up. "Chocolate mousse! It's my favorite." She started picking up dishes.

"I'll help," I said, and joined her clearing the table and taking the plates back to the kitchen.

She found the large bowl of the chocolate mousse on a shelf in the walk-in cooler. Simone brought us four small crystal bowls. We filled them to the brim with creamy mousse. I decanted the second bottle of Lynch-Bages and replenished our glasses. The combination of chocolate and superb Bordeaux was a perfect end to a perfect dinner.

The house was suddenly quieter. The shutters had stopped rattling and the sound of rushing wind was gone. I opened the French door that led to the patio and looked out. It was still raining, but there was no wind. The air was warm and smelled of wet grass and gardenias.

"I think the worst of the storm has passed," I said.

"Why don't we go into the parlor? We can open the shutters and look out at the rain, enjoy our wine, and the rest of a lovely evening," Simone suggested.

We all agreed that was an excellent idea. I grabbed the carafe and followed the ladies and the Captain into the very elegant, seldom-used, parlor. Each of us carried a candle to light the way.

A huge square grand piano was centered in a semi-circular corner of the room. Behind it were several large shuttered windows.

A wide shelf just behind the piano bench was filled with various small instruments including a concertina, ukulele, tambourine, several small Vietnamese drums and some kind of metal cymbals.

"Is this where you have family jam sessions?" I asked.

Simone went from window to window opening the shutters,

then said, "All this was here when I first arrived as a young woman. The governor general loved music. He played the piano and ask his friends to gather around after dinner to sing, sometimes for hours. There was always somebody who knew how to play the concertina, and the rest of the guests were expected to do the rhythm.

"It was the way they pretended they were back in France," she added.

The power was out all over the city, but various small lights, probably from other candlelit homes, flickered in the distance. The moon behind the clouds cast a slight glow that allowed us to see beyond the windows. The rain lessened to a gentle shower.

Melanie walked back to the dining room, retrieved the candelabra, and placed it on the piano.

"We have survived the storm and enjoyed a lovely meal. This setting now requires some beautiful music," Simone declared.

The Captain, never one to pass on the opportunity to play, sat down at the enormous piano opened the keyboard cover and tested the keys.

"Simone. When was the last time this was tuned?"

"*Je ne sais pas.* I don't know, *mon cher,*" she replied.

"Oh well. Any port in a storm," he declared, and started on a rollicking version of Fats Domino's "Let the Four Winds Blow."

Melanie and I loved it and sang along. Simone didn't join in.

When he finished, she sat down next to him, put her head on his shoulder.

"Could we have something more romantic, *plus gentil, mon cher,*" she asked in a sweet voice.

"I have the perfect song, but you and Melanie must sing with me, and I need Rob to play rhythm ukulele.

"Rhythm ukulele?" I replied.

"Yes. Just like rhythm guitar, but use ukulele chords. I know you know them."

"Okay. Just go through the chord changes first, and I'll follow."

"One thing more, " the Captain added. "For authenticity, I am going to play this concertina instead of the piano," he said, taking the small accordion off the shelf.

"Okay, *mes amis*, we are going to sing *"Sous Le Ciel de Paris"* ("Under the Skies of Paris") in French. I know you'll recognize the tune Rob, even if you don't know the words."

He then played several bars of the tune on the concertina and called out the chord changes as I tried to keep up. After a couple of times through, he started singing:

"Sous le ciel de Paris s'envole une chanson, hum hum...(Beneath the Parisian sky a song flutters away)."*

Melanie joined him enthusiastically, her beautiful voice rising to the front as he modulated back to let her lead. Soon, Simone joined in, her voice a reminder of Edith Piaf, the French chanteuse who had made that song so famous.

The two women made a sweet duo, and the Captain stopped singing and let them carry the tune while he played like a veteran Parisian street musician.

When they finished, the two women hopped up and down, hugged and clapped.

Simone radiated with joy. It was though the weight of the world had temporarily taken off her shoulders.

"Merci beaucoup, mon capitaine. One more *en Français, s'il vous plait."*

"Okay. Rob, you'll recognize this tune. It was one Bobby Darin's greatest hits. But Charles Trenet, a Frenchman, wrote the original. It is called, 'La Mer,' (The Sea)."

He put the concertina back on the shelf and went back to the piano. I'd played the chords to Darin's hit song many times, so when he started, I followed right along.

"La mer, qu'on voit danser le long des golfes clairs...(The sea, we see dancing along the shores of clear bays)."*

This time Simone did not hesitate as she and Melanie took over the lyrics while the Captain and I just smiled and played. At the end of the song, we all clapped and complemented each other's talents. I emptied the carafe, into our four glasses.

I offered to go for the third bottle, but Simone declared she had something better. She went to the kitchen and returned with a bottle of champagne. As she popped the cork we heard a sharp noise coming from the bay windows surrounding the piano.

Two people were waving at us from outside. I did a double-take and realized who it was.

"It's Andrew and his girlfriend, Kaneli."

"Melanie, go to the front door and call them to come around," Simone said.

I waved out at them, pointed to my right, and mouthed instructions to go around to the front door.

Small rivulets of rainwater were dripping off the large plastic garbage bags they had fashioned into makeshift rain slickers. They stripped them off as Melanie invited them inside. Except for their faces and hair, they were surprisingly dry.

Kaneli gave me a big hug. "How ya doing, mate?" she said.

"I'm doing great. But you two are crazy for going out in this storm," I replied.

Then I turned to Melanie and quickly introduced her to Kaneli.

"It is pleasure to meet you Kaneli, " she said embracing her and giving her a kiss on each cheek. Then she did the same to Andrew, adding. "It's about time you brought Kaneli to meet us."

"Come into the parlor, we're singing away the weather."

As we entered the parlor, Simone was returning from the kitchen with a second bottle of champagne and two more glasses.

"*Bienvenue*, welcome," she said. "You are very brave to be out in weather like this," she said.

After Andrew introduced Kaneli to Simone and the Captain, he explained that they wanted to see if we were okay.

"We were at the New Orleans when the power went out. Most of the crew, including Reyes was there. He told us that he'd dropped you off before the storm hit. When it let up a little while ago, we decided to make sure you were all safe," Andrew explained.

"The club owner, Cam, gave us some plastic bags to wear and had her busboy drive us over here in his little jitney. It's still raining, but there's no wind and the bags kept us pretty dry," he added.

The champagne flowed and the party continued until we'd exhausted most of the songs about wind and rain that we could remember, including "Rhythm of the Rain" by the Cascades, "Early Morning Rain" by Peter, Paul, and Mary and "Raindrops" by Dee Clark.

When we ran out of words, the Captain played Vince Guaraldi's "Cast Your Fate to the Wind."

As the Captain finished his number, I took Melanie's hand and led her out to the covered part of the patio, out of sight of the parlor.

"I just had the sudden need to kiss you," I explained as I put my arms around her and pulled her close.

She returned my kiss. "I was hoping you'd come to that conclusion a little earlier. Sing-alongs are great, but I reached my limit an hour ago."

I was more than a little drunk and felt deliriously happy.

I attempted to pull her out from under the overhang. "I think we should dance in the rain." She resisted, but I began the appropriate the tune.

"*Do, do, do do…I'm singin' in the rain, just singin' in the rain. What a glorious feeling I'm happy again…*"

Doing my best to dance like Gene Kelly, I did a few soft-shoe steps, reached for her hand, twirled her where she stood, then pulled her out into the rain with me at the very end of the spin.

"I'm laughin' at clouds, so dark up above, the sun's in my heart and I'm ready for love…"

She stood scrunched up for a few seconds, wiping the rain out of her face with her hands, then shrugged, grabbed my hand and joined me as we ate,[ted a poor shuffling imitation of Kelly's steps across the wet pavers.

The patio door swung open and Andrew and Kaneli joined us, then the Captain and Simone stepped out.

We became six crazy drunks singing as loud as we could, dancing, twirling and stomping as the rain continued to fall.

"Well, that's a new way to end a perfect evening," the Captain said.

"I should remind you, Rob and Andrew, that we have a situation meeting tomorrow at 0900 hours in the wardroom," he added.

"Oh God. I forgot," I declared.

"Me too," Andrew added. "How in the heck are we going to get back to ship at this hour?"

"You are not going anywhere tonight. I have several extra guest rooms and you and Kaneli can have your pick," Simone said, swaying slightly and slurring her words. She was as far gone as the rest of us.

"Not to worry. Reyes is picking us up here at 0830," the Captain announced.

Melanie took my hand and led me toward the stairs.

"Andrew and Kaneli, follow us. I'll show you where the guest rooms are," she declared.

Once we directed them to their room, Melanie and I returned to hers, quickly undressed, and made passionate, but somewhat clumsy, love before falling soundly asleep in each other's arms.

24

Our First Farewell
●●●●●●●●●●●●●●●●●●●●●●●

A NDREW AND I WERE BOTH surprised to find our civilian clothes from the night before dry and folded on chairs inside our rooms. We got up just in time to throw them on and head out the front door with the Captain.

Neither Simone nor Kaneli were there to wish us a good day. I know Melanie was still sound asleep in her bedroom.

Reyes was bright and cheerful as he opened the door for the Captain. Andrew jumped into the shotgun seat and I got in the back with the C.O., who also looked bright and clear-eyed. Such was not the case with Andrew and me.

"That was quite a storm last night," Reyes declared.

Nobody replied.

Finally, the Captain spoke. "How did the ship handle it?" he asked.

"No problems Captain. The XO and Harry made sure everything was tied down and we put out extra lines to the pier as you ordered."

"Good. It wasn't a typhoon – just one of those fast-moving squalls that come down the South China Sea. They can be nasty, but they usually don't last long," the Captain replied.

The car pulled up on the pier near the ship and the Captain got out first, leaning back into the car, where Andrew and I were trying not to throw up, he said, "You boys don't look so good. I think you should get some breakfast before our meeting starts."

"Aye, aye, Captain," we both managed to blurt out before following him up the gangway to the ship.

It was one of the days that are best filed away as reminders of what not to do when you're having so much fun that you don't keep track of what you're drinking. It's a shame, but resolutions that begin with "Never again," never seem to last.

The meeting, as best as I can recall, was a review of the engine repair (not quite done yet), watch schedule announcements, and concert plan updates, the latter of which I remembered I was supposed to announce.

"Binh. You and Andrew are supposed to meet with Master Lu at his school today at 1530 hours," I said. "And bring your music."

Andrew managed to groan out an okay.

"Do you have directions to his school?" Binh asked.

"It's next to that Buddhist temple a few blocks from downtown," I said, surprised that Binh didn't know his way around Vung Tau.

"There are at least four Buddhist temples here in Vung Tau," Binh said.

"Okay. I don't even know the name of the street. If we take the ship's car, I can find it by starting from the General's Daughter." I still felt drunk and desperately needed a nap.

The XO confirmed that neither Andrew nor I had the watch. We agreed to meet at the car at 1500 hours. I would drive them to their appointment and back.

After the meeting was adjourned, I was looking forward to sleeping off my hangover. Just then O.J. handed me a sealed envelope marked "Secret."

"This came in an hour ago. I need it decrypted ASAP."

As Communications Officer, I was also the ship's "Crypto Officer," one of only two on board capable of decoding a highly classified message by means of a special crypto machine that looked like a clunky cross between an electric typewriter and a multi-key Burroughs calculator. Learning to use it had been a significant part of my post-OCS training at Newport's Navy Communications School.

The crypto machine was locked in the "Crypto safe," which was a space smaller than a closet inside the locked radio room. Nobody with claustrophobia could ever have made it as a Navy Communications officer.

I had to lock myself into the tiny, stuffy, airtight space and breath my own toxic hangover breath while trying to concentrate on de-coding the message. It was a tedious process of reading a long series of random numbers, then feeding them, one at a time, into the machine.

Regulations required me to keep the door locked while I did this. I couldn't stick my head out to catch a breath of fresh air.

Fortunately it wasn't a long message, but still took more than an hour to decode. I managed without throwing up. The bad news was the message itself.

"Urgent. When operational, immediately proceed to Da Nang to relieve USS *Gerald County* for operation resupply Cua Viet. Recommend gunnery drills en route. *Gerald County* was severely damaged in an attack at Cua Viet."

There were a few more details, but essentially it meant that we were leaving Vung Tau as soon as our engine was repaired.

I delivered the message to O.J. who took it to the Captain and XO.

As I was staggering down the passageway toward my stateroom, I heard Harry tell the XO that he expected to have both engines ready to test by early the next morning.

That meant we'd be leaving for the northernmost part of South Vietnam shortly after dawn, assuming the engines checked out.

Such a plan required a flurry of activity from the engineering and deck crews in preparation for our departure.

Harry was rousing Andrew from his bunk, telling him to get his ass moving while I rolled into mine and pulled a pillow over my head to shut out Andrew's groans of dismay.

I slept through lunch and only woke up when Reyes shook me awake at 1400.

"Mr. Allen. I saved some lunch for you and then you've got to drive Mr. Cohen and Mr. Hoang to the music school," he said. "And the Captain wants to speak with you before you go," he added.

He'd washed, dried and laid out my one good set of civvies. I took a quick shower, changed, and went to see the Captain.

"Rob. You know our orders. If the engines work, we'll be out of here tomorrow morning. But I'm going to give Binh a special assignment to remain here while we're up north."

"Yes, sir. Do you have an idea of how long that will be?"

"We could be back here by Christmas, but more likely by New Year's Day," he replied. "But, Binh needs to stay here and work with Master Lu and Sister Josephine to get the musicians ready by mid-January."

"Yes, sir," I said, wondering why Binh wasn't in on our conversation."

"I need you to ask Master Lu, if Binh could stay with him while we're gone. And for a number of reasons, including the fact that we cannot tell civilians about our ship's movements, it must be confidential. I'm exceeding my authority by assigning Binh to stay here while we're gone. He's supposed to be a liaison to our ship. But, if the concert is going to come off by January 15, he has to stay," he concluded.

"Yes, sir. I think Master Lu will agree to any reasonable request from us," I said, and then added. "It would help if Binh had some kind of official document that looked like orders. The more official jargon the better. We could type it on Navy letterhead with lots of numbers and abbreviations that no civilian would ever understand. That way, if he ever gets questioned by Vietnamese authorities he has something to show."

"Good idea. Talk to O.J. and the XO. They should be able to cook up something that looks official but is mostly bullshit. We can give that to Binh before we depart in the morning."

"Aye, aye, Captain," I said, and then asked. "Does Binh know?"

"He will in five minutes. He's on his way to see me now."

I passed Binh in the corridor as I left the CO's office.

"I'll see you down at the car in a half hour," I said.

"Thanks, Rob," he answered then knocked on the Captain's doorframe.

I found O.J. and the XO and relayed the Captain's order about creating fake official papers for Binh.

Twenty minutes later I had the orders in hand and found Andrew and Binh in the wardroom reviewing parts of the score of the Mekong Suite.

"Okay, guys. Let's get going."

I drove through the base gate and headed along the route that I knew would take us to the General's Daughter.

"You're going to go in with us and ask Master Lu about Binh staying there, right?" Andrew asked.

"Yes. How do you feel about that idea, Binh?"

"If Master Lu will take me in and work with me, it will be a great privilege and honor," he replied.

"You'll also be working with Sister Josephine at the orphanage. In fact, the Captain is going to meet with her today and make sure that the three of you set up whatever practice sessions are necessary to keep the project moving forward," I said.

"I never imagined that I would have such an opportunity. I'm very grateful to all of you for what you are doing."

Without the distraction of a storm, finding the Buddhist temple and Master Lu's residence was easy. Hanh, his daughter, greeted us.

"My father is still teaching the music group. He asked that I show you in so you could listen and observe," she said.

We followed her through the house, out to the interior courtyard and around to the classroom from which lovely music was emanating, interesting, but alien to my ear.

There were ten children of various ages arrayed in a semicircle around Master Lu who was sitting on a low stool, his head cocked to one side, one hand rhythmically swaying back and forth. Occasionally he would point to a specific student, indicating that he or she should do something, but I wasn't sure what.

The one thing that I understood was that the children were accomplished on their instruments. The girl who had been so forward at our dinner previously looked at me and smiled.

Without acknowledging our presence, Master Lu continued running the group through various numbers. When he finished and stood up, he said something to them, and they all stood and bowed toward us. He finally turned, bowed, then came forward smiling and extended his hand, first to Binh, then Andrew, and finally to me.

"It is so nice to meet you Binh and Andrew, and to see you again Rob," he said.

Turning back to the children, he dismissed them, but several stayed, staring and trying to catch some of the conversation.

Binh turned toward them and said something in Vietnamese that made them smile and bow again.

"I told them that I enjoyed their playing very much and that they are excellent musicians," he said.

"Please, let's all go into the house for tea and more conversation. I see you brought your composition. I'm so glad," Master Lu said, pointing in the direction of the house.

After we all sat down, Hanh served tea and then joined us. I asked how they were after the storm.

"It frightened the younger children, so we invited them to bring their bedding into our room and spend the night with us. For them it became a party. There was lots of talking and whispering before I got them to settle down and sleep. But all went well and we had no damage," Hanh said.

"Before you discuss the music with Binh and Andrew, our Captain has asked me to ask you for a big favor," I said looking first at Hanh and then at Master Lu.

"Our ship must leave tomorrow for an extended period, perhaps four or five weeks. While Binh has been assigned to our ship as a liaison officer, our Captain would like to temporarily assign him to stay in Vung Tau and continue to work on his suite with you and Sister Josephine and your students. But he needs a place to stay."

"But of course. he must stay here with us," Master Lu interjected. "We have an extra bedroom and he is most welcome." Hanh nodded her agreement.

"That is most kind of you Master Lu. I would consider it a great privilege," Binh said.

"Thank you very much. Your hospitality will ensure that our plans for the concert will move forward, even in our absence," I said. "Now, I have to go back to the ship and pick up the Captain. Our next visit will be with Sister Josephine."

I excused myself, leaving Andrew and Binh to discuss the music.

The next two hours were a blur of activity. I returned to the ship. The Captain and Reyes came down the gangway as I pulled up. Reyes was carrying Binh's duffel, all packed and ready to throw into the car.

He took over driving. The Captain asked me to go with him to see Sister Josephine.

"We won't be there long. She's already agreed to the idea. I want to confirm with her that Binh and Master Lu will contact her regarding joint rehearsals and other details. I'm going to ask Melanie to help coordinate between the two," he said.

"That sounds like a good plan. So we'll be dropping by the General's Daughter too then?" I asked.

"Yes. I want to firm up some details with both Simone and Melanie. It will give us a chance to tell them we're going to be gone for a while. We can't tell them where or why, but at least they'll know we intend to return. And we really need their help to keep the concert on track while we're gone."

Our visit with Sister Josephine was short and to the point. She was a woman used to setting schedules and sticking to them and had already anticipated the need to coordinate between Binh, Master Lu, and herself.

"I will walk over to Master Lu's studio tomorrow. I've always wanted to visit that Buddhist temple and observe his music program. This will be the perfect opportunity. He, Binh and I can work out a plan. Don't worry Captain. We will keep our concert on schedule," she said confidently.

He thanked the nun and then we drove over to the General's Daughter where we found Simone and Melanie supervising the last of the clean up after the storm and the re-positioning of the tables and chairs in the dining area.

This time, neither of us was shy about embracing and kissing our sweethearts.

Simone asked if we could stay for a glass of wine and visit for a little bit.

"Yes. I need to tell you something and then ask you for help," the Captain said.

We followed Simone to a private nook in the dining area, and she asked one of her staff to bring us some wine.

Once it was served, the Captain announced that our ship had

to leave on a special assignment in the morning and that we might be gone for as long as five or six weeks.

I saw the look of concern on both their faces, but they remained silent.

"We need your help in keeping the benefit concert on track for our tentative January 15 date," the Captain added.

"Are you certain that you will return by then?" Simone asked.

"In the middle of a war I can't be certain of anything, especially when I and my ship have to go wherever the Navy orders us to," he answered. "But it appears that we should be back here sometime in early January, if not before. That is as much as I can tell you."

He reviewed the various things he hoped Simone and Melanie would supervise, including checking on Binh and making sure he, Master Lu and Sister Josephine had worked out a schedule.

"There are lots of other logistical details to work out, including where the orchestra will set up, how big a stage we will need. Will we serve food, drinks, and so on," the Captain said.

"*Mon cher*. I can do this. You have given me a task for which I am most suited. You must go where the Navy sends you. When you return, we will be ready to host a most beautiful concert," Simone responded.

Melanie nodded, then stood and reached for my hand. "Come walk with me for a few moments before you go," she said, a tone of resignation in her voice.

She led me around the corner of the building into a secluded part of the garden. A bench provided a place to sit.

"I will miss you," she said.

"I hate to leave now. All I can think about is you and how much I want to be with you – falling asleep with you in my arms and waking up to find you still there. It hurts to know how much I will miss that," I replied.

"Hurt is what we both understood would come from our impossible situation," she answered.

"I know. Duty has never been so hard to accept. But, I'm coming back," I said.

"Yes. This time. But for how long? One day you'll be gone and you won't be coming back," she said.

"I've been thinking about that a lot. I won't be in the Navy forever. We need to talk about what is possible once my obligation is finished," I said.

She looked into my eyes, a dead serious expression on her face.

"Yes. We will. But consider this: When is my obligation finished?"

She kissed me before I could offer any reply, then stood, took my hand and led me back to where the Captain and Simone were standing near the front door.

We embraced and kissed once more. Then the Captain and I walked back to the car. The two most important women in our lives watched us from the porch.

25

Victory at Sea
●●●●●●●●●●●●●●●●●●●●●●●

A FTER MORE THAN A MONTH in the bays and rivers of the Mekong Delta, the ship's rolling motion in the South China Sea took some readjustment. At our average speed of slightly less than ten knots, it would take us the better part of three days to get to Da Nang. The *Bell County* left Vung Tau Bay just after dawn.

I was standing the midnight to 0400 watch. The engines were running smoothly and the weather was calm and clear. Our course took us northeast, then due north following the coast of Vietnam. We were far enough off shore to avoid shoals and rocks, but close enough to see the land and mark our progress on the chart.

There were a lot of ships operating off the coast of Vietnam in 1967, many were U.S. Navy, while many more were commercial vessels bringing in supplies paid for by the U.S. All of them displayed navigational lights and were easy to spot and avoid.

Our naval and air power outmatched anything that the Viet Cong had in the way of boats. There was almost no chance that they would risk attacking a Navy ship in the open sea. They were too exposed with far too little firepower.

My main concerns on watch were the many small, unlit, fishing boats that the Vietnamese used to make a living.

It wasn't our ship we were worried about. It was their safety. A collision with us would most assuredly sink their boat and throw them into the water. At night, it would be a difficult rescue.

I felt certain that the fishermen didn't like risking their lives to eke out a living in the overcrowded shipping lanes caused by the war. But they had no choice. The least we could do was not run them over. That's why we didn't cruise at top speed and posted extra lookouts on the bow to watch for small boats.

Daytime watches were far more relaxing. Rehearsals for the ship's show were held every day in the crew's mess. I even had time to read the book the X.O. had loaned me.

The Captain's decision to hold gunnery practice interrupted our quiet routine.

It was prompted by a second secret message I decoded and delivered to him after we left Vung Tau. It disclosed that the LST we were relieving had been unloading ammunition and gasoline on the ramp at the mouth of the Cua Viet River, virtually on the DMZ, when an enemy artillery round hit their main deck, ignited the gasoline, and caused several shells to explode.

Three sailors were wounded and the ship's main deck was badly damaged.

He called us into the wardroom for a meeting. "We're sailing into harm's way, and we need to be ready. Gunnery practice starts tomorrow."

"Our target is all set up, Captain," Harry said.

He and Chief Mick had rigged a target of wooden boxes and pallets lashed together with rope and made to resemble a small boat. They sandwiched an old inflated weather balloon between two more pallets to create a partial cabin on top of the other pieces of wood. It was ugly, but they guaranteed it would float long enough for the ship's gunners to blow it to bits.

Harry added a finishing touch by painting a bright smiley face on the balloon.

Each drill began with the ship cruising at regular conditions. Then, the Officer of the Deck sounded General Quarters. Everyone went to their assigned battle stations. It was a test to see how fast and how efficiently we could be ready for combat. We had been at GQ on several occasions in the rivers, so getting to our battle stations went smoothly.

Everything was good until the shooting started.

Just before the drill began, the chief put the makeshift target in the water.

Then the ship made a slow, 360-degree turn so that we approached the target from behind with it off our starboard side and so that we'd be shooting away from land. The alarm sounded. O.J., the OOD, barked through the PA system, "General Quarters, General Quarters, All Hands Man Your Battle Stations!"

My station was on the bridge with the Captain and O.J., so I had a perfect view of what happened next.

Within minutes of going to GQ, all of the guns were manned and reported that they'd spotted the target off the starboard quarter.

"Commence firing!" the Captain ordered.

LST's were not designed to be fighting ships. They were supposed to carry tanks, trucks and other vehicles and troops to the beach, drop them off, and then go back for more.

The 40mm guns originally installed on them were intended to defend against air attacks, the theory being that if you put enough hot lead in the air, you're bound to hit something. The bluewater Navy ships, like cruisers, and destroyers had a lot more guns and well-trained gunners.

Fighting ship or not, the *Bell County* had its guns trained on the target that Chief Mick and Harry had thrown overboard. It was a virtual "sitting duck."

The 40mm gun crews opened a continuous salvo in the general direction of the target. In addition, the two .50-caliber machine guns on the starboard side of the main deck also commenced firing, as did the .30-caliber machine gun on the starboard side of the bridge.

The noise was deafening. The water all around the target was turned into a boiling froth. But, the ugly duckling not more than 200 yards off our starboard side continued to bob along.

The Captain kept looking at it through his binoculars, then toward the gunners, then back at the target, then shook his head.

"Shit! Cease fire! Cease fire!" he yelled in disgust.

The silence was a relief.

"O.J., turn this damn ship around and let's get into position to let the port side gunners have a shot," he ordered.

The ship made a slow 180-degree turn so that the next pass by the target would allow our port side guns to fire.

When the forward port gunner reported that he saw the target, the Captain once again gave the order.

"Commence firing!"

If loud noises could sink things, the target would have been at the bottom of the South China Sea twice over. But noise alone wouldn't do it, and the makeshift target that Harry and Chief Mick had crafted survived volley after volley.

By that time, the Captain's anger had turned to deadly resolve.

"O.J., close to fifty yards and blow that fucking thing out of the water," he ordered.

The starboard gunners didn't miss. When the cease-fire order came, only scattered pieces of wood were left, one of which was still tethered to a shredded piece of weather balloon.

The musically inclined *Bell County* crew started humming the theme song arranged by Richard Rogers for *Victory At Sea*, a popular TV documentary series about World War II. The ship's quartermaster had a recording of the song on tape. Within thirty seconds it was playing all over the ship through the PA system.

Around the wardroom dinner table that evening all present were waiting for the Captain to say something about the drill. When he didn't, Harry decided to speak up.

"You know how in World War II our fighter pilots used to paint zeros, or swastikas on their planes for each one they shot down? Maybe we could have Ortega paint a picture of our sitting duck on the starboard gun mount."

Nobody dared laugh or say anything. We all looked at the Captain for a response.

Finally, he looked up from his plate and spoke. "You know Harry. I have a better idea. Tomorrow, we're going to put you in a lifejacket and give you a really big sign to hold after we throw you overboard."

"What will the sign say, Captain?" the XO asked, playing along.

"There will be a giant bull's-eye and the words 'This is the Safest Target in Vietnam.'"

Then he continued. "And, if by some miracle, one of our gunners hits the sign; then, and only then, will I have Ortega paint something on our gun mount. "It will be a wonderful likeness of the ship's engineering officer," he declared

"Thank you, Captain. I'd be honored," Harry replied.

The Captain shook his head and laughed. We all joined him.

"The good news is our gunners can defend us against an attack. The bad news is that we'll need to wait until they're fifty yards away before we shoot," the Captain added.

Laughing at our poor gunnery performance was a lot like whistling past a graveyard. None of us were happy about going to a place where shells could drop out of the sky without warning onto our ship while it was loaded with ammunition and fifty-five—gallon drums of gasoline.

Nevertheless, that's where the Navy was sending us.

* * *

The bustling port of Da Nang was many times busier than the one in Vung Tao. Scores of merchant ships were anchored in the harbor waiting to be offloaded. There were also a large number of U.S. Navy ships as well as some smaller boats that were part of the brown-water Navy.

In addition, we had to avoid running over sampans manned by fishermen arrayed across our ship's course by the dozens. While weaving our way through them, we received orders over the radio to proceed directly to the loading ramp at the Navy base.

Once there, the Captain, XO, and OJ left for a briefing by the commander of the U.S. naval Support Activity, Da Nang. It was the Navy's largest overseas shore command, supplying more than 200,000 U.S., Vietnamese, and allied forces in the I-Corps Tactical Zone (the northern most combat zone in South Vietnam).

There was no question of our putting on a musical show in Danang. It was an all-business, move-it-or-lose-it place. As soon as our bow doors were open, several forklifts started loading us with the ammunition, food, gasoline and other supplies we would carry ninety nautical miles north to Cua Viet.

By late afternoon we were fully loaded and had our orders to proceed north immediately.

The Captain briefed us after dinner.

"The base just inside the mouth of the Cua Viet River is on the DMZ. It is a trans-shipment point, meaning they take what we unload there, put it on smaller boats, like LCU's (Landing Craft Utility) and ferry it upriver to Marine and Army bases further inland."

He paused and opened a chart that showed the section of the coast closest to the Cua Viet River as well as the river entrance itself. Pointing to a spot just offshore, he outlined our approach.

"There are shoals here, here and here, and the sand bar in front of the mouth is always shifting. On top of that, if it's foggy or cloudy, the North Vietnamese lob in artillery and mortar rounds hoping to land a lucky shot like they did with the *Gerald County*. They prefer bad weather because it is easier for them to fire their guns without us seeing where the shots are coming from."

"What do we do when they start shooting?" O.J. asked.

"All hands will wear flak-jackets and helmets. All guns will be manned while we are there.

"If shooting starts while we are already committed and crossing the bar, or beached out and unloading, there isn't much we can do. There's no way we can maneuver in that narrow space, and we can't retract from the beach and move out quickly either."

"Can we shoot back?" Harry said.

"If we can see where the attack is coming from, yes. But most likely we won't have a clue," the Captain replied.

"Damn, just when we were getting really good," Harry replied, causing everyone around the table to laugh.

26

Best DMZ Beach Party Ever

●●●●●●●●●●●●●●●●●●●●●●

A S THE SUN ROSE THE next morning, all of us were happy to see a bright, clear day. Before making our approach to the river mouth, the Captain put experienced crews in both of our LCVPs (landing craft) and lowered them into the water. Should we get stuck in the sand they could serve as our tugboats.

As it turned out, they weren't needed. The *Bell County*'s passage into the river went smoothly. Once inside, we made a turn to port and slowly put the ship's bow on the ramp the Seabees constructed on the Cua Viet sand. We ran our engines as though underway in order to keep the ship firmly on the ramp and counter the force of the current from upstream pushing against the side of the ship. One of the LCVPs was assigned to push on the port side of our stern to help keep us perpendicular to the shore.

The sailors driving the forklifts were speed demons. They didn't want to spend any more time than necessary handling gasoline drums and live ammunition in a zone that had been shelled repeatedly.

The base commander and his XO came aboard and the Captain invited them for lunch. He used the opportunity to explain our additional mission and asked if they'd consider allowing us to put on a show on the ramp after off-loading.

"If you don't mind the possibility that at any second a shitload of artillery shells could rain down on your band. I'm sure our troops would appreciate the diversion. They're used to the attacks and are always prepared to hunker down."

The Captain and XO suggested that it would be best to wait for our second or third trip, allowing time to get the word out, and for us to work out what we would do in the event of an attack in the middle of a show.

"Are the attacks coming from the other side of the DMZ or are they actually close to your base?" our XO asked.

"Mostly from guns in North Vietnam. They're have been a few attempted sneak attacks from small mortar teams closer to us, but even they were firing blindly. We always have Huey gunships in the air and there are Navy jets available at a moment's notice. It keeps them from exposing themselves and zeroing in."

The offloading of our ship was completed in less than two hours. The Captain backed us off the ramp, made the tight turn toward the sea with little room to spare, and we were on our way back to Da Nang. The next ten days passed quickly. We repeated the round-trip shuttle between Cua Viet and Da Nang a second time without incident, celebrating Thanksgiving cruising north on the South China Sea.

Freddie, our cook, had managed to find enough turkeys to feed the crew, adding mashed potatoes, gravy, cranberry sauce and sliced apples to our plates. There was also lots of meat left over for turkey sandwiches.

It was a foggy morning, with gradually improving visibility, as we made our third approach to the mouth of the Cua Viet River. This was going to be the day we would put on our show. Freddie had cooked enough turkey to serve for lunch for all the troops who might attend. The plan was to offload quickly then set up the bandstand in front of the loading ramp, start the show, and open the chow line two minutes after the last number.

We had just lowered the LCVPs and the crew was on station for maneuvering toward the river mouth.

"*Barrumpf!*" A large explosion shook the ship.

"That wasn't the engine blowing," O.J. said.

From the bridge we saw a small mushroom cloud emerge from behind the sand dunes near the base. A series of loud explosions continued. They were coming from an area 100 yards south of the ramp. It was where ammunition was stored inside a five-foot-high stack of sandbags. It didn't appear that the base was being shelled, but the explosions in the ammo dump continued.

The Captain ordered a sharp turn to starboard away from the beach and then repositioned us at dead slow several hundred yards from the river mouth. The fog lifted enough that we could see flames and smoke. More disturbing, were what appeared to be the bodies of at least a half-dozen sailors lying face down in the sand between the surf line and where the explosions had occurred.

"O.J., call Doc to the bridge," the Captain ordered.

"Aye, aye, Captain. Corpsman Hodges to the bridge," O.J. said over the PA.

Just as Hodges stepped onto the bridge and saluted the Captain, another large explosion went off causing all of our knees to buckle. The body count on the beach had gone up by two. We now saw eight sailors.

"Doc, we need to see if any of those sailors are alive, and if they are, we need to do what we can for them."

"Aye, aye, Captain," Doc responded.

"Lew, you and Rob both have had advanced first aid training. I want you to go with Doc and see what you can do for those men."

There was no new explosions, but I felt my knees buckle anyway. I was being sent in the exact opposite direction I wanted to go; all because I happened to take first aid courses while serving as a volunteer firefighter for two summers.

The Captain asked, "Doc, can you throw together two more quick first aid packs for the XO and Mr. Allen?"

"Yes, sir. I can have them ready in two minutes," Doc answered.

"Great. Make it so. We'll order the LCVP's to the starboard side and let down the rope ladder so you can get onboard. We have several stretchers in the hold. I'll have the chief send those down to the boats too."

The ship was rocking in the waves just outside the surf line. It made climbing down the rope ladder an adventure. But that was the least of my worries.

The XO told the lead boat driver to beach our boats a hundred yards down the beach from the eight prone sailors. Each of us would be accompanied by two stretcher-bearers. We'd make our way toward the explosion area, staying as far back in the surf as we could without floundering.

Once we were opposite the bodies, we would stay low and approach each to see if they were alive or seriously wounded. Using the first aid items in the packs Doc had given us, we would treat them as best we could, get them onto a stretcher and take them back to the boats.

There had been no additional explosions coming from the ammo dump, but lots of flames and smoke were visible rising above the sandbags. Bent over, we stayed as far out in the surf as we could while still being able to run forward.

Doc took the first body, the XO pointed me to the next, and he continued toward a third. As I approached the prone sailor, I told the two stretcher-bearers to stay back at the waterline while I checked to see if they were needed. The closer I got to the heat and flames, the lower I got, until I crawled the last thirty feet.

When I got next to the sailor I reached out and touched his shoulder.

He jumped. "What the fuck!" I heard him shout as he twisted his neck to look at me.

"You scared the shit out of me, man." He was black and looked no older than eighteen. His face was covered in wet sand, but there was no blood that I could see. He spotted the officer's bars on my collar.

"Oh shit. Sorry, sir."

"Don't worry about it, sailor. Were you hit? Are you hurt?"

"No, sir. I'm just staying low. I don't want my ass to get shot off," he replied, still staying scrunched down in the shallow hole he had dug for himself in the sand.

"Good. We've got a boat a little ways down the beach. If we both make like crabs and back our way down to the surf line we can get you to a safer spot," I said.

"If it's okay with you, sir. I think I'll say right here."

"Suit yourself. I've got to go see if any of your buddies are as lucky as you."

Just then another round cooked off inside the inferno.

"Sir, wait. I changed my mind, I would like to take your boat out of here," he shouted.

"Okay. Follow me. Stay on your belly and crawl backward."

When we got to the water I got to my knees and pointed toward the boat. "Stay low and go there. Tell the sailor in charge that Ensign Allen sent you.

"Aye, aye, Mr. Allen, and thanks."

I saw that Doc and the XO were also talking to two sailors kneeling in the surf, apparently unhurt.

I kept low, making my way toward them.

"Not a scratch on either of them," Doc said.

"Mine neither," I said.

The three of us made our way to the next bodies in line. They, too, were uninjured, and had simply dug in to avoid being hit by flying shrapnel.

Within thirty minutes, we had all eight sailors in our boats.

None of them had suffered a scratch. We radioed our situation to the Captain and were ordered to return to the ship. When we got back on board, the Captain informed us that he'd finally reached the base commander on the radio. He urged us not to send any more rescue missions.

Eventually the fire died, the ammunition cooled, and the explosions stopped. Not a single sailor or Marine was wounded. The base CO's account indicated that several mortar rounds had been fired into the base. One of them landed in the middle of the ammunition dump. All of the men on shore did as they were trained to do, find shelter and stay there until the shrapnel stopped flying. Nobody was near any shell that exploded.

Once we got to the ramp and started unloading, we took a lot of ribbing from the shore guys for our "rescue." Underneath all the joking around, we could tell they were grateful that we risked our necks believing they needed rescue. We made many friends on the beach that day. Unfortunately, our show and picnic were postponed to the next trip.

We were told that fighting further inland from Cua Viet had intensified, which also increased the need for more supplies. We spent the next three weeks ferrying one load after another from Da Nang to Cua Viet, hoping to find the right time for one show and picnic day on the beach. Everybody in our crew was exhausted from tension and fear that any moment a shell would drop on us. When we finally got the bright and clear day that made a surprise attack unlikely, we let it all hang out.

Hotdogs, beans, cookies, and lots of free beer were served while the show went on. The Captain agreed to allow a new act to be added, appropriate to the beach setting. Two sailors in the operations department and two others on the deck crew had formed a group they called the "Sons of Beaches." The drummer, a Korean-American from L.A., was the lead singer. One of the radiomen from my department played lead guitar, and a second played bass. The other deckhand played rhythm guitar. Three of the four were Californians and the fourth was from New Jersey. They all loved the Beach Boys and did great renditions of "Surfin' USA," "Little Deuce Coupe" and "All Summer Long."

It was chance for everyone on the base to blow off some steam and forget that they were in the middle of one of the most dangerous beaches in Southeast Asia. The only thing that stopped several rounds of encores was the falling light and the fact that we ran out of beer.

As we were reloading the bandstand, the base CO came over to where a group of us, including the Captain, were standing.

"That was one hell of a party. I can't tell you how much our guys appreciated it. You're the best thing that's happened here in months. Thank you," he said.

We all shook his hand and told him the truth – we loved doing it. The entire crew of the *Bell County*, musician or not, had taken its music mission to heart. Bringing joy to the guys most in harm's way brought joy to us. Of all the sailors, soldiers and marines sent to Southeast Asia, we were among the precious few who actually loved what they were doing there.

When we returned to Da Nang, the commander of the support mission informed us that the Gerald County was back in commission and ready to relieve us. We were ordered to return to Vung Tau and resume our resupply duties in the Mekong Delta.

27

Only in My Dreams
•••••••••••••••••••••••

W E SAILED OUT OF DA NANG harbor on December 22 bound for Vung Tau, with a scheduled stop in Cam Rahn Bay. The stop, just past halfway down the coast from Da Nang, was not originally in our orders, but the XO heard "reliable" scuttlebutt that the Bob Hope Show would be at the Cam Rahn Bay naval base on Christmas Eve.

Musical show junkie that he was, the Captain volunteered us to take a load of supplies to Cam Rahn Bay on our way south. We had a load of ammunition, food, beer, and other supplies in our hold for that base.

We passed through the dramatic narrow entrance to the bay early Christmas Eve morning. Beautiful green mountains rose steeply on three sides of the bay's deep, turquoise-blue water. Pristine beaches extended out from the emerald-colored jungle. Palm trees swayed in a light breeze and gentle waves washed back and forth on the white sand. It was beautiful.

If I had to be stranded on a tropical beach somewhere, this would be the place; except for the fact that somewhere in that dense jungle there were guys in black pajamas who could turn a day at the beach into hell in a matter of seconds.

One other small ship, a coastal patrol boat, was in the harbor. We tied up to a long pier. Except for a half dozen sailors waiting to catch our lines, the place looked deserted.

Because there wasn't much in the way of a shore crew, we used our own crane to move the loaded pallets from our hold to the pier.

While we offloaded our cargo, the Captain and XO asked one of the sailors on the pier to take them to the base CO. They got in a jeep with the sailor and disappeared up a narrow dirt road carved into the side of a steep, jungle-covered hill just 200 feet from the water.

They returned after several hours with bad news and good news.

The bad news was that the base CO had just gotten word that the Hope Show changed its itinerary at the last minute. Bob Hope was going to be in Da Nang for Christmas Eve, not Cam Ranh Bay.

"So what's the good news?" I asked.

"The base commander accepted our offer to put on a show, as long as we could do it on the pier," the XO said. "They'll supply the food, because we don't have nearly enough to feed the people at a base this large. We sort of saved his bacon. He'd planned a big dinner to go along with the show. And he was dreading the thought of telling his men that there was no show."

"So they will handle all the food service. All we have to do is the show?" O.J. asked.

"That's right. Their cooks will set up food service on the pier near our bandstand. All we have to do is put on the show," the X.O. said.

The gentle, grass-covered slope that ran along the pier provided a perfect seating area for our audience. Chief Mick and his team set up the bandstand between our ship and the hillside. It was a virtual natural amphitheater. The setting reminded me of the film of the musical *South Pacific*," starring Mitzi Gaynor and Rossano Brazzi.

The Captain held a meeting for the show in the ward room to work out the last-minute details. "We need to add something special to this show. It's Christmas Eve. These guys here were expecting a Bob Hope show, which includes comedy and beautiful women along with the music," he said.

"I agree, we're all too ugly to compete with that. Even our guys in drag leave a lot to be desired, no offense intended," Harry said. "We're damn good musicians, but not comedians."

"That's true for all of us, except you Harry," the Captain said. "You are our comedian."

"Me, sir? No way. I don't tell jokes. In fact, I'm not good at telling jokes. Wisecracks and funny asides are my specialty."

Andrew walked in during the exchange between the Captain and Harry, and sat down in the easy chairs, continuing to eavesdrop.

"Harry's right, though," Doc said. "They're expecting Hope and some jokes, and if Harry can't do it, I don't know who else can."

Somebody suggested Chief Mick might be able to open with a couple of his salty tales.

"We all laugh at the Chief's jokes, but that's because we understand him and his humor. I don't think it will work with the troops stationed here," the XO said.

Silence followed his comments for several seconds.

"I'll do it," Andrew said from his seat in the easy chair.

"You?" Harry exclaimed incredulously. "Do you know some good lines about what happens when Beethoven and Bach walk into a bar?"

"No, but that's not a bad start for a bit," Andrew replied.

"I have a little experience doing stand-up bits. I took a couple of acting classes at UCLA. One was taught by a professor who did stand-up comedy on the side. He was really good at accents and mimicking celebrities. He made us do our own stand-up routines as a way to get into character. He thought my stuff was pretty good," Andrew replied.

Everyone looked toward the Captain who had leaned back in his chair and was smiling up at the ceiling as though he knew something we all didn't.

"Thanks for volunteering Andrew. You're our opening act. Can you do five minutes?"

"Yes, sir."

"Okay then. Let's move on. I'd like to have our ship's choir lead everyone in some carols at the end of the show. But just before that, I'd like Archer's quartet to do "I'll Be Home for Christmas." It doesn't have to be doo-wop style. Just make it nice. Make sure they know the song, Reyes," the Captain ordered.

"Aye, aye, Captain," Reyes replied.

The meeting broke with everyone going about their various tasks.

Back in our stateroom, Andrew was busily scribbling notes on some three-by-five cards.

"Do you have a plan?" I asked him.

"I hope so," he said. There was a look of grim concentration on his face. "By the way, will you go ask the XO if I can borrow one of his golf clubs, preferably a driver? And, I need to borrow your San Francisco Giants baseball hat too."

As the afternoon shadows grew longer, I noticed that there were already small groups of guys sitting on the grassy slope facing the pier. With thirty minutes to go before show time, the whole area was full. There were more than 400 sailors, Marines and air-men on and around the pier. It was the largest audience we'd ever had.

I joined some of the other choir members standing to the side of the stage as the band members took their places.

Andrew walked onto the stage. He was wearing Harry's large horned-rimed glasses and my Giants hat, and carrying the XO's driver over his shoulder with one hand. In the other, he had his violin case. He pretended not to notice the audience at first, then, glancing to his left, he saw the crowd. Acting surprised, he stopped.

He spoke in a hesitant stuttering voice, squinting and peering out into the crowd. "Oh, hello. Perhaps you can help me. I'm looking for someone. Can you tell me where I might find a Mr. Hope? I think his first name is Bob?"

Everyone laughed.

"He's supposed to be a really good golfer. And I was hoping to get some tips."

He stopped, put down his violin case, and started fumbling around in his front pockets. "I hear you need a lot of balls to play here," he said.

More laughter.

"Maybe he went to DaNang to look for his balls," he added.

The crowd roared.

He slapped his forehead with his hand. "Oh! That's what the CO meant when he said the situation here was Hope-less."

The laughter continued.

"I'm new here. Just got in from New York City. The Navy recruiter asked me where I wanted to go. I told him Miami Beach or Hawaii would be nice; just somewhere with a lovely beach and warm weather in December.

"Am I in the right place?"

He got jeers, cheers, and more applause.

"In addition to looking for Mr. Hope's balls, the CO put me in charge of the base lost-and-found department. Do any of you know a Mr. Jack Benny?" He held up the violin case. A "Property of J. Benny" sticker was taped to it.

He made a show of opening up the case to see what was inside.

"Oh my! There's money in here. Two pennies, and a note. It reads: 'I will split the money with you if you return this violin. Best regards, J. Benny.'"

Andrew picked up the violin and bow and pretended to examine it closely. Then tried to play it. The sound was like a cat yowling.

He shook his head, and turned to the Captain who was seated at the piano on the side of the stage.

"Excuse me, sir. Can you help me?"

The Captain nodded and played a chord.

Andrew drew his bow across the violin, gradually bringing the sound in tune with the piano.

The Captain played another chord, which Andrew matched on the violin. Then another, and another, with Andrew matching each one. Gradually the tempo picked up and became a melody. Then, the rest of the band joined in and delivered a rousing rendition of the bluegrass classic "Fire on the Mountain." The most surprising thing to me about the number was Andrew playing the fiddle, something he vowed never to do.

The audience went wild, standing and stomping. Several sailors did do-se-does on the pier. When the number finally wound down and Andrew took his bow, everyone was standing, clapping and roaring with approval.

It was the best start to any show we'd ever done. Every act that followed got a warm reception. Then Archer and his quartet finished the show with "I'll Be Home for Christmas."

It began with Archer singing the first two bars a cappella, then the second singer picked up the next bars, and so on, through each singer. The Captain played piano softly for the final several bars.

Then, while the group hummed the tune in the background, Archer spoke to the audience.

"I know we'd all rather be home than here in Vietnam. Heck, we'd rather be anywhere but here. But that's just not possible today. So right here, right now, I like you all to stand up, close your eyes and join our ship's choir in another round of this song. And while you're singing with us, think of that special place in your heart where you want to be. And maybe, if only for a few seconds, together, we can all get there."

And so, on that warm night in one of the most dangerous places on the planet Christmas Eve 1967, 500 lonely, homesick sailors and soldiers sang together that sweet holiday song made famous by Bing Crosby.

Few eyes were dry by the time we finished.

While the base cooks served hot chow, Chief Mick handed out cold beers, from another one of those mysterious pallet accidents that happened on our way to Cam Ranh Bay. Naturally, we had no choice but to give it away, free, as long as it lasted.

I lost count of how many guys came up, shook our hands, and thanked us.

"You guys are fantastic."

"This was the best show I've ever been to."

"You made a really shitty Christmas a whole lot brighter, thank you."

Andrew was surrounded by admirers slapping him on the back, shaking this hand and complementing him. He seemed embarrassed by the attention.

The Captain, XO and Doc were sitting on the edge of stage sipping beers and enjoying the scene. I joined them.

"How did you get Andrew to play fiddle?" I asked him.

"I didn't. He already knew how. It was all part of the character for his bit. Andrew is a natural showman and has the talent to back it up."

"His whole act was amazing. Who knew he was such a natural?" I declared.

"Actually, one person did," the Captain said, putting his hand on the XO's shoulder. "Lew saw Andrew perform at UCLA and recognized him as the real thing. He never forgot, and when the time came, convinced me that we needed to make Andrew part of our merry band of music makers."

Harry chimed in. "Just look at all these guys. There's joy on their faces. Tomorrow or the next day they may be getting shot at or hunkered down in a bunker while mortars fall all around them. But right now it's Christmas Eve, we gave them a hell of a show, cold beer and hot food. They're as happy as anyone can be over here. That's why we love what we do. Merry Christmas everyone."

"Merry Christmas," we all said together.

28

The War Gets Personal
•••••••••••••••••••••••

B*ELL COUNTY* MADE GOOD TIME from Cam Ranh Bay.
By the morning of December 27 we were entering Vung Tau
Bay. The crew was at anchor stations and the ship was prepared to
make its mooring.

Suddenly, there was a loud thump from the stern of the ship.
Black smoke streamed out of the exhaust stack.

"Shit. Not again!" the Captain shouted in frustration.

Sure enough. In seconds the engine room had relayed the bad
news that the starboard engine had seized up.

We proceeded to our anchorage about a mile off the beach on
one engine. O.J. was already on the radio to the USS *Markab*, the
tender, talking to the officer charge of the engine repairs. We
dropped the anchor and shut down our one working engine. I had
the first watch; Archer was on the bridge with me. There were no
other ships moving on the bay. We were free to fill the time with
conversation.

"I'd like to listen in on what the Captain is saying about the
machinists who worked on our engine. He's as mad as I've ever
seen him," I said.

Archer nodded. "I heard Chief Mick and some of the guys in

engineering say that every time a ship breaks down, it's not good
for the Captain, because no matter what, it's his fault; even if it
was the machinists from the tender who fucked up."

"They're probably right. It goes on his record when his ship
fails to perform. It isn't fair, but it's the Navy's way," I said.

"The Captain's a good man," Archer said. "He knows his shit.
He's fair and he treats the crew, even the lowest-ranking seamen,
with respect. There's something wrong with a system that punishes
him when some other guy who's not even on his ship puts a part in
backward and fucks up the engine."

"He is a good man. And he probably won't get any credit for
all the goodwill and joy our shows have brought to the troops in
the outposts," I said.

"Which reminds me, Archer, you did a really great job with
'I'll Be Home for Christmas.' I liked it better the way you arranged
it than Bing Crosby's version."

"Thank you, sir," he replied.

Just then the XO came up to the bridge. We both snapped to
attention and saluted.

"As you were," the XO said, adding, " I have good news. The
pier is clear and we're going in right after lunch."

I felt bad for the Captain and guilty for the joy I felt about
being able to see Melanie so soon. It had been a long month
without her.

While the ship made its way to the pier gingerly on one engine,
the XO was calling the tender on the radio to request a meet with
its CO.

The commanding officer of a large ship like the *Markab* would
easily outrank the CO of any LST. The Captain's complaint about
the shoddy work on our engine would have to be tempered with a
considerable amount of tact. That was his afternoon's mission.

Harry and O.J. would be splitting most of the pier-side watches for the next forty-eight hours. The majority of the crew, myself included, was free to go on liberty.

Andrew was headed to the hospital to see if Kaneli was available. We talked about meeting later at the New Orleans Club, but left it tentative.

By 1700 hours, I was at the General's Daughter front door.

It was open and I could see the staff setting up for dinner. I walked out to the patio and saw Melanie placing vases with fresh flowers on each table.

She looked up as I came down the steps and gestured for me to come over to where she was standing.

As I got to her, she pointed to a hedgerow near the back of the patio and said sternly, "Go over there and get me two more vases."

"Aye, aye, Mademoiselle," I replied, perplexed but obedient.

I walked over to the hedge and looked behind them. There were no vases there. I was about to turn and ask her where I should look when she pushed me further into the shadows, threw her arms around my neck, and gave me a very long, sweet kiss.

"Where have you been? Someone saw your ship arrive three hours ago," she demanded, allowing me to catch my breath.

Still holding her body firmly against mine, I nibbled on her ear and whispered,

"I have this other job, which required my presence. In fact, my boss is still stuck there. No doubt your mother will be asking the same question of him."

"She's not nearly as impatient as I am," she replied, kissing me again.

"I am here now, my lady, at your disposal."

She broke our embrace and stood back.

"That's fine, but now I've got work to do. So go say hello to my mother and then find a seat in the bar, or take a walk. We will resume our conversation when I have time."

"Conversation?"

"Go!"

I found Simone Marquis in the restaurant kitchen talking to the head chef. She saw me, waved, then came over and greeted me with a kiss on each cheek.

"Rob, *mon cher, comment ca va?*"

"*Très bien, Simone, merci,*" I replied, then switched to English. "The Captain is tied up with some unexpected ship's business, but should be here in an hour or so."

"*Oui.* There is no hurry. He knows I am always busiest early in the evening. Thank you for telling me."

"Melanie is busy too. I'm going to walk over to Master Lu's school and see how Binh is doing. Please tell Melanie I'll be back in an hour or so."

"Of course," she said.

It was a pleasant walk to Master Lu's school. The quiet streets were shaded by large trees, which helped make the heat less oppressive.

When I arrived, I saw Binh, Hanh and Master Lu sitting around a small table in the open room facing their garden. Hanh looked up and saw me first.

"Rob! Welcome back!" she shouted.

Binh and Master Lu both waved, then indicted that I should join them.

"You're just in time," Binh said. We are going over the final changes to the score. How was your trip north?"

"Interesting and scary. There is a lot more fighting up there. I'm glad to be back with you and excited to learn how the music and the rehearsals with the children are going."

Binh and Master Lu each waited for the other to answer me.

Finally, Hanh, spoke up. "They're both being modest. They've been working night and day, and the results are promising. Sister

Josephine is also fully cooperating. The students from both schools have already played together three times, getting better each time. The children seem to love it, and are getting along very well."

"There is a lot to learn, especially for musicians so young. But their enthusiasm makes up for their lack of experience. They've learned more than half the suite already. I believe they will have it all mastered within three weeks," Master Lu stated.

Binh nodded his agreement.

"Three weeks is just about all we have before the concert," I pointed out.

"Yes. We were wondering about that. I believe Madam Marquis and Sister Josephine have been discussing January 15 as the actual date, but they were waiting for your Captain to return for final approval," Master Lu added.

"I think he was waiting to hear if the music and the children would be ready. He also needs final approval from Admiral Kirkpatrick, who wants to put out the word, and perhaps invite some diplomats," I replied

Hanh served tea and I listened as they tried to guide me through the suite's various parts.

"I've followed some of the patterns that Ferde Grofé used for his Mississippi Suite and the Grand Canyon Suite. The suite tells a musical story of the Mekong River from its origins on the high Tibetan Plateau all the way to the South China Sea. Elements of the music cover all the countries through which it runs, he said.

"I want the music to express how the river ties us all together. Even its name derives from several of our languages. It is the mother of water. It teems with life and ebbs and flows with the season," he added.

"It is a masterful piece. Binh has found his calling in creating Mekong Suite. I feel fortunate to be involved," Master Lu said.

"Without you, Master Lu, I could never have completed it. We have done this together and it is your work as much as mine," Binh said.

It was clear that Master Lu and Binh had formed a bond, much like a father and son. But it was Hanh who surprised me the most. She had obviously fallen in love with Binh, and her feelings appeared to be reciprocated.

I almost chuckled out loud to think that I'd played the role of a matchmaker for a couple from a country and culture so different from my own.

Binh's suite was a love story, a metaphor about how we are all connected, and our need to love and be loved is as natural and constant as the flow of the river that connects all the people of Southeast Asia. At that moment I felt true affection for the three of them, as though I, too, had somehow been included in that flow of love.

An hour later, I walked back toward the General's Daughter feeling that of all the things I'd done as an officer in the United States Navy, helping those three Vietnamese citizens and their students was the most meaningful – that, and falling in love with Melanie. What was going to happen to us? My days in Vietnam were numbered. Heck, my days in Vung Tau were probably numbered. There was a good chance the *Bell County* would get sent north again, and those orders could come without warning.

The war itself could turn worse. Vung Tau was peaceful at the moment. But what if the fighting moves into the city? What would happen to Melanie and her mother? The convent and the orphans? Master Lu and Hanh? Kaneli and Meg and the other civilians attached to various missions in this city?

These were people I cared about who would be in harm's way and there was almost nothing I could do to protect them.

"How did things get so personal so fast?" I asked myself.

Then it struck me: For the people of Vietnam this fight for

their country to be truly independent had always been personal. It's their country. They must fight on, putting themselves, their families, and friends in constant danger. Unlike me and the other Americans fighting here, they can't escape to a safer place. They're already home. It's not safe and probably won't be for a long time.

Melanie and Simone did have a choice. Simone might consider a return to France, but I was not at all sure Melanie would. My impression was that her French experience was mixed at best. As Simone's adopted daughter, she was legally French, but her heart was in Vietnam. When the time came to choose, I feared she would not leave – not for her mother, not for me, not for us.

Those thoughts gnawed on me as I slowly made my way back to the General's Daughter.

29

Fools Rush In
• •

T HE GENERAL'S DAUGHTER WAS FILLED with diners
when I returned. Melanie and her mother were busy hosting.
I spotted the Captain and XO in the bar and joined them.

"Rob, we were just talking about you," the Captain said.
"We're hoping you have good news about Binh's music and the
concert plans."

"Yes, sir. The news is good." I gave them a summary of my
meeting with Binh, Hanh, and Master Lu.

"Okay. The January 15 date is looking like a go. Lew has
exchanged messages with Admiral Kirkpatrick's adjutant and we
should hear in the next day or so if we can announce it," the
Captain said.

"Are we going to give it a more specific name or title? And
who is presenting it? The Navy? The General's Daughter? St.
Genevieve's Parish?"

The Captain and XO looked at each other and smiled.

"That's something right in your wheelhouse, Ensign Allen,"
the XO said. "We're expecting your suggestions within the next
forty-eight hours."

Just as the XO delivered that order, Melanie walked over and we all stood. She kissed them on each cheek before giving me the same, her lips lingering just a little longer on the last little peck.

"You all look like you are in very intense conversation. Please sit. I'm working and it appears that you might be too. I just came over to say hello," she said.

"We were just asking Rob to work up a title for our concert. Perhaps you have some thoughts, Melanie," the Captain said.

She nodded. "Perhaps, but Rob has already worked that out. I'm sure it will be just the right thing," she declared.

My jaw dropped. How in the hell did she know that?

She asked us for our drink orders, although she knew exactly what each of us would have. "Your usual gin and tonic, Rob?"

"Make it a double, and by the way. How did you know I'd already worked it out?"

She came over and whispered in my ear. "Sometimes you talk in your sleep."

The Captain and XO overheard and smiled. There was no keeping secrets from them.

"I'm not certain how Melanie knows, but there is something I have in mind. My meeting with Binh and Master Lu today settled it," I said.

"Some women have an uncanny way of reading minds. Melanie has that gift. Anyway, tell us what you've got," the Captain said.

"I'd rather sketch it out and show you," I said, reaching for a clean cocktail napkin and pulling out a pen.

I scribbled quickly. "This is a very rough draft and may need a little editing, but you'll get the general idea," I said.

On the napkin, I roughed out what could be printed as an invitation/announcement. I put it down on the table and turned it around so they could read it.

Mekong River - Mother of Waters
Premier of an original suite by
Vietnamese composer Binh Tien Hoang
Performed by the Vung Tau Student Orchestra
Co-directed by Nguyen Van Lu and Sister Josephine
of St. Genevieve's School
A benefit for Saint Genevieve's Orphanage and School
Saturday, January 15
1900 hours
General's Daughter, Vung Tau
Co-sponsored by Madame Simone Marquis
and the USS *Bell County*

They both leaned over and scanned it several times. Then the XO read it out loud.

"Hmm. The Vung Tau Student Orchestra? Composer Binh Tien Hoang? Those titles stretch the boundaries of hyperbole, but they sound great," he said.

"Who's to say Binh's not a composer? He composed this suite. And all it takes to name our combined group of music students the Vung Tau Student Orchestra is us saying it," I answered.

"This is good Rob. It's simple, direct and it gives credit where credit is due. The only thing that we might have to expand is the co-sponsor list. The admiral will have something to say about that," the Captain said.

"I bet O.J. will have some ideas too," I said. "We could offer sponsorships for significant donations."

"Yes. That's what I was thinking," the Captain said. "But there's also the South Vietnamese government and local authorities to be considered. They will want to be included. In fact, finesse may be required to keep them from taking it over."

"Could they really do that?" I said surprised that it was even a possibility.

"The General's Daughter, the church, orphanage, and school are in limbo with respect to the government.

"In theory, it could claim ownership of the property. The French no longer have authority anywhere in Vietnam," the Captain replied.

"So all the work that Simone and Melanie have done to keep the General's Daughter going could be undone by some South Vietnamese government hack?"

"Yes. The Saigon government is corrupt to the core. They've been enriching themselves at the expense of their people ever since the French left," the XO added.

"Then why are we supporting them?"

"Because they're opposed to the Communists," the XO responded, adding "You know that old saying, 'the enemy of my enemy is my friend.' Following that axiom can put you in bed with some real sleazy friends," he added.

"Shit. Then we're walking a very thin line. We want to promote *Mother of Waters* enough to make it a successful benefit, but not so much that it attracts attention from the crooks in Saigon," I said.

"You've got it, Rob. That is also why I need to talk to Admiral Kirkpatrick before we make the announcement," the Captain concluded.

"We need sponsors willing to support the children, but with no interest or intent to benefit directly themselves," I said.

"Sounds like a job for the *Bell County*'s best scrounger," the XO declared.

"Here's to O.J." The Captain raised his glass.

"To O.J.," the XO and I repeated.

I asked about the condition of our starboard engine and how the meeting with the tender CO went.

"The *Markab's* captain has put his best mechanic on it. They were already taking the engine apart when I headed over here. We probably won't know much until sometime tomorrow," the Captain said.

We talked about a host of topics for another hour or so, and then the XO excused himself, saying he was heading back to the ship.

"The XO is married, right?" I asked the Captain.

"Yes. He and his wife, Roxanne, have three children, two boys and a girl."

"A long tour like ours has to be hard on married people and their kids."

"It is. And it's one of the reasons I'm not married after sixteen years in the Navy."

"You've been in the Navy for sixteen years. What did you do, join when you were sixteen?"

"Close. I was seventeen. I got in with permission of my mother. I turned eighteen at boot camp."

"Wow. Do you ever think about getting out and going home to New Orleans? I think you could make a great living playing music there," I said.

"I think about it all the time. In fact, after I make lieutenant commander, I will have less than three years to serve before I can retire."

"When will you make lieutenant commander?"

"I just got notice that I did. I put the leaf insignia on next week."

"Congratulations, Lieutenant Commander Baillier," I said, offering him my hand.

"Thanks, Rob. Only you and Lew know so far. I'm going to tell Simone tonight and the crew next week."

"Simone will be happy. She's a sweet, interesting, intelligent, and beautiful woman and she loves you," I said.

"I've never known anyone like her before. Meeting her made me rethink my resolution to stay single."

"Do you think she'd marry you if you asked her?"

"We've actually discussed it. I asked her if she'd consider leaving Vung Tau and living in the States."

"What did she say?"

"She answered, '*Peut être.*' *Peut être* is French for 'perhaps.'"

"That sounds like a yes to me."

He shook his head at the dilemma that such a decision presented. "I believe that we will get married. We just haven't figure out the how and when. We're both bound by duties and obligations."

"I just had a vision. Some day in the near future you will be running a fancy jazz club together in New Orleans. Simone will handle the front of the house. You will play the music," I said.

He smiled and tapped my glass with his. "Let's drink to that bright future."

"I'm hungry. Are you? Let's find a table in the corner of the patio and see if we can get Simone and Melanie to join us." I followed him toward the dining area.

The majority of tables were empty but the patio was still open for dinner. We chose a spot near the bandstand. Neither of us needed to see the menu. The wait staff just started bringing the dishes that they knew we'd want.

As we finished off our last entrees, Simone and Melanie came over with our desserts and a bottle of Champagne.

"Are we celebrating something special?" I asked.

"I think every moment that we are together like this is worth celebrating?" Simone said.

Melanie nodded in agreement, popped the cork, and poured us all a glass.

The Captain extended his glass toward the center of the table so each of us could click to his toast. "To this lovely moment and many more."

"The only thing that would make it better is music," Melanie said, looking at me. "Rob. I think it is time for you to sing me another love song."

"The Captain is the musician in this group, not me. If I sing, the remaining diners will all leave."

"Don't sell yourself short, Rob. You've got a pretty good voice. It kind of reminds me of Elvis," he said, getting up and heading toward the piano.

I'd had enough to drink that my inhibitions about performing in public were muted. A guitar stood among the several instruments on the stage. I followed him and picked it up.

"Since you mentioned Elvis. How about "Can't Help Falling in Love With You."

The Captain played the opening series of chords exactly as it was played in the king's hit record. I strummed the guitar lightly, never taking my eyes of Melanie. The song flowed out of me as though Elvis was right there helping me stay on key.

After I repeated the last refrain and the Captain hit the final chord, there was dead silence.

Then the Captain whispered, "Best Elvis in years. Nice job, Rob."

The remaining diners started applauding. I didn't know what else to do, so I stood, bowed and returned to the table.

Simone hugged me, and whispered in my ear, "*Tres charmant, tres belle.* That was beautiful."

I saw tears on Melanie's face. There was love in her eyes. I also felt the sadness that neither of us could deny. I put both my hands in hers and pulled her close.

"We'll have plenty of time to be sad. Now is not that time. Remember the teachings of master Thich Nhat Hanh: 'Life is available only in the present moment.'"

She looked at me in surprise, then wonder. "You're quoting Vietnam's most revered Buddhist teacher now?"

Then she smiled. "You've been talking to Master Lu."

"You're right. He and I agree that Buddhists have a lot more pithy sayings than Christians."

She smiled, wiped the tears off her cheeks, and hugged me.

"Thank you, Rob. I don't want to be sad tonight."

After the Captain and I helped her and Simone close down the restaurant, Melanie led me to her room. When I started to say something, she put a finger to my lips and shook her head. The rest of the evening would not be for conversation.

No words were spoken. Our lovemaking was slow, sweet and tender. We sought to indelibly mark our senses, hers in mine, mine in hers, so that they would be as much a part of us as our own.

I awoke the next morning feeling refreshed and optimistic. I was surprised, because without really discussing it, Melanie and I had acknowledged our days together were numbered. Our love story would not have a happy ending. We would not ride off into the sunset to live happily ever after together. We both knew it was true.

Fortunately, Master Lu had given me enough Buddha quotes to fill a bucket, including one that applied to the moment: "There's only one moment for you to live, and that is the present moment."

With that in mind I began gently stroking Melanie's soft skin hoping to arouse her into sharing the present moment with me.

30

The Concert Must Go On
••••••••••••••••••••••

S IMONE AND THE CAPTAIN WERE making breakfast when Melanie and I came down to the kitchen.

"*Bonjour* my children," Simone said playfully. "Did you sleep well?"

Melanie looked at her mother and rolled her eyes.

I answered, "*Oui Madame, tres bien*, and you?"

"Oh, yes. My man is now a lieutenant commander. I feel much safer with such a powerful person sleeping by my side."

"Mother!" Melanie exclaimed in mock embarrassment.

I could tell that they were both happy for Captain Baillier, and teasing was just Simone's way of letting him know.

"Simone and I were discussing the concert and the delicate subject of the guest list and sponsors. We're in agreement that although we're proud of Binh and our children, we think we should keep our event below the Saigon government's radar. Do either of you have any thoughts on that?" the Captain asked.

"I agree entirely. We don't want any of Thieu or Ky's stooges anywhere near us and especially not the school and orphanage," Melanie said with surprising firmness.

Her mother looked at her in slight alarm.

"Have you been meeting with the WRL again?" Simone asked her.

"Yes, Mother. I'm a member. You know that."

"I also know how dangerous it is," Simone replied, her good mood suddenly turned dark.

"What's the WRL and why is belonging to it dangerous?" I asked.

"It is the Vietnamese Women's Movement for the Right to Live. We stand for peace and women's liberation through political action and diplomacy, not violence. We are politically neutral," Melanie replied.

"Saigon sees you as sympathetic to the communists. You know that," Simone said.

"We're not communists. In fact, we are against this war entirely and oppose what both sides are doing to our country," Melanie replied.

"What Melanie is not telling you is that the movement's leader, Ngo Ba Thanh, is highly critical of American involvement and conduct in the war. She is especially critical of your General Westmoreland," Simone said.

Melanie glared at her mother, but said no more.

"Okay. We're in agreement that we don't want any bigwigs from Saigon in attendance," the Captain said. "Let's move on."

Looking from Simone to Melanie then back to Simone, he asked. "Is it possible for the two of you to create a list of people, especially locals, who we could invite without creating more political controversy?"

"Yes." They both declared, nodding affirmatively.

"Good. Lew is working with the admiral's adjutant on possible military invitees, and I'd like to hear from Binh, Master Lu, and Sister Josephine on the subject as well. I'll ask Sister Josephine. Rob, you talk to Binh and Master Lu."

"We may be able to talk to all three at the same time," I replied. "Andrew told me yesterday that he was meeting them at the orphanage for a full orchestra practice later this morning."

"That's perfect. We can walk over together after breakfast. Would you ladies care to join us?"

"*Oui.* Of course," Simone replied. Melanie nodded yes.

As we settled into eating, the Captain began talking softly, almost as though he was speaking to himself.

"I believe that music has great power to bring people together. Binh's suite is by and for Vietnamese. It is influenced by an American composer, and will be performed and conducted in part by musicians trained by the French. We are working to bring it all together in a meaningful way that will also raise some money for the orphanage and school. These are good things. It is difficult to see any good in the rest of our work here."

I understood and agreed. Even career officers like him questioned our military purpose and strategy in Vietnam. Most of us didn't see any benefit to our country and doubted we were doing much to help the people of Vietnam. I was just grateful that the *Mekong Belle's* musical mission at least brought some pleasure and relief to the troops stationed in god-awful bases in the boonies.

After breakfast, Melanie asked me to read some of the articles she was preparing for her final job interview with the news service. Once we got to her room and she pulled out the papers. I could tell she was distracted by something else. I guessed it was the fight she'd just had with her mother.

"You know, parents never stop worrying about their children, even when their children become adults," I said.

"I know. I'm not angry with her. It's just that I feel trapped between two duties. The first is to honor and love my mother. The second is to honor and love my country. Vietnam is my country, not France," she said bitterly.

I nodded, but didn't say anything, letting her continue on to what I suspected was the heart of her dilemma.

"My mother is right. My involvement with the WRL, is dangerous, but not just for me, also for her. The men in government want to silence us. So far, it is only threats, but they could come after us and our families."

"It sounds like you both need to talk," I said.

"You and I must talk also." She replied.

"You mean about that huge elephant in the room?"

"What? An elephant?"

"No. It's an expression that we Americans use to describe a difficult topic that is as obvious as an elephant, but nobody wants to talk about."

"Yes. Our elephant is us," she replied.

"Okay. What about us?"

"One day you will leave. I cannot."

"Yes, my Vietnam duty will end many months from now, and then I will have to go where the Navy sends me, but only for another year. Then I am free to go where I want, when I want," I said.

I took both her hands in mine and pulled her closer.

"You could make me the happiest man in the world and say you'd go with me then."

She didn't pull away, but her eyes betrayed her resolve.

"I wish it were that easy. But, I can't just run away from my country in the middle of a war, leaving my friends behind. I must stay and do what I can. I wasn't at home in France. I would not be at home in the United States. In spite of my love for you, I would be lonely for my friends, for my culture, for my country."

"So you do love me?" I said smiling.

"You know I do."

"And I love you."

We hugged for a very long time, neither of us speaking.

"On this occasion, I would like to compose my own saying regarding life in the moment. I am borrowing heavily from Master Lu's Buddha sayings list. It goes like this:

Let's not think of sad goodbyes that fate brings tomorrow.

We are in love. Every moment together is a precious gift."

"Buddha could not have said it better," Melanie said, then kissed me.

"Now show me your stories," I said.

Melanie had re-written the series of articles based on interviews with local women, who spoke honestly about how the war had affected them and their families. They offered no opinion on which side was right. They focused instead on the pain and suffering of those caught in the middle.

"These are excellent, Melanie. Do you have photos to go with them?" I asked her.

"Not yet. And that may be a problem. Even though I've tried to keep the articles neutral, neither the South Vietnamese government nor the Communists accept neutrality. You are either for them or you are against them. I can use fictitious names for the women, but if I include their photos, then they could be exposed to danger of retaliation from either side."

"I understand. But you do realize that if these stories run under your byline, you also will be in danger," I replied.

"I know, which brings us back to the concerns raised by my mother. Most of the women I interviewed are either members of the WRL movement, or at least sympathetic with it. I could bring the wrath of Saigon down on all of us including my friends, Cam and Hanh, and my mother."

"You could write under a *nom de plume*," I suggested.

"If my mother insists on staying and I want to be a journalist, that is what I will have to do."

"Let's talk about your mother for a minute. The Captain loves her. He wants to marry her and bring her back to the states with him. I assume she's told you that?"

"Yes. But she will not consider leaving me behind," Melanie answered.

"It sounds like your mother and I have something in common," I said, then added, "For now, let's concentrate on making the concert a rousing success. In fact, I have an idea that popped into my head when I was reading your articles. All of those women and their women friends should be on the guest list."

"Yes. It could be a subtle but firm way for local women to stand up for children made orphans by the war. We don't have to carry signs, or march, or protest. We just have to be there. It is a wonderful idea my darling," she said grabbing me around the neck and pulling me onto the bed on top of her.

We managed to make it downstairs just as the Captain and Simone were about to head out the door without us.

It was a pleasant day for a walk. Worries about the future and the sadness that waited around the corner could be stuffed away in the back drawer of my mind. I was sure they would come out to haunt me when I was back on the ship standing a late night watch alone with my thoughts. They'd just have to wait 'til then.

We found Andrew, Binh, Master Lu and Sister Josephine standing in the large music practice room of the school. The students were busy tuning their instruments and reviewing their music.

Binh explained that they were ready to try the second half of the suite, and would be stopping frequently, but we were invited to find a comfortable seat and observe.

Then Andrew spoke up for the first time.

"Captain, we have one little problem," Andrew said. "We don't have a bass. And this suite must have a bass."

"Well, we can loan them our band's bass," he said, then realized the full meaning of what Andrew was saying. "You need the bassist as well."

He thought for a few seconds and started to smile. His smile grew wider and soon he was laughing out loud.

We all looked at him curiously.

"What is it?" Simone asked him.

"I'm imagining the look on Harry's face when I tell him he has to play bass in the Vung Tau Children's Orchestra."

"You'll order him to do it?" I asked.

"No. Not really. I won't have to. I'll suggest that it is the only solution that I can think of, but offer to accept any he might have. He'll huff and puff, and make a few wise cracks, but he'll do it."

We all sat back imagining the orchestra on stage; several rows of small children, most barely four feet tall, and, towering behind them, a huge bear of a man leaning on a bass fiddle.

"You know, the Mekong River starts in the Himalayas. Maybe Harry could represent the Yeti," I said. "What do you think, Binh?"

"What's a Yeti?" he and Melanie asked together.

"A Yeti, you know, the abominable snowman."

"Oh. You mean a *meh-teh*. Yes. Your Harry looks like the *meh-teh* mountain people talk about when they want to frighten their children into obedience. But our students will soon learn, as I have, that he is a very sweet and gentle bear on the inside. Not at all frightening," Binh said.

"But maybe, I could add a few bars of deep base for him alone, just to introduce the *meh-teh* to our audience."

"Perfect!" declared the Captain.

31

Mother of Waters
•••••••••••••••••••••••

T HE FOLLOWING THREE WEEKS PASSED in a whirl
of activity both onboard our ship and in Vung Tau, where
preparations for the *Mother of Waters* concert were coming together
nicely.

Repair work on the *Belle County's* starboard engine came to a
halt when the mechanics found that the damaged parts could not
be replicated on the tender due to the lack of the proper materials
and equipment.

This left the ship tied to the pier, its engine dismantled, and no
place to go.

To keep the crew occupied, the Captain ordered all spaces to
be thoroughly cleaned and all outside surfaces painted.

He shortened the workday so it ended at 1500 hours, leaving
the remainder of the afternoons for music rehearsals, free time
and liberty.

During our trip from Da Nang to Vung Tao, Doc Hodges surprised the Captain with a request to add a dance number. Doc's
morning calisthenics workouts had evolved into tap and jazz dance
lessons. He discovered that three of the six guys who showed up
every day had taken dance classes at some time in their youth.

Doc and Reyes both had taken tap and dance classes and performed in their schools' shows. Dancing was a good workout and the guys were having fun. It led to Doc's class doubling in size.

"We'd like to do 'There Ain't Nothin' Like a Dame' from *South Pacific*," he told the Captain. "Reyes and I have made the choreography basic. At least half the guys can carry a tune."

"Doc, it's a great idea, but how are you all going to fit on the stage?" the Captain said.

"I've already talked to Chief Mick. He can knock together front extensions for the stage that will give us the room. Of course, at some of the remote bases, we won't be able to do it for lack of room, but even if we only get to dance in some of the shows, it will boost morale. We can include guys who like music but are feeling left out right now."

"If you can get the chief to extend the stage, I'm willing to add it," the Captain replied.

On shore, Andrew was spending a lot of his time at the school working with the string section of the school orchestra.

As predicted, Harry, put up a fuss, then relented and was now practicing with the kids three times a week. He quickly became their favorite. They called him *"Cha Chiu,"* 'Papa Bear' in Vietnamese.

Sister Josephine was alternately irritated and delighted as the ebullient engineering officer clowned around in the practice sessions more than the most unruly of the children.

Harry loved the kids. So much so that he used his own money to procure, with O.J.'s help, a half-size standup bass designed for children. His plan was to give it to the school, volunteering to teach bass whenever he was in port.

December 31, New Year's Eve, came and went without a lot of fanfare or celebrating. Vietnam's Lunar New Year, Tet, would be January 30.

Melanie and her mother drafted a list of several dozen local women to invite to the concert. They hand-wrote special invitations, which they delivered personally. I spent afternoons walking around Vung Tao with Melanie as she handed out the invitations and stopped to chat with her friends.

The XO contacted the Navy officers that the admiral had invited to the show. In addition, the admiral invited the American embassy in Saigon to send a representative. They insisted on inviting one or two of their counterparts from the South Vietnamese government, a matter that the XO had stressed must be kept as low-key as possible.

O.J. managed to acquire a list of private U.S. and Thai businesses that were major suppliers to the Navy. He sent letters to their top executives and convinced them that a donation to the concert for Mekong Region orphans was something they must do.

As a result, he had pledges for more than $30,000.

The General's Daughter could accommodate an audience of approximately 200.

Simone had sketched out a rough seating chart and planned a champagne and hors d'oeuvre reception to precede the concert.

By January 7, the combined student groups were starting to sound like an orchestra. Virtually all of the local women Simone and Melanie had invited were coming. So where officers in charge of all of the military units based in Vung Tau, including the Australians, plus the medical personnel attached to the local hospital.

The special part for our engine also arrived on January 7. The tender machinist took one look at it and declared, "They sent the wrong fucking part." A second order went out. By that time, we were certain our ship would not be underway until after the concert on January 15.

None of us minded. We were all committed to the success of the show. The crewmembers not involved with the concert were happy with the short workdays and additional liberty.

I asked the Captain if all of the breakdown time would look bad on his record and hurt his career.

"Yes. If I was staying in for another ten to twenty years. But I've decided to retire at the first opportunity. The ship broke down and can't carry out its military mission. I consider it a sign that our real mission is to see this concert through."

And see it through we did.

We held our first walk-through rehearsal at the General's Daughter on the January 12. Several *Bell County* crew members, including Chief Mick, our electronics technician, Murdock, and Reyes all helped with the sound and lighting systems. Binh, Master Lu, and Sister Josephine took the orchestra through each part of the suite, explaining the timing and transitions.

Andrew, Melanie and I stood to one side watching it all come together.

"Andrew, your string section sounds fantastic," I said.

"It's not mine. Sister Josephine is the real genius, but I am proud of how good they sound."

"You all deserve credit. None of this would be possible if it weren't for everyone on your ship," Melanie said.

"I bet most of the guys over here prefer helping people to fighting them. I know we'd all be happier with a mission of peace, rather than killing and destroying. If we do nothing else, at least we will have helped do one good thing in Vietnam," Andrew said.

"Amen, brother," I said.

Melanie gave Andrew a hug. "I've saved two front-row seats for Kaneli and her roommate, Meg, for the show," she added.

Simone closed the restaurant the night before the concert so that the staff could concentrate on setting up for the next day. The Captain and I helped arrange chairs and move tables. By midnight, the place was as ready as it was going to be.

Our only concern was the weather. There were hints of possible rain squalls. While the large patio had some awnings, they didn't cover the expanded area where many of the seats were set. All we could do was hope for clear skies.

Melanie and I had a hard time falling asleep. Both of us had invested a lot of time and energy in the concert. It was personal, something we'd worked on together. We wanted it to be perfect. We finally slept, only to be awakened just before dawn by the crash of lightning, thunder and rain pounding on the roof.

"Shit!" I said, pulling the covers over both of us. "Maybe if we hide under this blanket it will go away and leave us alone."

We fell back asleep. Bright sun peeking through the shutters woke us two hours later.

"It worked. The storm went away. Your blankets have magical power," I declared.

We pulled our clothes on and went downstairs to join a gradually expanding work crew trying to clean up and dry out everything that got soaked. Fortunately the sun was out. By midday, the patio was habitable again.

Although many members of the military were on the guest list, everybody was asked to come in civilian clothes. For me, that meant my one-and-only pair of tan trousers and my well-worn aloha shirt. I was just toweling off from the shower when Melanie handed me a package wrapped in bright blue paper and tied with a silk ribbon.

"*Pour moi?*" I asked.

"*Oui, mon cheri*. I can't have you attending the concert in that old Aloha shirt," she replied.

I opened the package. In it was a nicely tailored cream-colored silk and cotton shirt.

"Mother and I had a friend of ours make it for you," she said.

"It's beautiful. I've never had a shirt so elegantly crafted. Thank you," I said dropping my towel and pulling her into my naked body. She lingered for a few seconds before sighing and pushing me away.

"Not now. We don't have time. Pull on your trousers, put on your new shirt, and join us downstairs in ten minutes."

"Aye, aye, Mademoiselle," I replied bowing as she headed toward the door.

I joined her, Simone, the Captain, and the XO in the salon for the reception.

"Admiral Kirkpatrick, his adjutant, and the diplomats from Saigon are due to arrive any minute," the XO said.

"Who are the diplomats?" I asked.

"I don't know, and I have no idea who is coming from the Saigon government," he replied.

As if on cue, one of the General Daughter's receptionist's led a small group of well-dressed men and women toward us.

I heard the Captain speak first.

"Admiral Kirkpatrick, welcome back," he said, stepping forward and extending his hand.

The admiral was a tall, thin man in his late fifties, with gray hair and a face creased by many days in the sun and salty air. The Captain introduced him all around. He had a warm smile and a firm handshake. His voice was deep and soft. His adjutant was a young lieutenant commander about the same age as our Captain.

With them were two women; one was Elizabeth Delong, our Saigon embassy's PIO (Public Information Officer). With her, was a Vietnamese woman, Mademoiselle Phan Van Mai, who was the personal assistant to Madame Nguyen Cao Ky, the wife of Nguyen Cao Ky, prime minister and vice president of Vietnam. This seemed to be exactly what we were trying to avoid. But it was too late to change.

As it turned out, Miss Phan and Miss Delong were not only good friends, they were also sympathetic with the goals of the WRL.

It was agreed that the Admiral and both women would be in the reception line with Simone, Sister Josephine, the Captain, Binh and Master Lu. Melanie, Hanh, Andrew, the XO, Harry, O.J. and I would serve as a secondary reception line and escorts for the guests with reserved seats. Simone and Melanie had assigned seating so that local women occupied at least half of the two first rows, alongside the military officers and guests from Saigon.

As the guests completed the reception line, we'd welcome them and point the way to the champagne and hors d'oeuvres. Once the salon filled up, we mingled and talked with the guests. We were all prepared to answer questions regarding the origins and purposes of the concert and about the good that the school and orphanage were doing for Vietnamese children.

With ten minutes to go before the start of the show, everyone was seated.

The lights dimmed and Binh, Simone, and Sister Josephine walked on the stage together. The audience applauded politely. Simone spoke first. She thanked everyone for coming and praised her staff, the Captain and the crew of our ship for planning and pulling the concert together.

Then she introduced Sister Josephine, who thanked Simone, her staff and our crew again, and told the audience a little bit about the school and orphanage. She also spoke on behalf of Master Lu and his cultural arts center at the Buddhist temple, praising him, Hanh and their students for their hard work and talent.

"Now," she said, "it is my honor to present Lieutenant Binh Tien Hoang, a very talented young man who has declared his love for Vietnam and its people in the most eloquent and beautiful way possible. The *Mekong Suite* is brilliantly written and will be lovingly performed by the talented young people of this community. Thank you for coming, and now here is our maestro."

Binh stepped forward and surveyed the crowd. I could tell he was deeply moved.

He bowed. Then in a clear, strong voice, first in Vietnamese, then in English, he told a short story.

"When I was a boy growing up in a small village on the Mekong River, I had the good fortune to have a father who loved the water. He loved swimming, fishing, and boats. He worked hard, but when we could afford it, we would take trips, always on the Mekong, and he would show me how this great river and all of its tributaries represented the lifeblood of our country. It quenches our thirst, it nourishes our rice, gives us fish, and transports us where we need to go. It brings us all together as one.

"No matter which side of this war we are on, the river is our constant companion. We call her 'Mother of Waters.' If she could talk, I believe she would tell us to stop wasting what she gives us and do our best to live as one as she has always intended.

"I am grateful to my friend, Captain Baillier, his officers, and the crew of the *Bell County*, and Master Lu of the Vung Tao Vietnamese arts school, and Madame Marquis and Sister Josephine. Thanks to them, I was able to finish translating the message of our *Mother of Waters* and share it with you here tonight. Like the waters of the Mekong itself, I hope the music will flow from here to all who love our country. Thank You."

The audience applauded enthusiastically. On cue, the lights over the stage brightened and the audience got their first view of the Vung Tao Children's Orchestra and bassist Harry "*Cha Chiu*" Haggert.

32

The Mekong Suite
••••••••••••••••••••••

B INH AND MASTER LU AGREED that Sister Josephine should be the conductor, not only because most of the students were hers, but also because she was the only one with previous experience as a conductor. Her diminutive stature allowed the audience a better view of the student musicians.

As her hands started to move, the beginning notes sounded like a soft rain falling in the distance. The violins, cellos and Vietnamese string instruments were lightly plucked on alternate beats. Each had its own distinctive tone. The volume increased gradually as other instruments joined in, creating the sound of a small stream tumbling over rocks.

A series of heavy thumps emanated from Harry's bass. Was that the heavy footstep of a bear crossing the creek?

The Mekong's story was beginning.

Andrew and Binh had collaborated on a printed program that led the audience through the tale, page by page. The suite's theme, the flow of the river, took us through each movement, from the prelude to the coda. Along the way, we were introduced to life on its banks in each country.

Binh borrowed ideas from Grofé's suites, including a thunderstorm sequence that was riveting. His use of Master Lu's traditional gongs and drums was especially effective in that segment. There was a floating market scene in which the strings made humming noises that hinted of the murmur of human voices.

As each scene unfolded, the theme moved us along the river.

The coda ended with a crescendo depicting the Mother of Waters flowing into the sea as the sun rose to greet it.

After forty-one minutes, when Sister Josephine brought the last note to a close and her arms rested at her side, there was a moment of silence, then a burst of applause as the audience showed its appreciation. Soon, everyone was standing and applauding while Sister Josephine asked each student to stand a take a bow. Then, Binh and Master Lu joined Sister Josephine on stage. All three pointed to the big guy at the back of the orchestra standing by his bass. He too took a bow to more enthusiastic applause.

It was a masterful performance, especially for a group with an average age of twelve (not counting Harry). Sister Josephine and Master Lu invited the students to put down their instruments and come forward so the guests could meet them.

The Vietnamese women were the most enthusiastic of all, praising them in their own language. Miss Phan from Saigon, tears in her eyes, seemed deeply moved. She was down on one knee holding the hand of one of the youngest of Master Lu's students, smiling and praising the child.

The military guests waited their turn to congratulate the students.

Simone and Melanie had set up a large food table to one side of the stage especially for the children. When everyone had congratulated the youngsters, Sister Josephine, gave them permission to go eat. They shouted with glee and, like locusts, swarmed over the food.

Sister Josephine, Master Lu, and Binh remained and mingled with the guests, many of whom had questions about the music and how the students had managed to play it so well. I noticed that Admiral Kirkpatrick, Captain Baillier, Miss Phan and Miss Delong were all huddled together in intense, but friendly conversation. I learned later that they were discussing the possibility of Binh leading a Vietnamese music goodwill tour to the states.

By the time the children and all of the guests left, most of the clean-up and rearrangement of the dining room was done. Andrew and Kaneli tried to persuade Melanie and me to join them at the New Orleans club for some late-night dancing, but we declined. Instead, we joined the Captain and Simone on the residence patio for a cognac. The evening had flown by. We were too excited to sleep.

"I can't believe how good those kids played," I declared.

"I have to say it was one of the most inspiring nights of music I've had in my life," the Captain said.

"We brought a lot of different people together to celebrate our culture. Without your leadership, it wouldn't have happened. This night is as much to your credit as it is to the children, Binh, Master Lu and Sister Josephine," Simone stated.

"Thanks, Simone, but it was all of us, you and Melanie, your staff, my crew, even the admiral," the Captain said.

"I especially enjoyed watching the women from the community. They loved it. And what they said to the children afterward put a lot of smiles on the faces of those kids," I said.

We sipped our cognac, talked about our favorite movements of the suite, and gradually allowed ourselves to unwind from the excitement of the evening. By 0100, Melanie and I headed upstairs, leaving the Captain and Simone to share another cognac. We had just enough energy to make love before falling sound asleep.

As usual, the Captain and Simone were up before us and had our breakfast on the table when we came downstairs. We were all still basking in the glow of the concert and expressing our amazement at Minh's talents and the competence of the young musicians.

"It's a remarkable work. It should be played before a wider audience than we can drum up here in Vung Tau," the Captain stated emphatically.

"Is that what you and the admiral were discussing with the two women from Saigon last night?" Melanie asked.

"Among other things, yes. We also talked about finding a way for the students to participate; even possibly making a tour to the States and Europe."

"Wow! That was an interesting conversation," I said.

"Yes, but for now it is all talk. Miss Phan's influence is only with her boss, Madame Ky, who has little or no real power. But she has some influence with her husband and she is unafraid to speak up. She might be persuaded to see the value and goodwill in a Vietnamese student orchestra playing a Vietnamese composition before international audiences," the Captain said.

"It would be a wonderful experience for the children and Binh," Simone added.

"I don't know how much longer we can convince his ARVN superiors to allow him to stay with us. The admiral is going to try pitching the music tour idea to his superiors too. Maybe their endorsement will help." the Captain said.

"The Admiral said one more thing. He wants to see the show, our ship's show, before he heads back to San Diego. He leaves February 1."

"Is that a problem? Our guys have been practicing almost every day?" I asked.

"We don't know when the engine will be fixed. We're stuck alongside a very crowded pier. There are forklifts, cranes, and stacks of pallets, hoses, cables and wires strung all over. There's very little room for a stage, let alone any kind of audience," he said.

"The Admiral surely understands that?" Simone said.

"Yes, but he still wants to see the show. So, I set the date as far out as I dared to give us time to figure things out."

"So what's the date?" I asked.

"January 28," he replied.

"Two days before Tet," Melanie said.

"Yes. I didn't want to hold it on the eve of Tet, because there's a possible truce in the works. If that happens, many of the civilian workers will take time off to be with their families. They won't be around to help with clearing the pier area for a show"

"At least we have plenty of time to get ready," I said, adding "Sounds like a job for Chief Mick."

"Exactly what I was thinking. In fact, you and I need to get back to the ship after breakfast and meet with everyone to work out a plan," he declared.

The *Bell County* looked clean and bright with its new coat of paint when the Captain and I arrived at the pier. At 1300 hours the entire crew of the ship crowed into the crew's mess to hear the Captain's announcement of the January 28 command performance.

"If it wasn't for Admiral Kirkpatrick, there would be no *Mekong Belle* shows at all. He went out on a limb to get our musical mission approved, and I want him to see that his faith in us is well-founded. Let's make it our best show ever," the Captain stated.

"You can count on us, Captain," Doc Hodges shouted from the back of the room. His declaration was followed by applause and shouts of support.

"Thanks, Doc, and thanks to all of you," he responded.

Then, he and the XO assigned various responsibilities for planning and preparation to some of the officers and key petty officers.

The XO, O.J. Doc, Reyes, Archer, Chief Mick, Harry, Andrew, and I were asked to stay for a discussion of the space problem specifically.

The XO pointed out the obvious. The pier was a jammed with

equipment, hoses, wires, crates and barrels, leaving us little room for a performance and an audience.

"Why not use the crap?" Andrew suggested.

"What do you mean?" the XO asked.

"One of the things we need to prove is that we can take our show anywhere, no matter the circumstances. Rather than try to get all of that shit moved out of the way, let's make it part of the set. All we really need is a stage for the dance number. Even that can be improvised to include the equipment, pallet stacks and other stuff."

The Captain rubbed his chin in deep thought then looked at Andrew then the XO.

"Interesting idea, Andrew. I'm thinking *On the Waterfront* meets *Anchors Aweigh*. What do you think, Lew?"

"The Admiral will love it. But it's going to be a challenge for Chief Mick and his team to set up. What do you say chief?"

"I only saw *On the Waterfront* once. It ain't a musical. The only thing I remember was Marlon Brando was in it. But I've seen *Anchors Aweigh* at least ten times. The songs, except for 'Anchors Aweigh,' aren't that good, but Frank Sinatra and Gene Kelly were great.

"We can make it work on the dock. The only question is who's going to keep those tight asses at base command off our backs when we start moving stuff around?" the chief asked.

"We'll take care of base command. And you're right, Chief, *On the Waterfront* wasn't a musical, but the score of the film, composed by Leonard Bernstein, was nominated for an Oscar. There's a lot of drama in that music," the Captain said. "I think we can get help with set up from the CO of the *Markab*, especially if we offer him and his crew the best seats in the house."

"Seats? Where are we going to get seats? And if we do, where are we going to put them?" Harry asked.

"O.J. will find a way," the XO said, looking at the operations officer, who gave him a thumbs up.

Andrew was assigned to work with the chief and Harry on the pier side arrangements. Doc, Reyes and Archer were directed to plan each musical number so that it could be mobile.

I would assist O.J. with his scrounging and work on an announcement flyer.

"Okay. Andrew has given us an excellent idea, and you all have your assignments. Meeting adjourned," the Captain declared.

Two weeks was plenty of time to pull everything together. We all kept busy. I still had most evenings free. Melanie and I spent several of them together with Andrew and Kaneli, dining and dancing. There seemed to be a lot of sailors and other military personnel on liberty. The bars were hopping.

Melanie's friend, Cam, who owned the New Orleans Bar, joined us for drinks at her club one night. The discussion got around to the war, and how much it was hurting the country. I already knew that Cam, along with Melanie and Hanh, were members of WRL, the Vietnamese women's anti-war group.

"Those of us who own restaurants and bars near American bases are doing good, but the people out in the countryside are starving and getting caught in the crossfire," Cam said.

"That is the tragedy of a civil war. Innocents in the middle have nowhere to hide. And we make it worse, because we can't tell the good guys and from the bad. We're also in the middle of something that we don't understand," Andrew said.

"What you need to understand is that most Vietnamese people just want to live in peace. They don't want to choose a side, and they don't see Americans as their saviors either," she answered.

This revelation didn't surprise us, and it added to our sense of futility – our feelings that this war, and America's role in it, was a terrible mistake.

As a war correspondent, Melanie would be in the middle of it too. Her interviews had gone well. The editors liked her stories. She was waiting to see if she got the job. If she did, she would leave Vung Tau. Our days together ended.

"Have you discussed the job with your mother?" I asked.

"Yes. She's worried for my safety and doesn't want me to leave. But she knows she has to let me go. I told her I had to let her go, too."

"Let her go? Like go back to France?"

"Yes. Or marry Captain Baillier and go to the United States."

"You'd be okay with that?"

"Of course. She loves him. They would be happy together, no matter where they were."

"But that would mean leaving the General's Daughter, the school, and you behind."

"Rob, The General's Daughter cannot survive without the American and Australian military here. They are our best, almost our only, customers. The French Catholic church has already spoken of recalling their priest and the nuns and turning the school over to the local government. Things are changing, and the changes will not be good for my mother."

"You could go with her," I said knowing that choice had already been rejected more than once.

"You know I can't. I won't. Vietnam is my country. I'm staying."

Up to that point, I'd held onto a sliver of hope that she might change her mind. But I realized that accepting her decision was my only choice.

If we were forced to part sometime in the weeks and months to come, it would be with unquestioning love and acceptance of the impossible choices we both must make. The rush to put together our show for the admiral would leave little time to dwell on Melanie's decision.

The Captain and X.O. were determined to make our Vung Tau pier-side event a true demonstration of the best of the *Bell County*, not only the best of our talented artists, but also of the entire crew and what we could all do together.

We had just a few days to make it happen.

33

Anchors Aweigh
•••••••••••••••••••••••

W ITH JUST FIVE HOURS UNTIL show time, Chief Mick had to shout at the crane operator to be heard above the din of saws, hammers and forklifts on the pier alongside the ship. A 25-foot-long gangway swung from the crane's cable as he tried to position it between the ship's main deck and a large forklift parked on the dock, its forks elevated to their maximum height.

"Okay, raise it a little higher. That's it. Now swing it to port another thirty degrees. Stop! Hold it right there."

The half-dozen sailors working directly below it on the pier seemed worried that it could slip off the cable and crush them. When secured, it would hang over the main stage and become the focus of the show's big tap dance number.

The pier was swamped with sailors moving pallets, lines, hoses and boxes to resemble the set of the movie "On the Waterfront." The X.O. and Andrew were directing their movements from the middle of the stage.

To them, the disorder had meaning. It was stagecraft, their vision of the set for our live musical show. Anyone passing by might have thought it looked more like a scene of a terrible disaster. Such was the case of the hapless supply lieutenant with whom Harry and Andrew had a previous run-in.

This time, it was Harry and I who were standing on the edge of the chaos when he, aka Lt. Buttlicker, drove up. He exited his car and looked down the pier where the sailors were as busy as bees around a hive. He turned toward us with a dazed and confused look on his face, as though he couldn't believe the mess he was seeing.

"Jesus Christ! The pier looks like somebody emptied Fibber McGee's closet all over it." He pointed an accusing finger at Harry. "Are you responsible for this?"

Harry shrugged his shoulders; then nodded his head toward the end of the pier where a large black Cadillac was approaching. "No. I'm not. But he is," Harry said.

The lieutenant turned and looked toward the approaching vehicle. Then did a double take when he saw the flutter of a flag mounted on it, which indicated the rank of its occupant.

"I think you're about to have one of those 'oh shit moments,' Lt. Buttlicker. I suggest you move your car out of the Admiral's way," Harry said.

Unfortunately, it was too late. The Admiral's driver pulled up to within an inch of the supply officer's car, then stopped, exited, and opened the back seat door for Admiral Kirkpatrick.

He was wearing the blue dungaree work uniform of an ordinary seaman, complete with a white sailor's gob (sailor hat.) Only the stars pinned to the shirt's collar, gave him away.

The entire cast would be costumed in dungarees.

The Admiral's appearance pushed the poor supply guy into a state of temporary paralysis. He couldn't seem to loosen his grip on the car door handle to offer a salute.

Harry and I saluted, and the Admiral returned our salute and shouted, "As you were." Then he turned to Lt. Buttlicker and pointed to an open space nearby. "Lieutenant, after you move your car, will you park mine there, so that I may leave right after the show." He didn't wait for a response. Instead, he nodded to his driver, who reached back into the car and pulled out his saxophone case and followed him as he walked purposefully into the chaos on the dock.

The supply officer managed to unfreeze himself long enough to complete his parking attendant duties and depart the scene to be never heard from again.

Because he was in dungarees, most of the men moving to-and-fro kept right on working, not realizing that an admiral was in their midst. The X.O. and Andrew saw him approaching, stood to attention, and saluted.

"As you were. Can I leave my sax here by the piano for now?" he added.

"Of course, Admiral," the X.O. said. "Captain Baillier is in the wardroom going over some final notes with Doc."

"Is that you're set design?" the Admiral asked, nodding toward the large piece of butcher paper that Andrew held in his hands.

"Yes, sir. We're just getting the last things moved into place."

"So that gangway you have suspended over our heads is going to be a dance stage?"

"Yes, Admiral. Doc and a few other guys will be tapping and singing to the song 'There Ain't Nothin' Like a Dame.'"

"And what about the crates, and other cargo scattered around the stage?"

"They're all props. We'll be using them during the show," Andrew answered.

"I'm glad I only have to play the sax on this stage. You'd have to be quite an athlete to move around on this set."

"You, the Captain, me, and the rest of the band get to stay in one place and play good music. The singers and dancers will be the moving parts of the show," the X.O. said.

"Clearly, you don't do this kind of setup for every performance."

"No, Admiral. This one is for you. Most of the set was Andrew's

286

idea. We wanted to show you the full range of talent and abilities of our crew. We are turning a typically cluttered dock into a musical set using only what is here."

"Well. I'm already impressed. By the way, when's rehearsal? We've only got a few more hours before the actual show."

"Rehearsal is at 1300, but we don't have time for a full run-through. As you know, the band's been working on the music for the last three days, and the dancers and singers have all been going over their numbers. We're just going to walk through each part, set up, transition, but skip the actual music, although we will run through the finale, 'Anchors Aweigh.'"

The audience started arriving a half-hour before curtain.

The Captain had arranged passes and seats for Simone, Melanie, Master Lu, Hahn, and all of the nuns from the convent and members of the student orchestra, plus several of the local Vietnamese women's group.

Elizabeth DeLong arrived with a small contingent of corre-spondents and photographers from news bureaus stationed in Saigon. The rest of the audience consisted of officers and sailors from the U.S. and Australian bases. We managed some folding chair seating near the stage for special guests, but the rest of the audience managed to find seats and perches on and around the various pieces of flotsam scattered around the pier.

Of course there was no curtain, or any other trappings of a real theater. The show was blue-collar all the way, with the entire cast in dungarees.

Chief Mick had managed to rig a machine that pushed steam clouds up at various points around the set, giving the impression of fog moving in and out.

At 1600 hours, the ship's choir opened the show with the "Navy Hymn." Then, the Captain came to the microphone.

"Ladies and gentlemen, welcome, *bienvenue, chao mu'ung*. I am proud to present the man who made this all possible, Admiral Richard Kirkpatrick, Commander of Amphibious Forces Pacific."

The Admiral stood next to the Captain, the saxophone hung from his neck.

"I want to add my welcome to you all, and thank Captain Baillier for what he has done for the Navy and all the men who will be able to enjoy a great live musical show, even while stationed in the most dangerous places in Vietnam. He has brought together the most musically talented and dedicated sailors in the Navy. He, and they, make this show possible."

When the full band began to play, I noticed how Andrew and Bihn, each on violin, added a richness to the sound, which seemed to bounce off the ship's hull and dock structures as though it was especially designed as a concert hall.

What followed was the most spectacular show of the *Mekong Belle's* Vietnam tour. The voices never sounded better. The Andrews Sisters sketch was outstanding, and the tap dance number drew applause that stopped the show for several minutes.

When the last bar of "Anchors Aweigh" ended in a crescendo, everyone applauded and cheered, including all of the performers. Nobody wanted to leave.

The correspondents traveling with Elizabeth Delong interviewed the Admiral, Captain Baillier, Doc Hodges, and Binh. Some of them even took quotes from Simone, Melanie, and the Vietnamese guests. Photos and stories were sent out on the wire services and we got a big write-up in *Stars and Stripes*.

It was the musical high-water mark of the *Belle County's* Vietnam tour.

While the Captain and I enjoyed the post-performance glow chatting with Simone and Melanie, Admiral Kirkpatrick made it a point to go to each member of the crew, shake their hands, and congratulate them on a job well done. We were all standing together watching when he finished and walked over to us.

"Bill, the only regret I have is that I can't go with you to one of those upriver firebases to be part of the joy you bring with you," the Admiral told the Captain.

"We'd love to have you with us. The band needs a good saxophone," the Captain replied.

"Maybe, but I'm certain my boss won't approve a transfer. Otherwise, I'd be here tomorrow. Speaking of which, I understand your engine is fixed and you'll be moving to the loading ramp the day after tomorrow."

"Yes, sir, we're back online. We should be loaded and on our way, before your plane takes off for home."

"Excellent.

"Oh, about that other matter we spoke of," the admiral paused and smiled at Simone. "It's approved. You are good to go whenever you can make the arrangements." He then turned to Simone and Melanie, who were standing with us. "Simone and Melanie, there's plenty of room in my car. I'd be happy to drop you off at the governor's mansion."

Simone smiled. "Thank you admiral, for everything. And, of course, we hope you will join us tomorrow at the General's Daughter for an early Tet Eve celebration."

"That would be absolutely delightful," he replied. Then offered her his arm. "May I escort you to the car?"

I gave Melanie's hand a quick squeeze. "I'll see you later tonight."

"*Oui, mon cher,*" she whispered. Then turned and followed her mother and the admiral toward his car.

As the Admiral's Cadillac moved out of sight I turned to the Captain, expecting him to tell me why Simone was so pleased with whatever it was that the Admiral approved. Instead, he changed the subject.

"I've asked Simone if she would join me at the New Orleans

Club tonight. A bunch of us feel like a good old-fashioned jam session. She said yes and said you and Melanie should come too."

"I know Melanie would love that," I said.

"Okay then. Be ready to head to the mansion at 1930 hours."

"Aye, aye, Captain," I said, then asked, "Are you going to tell me about that other matter the Admiral mentioned?"

"All in good time, Rob. All in good time," he said, heading up the gangway to the ship.

Later, when we arrived, the General's Daughter was closed in preparation for the next evening's Tet Eve party. Simone and Melanie were directing the setup. They expected a big crowd. We volunteered to pitch in with the tables and chairs.

As we finished the work, Simone brought out a tray of food and a bottle of wine for the four of us to share. The Captain raised his wine glass. "Here's to Admiral Kirkpatrick for all he's done for us."

Melanie and I looked at each other, then at Simone and the Captain.

"Okay. What's going on?" Melanie said.

Simone got out of her chair and walked over behind the Captain, leaned over and kissed him on the cheek.

"I think it is time to tell the children," she said.

"I was going to wait and announce it to everyone tomorrow night at the dinner," he replied.

"That's fine for your other officers, but Melanie and Rob are family."

"You're right," he said to her, then turned to Melanie and me. "She's usually right, which is why I've asked her to marry me. Thankfully, she has accepted. I had to work out a few official details with my boss. Now that's done."

I looked and Melanie and she looked at me. We both started laughing.

"We've wondered when you'd quit stalling and get on with it," Melanie said. "Rob guessed February near Valentine's Day. I expected sooner."

"In any case, it is wonderful news," I said and I raised my glass. "Congratulations to you both." Melanie joined me in the toast.

"We want to have the wedding here sometime within the next thirty days. We're working out the details. The captain of the *Markab* has agreed to perform the ceremony."

"So soon?" Melanie said, surprised.

"Yes. It gives your mother full status as the wife of an American officer, and makes her eligible for all of the protection and privileges that go with it, including emergency evacuation as a dependent, if that was ever necessary."

I didn't want to look at Melanie because I knew she could read my thoughts. If the decision was only up to me, I would have gotten down on one knee and asked her to marry me, making way for a double wedding within the next thirty days.

Instead, we offered to help plan her mother's wedding.

By the time the four of us arrived at the New Orleans Club the place was rocking. Doc was on the piano, the XO on the drums, and Harry on the bass. The New Orleans house band accompanied them as various members of the crew, some solo, some in trios and quartets, did their renditions of various pop hits currently playing on Armed Forces Radio.

Kaneli and Andrew walked in just after we arrived and joined us. Many drinks and songs later, we staggered our way back to the mansion and slept until noon the next day. I made it back to the ship just in time for an officer's meeting in the wardroom.

"As you may have heard, both sides have agreed to a cease-fire for Tet. It began at noon," the Captain announced.

"Some of our intelligence people are not convinced that it will hold. But many of the South Vietnamese troops have already been given the weekend off.

"We, on the other hand, will be back at work. At 1300 hours tomorrow, we will make our way from this pier to the supply ramp where we'll be loaded for a run upriver to My Tho."

"Will we be putting on a show there?" Harry asked.

"Yes. The base CO sent a message yesterday that he's making room on the ramp for us," the XO answered.

The Captain stood, indicating the meeting was adjourned. But added, "John has volunteered to stand watch tonight, so all of the rest of you can be my guests for dinner at the General's Daughter. The admiral will also join us. I made it early, 1800 hours, so you can make it back to the ship for good night's sleep," the Captain announced.

With that, the meeting broke up and I went to my stateroom to take a nap. Andrew followed a few minutes later.

"What's the deal with this big dinner?" He asked.

I didn't want to spoil the Captain's wedding announcement.

"I think it's his way of saying thank you for the good show we put on."

"But, I was going to meet Kaneli for a lobster dinner later at the beach club," he added.

"You probably can. We're eating early. Just plan on having two dinners," I said.

"One other thing. Kaneli heard rumors that there may be trouble in Vung Tau. The locals are talking about Viet Cong movements just north of here."

"Shit. I hope not. This has been such a peaceful place. I'd hate to see it change."

"At least there's a truce for Tet."

"Yeah, we're safe for now," I said, and I drifted off to sleep.

34

Tet Changes Everything
● ●

A NDREW WENT TO TELL KANELI about the changes in their plans for the evening. The Captain and I arrived at the General's Daughter an hour early to confirm the size of our party. Simone and Melanie were frantically helping the staff set up the tables when we arrived. They looked stressed. Simone saw us first.

"What's wrong?" the Captain asked her.

"Half of our wait staff and a third of our kitchen staff didn't show up for work. I know it's Tet, but it's unusual that they didn't ask to leave early," she said.

"Can Rob and I help?" he asked.

"No. We are just about done. But, it means that Melanie and I will be waiting tables tonight."

"We'll try to keep it simple and not add to the stress," the Captain volunteered.

"*Merci mon cheri*. I'm sorry I won't be able to spend much time with you until later," she said. Then, kissed him on the cheek and hurried off.

The rest of the *Bell County*'s officers arrived twenty minutes later, followed shortly thereafter by Admiral Kirkpatrick and his adjutant.

"We got here earlier than I thought we would," the Admiral said. "I assumed the streets would be jammed with traffic because of the Tet holiday, but except for our sailors, they were nearly vacant."

"Lots of the stores are already closed and shuttered, and there are no vendors on the streets. It's kind of eerie," his adjutant added.

"Hmm. That is odd," the Captain replied. His forehead wrinkled and he looked concerned. Just then Melanie came over.

"Gentlemen, welcome to our Tet Eve dinner. Please sit down. I will be back in a few minutes to take your drink orders." As she circled around our table, she reached out and gave my arm a squeeze.

"They're a little short-handed tonight so it's a good thing we got here early," the Captain said.

Everyone was in a good mood. Melanie took and then delivered our drink orders while the Captain suggested that he order for the table.

"There is a special Tet menu tonight, it includes most of my favorites. I think you will like them to," he said.

The Admiral spoke next.

"Before we get busy enjoying our dinner, I want to say again how proud I am of all of you and your crew. The *Bell County* has exceeded all of my expectations. I have recommended that the ship and its crew receive the Navy Meritorious Unit Citation for its extraordinary work on behalf of all of our sailors, soldiers, and Marines."

He stood and raised his glass, we all followed suit.

"Here's to the best and most entertaining ship in the Brown Water Navy, the USS *Bell County.*"

We all repeated, "To the *Bell County*," then, clicked our glasses.

By the time our first course arrived, we were through our second round of drinks and working on a third. As the dinner plates were cleared and dessert was being served, the Captain rose to his feet and we all started to follow.

"No. Please remain seated. I just have a brief personal announcement." He paused and waved at Simone to come over. As she did, he took her hand, and pulled her close to his side.

"I am very happy to announce that Simone and I are going to be married, and that you are all invited to the wedding, which will be right here sometime in the next month, assuming we can make all the necessary arrangements."

We all stood and raised our glasses.

"To our Captain and the future Mrs. Baillier, congratulations," the XO said.

"*Salut!*" we all added.

"*Merci beaucoup.* Thank you all very much. It will be a wonderful wedding. Now, I must excuse myself. We are very busy tonight," Simone said, kissing the Captain on the cheek and returning to the kitchen.

Everyone congratulated the Captain.

"Does this mean we can break out our dress whites and actually wear them?" Harry asked.

"And our swords too?" I added.

"Absolutely. We're going to celebrate in grand Navy style," the Captain replied.

One of the waiters appeared with four bottles of Champagne. Our celebration continued for another hour and a half.

Sometime after 2200, I saw Melanie's friend Cam run in. There was a look of alarm on her face as she searched the room for Melanie. When she spotted her, she hurried over and whispered something in her ear. Melanie said something back and Cam shook her head. Their hurried conversation lasted another minute, then Cam left and Melanie went to her mother. Then both of them came to our table.

"Admiral, Captain. May we speak with you privately?" Simone said.

They left the table and went to an unoccupied part of the dining area. While they were talking, Reyes rushed in and joined their conversation. I saw both men's faces go deadly serious. They walked back to the table stiffly.

The Admiral spoke first.

"Gentlemen, it appears that the truce has been broken. The air base outside of town is under attack by a large force. All Allied forces have been put on high alert. We must report back to our duty stations."

The Admiral went around the room, repeating his message to the other diners, virtually all of whom were military personnel. We had two cars, the ship's and the Admiral's; enough to get us back to the base. But, as we were exiting the restaurant, the Captain pulled me aside.

"I am ordering you to stay here and see to it that any Americans, Australian, French or other civilians get to a safe place. Remember the cellar at the church I showed you?"

"Yes, sir."

"Okay. As soon as I can, I will send armed sailors to cover you. After we leave, start herding people toward the church. Do not let Simone and Melanie stay behind to protect their restaurant, which they will want to do. You may have to spend the night in that cellar. The car and the sailors I send should also stay."

"Aye, aye, Captain," I replied.

I followed them out to the street and looked in the direction of the air base. It was several miles away, but I saw a glow in the sky and heard muffled explosions. Simone and Melanie were standing on the porch as the remaining diners filed out. Some customers had cars waiting, others started to walk toward their respective bases.

All over Vung Tau, American and Australian sailors, soldiers and Marines would be making their way back to their ships and bases by any means they could find.

"The Captain wants me to get you both and members of your staff to the church wine cellar now," I told Simone and Melanie.

"We've already released the staff to return to their homes and families. There are another six customers who are attached to the merchant ships in the harbor who are stranded," Melanie said.

"I must stay here to protect the restaurant," Simone said.

"I'm staying with my mother," Melanie declared.

"The Captain told me you'd say that. But he believes you are in great danger here because it is known to cater to us and our Australian allies. So far, the attacks have only been on military targets. Not the town itself. But the General's Daughter is about as close to a military target as there is inside the city. It's too risky to stay, at least until things settle down," I said.

"No! No! If they come, I must stop them," Simone cried in anguish.

"They are trained soldiers who hate Americans and the French. They will have guns. What are you going to do, scare them off with a kitchen knife? The Captain ordered me to get you out of here. There's no way I can force you. So, I'm just asking. Please, if you don't trust me, trust your future husband," I said.

Simone looked at me, then at the door, then her shoulders slumped.

"You're right. Give us three minutes to grab some things," she said.

Melanie nodded her agreement and each of them took off for their rooms, returning a few minutes later with small bags in which they had shoved a few personal items.

"One more thing," Simone said as she headed toward the kitchen, returning a minute later with three long carving knives.

"Maybe three of us with knives will frighten them," she said smiling and handing one to each of us.

The stranded men from the merchant ship spoke Spanish and a little bit of English. I did my best to explain that they should follow us to a safer place. They nodded in agreement and the nine of us headed out the door and turned toward the church and school.

The glow from the direction of the air base had gotten brighter and the explosions louder. I heard the chatter of machine guns in the distance. There was no need to run, but we walked as fast as we could. A block from the General's Daughter, the lights all over the city went out. It was nearly pitch black.

The sounds of the fighting seemed closer now. Melanie had a flashlight.

We continued to walk as fast as we dared without stumbling over something. When we got to the church we could see several people with flashlights herding the children toward the back area where the cellar was.

Sister Josephine was standing at the open door of the orphanage checking for stragglers. She spotted us and waved us forward. Simone rushed to her and gave her a hug.

"Are the children alright?" She asked.

"Yes. Everyone is accounted for. We are prepared. The children have been through drills. Come. It is time for all of us to get to the cellar," she said.

Sister Josephine's declaration that she was prepared didn't surprise me. If there was ever a natural-born drill sergeant, it was she. When everyone was secure, the door was barred and candles were lit. Sister Josephine and three other nuns went around setting up the bedding and blankets for the children. We found several benches set around two tables and sat down. Sister Josephine returned and in perfect Spanish told the merchant marine officers that they were welcome and safe.

"Where is Father Daniel?" Simone asked.

"He left for France two days ago. I do not think he will be returning," the nun replied.

Just then we heard banging on the cellar door, followed by a familiar voice. "Mr. Allen. It's me, Reyes. Archer is with me. The Captain sent us to protect everyone."

I sighed with relief and opened the door. They were carrying three .30-caliber carbine rifles and three .45-caliber pistols.

I wasn't sure that the three of us could hold off a company of Viet Cong, should they attack the school, but it felt better than the idea of fighting them off with a butcher knife. They also had a walkie-talkie with which we could call the base for help. Unfortunately, we had no way to talk directly to our ship.

"Is the Navy base under attack?" I asked.

"No. Not yet, but everyone is on full alert. There are two squads of Marines covering the gates, and our ship and the *Markab* are at general quarters. We've stationed men with rifles at both ends of the pier. There are also a bunch of Huey gunships in the air circling over the base and the town," Reyes said.

"The Captain has the engines running and teams ready to cast off the lines just in case we have to move the ship in a hurry," Archer added.

"Our job is to hold on until daylight; then we can call for air cover if we need it," I said. "For now, one of us needs to stand lookout outside just in case they try a sneak attack. There's a stack of wooden barrels just to the right of the door. We can use that as a partial cover.

"We'll rotate the watch every two hours. Archer, you go first. Then I'll relieve you, then Reyes will relieve me. If you see anything that looks like a threat, get inside fast and we'll use the radio to call for help," I ordered.

"Aye, aye, Mr. Allen," they both said.

Melanie and Simone had set up some pads and blankets in the corner nearest the door. I joined them.

"We're okay for now," I told them. "Archer's keeping watch outside. I'll relieve him in a couple of hours. We have a radio to call for help if we need it."

They both nodded. Melanie pulled me down next to her and put her arms around me.

"Don't worry. We're in a safe place. The attack seems to be focused on the air base," I said.

I was worried. It was no coincidence that so many locals, including some of the General's Daughter's staff, seem to have known about the attack before it happened. If so, whose side were they on?

Vung Tau wasn't the only place in which the war had taken a ugly turn for the worse. We later learned that on the first night of Tet, nearly every city and village in South Vietnam came under attack. Many of them were completely overrun. More than half the soldiers of the ARVN divisions assigned to protect the Mekong Delta towns were on leave for the holiday.

Caught off guard by the initial night assaults on their Mekong bases, the American Army soldiers and Navy sailors recovered quickly. There were many close calls, but within forty-eight hours, the Viet Cong were forced to retreat. Those hours were hellish for many of our guys, especially those assigned to remote outposts. Boat mechanics, clerks, cooks and other personnel, not normally expected to fight, were handed rifles, given on-the-spot training, and put out on the perimeter to help fend off the attackers.

In Saigon, Hue and other places in South Vietnam, equally ferocious attacks on American and ARVN targets were underway. Viet Cong soldiers attacked our Saigon embassy by blowing a hole in its exterior wall. U.S. Marine guards were killed in the first wave. The VC managed to get inside the embassy building and held it until our reinforcements arrived and took it back after an all-night fight, killing all of the invaders in the process.

In the former imperial capital of Hue, it was far worse. Between January 30 and March 3, in the longest and bloodiest battle of the Vietnam War, eleven battalions of ARVN, four U.S. Army battalions and three Marine Corps battalions defeated ten battalions of the People's Army of Vietnam and Viet Cong. Hundreds, including civilians, died. Thousands more were wounded. Civilian casualties were high in every city and village that came under attack during Tet.

The U.S. airbase at Vung Tao took the brunt of the attack nearest us. There were isolated incidents of fighting near the harbor. I saw tracer rounds flying through the air and several rockets exploded near the breakwater. It was impossible to tell one side from the other. By dawn the fighting slowed.

Reyes and I cautiously made our way out to the street. We saw two Shore Patrol jeeps, each with four armed sailors, approaching.

"Are you from the *Bell County?*" the Chief Petty Officer in the first jeep asked.

"Yes. I'm Ensign Allen and this is Petty Officer Reyes," I replied.

"We were sent to protect the civilians here. You and your men are to return to your ship ASAP. It's at the supply base ramp," the Shore Patrol chief said.

I jogged back to the cellar and told everyone that it was safe to come out. Simone and Melanie walked out to the car with us.

"We've been ordered back to the ship. I expect we'll be sent somewhere upriver later today. We could be gone for several days," I said.

Simone hugged me and told me to be safe. Then Melanie hugged me long and hard. She spoke softly in my ear, "This is not the way we will say goodbye. Come back soon my love."

35

The Beginning of the End
●●●●●●●●●●●●●●●●●●●●●●●

THE SAFE LITTLE BUBBLE IN which Melanie and I had lived and loved burst on that first terrible night of Tet. Thereafter, each of us was dragged by war, fate and duty along separate, rarely intersecting, paths. The Navy set mine.

When Reyes, Archer and I got back to the *Bell County*, it was nearly loaded. We were packed with a double load of gasoline and ammunition stacked in our hold and on our main deck, rail to rail, protected from sniper's bullets by two layers of sandbags.

The ship backed off the ramp, dispatched posthaste to My Tho, which had been overrun ten hours previously. Our soldiers there were fighting for their lives and running out of ammunition. The PBR's and other boats of the mobile riverine force were not only low on ammo, they were also out of gas.

Once we were clear of the bay anchorages, the Captain ordered flank speed, putting our newly rebuilt starboard engine to an immediate test. LSTs, even at flank speed, can barely do eleven knots with a strong following wind. But we managed to make it to the river mouth before sunset.

The tide was barely high enough for us to clear the mud, but the Captain chose to cross the bar and enter the river anyway, even though it might mean traversing the last of our journey upriver to My Tho in the dark.

From that point on, we were at general quarters. All guns were manned and all hands wore flak jackets and helmets. Two sailors on the bow shot into any piles of flotsam that might touch the ship. We proceeded as fast as we dared, trusting that the course we'd followed previously had not silted in. Light was fading fast. The Captain reduced our speed to dead slow and ordered the lowering of both LCVPs (landing craft), each with three crewmembers on board. They took position fifty yards ahead on each side of our bow. They carried portable signal lights visible from the *Bell County*'s bridge. We kept our bow between the two lights.

It was a funky, makeshift solution, but it kept us moving upstream, albeit slowly. All exterior lights on board the ship were extinguished. Only very dim red lights allowed those of us on the bridge and wheelhouse to read the compass and the charts. Brilliant flashes from parachute flares appeared in the sky miles ahead of us. After another hour at dead slow, the flares were closer and we could hear the sounds of explosions and gunfire. Twilight had turned to night.

We rounded a wide bend and the battle scene spread out before us. It was a hellish mix of smoke and fire, punctuated by explosions. The whole town of My Tho appeared to be in flames. Artillery rounds exploded inside the city. Tracers flew through it in all directions.

Fighting raged on both sides of the river. There was no way to tell who were friend or foe, and no safe place to be. The supplies we were carrying to that base were needed, but we could not unload them with the battle raging around us. Base command ordered us to anchor in the middle of the river under blackout conditions and man our guns. Had we been attacked, we could have defended ourselves, but instead we were just frustrated spectators.

Overhead, Huey gunships swarmed like angry hornets, spitting out machine-gun rounds down toward the jungle so fast that there was no space between the tracers. They looked like ray guns, from which glowing, red-hot beams burned anything and anyone, they touched below. Red, green and brilliant white flares lit the sky and tracer bullets crisscrossed through the air around us and in the jungle on both sides of us.

The Captain assigned our two LCVPs to patrol in a circle around the ship, randomly dropping concussion grenades into the water to thwart any attempt by Viet Cong swimmers to attach mines to our hull.

Our ship was incredibly lucky. It would have taken only one bullet hitting one drum of gasoline to set off a chain reaction that would have incinerated our ship and all on board. We made it through the night.

By the time there was enough light to make our way to the ramp, all of the close-in fighting had ceased. Navy jets were dropping bombs in the surrounding jungle less than a half-mile from the base. The town was still burning and our ships and boats were shrouded in what looked like fog but smelled of cordite and burning wood.

Lieutenant Commander (LCDR) Jones, the base commander, was waiting for us on the ramp.

"Boy are we glad to see you guys. We were so low on ammo, we were ready to start stacking up rocks to throw at the VC. Our boats are out of gas and dead in the water," he said.

Our forklifts rushed to offload the barrels of gasoline and pallets of ammunition.

"I'm sorry we couldn't get here sooner. And we can't stay. We've got orders to head upriver to firebase Houng No. On the chart it looks like it's practically in Cambodia," the Captain said.

"Shit. You are headed into a hornet's nest. Several of our boats came under heavy fire just south of there, near Chau Phu," LCDR Jones said.

"We've been told that the troops at Houng No are in desperate shape. We're going to try to get our supplies to them today," the Captain said.

"Now that we have the gas and ammo, let me assign some of our boats to escort you there. We need to get back into that zone, anyway."

"Thank you, Commander. We will gladly pay you back with our best show and food whenever all of this other shit blows over," the Captain replied.

During a lull in the conversation I asked the base commander about my OCS buddy, Alex, who commanded one of the PACV boats out of his base.

"I'm sorry. A Viet Cong rocket squad ambushed Alex and his crew three weeks ago. All three were killed and their craft was destroyed."

It was hard to imagine my brave, happy-go-lucky buddy dead. He seemed like the kind of person that was so full of life that he could survive anything. The news really shook me, but there was no time to grieve.

We pulled off the ramp and prepared to continue upriver, hoping to make the Houng No outpost before dark.

The PBRs were fueled, loaded, and ready to go with us.

We used walkie-talkies for ship-to-boat communications. Three boats were stationed ahead, two astern.

We made good time until we got to a very sharp, narrow bend in the river. The map showed it to be near the village of Chau Phu. When we rounded the bend, we saw that Chau Phu was no more. Smoking rubble was all that remained.

In the middle of a narrow, nearly 180-degree turn, several rockets shot out of the jungle 100 yards forward of our starboard bow. One splashed into the water before it got to us. The second sailed overhead and hit the opposite shore. The three PBRs opened fire on the patch of jungle from which the rockets came. Our forward forty mm guns did the same.

Just to be safe, the Captain ordered all guns to rake the jungle on both sides of the ship, in case any other snipers were waiting to ambush us at that narrow choke point. There was no return fire. Once we got to a wider spot in the river, the Captain ordered a cease-fire.

It was a tense, two-hour journey the rest of the way. The river got narrower. The chart we had was nearly useless. We had no idea of how deep the water was. The sun was low on the horizon when we reached the firebase, little more than a wide place in the jungle on a muddy riverbank.

With our LCVPs acting as tugs, the Captain was able to shoehorn our bow onto the ramp. The base's only forklift had been destroyed the night before by a VC mortar round, so we had to use our ship's hand trucks and the crane to get things off the ship as quickly as possible.

The last of the off-loading took place in the twilight.

The base commander, a very young-looking Marine Captain, met us at the side of the ramp. His face was marked with soot and mud, and he looked like he hadn't slept for several days. In fact, all of the men around us looked exhausted.

"You guys saved our asses. We're nearly out of everything, especially ammo," he said.

"How about food, Captain? Do you have enough?"

"We've got C-rations and enough tablets to treat water for drinking. That's what we've been living on for the last forty-eight hours." .

"Assuming you don't need all of your men guarding the perimeter tonight, we'd be happy to bring them on board in shifts and feed them good, hot, Navy chow until everyone is full," the Captain said.

The Marine smiled for the first time.

"If you'd do that for us, sir, I'll get our men here. Thank you," he said, his voice nearly choking with emotion.

"It's the least we can you for you and your brave men. We can be ready to start serving the first shift in forty-five minutes, and if need be, I can spare a dozen of our crew to supplement your guard force so you can send more to eat. They're not Marines, but they've had firearms training."

"Thank you, sir. The VC probably won't hit us again until sometime after midnight. By then, thanks to you, our men will be fed and rested."

They came on board in full combat gear, rifles slung over their shoulders, a mixture of weariness and fear on their faces.

Several of our crew acted as greeters, guiding the Marines to the mess below decks, showing them the location of the heads, and making sure they all had seats at the tables. Rather than eat our dinner in the officer's wardroom, all the ship's officers ate with the Marines and their officers in the crew's mess.

It was amazing to see what a safe, steel deck overhead, hot chow, and friendly conversation did to remove the tension from their faces. Most of them were just kids, a long way from home, lonely, and scared shitless. Several, their bellies full, put their heads down on the table and fell sound asleep, probably the first they'd had in two days.

The Marine captain was one of the last to eat. Several of us joined him. We asked about the attacks on the base.

"It started three nights ago with periodic probes. They'd drop some mortar rounds in and then fire a bunch of shots at certain points around our perimeter.

"Then, on Tet eve, the jungle around us erupted and they came at us from all directions. It was close combat. The kind we're trained for, but most of us had never seen until then. We drove them back. Then they'd attack again, and we'd drive them back again. Just before daylight, they just melted back into the jungle."

"How many casualties did you have, Captain?" the XO asked.

"Two killed, five wounded. We called in a medevac Huey to take them out once the sun was up."

The conversation then focused on preparation for a possible attack later in the evening. It was decided that the ship would close its bow doors, but remain on the ramp, prepared to back off into the river if necessary.

Our Captain set a modified combat watch, with all guns manned, an officer on the bridge and a fully manned wheelhouse and engine room. Just before the Marine base commander returned to shore, Captain told him that all of his men could expect a hot breakfast in the morning, assuming nothing prevented the same kind of rotating meal service from working. Once again I saw the look of gratitude brighten the young officer's face.

"Thank you, Captain Baillier. What you're doing for us is above and beyond," he said.

"As I said before, Captain. It is the least we can do," our CO replied.

No attacks came that night. In the morning, Freddie and his team had hot cakes, bacon and sausage, and lots of hot coffee, ready to serve as the first of the Marine shifts came on board. By the time everyone was fed and we were ready to depart, we'd been thanked profusely by just about everybody at the base.

It was we who should have thanked them. They were the brave men sent to the most hostile and dangerous places in that war. They had to fight who knows how many Vietnamese on behalf of other Vietnamese, who probably didn't want us there anyway.

Yet, they did their duty bravely and honorably. I will never forget them.

36

Until the End of Time
•••••••••••••••••••••••

POST-TET REPORTS INDICATED THAT North Vietnam's General Giap had high expectations of the Tet offensive. It was, instead, a catastrophic tactical defeat for his forces everywhere in Vietnam. The mobile riverine force, of which the *Bell County* was a part, was particularly effective in preventing the Viet Cong from gaining any permanent footholds in the region.

But for Americans at home, and those of us in the war zone, the war had changed. We won the battles, but lost whatever sense, or pretense, of purpose we'd had before Tet. There was a growing realization that we didn't belong – that we were seen by Vietnamese as either invaders, occupiers, or unwelcome guests, little better than the French or the Japanese before them.

Tet also spelled the beginning of the end for Melanie and me. The next months went by in a blur, with little rest or sleep. Even when the *Bell County* got a full day in Vung Tau, she was not there. She was on assignment with the news service that hired her. I missed her terribly.

Vung Tau was safe. The General's Daughter was still in business, as was the New Orleans Club. But when Melanie was not there, I had little interest in going on liberty.

Andrew and Kaneli did their best to cheer me with invitations to join them when they went out. But being with them just emphasized who was missing. Without Melanie, no matter who else was with me, I felt alone.

Several months after Tet, the Captain told me that Simone received a visit from a very polite, but firm, ARVN officer, who informed her that the General's Daughter was now the property of the government and would become the headquarters for the ARVN colonel in charge of Vung Tau. She was given ten days to vacate.

Although not entirely surprised, Simone was nevertheless in great distress over the sudden loss of the legacy she had done so much to preserve. She was most upset about her Vietnamese staff, many of them former orphans, who would lose their jobs.

Worse still, ARVN recruiters had swooped down on the school and taken away several boys, just seventeen, forcing them to join the military. They tried to take two of the older teenaged girls as well, but Sister Josephine threatened to call down the wrath of God on them if they did.

Sadly, the handwriting was on the wall. The Catholic Church in France had not sent a priest to replace Father Daniel. The Ursuline Order in France planned to close the convent and call their remaining nuns back to France.

The only happy point in that depressing series of events was the wedding of Captain Baillier and Simone.

They made plans for a hasty, somewhat informal, ceremony at the General's Daughter just two days before it was to be turned over to the Army of the Republic of Vietnam.

Melanie arrived on the morning of the wedding. She'd lost weight. Her beautiful long hair had been cut to a short bob. I greeted her at the door of the mansion. She looked as exhausted as I felt.

She hugged her mother and the Captain. Then she put her arms around me and we hugged for a long time. Then, without saying anything, she took my hand, as she had the first time on that stormy evening so many months ago, and led me upstairs to her room. We undressed each other and made passionate love twice before either of us said a word.

"I probably stink. I haven't had a shower in five days," she finally said.

"You smell wonderful. In fact, I will never take a shower again, just so I can preserve your essence on my skin," I replied.

"Okay, but I still want to shower. You are invited to join me of course."

It was as though nothing had changed between us. After showering we returned to bed and neither one of us wanted to leave it. But then we had to, to get ready for the wedding.

A majority of the ship's company and its officers were able to attend. We wore our dress white uniforms. It was the one and only time I got to wear my sword.

Binh, who had been ordered to return to ARVN headquarters in Saigon after the Tet attack, arrived at the wedding with Hanh and Master Lu.

He offered the only piece of good news related to the confiscation of the General's Daughter.

"When I heard that they were upgrading the ARVN presence in Vung Tau, I talked my way into a transfer here as part of the regional headquarters staff," he told Simone and the Captain.

"At least there will be somebody we know and trust here," Simone said.

"I'm sorry my change in fortune came at your expense," Binh said.

"You had nothing to do with ARVN's decision to take the General's Daughter. At least some good came of it," she replied.

Many of Simone and Melanie's friends from town also attended. The captain of the Markab did a splendid job of officiating, and the champagne flowed freely for everyone. For the first time in months, the ship's band got to play. Several of the ship's groups sang. It was, in many ways, our last hurrah in Vung Tau.

For Melanie and me it was a bittersweet evening. She had to leave in the morning and didn't know when she'd get back.

"We're heading to Cambodia and hoping to report what is happening there and in Laos," she said.

There was a brightness in her voice when she talked about her co-journalists and the work they were doing reporting on the war.

"I decided against a *nom de plume*, but I am using Tran Vi Gian, my given Vietnamese name. It is truly who I am. Our news service's reporting is from an Asian perspective. Using my real name makes that clear."

"Does your mother understand?" I asked.

"We had a long discussion before I accepted the job. I told her I wanted her to be happy and not worry about taking care of me, and that I had to let her go and she had to let me go."

There was finality in her voice. This was it. The end that we both knew was inevitable. I was suddenly overcome by deep sadness.

"I guess that goes for us, too," I said.

"Yes, my love. Us, too. Tomorrow the Melanie Marquis you knew will be only a memory, but Tran Vi Gian will carry Rob Allen in her heart for as long as it beats."

"I can't stand the thought of a world in which I cannot be with you," I said.

"Then don't think of it that way. Nobody can take away our memories of each other."

The reception went on around us. Except for one dance with Simone, I spent every minute with Melanie.

After everyone left, the Captain and Simone sat us down and

laid out their plans. Simone was working with Hanh and other women in the town, who agreed to take over the orphanage when the nuns left. Simone would live in the convent until the turnover was complete, then fly to Bangkok, where, as the wife of an American officer, she could fly to the United States.

The Captain made arrangements for her to stay with his parents in New Orleans until our Vietnam tour was complete and he returned to the States.

"Do you know what your next duty station will be?" I asked him.

"No. Not yet. But I've requested shore duty somewhere on the east coast, the closer to New Orleans the better. Charleston or Norfolk would be good."

"Shore duty? Isn't that a bad career move?" I asked.

"Yes. But I intend to leave the Navy in two years. Spending those final two years in a place where Simone and I can be together is the important thing."

I understood the Captain's thinking perfectly. I'd hoped for the same thing for Melanie and myself. In fact, I'd already sent a message to the Bureau of naval Personnel requesting my next assignment to be as a Public Information Officer somewhere on the West Coast. At the time I made the request, I was still hopeful that Melanie would agree to come with me. Now, the thought of being anywhere without her left me feeling hollow inside.

We said goodnight to the Captain and his bride and went upstairs together for the last time. I didn't want to fall asleep and I don't remember how many times we made love, but sometime before dawn, exhaustion caught up with me.

When I woke up she was gone.She left a note. It was the last verse of the song I'd sung to her at our dinner with Master Lu and Hanh ending with:

"...And last, 'til the end of time..."

EPILOGUE

April 2018
● ●

T HE AIRPLANE CAPTAIN'S ANNOUNCEMENT THAT
we were landing in New Orleans in twenty minutes woke me.

My wife, Helen, asked, "Are you okay? You were groaning and mumbling something in your sleep," she said.

"Yeah. I'm fine, just the same old nightmare."

Early in our relationship, I had told her about Vietnam, my ship, Captain Baillier, Simone, and especially Melanie. She knew it all, even the details of our final months in Vietnam.

Helen's ability to understand and empathize helped me move on. But my memories of those last days in Vietnam still haunted my dreams.

After the Captain's wedding in Vung Tao, the *Bell County* returned to a seemingly endless series of re-supply missions between our base and the river bases. O.J.'s tour was up and he flew home. I was promoted to Operations Officer. We were finally able to put on our shows again. Toward the end of our tour, Kaneli and Meg flew back to Australia. Simone's stay in Vietnam was ending.

I went with the Captain to see her off at the air base. He managed to arrange a flight for her to Travis Air Force Base in California. From there she would make her way by commercial airline to New Orleans.

She had lost all contact with Melanie. The news team had been operating near the borders between Vietnam, Cambodia and Laos.

It would be years before we would know her fate.

The Captain received his orders to report to the naval base at Norfolk, where he would wear two hats, one as a senior amphibious warfare instructor, the other as the director of the U.S. Navy Band stationed there.

His transfer orders were effective the day after our arrival in San Diego.

The day before our departure from Vietnam, the Captain, Andrew, and I had dinner at Master Lu's home. Binh, who was now engaged to Hanh, joined us. So did Melanie's friend Cam.

They were the last of our closest friends in Vung Tau.

We ate heartily, shared lots of rice wine, and reminisced about our good times together.

"One day, this war will be over. I hope that we are all alive to see that day, and will find a way to celebrate together once again," Binh said.

I could not stop my tears as I hugged each of them. They were my last connection to Melanie. For a brief time, fate had allowed me to find friends and a great love where I never expected them. Vietnam and its people would always have a place in my heart.

The ship's voyage home was long. While most of my shipmates looked forward to getting back to "the world," I was afflicted with unrelenting melancholy. They would have their wives, families and sweethearts. The Captain would have Simone. I had people at home, including my grand Aunt Celeste, whom I loved and cared about, but the void left by Melanie swallowed all the joy I might have felt.

When the ship was just one day from its home port of San Diego, the Captain called me to his cabin. He handed me a message from the Bureau of naval Personnel.

"Congratulations, Rob, you've been promoted to Lieutenant Junior Grade (Ltjg) and assigned to the Public Information Office at Treasure Island naval Base in San Francisco," he said.

"Yes, sir. Thank you, sir," I replied flatly. Under other circumstances I might have been happy. But the long voyage had only deepened my sadness and worry about Melanie.

"Rob, Melanie told me not to let you be sad. She insisted that I remind you that you both agreed to move on. She said you will love and be loved again. So. I'm reminding you," he said.

Always the more pragmatic of the two of us, Melanie would not waste her life pining away for me. She was telling me I shouldn't pine away for her either. It would take me a long time for me to figure out how to do that.

A decade passed before I learned anything of her fate.

On the day the Captain Baillier left the *Bell County*, our band played "Won't You Come Home..." as he walked down the gangway.

Before he left I had one last meeting with him.

"I just want to say thank you. I will always remember everything you did for our crew and me especially. You taught me more and gave me more than I can ever repay," I said.

"I'm proud of you, Rob. I know it's not what you choose, but you could have a great career in the Navy. More importantly, you are a good man. It was a honor to have served with you."

"One more thing," he added. "This is my last order as your CO. Simone's right. We're family. I'm like an uncle or wise grandfather. So, the order is: we stay in touch. We exchange Christmas cards and phone calls, and maybe even some visits."

I saw tears in his eyes as he offered me his hand.

* * *

We did stay in touch even though we were on opposite coasts. I kept hoping that Simone would have news about Melanie. Sister

Josephine returned to France. She and Simone corresponded regularly. Finally, in 1978, Sister Josephine forwarded a letter from a Catholic missionary who had gone to Vung Tau to see what had become of the church, school, and orphanage. Under authority of the new government of Vietnam, it was still caring for children orphaned by the war.

In the letter, the missionary mentioned that Hanh, an old friend of Simone's, sent best wishes, and news that Melanie was alive and living in the north near Hanoi. That was all we heard until 1995 when a letter from Melanie finally reached Simone.

In it, Melanie explained that in late 1968 she had been wounded in a B-52 strike in the mountains between Vietnam and Laos. She suffered a severe concussion and a broken pelvis and spent the next three years recovering in a small village near Luang Prabang, Laos.

There was more to the story, but the bottom line was that she recovered from her injuries and re-entered Vietnam, hoping to make her way back to Vung Tau. Instead, she was captured by the North Vietnamese, labeled a spy, and held prisoner in a jungle compound for the remainder of the war. Noting her fluency in English and French, her captors allowed her to teach in the small village school near the camp.

She was freed once the war ended, but chose to follow her former captors back to Hanoi, where, after a long period of re-education by the communist government she was employed to teach English and French at a school on the outskirts of the capitol. Because she was labeled a former spy, her correspondence with the outside world was restricted; her travel, forbidden.

Years passed. She met and married a fellow teacher at the school. In 1994 her husband died. By then, all restrictions were lifted and she was free to move. She resigned from teaching and made the long journey back to Vung Tau. To her surprise and delight, Binh and Hanh had survived the war together and were still running the school at the temple. She moved in with them.

I kept a copy of that letter and shared it with Helen, along with the honest feelings of regret that I had left Melanie behind.

Twenty more years passed. Then, I got an invitation to the fifty-year reunion of our crew in New Orleans, our Captain's hometown. The Captain added a note to the invitation saying that he and Simone had something they wanted to share with me. What was it?

Buddha says, "In the end these things matter most: How well did you love? How fully did you live? How deeply did you let go?"

Now, on my way to a rendezvous sure to revive long-buried memories, I wondered if I'd ever truly let go.

Helen and I checked into a New Orleans vacation apartment that we'd rented on the edge of the quarter two blocks from Big River Belle, the Captain and Simone's music club on Frenchman Street.

We arrived at the club a little after 8:00 p.m. Live music had already started. As we followed the receptionist to a table toward the back, two huge, hairy arms wrapped around me, pulling me backward.

"Well, if it isn't the surfer dude from California," the booming voice declared.

"Harry?" I exclaimed, turning to see the big guy's bright smile through a mostly grey beard.

"None other. Welcome to the first annual reunion of the old salts of the *Mekong Belle*," he said.

Other than a few extra pounds and a lot more grey in his hair and beard, he looked the same. I introduced Helen.

Harry took us over to a cluster of tables around, which I saw lots of familiar faces, older, but unmistakable – Doc, Archer, Reyes, and O.J. All, except Reyes, were with their wives. Reyes, to no one's surprise, had come out of the closet once it was safe. His partner, with whom he lived in New York, was a choreographer and on the road with a Broadway show.

Just as we started catching up, I heard Harry shout again and looked toward the door. My old roomie, Andrew, walked in with Kaneli on his arm. They lived in New York City, but had visited us in California on several occasions. Kaneli and Helen had become good friends and kept up with each other via texts, Facebook and phone calls.

Over the decades, we'd also exchanged a few visits with the Captain and Simone.

Helen had never met any of the other old shipmates before, but she knew them through my stories. I saw that she was comfortable with the joyful "remember when" chatter that gathered momentum as the evening wore on.

Shortly after 9:30, I heard Andrew and Kaneli both gasp in surprise. Then Harry loudly whispered, "I can't believe it!"

I turned.

Her eyes caught mine first. I looked. Blinked. Looked again.

"It couldn't be, not after all this time," I thought.

Then she smiled and I knew it was no mistake. I took Helen's hand and brought her with me. I had openly shared with her my feelings about a love found, then lost, more than a half-century before. I instinctively knew Helen would accept without jealousy, the joy I felt at that moment.

"Helen," I said, "I would like to introduce you to Melanie."

Then I turned and said. "Melanie, this is my wife, Helen."

The two great loves of my life hugged as though they'd known each other forever. Then it was my turn to hug. It felt like a long-lost part of me had been re-attached. I was overwhelmed with gratitude to the Captain and Simone for making Melanie's visit possible.

It was a glorious evening, filled with shared stories old and new. I wanted to reconnect with everyone, and most especially, Melanie.

The romantic love we'd shared so long ago had been replaced by a sense that I had been reunited with my long-lost sister. It was an oddly peaceful recognition that I had, indeed, moved on.

The Captain finally said he had to close the club for the night. He reminded us the real reunion was the following night.

More shipmates arrived the next morning for the main event. Not everybody made it. Lew, our XO, died in 2005. Chief Mick stayed in the Navy for thirty years and died in 1999. John Walton was living in Alaska and sent his regrets.

Dozens of the crew did manage to come, including most of the talent from our road shows. Musicians and singers love nothing more than free-wheeling jam sessions, where they are also each other's most appreciative audience.

I told Helen she was about to experience an evening of the *Mekong Belle's* greatest hits. The music brought us all back to the year we rocked the Mekong.

During a break, Helen, Simone, the Captain, and I sat with Melanie while she told us about her ordeals as a prisoner and then what it was like as Vietnam recovered from the devastation of the war. We learned about her late husband, and their life together as teachers near Hanoi. They had no children.

She seemed content – happy to see us, but proud that she had stayed and help rebuild her country.

"Helen is beautiful, she is exactly who I knew would make you happy," she said to me.

"It took me a while to move on. She made it possible. We've had a wonderful life together," I replied.

"We are both fortunate to have moved past our regrets," she said.

"I live in a small cottage next to Binh and Hanh. They send their love by the way. They have two adult children and four grand-children. They run the school. Binh still writes music. His Mekong

Suite is now played by the Saigon Orchestra as a regular part of the celebration of Vietnam's independence. He is an honored citizen."

"And you. Does your country recognize what a true patriot you are?" I asked.

"I am at peace with the choices I made. Vietnam has moved on. I live among good friends and help teach our children about Vietnamese culture. It is more than enough for me now."

"It is our fate to be happy, though the choices we made were sometimes painful," I replied

"Do I sense that you have another Buddha quote for me?" she answered smiling.

"Actually I was thinking of the poet Tennyson.

"He said, 'Tis better to have loved and lost than never to have loved at all.'"

"I don't regret loving you, although it was devastating to leave you. It was never lost and now I'm grateful for having found you again."

As the second evening's party wore on, we wore out. For a while, it was as though nothing had changed and we were still in our twenties and thirties. Our bodies, however, reminded us of our status as senior citizens.

Helen and I joined the Captain and Simone at a quiet corner table. Melanie, Kaneli, and Andrew came over to join us; then Harry, then Doc, and so on, until we were all back in the present, content with lives well-lived and bonds of friendship that time had not erased.

I looked around the table and smiled. The band was back together for one last hurrah. It felt right. The conversation stopped as though everyone had the same thought at the same time.

Archer's familiar tenor voice broke the momentary silence. At the chorus, we all joined in: *"...stand by me, stand by me, stand by me."*

A *Mekong Belle* Song List

MEKONG BELLE IS NOT ONLY a story about love between a man and a woman, but also a story about how music, and the love of music, can bring us all together. Below is a list of tunes to which I referred, and which carried me along as I wrote this story. Most are readily available via multiple downloadable music sources. I highly recommend that you create your own playlist of tunes like these and play them softly in the background while you read *Mekong Belle*.

"Beyond the Sea" – Bobbie Darin

"Almost Like Being In Love" – *Brigadoon*, Gene Kelly

"Surfin' USA" – The Beach Boys

"I'm Walking" – Fats Domino

"Boogie Woogie Bugle Boy" – Andrews Sisters

"Some Enchanted Evening" – *South Pacific*, Ezio Pinza

"Won't You Come Home Bill Bailey?" – Various

"The House of the Rising Sun" – The Animals, many others

"Navy Hymn" – Traditional

"Oh Happy Day" – Old gospel song, Edwin Hawkins Singers, many others

"Bill Bailey" – Louis Armstrong, many others

"Sh-Boom" – The Chords (1954)

"Why Do Fools Fall In Love?" – Frankie Lyman and The Teenagers

"When the Saints Go Marching In" – Louis Armstrong, many others

"Old Man River" – *Showboat*, Paul Robeson

"A Change Is Gonna Come" – Sam Cooke

"*Bei Mir Bist du Schon*" – Andrews Sisters

"Iko Iko"– The Dixie Cups and others

"You Don't Have to Say You Love Me" – Dusty Springfield

"The First Time Ever I Saw Your Face" – Roberta Flack, Joe & Eddie

"Misirlou" - Dick Dale

"Surfer Girl" - The Beach Boys

"Johnny B Goode" - Chuck Berry

"Waltzing Matilda" – Australian folk song

"All I Have to Do is Dream" – Everly Brothers

"If You Go Away" – Jacques Brel (English lyrics by Rod McKuen)

"Do-Re-Mi" – *Sound of Music*, Julie Andrews

"Victory At Sea Theme" – *Victory at Sea*, Richard Rogers,

"Fire On the Mountain" – The Marshall Tucker Band

"We Gotta Get Out of This Place" – Eric Burton and The Animals

"I'll Be Home For Christmas" – Bing Crosby

"In The Still of the Night" – The Five Satins

"Let the Four Winds Blow" – Fats Domino

"*Sous Le Ciel de Paris*" – Edith Piaff

"La Mer" – Charles Trenet

"Rhythm of the Rain" – the Cascades

"Early Morning Rain" – Peter, Paul and Mary

"Raindrops" – Dee Clark

"Cast Your Fate to the Wind" – Vince Guaraldi

"Singing in the Rain" – Gene Kelly

"I Can't Help Falling in Love With You" – Elvis Presley

"Stand By Me" – Ben E King

www.hellgatepress.com

Made in the USA
Las Vegas, NV
14 December 2023

82754277R00184